Foot thuds sounded, spu... leather soles. As if out of a dream, a figure materialized— slender and curvy, long, blond hair tumbling over shoulders clad in a striped brown serape. As the stranger stepped closer to the cave entrance, Prophet blinked, trying to clear his vision.

He looked down at brown boots trimmed with silver spurs and followed the lithe, denim-clad legs up to a cartridge belt and two cross-draw holsters strapped to slim hips, over the serape. A kid-gloved hand still held a cocked, silver-chased, pearl-gripped .45, gray smoke curling from the barrel . . .

Prophet cleared his throat and raked out, "Fancy meetin' you here, Louisa."

HELL'S ANGEL

— A LOU PROPHET NOVEL —

PETER BRANDVOLD

BERKLEY BOOKS, NEW YORK

THE BERKLEY PUBLISHING GROUP
Published by the Penguin Group
Penguin Group (USA) Inc.
375 Hudson Street, New York, New York 10014, USA

USA | Canada | UK | Ireland | Australia | New Zealand | India | South Africa | China

Penguin Books Ltd., Registered Offices: 80 Strand, London WC2R 0RL, England
For more information about the Penguin Group, visit penguin.com.

HELL'S ANGEL

A Berkley Book / published by arrangement with the author

Berkley Books are published by The Berkley Publishing Group.
BERKLEY® is a registered trademark of Penguin Group (USA) Inc.
The "B" design is a trademark of Penguin Group (USA) Inc.

For information, address: The Berkley Publishing Group,
a division of Penguin Group (USA) Inc.,
375 Hudson Street, New York, New York 10014.

ISBN: 978-0-425-25070-9

PUBLISHING HISTORY
Berkley mass-market edition / June 2013

PRINTED IN THE UNITED STATES OF AMERICA

10 9 8 7 6 5 4 3 2 1

Cover illustration by Bruce Emmett.

ALWAYS LEARNING   PEARSON

For my high school English teacher in North Dakota
—Kerry Jaeger

1

"*DIOS MIO.*" THE senorita said through a gasp. "Lou, you must go! My husband is home!"

"Husband? *Ramonna*, you're a *whore*!"

"Not anymore, Lou."

The senorita gasped when another sound rose from the hotel/saloon's first story, and clamped her hands to Lou Prophet's face. She stared up at him, chocolate eyes wide and bright with terror. She squirmed beneath him. Her full breasts raked warmly against his chest.

"Lou, *vamonos*! He is an angry man! Very jealous! If he sees us together, he will *keeel* you!"

Lou Prophet stopped bucking against the lovely *puta*, Ramonna Oscuro, whom he'd met a couple of years before, here in the little border village of San Simon, when he'd been on the run from the Federales. He stared down at her, incredulous.

It was deep night, but downstairs, in the hotel's little cantina, boots thudded. A contented whistling sounded. It stopped.

The man's burly voice barreled up the stairs in Spanish,

echoing off the mud brick walls—"*Hola*, my hot little chili pepper—your husband is home!"

"Shit!" Prophet said, scowling down in disbelief at the frightened *puta*. "That ain't Colonel Campa, is it—commander of the local Rurale outpost?"

"*Si,*" Ramonna said, nodding, as boots tapped slowly, heavily on the stone stairs. "He is very jealous man, Lou! He married me to keep me pure, though I have it on good word he still tumbles with any girl he gets heated up for!"

Prophet cursed again and rolled off the bed, climbing to his feet and looking around on the scarred wooden floor for his underwear. "The son of a bitch was dogging me for three days through Chihuahua. Accused me of holdin' up a stage on the old Comanche Trail. Knows damn well I didn't. That was Missouri Charlie Black and Pancho Scudder. Campa just soured on me after I cut his ear off in a fair knife fight in Juarez, two years ago last Christmas."

"That was you?"

"Didn't mean to. Meant to cut his throat, but I was too drunk to see straight. He said if he ever saw me in Mexico again, he'd see me shot down in front of the nearest adobe wall."

Prophet stepped into his balbriggans, drew them up his legs, having to squat and wriggle around to get the skintight, threadbare garment up his thick, brawny, six-foot-four-inch frame without ripping out the seams. "Lost him two days ago. Didn't figure on him thinkin' to look for me here—in the same little village he's *headquartered* in!"

The colonel's deep voice, slurred from drink, shouted, "I have brought you a present, my little mountain flower!"

Prophet glanced at Ramonna skeptically as he scooped his denim trousers off a chair back. *"Mountain flower?"*

"He's quite a poet, the *bastardo*! I only married him because I was tired of going from man to man, and I was drunk. I'm not as young as I used to be. I'll be twenty next month. The years catch up to us all. Hurry, Lou—he's in the hall!"

Prophet clamped his pants under his arm, then stooped

to grab his boots into which he'd stuffed his socks when he and Ramonna had come up to her room after the fandango in the village plaza, to get down to the business of the flesh. He could hear the colonel's boot thuds growing louder in the hall. Campa was whistling and humming, sort of shuffling along, likely three sheets to the wind. But Campa was the sort of man who sobered up fast when riled, and he was known as a good and willing hand with a six-shooter.

Prophet clamped his boots under his arm with his pants. He slung his cartridge belt and holstered Peacemaker over his shoulder, retrieved his sawed-off, ten-gauge, double-barrel coach gun from where he'd hung it by its leather lanyard from a wall spike, and picked up his Winchester '73 repeater that he'd leaned against the wall by the door.

As well armed as he himself was, he could blow Campa into bits the size of a cow's cud, but if he ambushed him here in his own town, he'd have every Rurale in northern Chihuahua after him, and he'd never again be able to hunt bounties south of the border. Mexico was the primest of hunting grounds. Whenever the outlaw herds were holed up tighter than ticks in a cur's ear up north, Prophet knew he could fund at least another year of stomping with his tail up by turning his sights on the other side of the Rio Bravo.

"Ah, my lovely Ramonna, I can't wait to impale you with my razor-edged love dagger!" Campa guffawed, his laughter alternating between deep and raspy, and high and brittle. He'd greatly amused himself.

"Christ, Ramonna—couldn't you have done a little better than *that*?"

"I told you I was drunk!" she hissed, sitting up in the rickety bed, the single sheet falling to her waist and exposing her full, brown breasts. Her rich, dark brown hair was piled high atop her head. "That scar where you cut off his ear did nothing for his looks, either!"

"Hey, you married him!"

The boot thuds stopped just outside the bolted but insubstantial pine-board door. "Who are you talking to, *chiquita*?"

Ramonna hissed and clamped her hands over her mouth, brown eyes appearing about to pop out of their sockets.

Prophet had just opened the wooden shutters over the window. Now he swung around and cast an anxious glance at the door. "Ah, shit," he whispered. "You gonna be all right, Ramonna, girl? I'd hate like hell for—"

"Lou, go!" the girl hissed again, thrusting her arm toward the window.

"'Lou'?" came the colonel's soft, mocking voice from the other side of the door. "Lou *who*, my darling Ramonna? You don't have a big, ugly bounty hunter by the name of Lou Prophet in there, do you?" His voice was soft, but Prophet noted the restrained fury in it. The Rurale colonel had switched to Spanish. "The one whose trail I was fogging across half the Chihuahuan Desert?"

"Lou?" Ramonna called, stretching a brittle smile and ensconcing her voice in sugar. "Lou who, *mi amore*? You know I have eyes for no one but you!"

She kept waving frantically at Prophet, who looked out the window and into the straw-strewn yard at the back of the hotel/saloon. He was about thirty feet above the ground, but there was a rear gallery roof of woven ironwood branches roughly fifteen feet below him and slightly to his right.

Possibly, he could land on that and then leap the rest of the way to the ground without killing himself.

Possibly . . .

Campa was rattling the door latch. "Open the door, *chiquita*," he said in a singsong, menacing voice. He hammered on it loudly, with such power that the door lurched in its frame. "Open the door right now or I will *blow it open*!"

"Coming, my bull!" Ramonna shot Prophet another tense, frantic glance as she bounded up out of the bed and uncoiled her cool, naked brown body, starting for the door. "Just one second, my wild stud horse!"

Too late.

There was what sounded like the blast of a Napoleon cannon. The rickety door flew open, shedding parts of itself including the locking bolt, as it slammed against the dresser behind it, knocking Ramonna's wooden Our Lady of Guadalupe off the wall above it.

Prophet was crouched atop the windowsill now, but as the burly, shaggy-headed Campa bounded into the room with his two pearl-gripped pistols drawn, the bounty hunter threw himself, his load of clothes, and his small arsenal off the casement, angling toward the brush roof below.

The brush grew until he could see the sides of each branch limned by lilac starlight. He bent his knees slightly to best absorb the impact. But when his feet struck the roof, there was only a slight impact.

The woven branches sagged briefly before breaking apart, and suddenly the big man was falling on through the roof to pile up in a heap on the gallery floor below.

Prophet had dropped his gear and lay writhing, bells tolling in his ears, pale doves flapping before his eyes, his feet and ankles burning. An Apache war lance of pain impaled the left shoulder and hip he'd landed on.

"Yanqui son of a bitch!" Colonel Campa shouted, and Prophet looked through the ragged hole he'd made in the roof above to see, slightly to one side, the Rurale's round, dark face shrouded by his shaggy hair, glaring down at him, white teeth showing between lips sheathed in long, drooping mustaches. "Die, you bas-*tard!*"

The gun the colonel was extending toward Prophet stabbed red yellow flames as it roared. Prophet rolled to one side, and as the bullet plowed into bits of brush protruding into the hole in the roof, diverting it, he began quickly gathering his gear.

Bam! Bam! "Die, you son of a bitch!" *Bam-bam!*

The bullets plowed through the roof. Two thudded into the gallery's worn wooden floor within a foot or two of the bounty hunter's large, pale, bare feet. Another pinged off the casement ledge beneath a lower-story window. Ricocheting, the third slug sliced a burr across Prophet's right shoulder before screeching off into the dark night.

"No!" Ramonna was screaming above the shots' dwindling echoes. "No, Arturo, no! He means nothing to me!"

"Thanks a bunch, Ramonna," Prophet raked out through gritted teeth as, his hands and arms full of his gear once more, he bolted out from under the gallery roof, heading for the cover of brush and stock pens beyond the saloon. The livery barn in which he'd stabled his horse lay in that direction, north, though a good seventy or so yards away. He hoped like hell he'd be able to find it on so dark a moonless night.

Campa fired both his pistols now as he shouted Spanish epithets. The bullets blew up dust, straw, and chicken shit around Prophet's hammering heels.

Crouching, knees pumping, clutching his gear to his body, his shell belt and holstered .45 flapping against his right side, he traced a serpentine path to make himself as hard a target as possible for the drunken Rurale colonel. Still, several of Campa's bullets came close enough to pelt the bounty hunter with dirt and rocks as well as with chunks from the mud bricks of the chicken coop he skirted, hearing the roused hens squawking and quarreling inside.

He was halfway to the thick brush beyond the chicken coop, Campa's pistols continuing to bark behind him, when Prophet heard an angry snarl. There was the quick pad of four feet.

The low, angry snarling grew louder. Prophet glanced over his left shoulder to see a medium-sized dog tear after him, starlight showing in the beast's shaggy fur and reflecting off its small, angry dark eyes.

"Ah, shit!" the bounty man lamented breathlessly, turning his head and continuing to pump his legs, ignoring the pain of pebbles and cactus thorns biting into the soles of his bare feet. "A goddamn dog—just what I need!"

There was another shot from behind. Then another.

Just as the dog was about to clamp its mouth around one of Prophet's ankles, Campa's last slug tore up dirt within an inch of the pesky devil. It yipped sharply. Deciding it wasn't as angry as it had thought, the mutt veered off course to disappear in the heavy shadows behind the coop.

Prophet kept running until he was sure he was out of

range of Campa's pistols. Shouldering up to the rear corner of a small, dark casa, he dropped his gear on the ground, then picked through until he'd found his socks. Breathing hard, looking around cautiously, he pulled the socks on and then reached for his pants.

A shrill cry rose behind Prophet from the direction of the hotel. Campa was shouting in Spanish, the words muffled. He must have been out front of the place now and yelling toward the Rurale headquarters on the south edge of town.

The echoing cries set a couple dogs to barking. From what Prophet could make out, the colonel was ordering his underlings to sound the alarm. The thought had no sooner passed through the bounty hunter's brain than a bell began tolling loudly, wildly, alerting every Rurale in town.

The bounty hunter cursed again sharply and muttered, "Whoever heard of a whore gettin' married? Especially one as talented as Senorita Ramonna . . . !"

Prophet picked up his pants, quickly stepped into them, and then into his boots. When he'd pulled on his buckskin shirt and thumbed his suspenders up over his broad shoulders, he wrapped his shell belt around his waist, buckled it, and tied the thong securing the holster housing his walnut-gripped .45 Peacemaker low on his right thigh. He looped his shotgun over his shoulder, picked up his rifle, and set off running through the brush and scattered casas and stock pens, in the general direction he remembered the livery barn to be.

The bell kept tolling, sounding inordinately loud in the quiet night. Campa quit yelling, but as Prophet ran around the corner of a house and started east, someone else started yelling in the west.

He whipped a look to his left. Two men in dove gray uniforms and straw sombreros were running toward him.

"Stop!" one of them shouted, bringing his Trapdoor Springfield rifle to bear. He had a cigarette or a cigar smoldering between his lips, the coal glowing redly. They'd likely been out on patrol against renegade Comanches or the particularly savage breed of bandit that haunted this border country, when they'd heard the bell and the colonel's indignant shrieks.

Prophet extended his double-barreled coach gun in his left hand. He triggered the left barrel. The explosion sounded like a detonated keg of gunpower. The flash of the heavy flames lapping from the maw showed the nearest Rurale flying two feet up and straight back with a scream, his sombrero tumbling down his chest.

As the other Rurale stopped and, also screaming, jerked his rifle stock to his shoulder, Prophet's sawed-off gut shredder blossomed once more, the flames reflecting off the second Rurale's pale uniform before the fist-sized wad of buckshot tore through the man and hurled him over his partner. He bounced off a stock trough, his back breaking audibly, and landed in the street with a heavy thud, his rifle crashing to the ground beside his quivering corpse.

"Sorry, amigos," Prophet said. "But better you than me!"

Prophet swung away from the dead Rurales and continued running for his horse, hearing more shouts rising beneath the consarned tolling of that damned bell.

2

PROPHET APPROACHED THE livery barn that sat near the north edge of San Simon, near the old, crumbling adobe church that humped up beyond it, blotting out the stars. He'd chosen the barn because it was off the beaten path, and he figured no Rurales would house their own horses there and recognize his own rather conspicuous, somewhat notorious beast, the appropriately named Mean and Ugly.

Now he slipped between the wooden doors and drew them closed behind him. There were only four or five stalls in the place, with a paddock out in back.

As he latched the doors and quickly lifted the bale on a lantern to light it, a voice said in Spanish from the dense shadows, "If you're here to rob me, I must inform you that I am old and blind, and the merciful *Jesus* watches over me and my horses from the cathedral next door! Stealing pesos from me will get you sent straight to hell!"

Prophet hung the lantern on a rusty nail. "Go back to bed, old man. It's only me—Lou Prophet. I'm just gonna saddle my horse and fog the sage. I'd appreciate it if you'd

never heard of me, if anyone asks—especially the men of
Arturo Campa."

"Oh, you." The old man, whose name Prophet remembered was Santiago Sandoval, materialized like a lumpy
ghost in the murky shadows, carrying his own, spy-flecked
lantern by its handle. "The bell tolls for thee?" He rolled his
dark eyes toward the front of the barn, to indicate the continued tolling of the bells at the Rurale headquarters.

"They toll for all of us, sooner or later," Prophet said,
stepping into his horse's stall, the mean, hammer-headed
roan twitching his ears devilishly.

"I should have known it was you."

"What do I owe you?" Prophet asked, throwing his saddle blanket over Mean's back.

"Six pesos. And an extra one for the patience required
to house and feed such a wretched, contrary beast. He tore
the seam in my serape earlier, when I was only trying to
comb him."

"I'll make it seven," Prophet said, understanding.

A woman's voice said from a lean-to partition in which
the old man and his wife lived: "Come back to bed, Santiago. My feet are cold."

The old man gave a wan smile and shrugged. "Leave it
on the water barrel."

He and his lantern slipped back into the shadows, and
Prophet quickly rigged up the dun in the darkness.

Mean stomped and snorted, playful and excited despite
the lateness of the hour to hit the trail again. Mean and Ugly
didn't care to be housed in livery barns unless there were a
frisky mare or two for him to touch noses with, stomp with,
and to generally try to impress despite the fact he'd lost his
balls to the gelding knife many years before. Prophet had
just turned his back on the horse to grab his saddlebags off
the stall partition when out the corner of his eye he saw the
dun lower his long snout toward the bounty hunter's shoulder and peel his leathery lips away from his teeth.

"Goddamn your cussed hide!" Prophet hissed, jerking
around and smashing his left elbow against the side of the

horse's stout jaw just in time to keep the shoulder of his tunic from being ripped out.

The horse lurched back, blowing, snorting, shaking his head, twitching his ears, and showing his teeth. If there were ever a horse who could laugh in ribald mockery at its rider, that horse was Mean and Ugly.

"Why the hell do you do that?" Prophet asked the wicked beast, tossing his saddlebags over the horse's back, behind his saddle. "As if I got all night to dance around in here with you, sportin' for a fight. We got them Rurales on our asses again, no thanks to Senorita Ramonna—if you can't trust a whore, *who can you trust?*—and I got no damn time for your nonsense. You know, if I had a lick of sense, I would have listened to everyone who's so willingly given their opinion on the subject and ridden you off to the damn glue factory years ago!"

He led the horse to the front of the barn, blew out the lantern, tossed some coins onto the rain barrel's wooden cover, and then slipped out between the doors, closing them quietly behind him.

He cocked his head to listen. The bells had stopped tolling. The silence was even more menacing than the tolling had been. Campa's Rurales were after him, but where were they searching?

Oh, well, he thought as he stepped into the leather—*at least they don't know where I am, either.* He slid his shotgun over his shoulder, letting it dangle down his back, and booted the horse around the side of the livery barn, wanting to light a shuck out of San Simon as quickly as possible but also get as far away as he could from the Rurale outpost on the south edge of town.

He steered the snorting horse between unlit shacks, stock pens, and corrals.

The flat roofs around him were limned in starlight. Low hills humped darkly in the north, and a lone coyote's keening cry beckoned him. Ahead on his left, lantern light guttered, and he was about to turn away from it when he saw a figure kneeling on the rear stoop of a small, adobe house.

Another silhouette, this one with a rounded figure and with long hair—a girl—crouched over the one kneeling and leaning forward, loudly convulsing.

Prophet drew up to the rear of the house, a few yards away from the stoop, and rested his hand on the butt of his Winchester '73 jutting up from the sheath under his right thigh. The girl was speaking softly in Spanish to the young man airing his paunch in the wiry brush of the neglected yard.

A spindly looking creature, the kid had long, copper red hair, and he was dressed in only threadbare balbriggans and socks. He looked up, and the long strands of his copper red hair fell away from his face, revealing what appeared to be a palm-sized S that had been burned into his left cheek, at a slight angle tilting from the bottom corner of his right eye to the upper right corner of his thin-lipped mouth.

In the light of the lantern that the girl held, Prophet saw the kid curl his lip and say raggedly and with a good degree of self-deprecation, "Haven't learned how to mix tanglefoot with tobacco and women yet, but I'm workin' on it!"

"Don't be in a hurry, Red." Prophet stared at the S-brand on the kid's face that looked familiar, shuffling through memories. "Have we met?"

The kid regarded him skeptically, cautious as a desert coyote. "Have we?"

"What's your name, kid?"

The pale, gaunt-faced younker gave a wry grin. "What's yours?"

Prophet returned the smile. Hoof thuds sounded from the other end of the shack, and men's voices rose. He could hear the squawk of tack, the rattle of bit chains, and he cursed under his breath.

Someone must have seen him light out from the livery barn.

He looked at the scrawny, redheaded kid still grunting sickly on his knees and said, "Do a fellow gringo a favor—will you, junior? If anyone in dove gray inquires about a man named Prophet . . ."

"I hear you," the kid said, tilting his head toward the

shack behind him, listening to the thuds of approaching riders rising in the south.

Prophet booted Mean and Ugly on along the broad alley
he'd been following, angling northwest, letting the sure-
footed horse pick its own way through the darkness. When
he was sixty or so yards from the shack, he hipped around
in his saddle to see several riders stopped near the edge of
the lantern light. They wore gray uniforms and gray hats
with black visors.

The kid was standing and pointing straight out from the
rear of the shack, and Prophet could hear his voice speaking
Spanish about as proficiently as Prophet himself would.

When the Rurales veered off to the northeast, Prophet
heaved a relieved sigh, muttered, "Thanks, junior," and
booted Mean on out of the village, following an angling
horse trail northwest into the hills toward the Rio Bravo that
cut through the desert along the southern edge of the boot
heel of Texas, too damn many miles beyond.

He was climbing a long hill when the drum of hooves
sounded behind him.

Glancing back, he saw two riders galloping down a hill
about fifty yards behind. In the darkness he could see their
pale uniforms and the silver insignias on their sombrero
brims reflecting starlight, gray dust rising behind them.

Prophet stopped Mean just beneath the brow of the hill
and slid his Winchester from its saddle boot. He cocked a
round, aimed, and fired two shots quickly, watching the
gray dust fan up on each side of the riders. They drew so
sharply back on their reins that the horses ground their rear
hooves into the tough terrain and skidded several yards before stopping.

Prophet triggered two more rounds in front of the riders
then heard them both curse in Spanish. He watched as they
neck-reined their mounts around, batted their heels against
the mounts' flanks, and galloped back up and over the hill
and out of sight. The rataplan of shod hooves dwindled
quickly, and then the only sound was the indignant yammering of two coyotes in the dark hills to the east.

Prophet waited, listening, watching for more riders. When none came, he plucked four fresh shells from his cartridge belt and thumbed them through the Winchester's loading gate. Sliding the rifle back into its scabbard, he pointed Mean north once again and touched spurs to the horse's flanks. He did not gallop the mount and risk Mean breaking a leg and stranding him out here at the mercy of Campa, but only trotted up and down the long hills cloaked in starlight.

Several times he stopped to let the horse rest and drink from his hat. He'd left San Simon so quickly that he hadn't had time to fill his canteen, so he continued north across the dry Chihuahuan Desert with only a little brackish water sloshing around in the flask. There was a Mexican stage line that ran through this part of the desert, and there were of course wells at all of the stations along the line, but since he didn't know their exact locations, finding one in the dark would be almost impossible.

Best to avoid the stations for as long as he could. As few folks who saw him on his run to the border, the better.

He'd stay clear of the country's main trails, as well. If he was lucky, he'd run into a spring. If not, he and Mean would have to wait to refresh themselves at the Rio Bravo. They'd gone without water before.

He continued riding, slowly but steadily widening the distance between himself and Campa. Staying off the main trails should buy him enough time to get across the border before the jealous Rurale colonel could catch up to him. It would be damn near impossible for Campa's men to track him out here in the dark. There was no moon, and it didn't look like there was going to be one, and while the stars were bright, they weren't bright enough for efficient tracking.

After an hour of relatively hard riding, hearing no one behind him, Prophet allowed himself a saddle snooze. When he awoke, he rested Mean, dampened the horse's mouth and nostrils with a wet bandanna, and then set off once more. Dawn found him skirting a broad canyon that he knew fed into the canyon of the Rio Grande, which meant he was getting close to the border.

The gray light turned a soft red, and shadows drifted out from rocks and small bunches of dry, brown grass. Sotol cacti sent their saber-like stalks straight up from their ragged bases around him.

The sky turned slowly from green to a cobalt blue. To each side were mountains. Behind were the rolling, brown, rock-stippled hills he'd passed through in the dark.

Around nine o'clock, judging by the sun's angle, he spied some relatively heavy growth sheathing an arroyo just east of him. He reined Mean into the shallow wash and loosed a ragged breath when he saw shiny water bubbling up from tan shale rock along the wash's southern bank, nourishing the galleta grass and a few spindly willows drooping around it, offering shade. The water winked gold in the intense desert sunlight. A kangaroo rat scurried behind a hump of gray rock on his left, and he could hear the rapid thumps and grunts of what was likely a javelina that had probably been enjoying the water before Prophet and Mean had interrupted it.

Mean smelled the water and shook his head in eager anticipation, rattling the bit in his teeth.

Prophet rode the horse ahead and climbed heavily out of the saddle, looking around carefully. When water was this scarce, there were likely to be more critters nearby than wild pigs and kangaroo rats. Border toughs, maybe. Possibly Kiowa, as this was their traditional stomping grounds, though he was glad he'd seen no recent sign of the fierce nomadic warriors.

When he'd slipped the bit from Mean's mouth and loosened his latigo strap so that the hammer-headed dun could drink freely, Prophet dropped the reins and let the horse have at the chuckling spring. He'd ridden slowly, easily for the past hour or so, so the dun didn't require the obligatory cooling. Even if he tried, he doubted he'd be able to hold the stubborn beast back from the faintly murmuring springs.

While the horse drank, Prophet climbed the arroyo's north bank, starting a little at a sand rattler that had been sunning itself on a flat rock but now slithered quickly off into the rocks beyond a paloverde tree. Mean continued to drink loudly, twitching his tail at flies, as Prophet scanned the area for interlopers.

When he figured Mean had had enough, he went down, pulled the horse back away from the spring, and crouched beside it, doffing his hat and lowering his mouth to catch a slender freshet tumbling over the shelving sandstone.

The water wasn't over cool but it was fresh. It tasted richly of minerals. Instantly, he felt it reviving him. When he'd had a bellyful, he walked over to where Mean stood hip-cocked, and unslung his canteen from his saddle horn.

The flat, unechoing crack of a rifle exploded the sunny stillness. The canteen jerked wildly in Prophet's hand. The bullet crashed through it and ricocheted off a rock near the springs.

"Shit!"

Prophet dropped the ruined flask and lunged for his rifle.

3

AT THE SAME time but fifty miles north of the Rio Grande, the dwarf Mordecai Moon sat back in his child-sized wicker rocking chair on the porch of his big, gaudy saloon called Moon's House of a Thousand Delights and stared out at the broad, dusty street of the town that was formerly known as Chisos Springs but which the dwarf himself had renamed in his own honor—Moon's Well.

Moon had renamed the town when he'd purchased the saloon from the old trader and prospector, Chisos La Grange. La Grange had been a half-mad prospector who'd haunted the Chisos Mountains to the west for nearly thirty years. Around his precious well, which offered the only steady supply of water in a hundred square miles, a small town had gradually grown after La Grange himself had built a saloon fifty feet from the well. Suffering from multiple afflictions in his later years, La Grange later sold the land grant as well as the well and the saloon to the dwarf Mordecai Moon. Moon razed the saloon and built another, far grander affair than La Grange's humble little watering hole, and named it with the dwarf's own personal flair and unabashed aplomb.

Now La Grange's diminutive successor, Mordecai Moon, sitting on Moon's House of a Thousand Delights's broad front gallery, poked his black bowler hat off his round head and hauled a folding barlow knife from a side pocket of his black clawhammer coat. He ran the razor-edged blade along the edge of his left thumbnail and pooched out his thin, chapped lips in concentration.

With his beak-like, bulb-tipped, bright red nose, his deep-set, cobalt blue eyes ringed with sickly yellow whites, and a knobby chin fringed with colorless goat whiskers, the dwarf was considered by most to be the ugliest specimen— man or beast—to be found within all of West Texas. "And that took in account," so the saying went, "a good many rattlesnakes and wild shoats!"

No one ever said this to Moon's face, however. At least they didn't and live to laugh about it . . .

The dwarf shaved off a narrow bit of the grime-encrusted nail, let the shaving drop to the floor of the broad wooden veranda · painted lime green, then closed the knife and shoved it back down into the pocket of his frock coat, which he'd had specially made to fit his diminutive frame. Usually, the clothes of a six- or seven-year-old child would fit Mordecai Moon, but no one seemed to make frock coats for small boys, so Moon had them made by a Russian tailor in El Paso. He had three—black, burgundy, and Irish green, but he had only the one black bowler hat that he trimmed with a red feather from a hawk's tail.

The hat was actually more copper than black, owing to its age and the ground-in desert dust. Moon might have been a wealthy man, but he was far from a well-heeled one.

Mordecai Moon sat back in his chair, which he'd pulled up close enough to the gallery's front edge that he could extend his stubby, bowed, two-foot-long legs and hike his little boy's black boots atop the rail, and cross them, which was what he did. Moon was fixing to take a midmorning nap so he'd be well rested for the night's business when he spied movement on the sun-blasted, rock- and cacti-tufted desert to the north, just beyond the town.

Two riders were following the old Chihuahua Trail, which was the only trail through Moon's Well and which became the town's broad main drag and remained so for a hundred yards before it slithered off into the desert once more—a floury pale line twisting and turning and rising and falling through one watery mirage after another, all the way to the Rio Grande and beyond.

Boots clomped behind Moon, issuing from inside the saloon, the two broad front doors of which had been propped open with rocks. No common batwings for Moon's place but grand oak doors carved in the ornate Spanish style and hauled in from an old Mexican church to the west.

The clomping grew louder and stopped. In the corner of his right eye, Moon spied movement, and he raked his eyes from the two oncoming riders to see his girl, Griselda May, leaning against the door frame, her long, dark brown hair dancing in the hot, dry breeze.

The girl yawned. "Anything happening out here yet, Mordecai? I'm bored."

Griselda pooched her lips out in a pout. Mordecai smiled, his little, dark blue eyes turning shiny and round, his thick lips stretching back from his large, tobacco-crusted teeth— teeth too large for his mouth. "You just hold on, Griselda. Things'll be hoppin' soon. George Montgomery's bull train is due through here in a couple hours, and then we'll wake the band."

Mordecai clapped his oversized hands twice, loudly, and cackled in his eager way that appalled and horrified most folks, his eyes swelling and nearly popping out of their sockets. The dwarf repelled most people, but in Griselda May he evoked nothing but a lusty flush.

"Is this Friday, Mordecai?" she said in her lazy, Texas drawl, her brown eyes coming alive.

She'd been born to a saddle maker and part-time sheriff's deputy in Tularosa but had left home when she was only twelve, hitching her star to a trail herd heading to Kansas. While all agreed that Griselda was one of the most beautiful women within a thousand square Texas miles, the joke was that she smelled like a thirty-and-found cow waddie, though that wasn't true.

They only said that because of how she dressed—in rugged trail gear complete with matched Colts. She hadn't punched cows in several years, since she'd thrown in with Mordecai Moon. Now she was Moon's girl as well as his business partner, and while she outshone him in looks, her soul was just as rotten.

Like Mordecai Moon, Griselda May was a cold-blooded killer. They were two peas of the same pod.

"It is that, Griselda. It's Friday!" The dwarf cackled again, rubbing his hands together in eager anticipation. He loved dancing to his own four-man mariachi band comprised of Mexicans who were of the Spanish grant's original tenant families. Moon also loved to gamble, though he was terrible at it, and no one wanted to gamble with him and risk incurring his wrath and a .36-caliber bullet fired from point-blank range between their eyes.

"Ah, shucks. Now I'm really bored. Bored and anxious. I'm so hot . . . so tired of the sun, Mordecai. I want it to be *night*." Griselda sauntered over in her undershot stockmen's boots, swinging her hips inside her skin-tight, black denims behind brush-scarred, red-stitched, black leather leggings, and cuffed the dwarf's hat off his forehead.

She planted a wet kiss his on his freckled cheek. "What do you say we go upstairs and tussle till dark?"

Griselda ran her hand up and down his short, willowy thigh clad in orange-and-black-checked broadcloth with patched knees. Moon winced and brushed her hand away.

"Oh, no, you git. Don't you go gittin' me worked up again, Griselda. I ain't as young as you. I'm liable to turn into old Frank Rose over yonder." He chuckled at that, glancing at the saloon sitting a ways west and on the other side of the street from Moon's place.

The Rose Hotel and Saloon was far less grand than Moon's place. It was an old, mud-brick affair with two stories and a brush roof. Originally, the Mexican tenants had

built it with Chisos La Grange's blessing—he'd had more
business than he knew what to do with—and then abandoned it for unknown reasons. The saloon was now owned
by Frank and Ruth Rose, who'd bought it from Moon. They
were now his tenants, as was everyone else in the town
of Moon's Well, though their dream of prospering here in
Moon's Well along the old Chihuahua Trail had withered
the day, nearly a year ago, Frank Rose was cut down and
bedridden by a brain stroke.

"Please, now, Griselda. I'm gonna end up like Frank
Rose, and you'll be feedin' me mush with a spoon, you keep
workin' my tired old bones like you been," Moon said.

"Sure couldn't tell that by this mornin'," Griselda said,
sticking the tip of her tongue in the dwarf's ear. "You per-
formed right well, Mr. Mordecai Moooon. . . ."

Moon chuckled and shuddered at the sensation of the
girl's, soft, warm, wet tongue. "No . . . now, you stop or
you're gonna git the old snake stirrin' in its hole!"

"I want it to stir. I like your snake, Mordecai."

Moon cackled in delight, basking in the girl's obvious
adoration and desire for him, which was so unexplainable to
so many. "Look there—we got someone comin'!"

He pointed toward the riders just now swimming up out
of a brassy mirage and entering the outskirts of Moon's
Well. Long, tan dusters flapped out around them as their
horses loped past the town's original mud shacks and stock
pens and corrals constructed of brush and ocotillo stalks.
They both wore Stetsons and string ties, and pistols were
tied down on their thighs. Badges of some sort flashed silver
whenever their flapping dusters exposed the lapels of their
wool vests to the sun.

The lawmen slowed their horses and came on toward the
saloon. Moon sat up straight in his chair, boots still crossed
on the porch rail before him. Griselda kept her hand on his
left shoulder, and he held his hand over hers, vacantly returning the affection though the dwarf's interest was mainly
on the newcomers now.

"Want me to wake Manco and Loot?" Griselda asked in her lazy drawl, pitching her voice at the end of the question with vague menace.

"Nah, hell. Let 'em sleep. They're gonna need to be in top form when the bull teams pull in, watchin' the gamblin' tables and makin' sure the girls get paid."

The lawmen trotted their horses from Moon's left, their horses' hooves clomping, their tack squawking and rattling. Tan dust, a good six inches deep in the street, puffed up around the mounts' hocks.

The men stared straight ahead from beneath their low-canted hat brims, mustache-mantled mouths moving as they conversed. They and their horses were covered beneath a golden sheen of trail dust. Drawing up to the well that sat directly in front of Moon's saloon, they swung heavily down from their saddles, giving weary grunts as though they'd ridden hard and far.

The taller man was looking at one of the two signs mounted on posts abutting the well on which Moon had written the cost for water, and he turned to the other one and said, "Dick, look at this."

The other one slapped his hat against his leg, causing dust to puff thickly around him, and hitched his big Colt pistol high on his right hip. He came around to stare up at the sign. "What in the *hell*? Chisos never charged for water."

"And I'll be goddamned if I'll pay for it!" said Dick.

They both snickered in disgust, shaking their heads, while the taller lawman took the bucket off the hook under the peaked, shake-shingled roof over the well that was rimmed with stones forming a wall four feet high. The well itself was about as big around as the trough of an average windmill—maybe eight feet in diameter. Chisos La Grange had dug it fifty feet deep, tapping into an aquifer that flowed out from under the Chisos Mountains to the west.

The taller lawman turned the handle on the winch, which went *sheep!-sheep!-sheep!* as the bucket dropped down into the dank, humid depths of the well that sent the refreshing smell of cool mushrooms and the iodine odor of minerals upward, and which set the taller lawman's throat to aching with thirst.

Mordecai Moon said from his perch on the porch of his gaudy saloon, in a voice soft with casual menace, "I'll say you *will* pay for it. Ten cents for a bucket, just like the sign says."

Griselda said in her saucy way, fists on her hips, thrusting her breasts out beneath her calico blouse, "Don't matter how much you drink, neither. You winch up a bucket, you pay for a bucket."

Both men turned to him while the taller one continued to winch the bucket into the well. Their eyes slid up and down the saloon's three stories, the whipsawed lumber painted purple while the doors and window casings and the floor of the gallery were painted lime green. The Rangers looked at Moon, and their scowls deepened.

"Who the hell are you?" asked Dick, poking a finger out at the dwarf with an expression of incredulity and revulsion. He flicked his eyes to the sprawling, gaudy saloon once more. "And what the fuck is *that*?"

"Read the sign." Moon climbed up out of his little, toy-sized chair, muttered, "Let me handle this, darlin'," to Griselda, and then walked in his sway-shouldered, bandy-legged fashion to the top of the gallery steps. "Even Rangers can read, can't they?"

He'd been able to tell by their five-pointed silver stars that they were Texas Rangers.

Moon hiked up his pants and his cartridge belt and hol-stered six-shooter—an 1877 Sheriff's Model Colt Lightning with a nickel finish, ivory grips, and a four-and-a-half-inch barrel—that hung relatively well on his spindly left hip, in the cross-draw position. He dropped heavily, grunting, down the steps.

As the taller Ranger winched the bucket back up out of the well, his partner pointed out the words on the grand sign over the front gallery and read them aloud: "Moon's House of a Thousand Delights." He offered a half smile in amazement and then looked at the little creature in a clawhammer coat and age-coppered bowler hat ambling toward him, the creature's head looking inordinately large on his otherwise childish, little, bow-legged body. His hands hung nearly to his knees.

"And you—don't tell me—you're Mr. Moon!" Dick said, chuckling. "And you think you own this here well and you can charge for water out here in the middle of nowhere where they ain't none around for a hundred miles in any direction, unless you count the Rio Grande."

"That's about the size of it, yes," Moon said, stopping about ten feet away from the dusty Rangers and their dusty, sweat-silvered horses. "And if you don't go ahead and pay the box for the bucket you pulled up"—he dipped his chin to indicate the wooden payment box attached to the sign flanking Dick—"I'm gonna blow you both to the Devil so fast you'll think you was swallowed up by a hell-breathin' cyclone."

The tall Ranger set the filled bucket on the side of the well coping and glowered at Moon. "Listen, you little sawed-off son of a bitch—we're both Texas Rangers, and we been out of water since nine o'clock last night, and if you think we're gonna pay you a *penny* for this here bucket, you got another think comin'!"

Moon stared up at him. His ugly little pig's face with its tuft of chin whiskers was bland but his cobalt blue eyes gradually acquired a golden sheen as though they'd become two windows opened now to the fires raging in the dwarf's soul.

"What'd you call me?" he said so softly that neither Ranger had heard.

They knew he'd said something, though, and they frowned down at him.

"Huh?" said Dick.

"I said . . ." Moon licked his lips and drilled the taller Ranger with a primal look. ". . . What did you just call me?"

"I called you a sawed-off little half-ounce son of a bitch—that's what I just called you," the taller Ranger repeated, his rugged, mustached face flushed behind its liberal coating of dust.

Neither Ranger saw the gun come up until the dwarf had fired it, the crack echoing flatly around the broad street.

Both Rangers stood frozen, as did Moon, for a full five seconds before the taller Ranger swallowed hard and swayed a little before looking down at his belly. He chuckled skeptically at the smoking hole in his brown wool vest, just beneath a gold watch chain, and the blood that began to dribble out of it.

"Holy . . ." he said. "Holy shit—this little cocksucker just shot me, Dick."

Dick looked in horror from his partner to Moon, who glared up at him, recocking the Lightning. A tendril of gray smoke curled from the barrel.

"Hey!" Dick shouted, dropping his horse's reins and reaching for the long-barreled Remington thonged on his right thigh. "Hey, you—!"

Plang!

As a thin wand of orange flames flicked toward Dick, the Ranger screamed and twisted around as he fell back against his horse, which shied slightly, twitching its ears. Dick dropped to his knees and then screamed again, glancing in horror back over his shoulder at Moon, whose Lightning popped again.

Dick jerked forward as a round hole appeared in the back of his duster, just beneath his left shoulder blade, making dust puff from the filthy garment.

"Teach you to try to rob Mordecai Moon, Ranger!"

Dick lurched to his feet and ran, stumbling and grunting, off toward the other side of the street. Mordecai Moon shambled past the horses that had curveted away from the action, lazily swishing their tails, and extended the gun once more as the Ranger stumbled off down a break between Grieson's Saddle Shop and Waymer's Drug Store. "Here, have one more!"

Moon's pistol popped again.

Dick loosed another shrill scream and continued to run off down the break, heading for the shed and scattered Mexican shanties on the far side of the little town. Mordecai drew a deep breath, wagged his ugly head, and said, "If there's anything I can't stand, it's a goddamn Texas Ranger. Bastards think they own the whole frontier." He raised his voice. "Hope ya die slow in the desert, you son of a bitch!"

He walked over to the other Ranger, who sat against the well, staring up at his killer in shock, holding both hands across his belly as though to try to keep the blood and viscera from oozing out the quarter-sized hole. The Ranger's hat had fallen off his head, revealing his nearly bald, freckled pate behind a few sweaty wisps of sandy blond hair.

"Where the hell . . . ?" the man panted, gritting his teeth at Moon. "Where the hell . . . is . . . La Grange . . . ?"

"Said somethin' about goin' back East to live with his grandkids," said Moon. "Sold the grant to me two years ago. All mine now. Just like your ass is, dead man!"

"Nooo!" the Ranger screamed.

Moon silenced him with a bullet between his eyes.

He turned to face the saloon.

Griselda sat on the porch rail, her long legs behind the black leather chaps dangling over the side. She was smiling, showing all her fine, white teeth, her long, brown hair blowing in the wind beneath her round-brimmed, low-crowned black hat.

"Mr. Mordecai Moon," she said in a high-pitched little girl's voice, raising her right hand and holding her thumb and index finger a half inch apart. "I love you just a little bit more every day!"

Moon chuckled and ambled toward his House of a Thousand Delights.

Ruth Rose's brown eyes darkened in horror as she stared out of her and her husband's second-story bedroom window in the Rose Hotel and Saloon. She was standing so that she could see up the street on her right, where now only dust wafted around the two saddled horses that stood near the well, waiting for water.

One Ranger sat slumped against the stone coping of the well, chin dipped to his chest, arms hanging straight down at his sides, hands in the dust. The other Ranger had run off to die, most likely.

Now Mordecai Moon cackled loudly, throwing his head back as he sashayed in that proud, evil way of his, toward his giant, gaudy saloon, where the malicious, tawny-haired girl lounged on the rail, laughing, sharing in the dwarf's delight.

Ruth Rose swept a strand of light brown hair from her cheek and turned to where her husband, Frank Rose, lay in their bed, staring dully, slack-jawed, his eyes as vacant as marbles. Another of Moon's victims though this one was taking longer to die.

Ruth looked down at the bowl of oatmeal she'd been feeding her bedridden husband and said with hushed horror, "Lord, please spare us from whatever horror is fated to happen next in this hellish town!"

4

LOU PROPHET'S WINCHESTER leaped and roared in his hands.

The Rurale running toward him through the brush dropped his rifle and reached for his knee as he stumbled sideways and tumbled into a cactus snag, screaming shrilly. Dust lifted around him, and Prophet saw a wash of red painting the cactus though he could no longer see the Rurale.

Resting his rifle atop the ledge above the spring, the bounty hunter ejected the spent cartridge casing to send it careening over his shoulder and clanking onto the rocks behind him. He waited, staring through the scrub south of the springs.

Nothing moved now, not even the Rurale who lay belly down in the cactus snag, giving a soft, keening cry.

The dying man was likely a scout rider for Campa. As far as Prophet could tell, the scout was alone. Wary of being trapped here around the spring, and possibly surrounded, Prophet wheeled, slid his rifle into its boot, grabbed Mean's reins, and swung into the saddle.

He put the horse back down to the faint horse trail he'd been following, looked around carefully, spying only a thin mare's tail of dust rising in the southwest—a column of cream-clad riders on brown horses angling toward him. They'd heard the rifle fire and were headed in the bounty hunter's direction.

Giving the east, south, and west a thorough measure, he saw no other signs of movement. The main column of at least ten men—no doubt every Rurale Campa had stationed at San Simon, minus the two Prophet had killed the previous night—was a good mile or so away, and their horses were probably as blown as Mean was.

If he didn't linger, Prophet had a good chance of making it to the Rio Grande ahead of them.

Twenty minutes later, he followed a switchback deer trail down into the broad, deep canyon. Since he and Mean had watered at the spring, he didn't waste much time at the canyon bottom, where the muddy waters of the Rio Grande rippled over gravelly sandbars between the twisting canyon walls. He'd have liked to enjoy a bath with his clothes on, thereby scrubbing himself as well as his trail-sour, dust-caked duds, but he'd taken a whore's bath back in Ramonna's room, before putting the so-called wood to the comely senorita. That would have to tide him. Besides, he had no one to offend besides himself and his horse, and Mean didn't seem to mind.

When he and Mean were halfway up the north ridge wall, rifles began cracking behind him. He glanced back to see Campa's men lined up on the opposite rim, aiming their rifles at an angle, triggering lead at him.

Campa stood off to the right of the line of Rurales, wearing his customary wagon-wheel sombrero with the eagle insignia pinned to the steepled crown. The colonel was shaking his fist at Prophet and shouting. Prophet couldn't make out what he was saying beneath the crackling of the Trapdoor Springfields, but he had a pretty good idea he wasn't being complemented on his good breeding.

Prophet hummed, whistled contentedly. He and Campa both knew he was too far away for those old Springfields to be any danger. The bullets dropped harmlessly in the sand

and rocks at the base of the ridge. The Rurales kept firing, however, and Prophet kept whistling as he and Mean continued on up the game trail snaking up the face of the cliff. At the top, on Texas soil, he swung down from the leather, stepped up to the edge of the canyon, turned his back to it, dropped his buckskin trousers and longhandles to his knees, and bent forward, giving Campa's men a round, pale target to aim for.

There was a momentary increase in the firing and in the volume of Campa's tirade.

Prophet grinned.

He pulled his pants back up, mounted his horse, and rode off to the north, hearing the crackling of the Springfields continuing only sporadically now while Campa continued to pump his fist and berate him shrilly.

"Well, it ain't Georgia," the big bounty hunter said, swaying easily now in his saddle, gazing around at the vast, forbidding country around him, which looked like an endless rug of irregularly ridged corduroy stretching away for as far as the eye could see, spiked with mean and nasty-looking cacti of all shapes and sizes. "But at least it's America, by damn, and Campa won't cross the Rio Bravo less'n he wants to get crossways with the U.S. Army."

He glanced over his shoulder once more. Campa's men had finally now lowered their rifles and were walking off to retrieve their horses. Prophet chuckled.

And then, to keep his mind off his ruined canteen out here in this merciless desert where no man wanted to be long without water, he started to sing: "In Dixie's land where I was born, Early on one frosty mornin', Look away! Look away! Look away! Dixie Land!"

He didn't sing for long, though. The parched air soon turned his throat to leather.

He thought he could feel his tongue swelling, though it hadn't been long enough since he'd had a drink for that to happen. It was just his imagination, his anxiety over the lack of water, and the sun burning down through his weathered, funnel-brimmed hat and reflecting off the adobe-colored ground all around him.

He probably should have stayed closer to the river, but a canteen wasn't going to just rise up out of the rocks. Sooner or later, he had to head north. Chisos Springs was somewhere out here, between the Rio Grande and the Chisos Mountains, but he hadn't been through the settlement in several years, and he couldn't recall its exact location.

He remembered only the humble saloon run by the colorful old desert rat Chisos La Grange, and the man's well that teemed with cool, dark spring water that issued from cracks in the underlying Texas strata, deep underground.

La Grange's well was the only water for a long two-days' ride in any direction, under a pulsing sun raining liquid fire. Just the thought of a drink from it now made Prophet's throat all the drier, his tongue feel like a dead, swollen snake in his mouth.

An hour later, when the sun was about an hour past its zenith, he rode up a low rise and looked around to the north and west through his ancient, Confederate-issue field glasses. He spied what looked like a trail running from north to south a little west of his position. The trail was east of the gentle foothills rising gradually toward the craggy, copper ramparts of the Chisos Mountains shouldering dramatically against the western horizon.

And in the north, along the trail, there was a dark brown clump of what appeared more regularly shaped objects than boulders would be.

They were buildings.

Returning the glasses to his saddlebags, his heart quickening at the thought that he'd just located Chisos La Grange's settlement of Chisos Springs . . . and that he and Mean and Ugly might not die of thirst out here, after all . . . he rode on down the rise and deadheaded for the place in the godforsaken desert where he'd spied the brown blur.

When he'd ridden nearly another hour, and he was beginning to sag wearily in the saddle, and Mean's legs were beginning to splay and give him a jerking gait from the merciless sun and fatigue, Prophet reined up suddenly.

Straight out in front of him, not ten feet away, lay a dead man.

Prophet had seen enough dead men to know right away the man had given up the ghost. He lay belly down but twisted back on one shoulder, left cheek facing the sky. The other cheek rested on his outstretched arm. He wasn't moving even a little; he could have been a lump of man-shaped clay, just lying there, his upper lip and thick, brown mustache stretched back slightly from his upper teeth.

Prophet slid his Winchester from the saddle boot, and with a sudden spark of caution, he swung his right boot over his saddle horn and dropped smoothly to the ground, cocking the rifle and holding it straight out from his right hip.

"Kiowa" was a soft, menacing whisper all around him, emanating from the land itself, from a nearby mesquite and the far, red, shadowy Chisos range rising in the northwest. It set miniature snakes of apprehension slithering around beneath the skin of his lower back. He looked around carefully before deeming himself alone—at least within a couple of hundred feet or so—and then dropped to a knee beside the dead man.

The man was tall and relatively well dressed. His hat was nowhere in sight. His brown hair was thick and wavy though badly mussed and threaded with sand and dust. His long, tan duster was twisted around his legs and the tops of his worn, black boots trimmed with Texas-style spurs.

Prophet rolled the man onto his back. A five-pointed star flashed in the sunlight, the flash sparking off the bounty hunter's retinas for a moment, blinding him. Just when his vision had cleared and he found himself staring down at a badly bloodied Texas Ranger, a rifle report sucked back its own echo.

The slug plumed sand a few feet away.

A man's voice shouted, "Hold it right there, you Ranger-killin' son of a bitch!"

5

PROPHET LOWERED THE Winchester's barrel as the echoes of the rifle's screech chased each other skyward.

Behind him, Mean and Ugly snorted and shifted his weight uncomfortably. The bounty hunter looked to his right, saw a hatted head staring at him from over a rifle barrel. The man was belly down on a low, gravely dike about fifty yards away. The maw of the rifle remained trained on Prophet.

Apparently, he hadn't checked the layout closely enough. He wondered how long the man had been there. Likely, he was the shooter who'd shot the Ranger, which meant that Prophet, having discovered the dead Ranger, was probably next.

He scowled at the rifle, expecting it to blossom at any moment. But then it tilted upward, and the man wielding it stood, holding the rifle on Prophet with one hand, using the other hand to brush the red sand from his dark blue shirt, brown vest, and black denim trousers, the tops of which were stuffed down into high brown boots.

"Drop the rifle," the man said. He was young, and a pale

Stetson with a braided rawhide band was snugged down atop his head. Sandy hair feathered down over his ears and his collar.

Prophet squeezed the neck of the rifle's stock in frustration, then tossed the gun to the ground, muttering a curse. Nothing graveled a man who hunted for a living like being snuck up on.

"Now, the hogleg," the kid with the rifle said. "Slow as a winter rain."

Prophet slid his hand down to the Peacemaker holstered on his right thigh, unsnapped the keeper thong, and tossed the gun down next to the rifle. As the kid began climbing down the front of the dike, keeping the rifle trained on Prophet, the bounty hunter glimpsed a badge peeking out from behind the left flap of his vest.

Another Ranger?

The kid crabbed down the dike, loosing sand and gravel in his wake, and then walked around several tufts of cactus before drawing up within ten feet of the bounty hunter. The kid wore a smug grin, revealing a chipped front tooth.

His eyes were pale blue. A thin caterpillar mustache stretched across his upper lip, and scraggly sideburns dropped down to his jawline. If you didn't look closely, both the mustache and the sideburns could have been mistaken for a thin coating of soot.

The kid was almost as tall as Prophet though not quite as muscular. He was rawboned, with knobby wrists and shoulders.

"Killin' a Texas Ranger's a hangin' offense, you know, mister," he told Prophet with a sneering solemnity, glancing down at the dead man.

"It sure is."

"Why'd you do it?"

Prophet curled his upper lip. "I didn't do it, and I gotta feelin' you know that."

"How would I know?"

"When'd you come along?"

"Just now."

Prophet toughened his glare. "Then how'd you know he was a Ranger?"

The kid looked down at the dead man and then quirked a half smile as he raised his mocking, arrogant gaze again to Prophet. "I seen the badge when you rolled him over. I seen you headed this way, and then I came down to meet you, but when I got to the shelf yonder, I seen you crouched over a dead man. I think you killed him, and I reckon I'd best kill you right now. You wanna put some fun into it?"

Prophet wrinkled the leathery skin above the bridge of his thrice-broken nose. "Huh?"

"With pistols. We could go at it fair an' even-like."

Prophet stared at the kid, trying to decide if he was even younger than he looked or soft in his thinker box. "You're challenging me to a draw. . . ."

The kid grinned. A lock of thick, sun-bleached sandy hair licked down to just above his right brow. A mole shone just right of his nose, above his mustache. That, with the feral glitter in his eyes, gave him a wild, crazy look. "Yeah, that's right. I'm challengin' you to a draw. Just like a Friday night in Tularosa."

"Who the hell are you?" Prophet asked him.

"Me? Why, I'm the Rio Bravo Kid."

"The Rio Bravo Kid," Prophet said.

"Is there an echo?" The Kid's arrogant grin faded slightly. "I am the deputy sheriff of Moon's Well over yonder. I heard a Ranger come up missin', and I was sent by my superior, Sheriff Lee Mortimer, to come out here and look around, see if I couldn't scare him up."

Prophet studied him again, skeptically. The Kid was both young and daft. He had sharp but stupid eyes, the kind of eyes that could kill a man without blinking. "You keep that goddamn rifle aimed at me," the bounty hunter said, seething, "somethin' bad's gonna happen to you, son."

The kid laughed. "Yeah, like you gettin' gut-shot and left out here with him."

Prophet tried a different tactic. "Let's have us that contest."

The Kid's eyes brightened like it was Christmas and he knew he had a new rifle under the tree. "Yeah? Really?"

"Sure."

The Kid started to raise the Winchester. Prophet lurched forward with more speed and agility than anyone would have expected in a man his size.

With his left forearm he swept the Kid's rifle aside while hammering his right fist against the underside of the Kid's lower jaw with a solid smack. He jerked the rifle out of the Kid's hand as the younker twisted around and fell facedown in the sand, losing his hat and shaking his head as though a spider were chomping into his chin.

"Son of a *bitch*!" the Kid cried, scrambling to his feet.

As he charged Prophet, head down, the bounty hunter sidestepped, grabbed the Kid's collar, and jerked him in the same direction he'd been headed, only faster now. His forehead smacked a boulder resoundingly, and he crumpled up at the rock's base, wheezing and grunting, working his legs as though trying to regain his feet.

"Ach!" he said. "Oh, shit!"

Catching his breath, Prophet said, "Where I come from, fair warnin's as good as a promise."

With a shrill sigh, the Rio Bravo Kid sagged against the ground and lay still on his side.

Prophet tossed the Kid's rifle away and then went over and plucked the Kid's silver-chased Colt with gutta-percha grips from the Kid's tied-down holster. He tossed that away, too, and then walked over to Mean and Ugly and fished around in his saddlebags. The horse craned its neck to regard him wistfully with its brown eyes, which owned an orange cast in the sunlight, as though to say, "Out of the frying pan and into the fire. Way to go, champ."

Mean showed his yellow teeth and shook his head.

Prophet found the Rio Bravo Kid's black-and-white pinto pony ground-tied on the other side of the dike.

The horse shied a little when the stranger walked toward it but did not run. When Prophet had led the horse back to where the dead Ranger and the Kid lay, the Kid with his hands cuffed behind his back, Lou back-and-bellied both up over the pinto's back, the Kid across his own saddle, the Ranger behind.

The Kid was moving his head a little now, but mostly just wheezing and groaning, and Prophet had to smile at what must have felt like a giant fist wielding a smithy's hammer against the anvil of the Kid's tender brain.

"Serves you right, you purple fool."

The Kid had only a little water in his canteen, and it was brackish at best. He shared it with Mean but it did little to sate his thirst. He mounted Mean and led the pinto on across the desert across which long shadows were sliding as the sun angled down toward jagged peaks in the west.

As the town came into view, he was vaguely surprised by how much the place had grown since he'd last been through here. The Kid had called it by a different name than the one Prophet remembered, but, hell, things change. He wouldn't doubt if old Chisos La Grange was dead and pushing up century plants out here somewhere, or maybe fertilizing the ponderosas up in the Chisos Mountains, where he'd felt more at home.

Prophet grew more and more amazed as he followed the old Chihuahua Trail north where it broadened into the settlement's powdery, horse apple–littered main drag. A sign was calling the place Moon's Well as opposed to Chisos Springs, as Chisos had dubbed it.

Prophet recognized only a few of the old Mexican shacks that must have been here since the time of the hacendados, before this part of the Southwest was acquired by America. He remembered little else about the settlement. Chisos's old saloon and hotel was gone, another, grander structure taking its place. Moon's House of a Thousand Delights was a garish, wooden sprawl three times larger than Chisos's old, flea-bit flophouse, and three stories high, with a broad front gallery and two upper-floor balconies.

The roofed stone well sat across from it, flanked by a good dozen or so business establishments, including a hotel

and saloon that Prophet remembered from his last trip
through here. A humble, two-story, mud-brick affair, it had
been one of maybe three or four other businesses sheathing
the trail with Chisos's hotel at the time, on La Grange's
claim around the well.

Prophet saw the sign for a TOWN SHERIFF farther on.

He continued on past the well, wanting to get rid of his
cargo so Mean could cool down first before they both drank,
and so he himself could give the water the attention it de-
served. As he passed the sprawling, peacock-colored hotel,
trailing the pinto with the two men draped across it, one
dead, the other alive but sporting one hell of a headache,
he saw two faces in a second-story window.

Closing one eye against the sun, straining his eyes, he
saw the face of a tawny-haired girl staring down at him from
the window. She was crouching beside a little man with an
extraordinarily unappealing face. It must have been the
angle of the light, but the man appeared no taller than a
small child though his round, pasty face was that of an old,
ugly man.

Adding to the oddness of the visage, the girl was holding
a sheet to her otherwise naked body, which something told
Prophet was fine indeed, while the little man appeared to be
clad in only balbriggans. A fat stogie poked out a corner of
the haggard, large-nosed face that sprouted a colorless beard
from its spade-shaped chin.

The girl turned to the little man and moved her lips, saying something. The little man merely stared obliquely into
the street at Prophet, who turned his head forward as he
continued toward the office of the lawman that the Rio
Bravo Kid had mentioned.

It was on the right side of the street, between a livery
barn and a small, adobe-brick building sporting a barber's
pole on its stoop. A man who Prophet took to be the barber,
a slender gent with even features and pomaded hair parted
in the middle, sat on the stoop in a wicker rocking chair,
reading a book through round, silver-framed spectacles sagging low on his nose. The barber looked up from his book

and over his dusty spectacles as Prophet passed. He wore a small tattoo in the shape of a cross on his broad, tan left cheek. The tattoo looked completely out of place on the man's otherwise refined features.

"Sheriff in?" Prophet asked.

The barber studied the burdened pinto clomping along behind the stranger. "I don't keep track of Mortimer."

Prophet reined up in front of the small, whitewashed adobe-brick building on the far side of the barbershop. A wooden shingle over the front door announced simply: MOON'S WELL SHERIFF. Just as Prophet began to swing down from Mean's back, the door opened and a straight-backed, broad-shouldered, middle-aged man ducked under the low jam, puffing a meerschaum pipe.

He wore a three-piece suit but no hat, and his eyes were long, dark, and cunning as they swept Prophet quickly and then the pinto and its human cargo. Too quickly and furtively for most men to catch, he used his right thumb to flick the keeper thong off the hammer of the Schofield .44 holstered slightly left of his belly, in a hand-tooled, black leather holster.

He stood on the porch in front of his open office door, scowling at Prophet and smoking his pipe. Despite the black shirt he wore under a black leather vest under a tobacco tweed coat, he somehow didn't look hot. A town sheriff's star glistened on the black vest.

He had more the look of an aging gunman than a lawman. "Mortimer . . . ?"

Holding Mean's reins in one hand, Prophet stared at the man and riffled through memories the way he'd often riffled through old wanted dodgers, trying to put a name to a face.

"Prophet?" The sheriff of Moon's Well returned the foxily pensive stare. "Lon? No, Lou Prophet. Rebel bounty hunter from Georgia. Sold his soul to the Devil after the war."

"Lee Mortimer." Prophet nodded his surprise to see the old gunman after all these years. Funny how when you hadn't seen a noted outlaw in a while you just naturally assumed they'd taken a pill they hadn't been able to digest and were slumbering long and hard on a boot hill somewhere in the frontier outback.

"One and the same."

"Someone said you was back-shot by George Deushay in Sioux City."

"Iowa City. Amazing what a good doctor with a sharp scalpel can do nowadays."

Prophet poked his hat brim off his forehead. "Well, now I seen everything. An old, no-account gunslinger wearing a sheriff's star. How old are you, anyways?"

"Forty-five."

"Shit."

"All right! I won't own up to a day past fifty." Mortimer canted his head to indicate the pinto and narrowed one dark eye with menace. "One of those dead men you're haulin' around like firewood is the Rio Bravo Kid—my deputy."

"Ah, hell, he ain't dead." Prophet walked toward the pinto's cargo. "I just ran him against a boulder when he played like he was a farmyard bull and I was a younker too dumb to step out of his way." He chuckled. "Of course, I might have had a hand in helpin' him to smack the rock so hard, but rest assured, Mortimer, he had it comin'."

"Don't doubt it a bit," the Moon's Well sheriff said.

Prophet reached up, tucked his hands behind the Rio Bravo Kid's cartridge belt, and pulled him down off the pinto's back. He propped him against the horse while he dipped a key out of a pocket to unlock the cuffs securing the Kid's wrists.

The Kid grunted and blinked. His eyes were hard but vacant, like he wasn't sure who he was or what had happened to him yet.

Prophet turned to Mortimer, who'd walked around the front of the pinto to regard his deputy with grim despair, continuing to puff the stately-looking meerschaum. "What's his real name?" Prophet asked.

"Vernon Cartwright."

"And he grew up along the Rio Bravo, did he?"

"Nah." Mortimer shook his head. "Somewhere up in Nebraska. He just liked the sound of the name."

"It does have a ring to it, but couldn't you have found a better deputy?"

"I didn't find him. My boss did."

"Boss?"

Mortimer dipped his chin toward the big hotel up the street on the right.

Prophet looked at the Rio Bravo Kid. "You best keep a shorter leash on him. He might run into some jake who doesn't have a heart as big as mine and drills a bullet through his."

Mortimer was staring at his deputy, who was leaning back against the pinto, glaring at Prophet between hard, quick blinks of his pain-racked eyes. He had a lump the size of a horseshoe high on his forehead. It was gunmetal blue and there was a small, dried cut in the middle of it. "Rio, go on inside. Have a drink. The bull teams will be here soon, and we're both gonna need to be on our toes."

The Rio Bravo Kid bunched his fists at his sides as he leaned forward and said through gritted teeth, "This bastard rammed me into the side of a rock!"

"Get on inside!"

"I want my gun back!" Rio held out his hand.

Prophet pulled the Kid's nickel-plated Colt out from behind his own cartridge belt, flicked open the loading gate, and turned the wheel until all six cartridges were lying in the dust at his boots. A rising breeze, chill with the coming night, brushed a few grains of sand over them.

Prophet set the gun in the Kid's hand. The Kid stared down at the six brass bullets in the street, as though he were looking at his own manhood down there, and then shoved the pistol down hard in his holster.

"This ain't over by a long stretch," he told Prophet and stomped off toward the jailhouse.

Prophet looked at the man still draped over the pinto's back. "Now that fella there is dead," he said. "And if I killed him, I'd have killed your deputy there, too, instead of wrappin' him up like a damn Christmas present and settin' him on your doorstep. Just so we understand each other. I've had my fill of runnin' down in Mexico. I'd just as soon take it easy for a while."

He smiled, but the corners of his mouth were tight, and he kept an edge in his gaze as he waited for Mortimer's response.

The man didn't look at the dead Ranger. He knocked his pipe against his hand until the dottle dropped into the tan dust around the Kid's cartridges. "You look like you could use a drink and a bath, Prophet," he said in a leisurely way. "May I recommend the dwarf's place?"

"Moon's House of a Thousand Delights?"

"It's second to none, which is good, since there's none even remotely like it within two hundred miles in any direction. He has some of the best women in Texas." Mortimer lowered his voice and glanced along the street toward the big, purple saloon, as though he was afraid someone might hear. "It's not bad."

"I saw it." Prophet stepped into Mean's saddle. "I do believe me and my horse could a use a drink of water first, though."

6

LEE MORTIMER WATCHED the big, broad-shouldered bounty hunter lead his horse back in the direction of the well. Prophet had left the Rio Bravo Kid's horse behind, the dead Ranger still strapped behind the saddle. Unease gripped the sheriff of Moon's Well, causing snakes to writhe beneath the buckle of his cartridge belt.

He took one last drag off his cheroot, tossed the three-quarter-smoked cigar into the deep, floury dust of the street beyond the worn wooden stoop, and then swung around and walked into the jailhouse.

There were two, cage-like iron cells at the back of the shack, which had been a Mexican casa at one time, long before Chisos La Grange had bought the Spanish land grant certificate from some old Spaniard who'd inherited the certificate but wanted nothing more than to be rid of the oozing boil on the devil's ass. That was before La Grange had dug the well, of course, and made the land around it worth something again.

Before that, in wetter, more prosperous times, there'd been a spring about a quarter mile out of town, in the direction of the Chisos Mountains. The precious water had had

to be hauled into the settlement daily by the Mexican inhab-
itants who'd served the local *patron*, whose ruin of a hacienda sat west of town, in the Chisos Mountain foothills.
There had also been several springs near the old rancho, but
when they had gone dry, as the one near the village had
gone dry after a prolonged and devastating drought, the
ranch had failed and been abandoned by the grandees who'd
inhabited it—descendants of an old Spanish family who had
dwelled here for over two hundred years.

Now the grandees were gone, and Chisos La Grange was
gone. But the dwarf was here, having bought the land grant
for a measly two hundred and fifty dollars. And Mordecai
Moon's girl, Griselda May, was here, of course, as well.

Who could forget her?

Moon and Miss May had hired Lee Mortimer to oversee
the place. He wore a badge that Moon himself had cut from
a peach tin lid and had pinned to the sheriff's vest with
somber seriousness. Just as seriously, Mortimer was to en-
force the dwarf's laws governing the well and the sprawling
grant that the grandees had abandoned a hundred years ago,
though most of the permanent residents were a handful of
Mexicans and the ten or so businessmen who operated the
shops.

The rest of the grant was populated mostly by rattlesnakes, Gila monsters, wild pigs, roadrunners, and the
occasional old Kiowa warrior who, abandoned by his tribe,
returned to his ancestral homeland to die in some cave up in
the mountains. Mortimer rarely needed to leave town. The
dwarf and Miss May had, only two months ago, directed
him to hire the Rio Bravo Kid as his sole deputy, who lay
now on a cot in one of the two cells at the back of the shack
that served as a sheriff's office and jail here in Moon's Well.

The Kid had been Griselda's whimsical idea, apparently
for no more reason than she liked the sound of the Kid's
name, though the Kid's actual handle was Vernon Cartwright. Only lately had Mortimer begun to suspect there
were other reasons that Miss May had wanted a peach tin lid
pinned to the Rio Bravo Kid's pinto vest.

Mortimer didn't want to think about that. He'd come here nine months ago, on the dodge from several federal arrest warrants, seeking only peace and quiet. He'd accepted the sheriff's job because the dwarf had offered to pay him well, and up till now, at least, there hadn't been much to it.

And the weather out here was good for his girl, Wanda Copper, who was hacking her consumptive lungs up out in the shack they shared behind the sheriff's office.

"Why the hell didn't you shoot that man?" Mortimer's booming voice thundered around the cave-like adobe casa. He stood between his rolltop desk and the Kid's cell, pointing a finger in the general direction of the well to which Lou Prophet had headed. "When you had the chance out in the desert? Why didn't you take it?"

The Kid had been lying belly down on the cot. Groaning now, he rolled over and sat up, clamping his fingers to his temples. "You gotta yell so consarned loud?"

"Rio, you're sneakier'n a damn cat," Mortimer said, not lowering his voice an octave. "You had the drop on that bounty hunter. Why didn't you kill him and bury him out there with the Ranger?"

Mortimer had sent the Kid out to make sure the Ranger was dead, and to bury him. Now, not only did Mortimer have the Ranger's body to contend with here in town, where anyone might see it and get the word out to the Rangers what had happened, but he had a bounty hunter sniffing around.

Prophet would likely die in a few minutes, if he didn't pay for his water, that was—and he didn't look like a man who would—but that wasn't such a good thing, either. If the dwarf kept killing men who didn't pay the outlandish price for his water, the powder keg that was Moon's Well would surely explode before Mortimer was ready. Before he'd made enough money to pull his picket pin and drift for Mexico, and before his woman, and the mother of his deceased son, was well enough to travel.

Mortimer was in a tight spot. As tight a bind as he'd ever been in, even when he'd had posses hot on his heels.

"Rio, goddamnit, why didn't you kill Prophet?"

"I heard you the first time, Sheriff!" the Kid cried, dropping his boots to the floor and holding his head like a tender, oversized egg in his hands. "I don't know, I tell you. I reckon . . . you know . . . I thought I'd gun him fair. You know—not just shoot him with my long gun when he didn't even have his pistol drawn."

"That's exactly what you should have done, you simple fool!" Mortimer scowled into the cell at the Rio Bravo Kid, who leaned forward with his elbows on his knees, lightly massaging his temples with his fingers. "Look what happened to you! You think the dwarf didn't see you being hauled into town belly down across your horse? You think he didn't see the dead Ranger, too? Prophet sure as hell saw him, and he'll probably put it together who shot him. And who else might have saw? In an hour or so, the bull trains are gonna come stormin' in here. If the wrong person sees a dead Ranger and they get word to the Rangers up at Alpine . . ."

"Ah, hell, Mr. Moon ain't afraid of no Rangers," the Kid said. He chuckled. "You seen what he did to them two this afternoon."

"That was madness. He won't get by with any more of that or we'll get ten, fifteen Rangers ridin' in. Possibly with that many territorial marshals backin' 'em."

"You tell him." Rio stretched a faintly jeering smile at Mortimer. "Go on—I dare ya, Sheriff. Tell Mr. Moon to stop shootin' Rangers and anyone else who won't pay for his water."

Rage boiled in Mortimer. He had a mind to haul his old Remington out and gut-shoot the Kid. But that would only lead to more trouble. He was stuck with the Kid whether he liked it or not.

He extended a long, tan finger at the Kid in the cell and narrowed a glinting brown eye. "Get out there and bury that Ranger in the desert with the other one. Bury him deep—don't just scratch out a hole. I don't want the coyotes drag-

gin' the bloody parts around. And then get over to the well
and see if you can rein in whatever's goin' on over there."

He'd heard voices raised in anger, and it had caused the
snakes in his belly to coil up tighter than hang-rope knots.

"My head hurts!" Rio groaned.

"You heard me, Rio!"

Mortimer wanted nothing more to do with the dwarf
today. He stomped, spurs chinging loudly on the hard-
packed earthen floor, past the Kid's cell to the office's back
door. He pushed out into the dwindling sunlight. He walked
out past a small privy and into the brush flanking it, down a
slight hill, across a narrow, gravelly wash where little birds
flitted amongst the mesquite branches, and into the yard of
the shack that he shared with Wanda Copper.

It was a crumbling, pink adobe—two rooms downstairs,
a small loft in the upper story for sleeping. Home to mainly
spiders before Mortimer had moved in, Wanda had made it
a home crudely but pleasantly outfitted with whatever mis-
matched furniture and eating utensils she'd managed to
scavenge on days she felt up to it.

The chubby Mexican woman, Bienvenida, who raised
chickens a ways off in the desert and whose husband supplied the dwarf's massive saloon with firewood in exchange
for free water, looked up from her needlework as Mortimer
walked into the stone-floored casa. He closed the door quietly behind him, hung his hat on a wall spike. Inwardly, he
recoiled at the cloying, copper smell of blood, the musk of
human sickness, and the boiled-mushroom smell of medicinal herbs and roots hanging from the rafters to dry.

Bienvenida sat in the shack's living area, at the foot of
the bed on which Wanda lay in her rumpled nightgown, a
single sheet covering her. Wanda's red hair spilled across
her pillow. Blood flecked the pillow as well as the white
handkerchief she held in her hand in front of her mouth. Her
pale blue, red-rimmed eyes were open, and they had that
strained, wild look they acquired on days when her afflic-
tion was especially acute.

"Bad?" asked Mortimer.

She smiled weakly. "Better now. Are you home to stay?"

Mortimer half turned his head toward the door, listening for sounds from the street despite his wanting to know nothing of what was occurring by the well. Dread pressed its cold hand to the small of his back. He had to get himself and Wanda out of here soon, before the dwarf took Mortimer and Wanda—not to mention everyone else in the town he'd named after himself—down with him.

The sheriff glanced at Bienvenida and dipped his chin, his signal that he'd take over Wanda's tending now. The woman, clad in a sack dress and sandals, her long, coarse, black hair flowing back over her heavy shoulders, rose from the hide-bottom rocker and shoved her needlework into a small burlap pouch.

Bienvenida, who had cared for Wanda since Mortimer and the ex–saloon girl had come to Moon's Well, claimed that she was a descendant of the rancho's original *patron*, her great-grandmother being the love child of his with a half-wild Kiowa girl.

Now the stubby Mexican woman, whose stomach and heavy, sagging bosom bowed out the front of her shabby dress that was adorned with ancient talismans, glanced at the little monkey stove in the corner, on which a steaming kettle sat, and told Mortimer in Spanish to administer the tea in a couple of hours. It would fight the demon in the girl's lungs and help her sleep.

Bienvenida held up a stubby, admonishing finger, glanced at a bottle on the shelf above the stove, and wagged her jowly head. "No busthead," she said in English. "No busthead! Good for the demon, bad for Wanda!"

Mortimer held up his hands in capitulation. "No busthead, Bienvenida."

The Mexican woman leaned over Wanda and pressed her lips to the ex–saloon girl's forehead, muttered some quick Spanish, and then waddled over to the door and headed out to her own little shack, her irrigated gardens, and her husband and three young grandchildren, all awaiting supper.

"Sure could use a shot of busthead," Wanda said, her voice raspy from coughing.

"I ain't tanglin' with that old catamount."

Mortimer took a knee beside the bed, slid Wanda's hair back from her cheek, not liking how cool and clammy she felt despite the heat in the casa. It meant the fire inside her was dying. Despair was a living thing within Lee Mortimer—a feral cat gnawing on his guts. He'd had her for such a short time, and now he was going to lose her.

Where and what would he be without her?

Mortimer smiled at Wanda reassuringly, but inwardly he cursed. A damn renegade his whole life, and here on the lee side of fifty, he'd fallen in love with a saloon singer from Denver who was nearly half his age. A saloon girl dying from the consumption she'd probably acquired from too many winters as a child living in a drafty, old prospector's shack up in the Colorado Rockies with her surly father who'd died penniless, leaving his daughter destitute.

"You look good, Wanda."

"Your left eye rolls inward just a little when you lie to me." Her voice was gently teasing.

"All right, a slight exaggeration, but I'll be damned if you're still not the most beautiful girl I've ever seen in all my days."

She pressed her lips to the wrist of the hand he held against her face.

There was the flat crack of a distant pistol. Mortimer jerked slightly with a start, but managed to keep his smiling eyes on the girl. Her thin brows pinched as she studied him.

"What was that?"

"Someone shootin' a snake, most likely. The Kid will see to it."

"Must be lots of snakes in town today," Wanda said skeptically. "I heard shootin' earlier, too." She paused, held her anxious, probing gaze on his. "What's happening out there, Lee? I can tell it's got you bothered. I know you well enough by now to know when you're rattled."

She gently squeezed his wrist.

He lowered his hand, leaned against his elbow that he propped on the edge of the cot. "I been thinkin', Wanda. . . ."

He jerked again at the crack of another pistol shot.

"I been thinkin' that we need to get you feelin' better soon, so we can pull our picket pins."

Wanda cast a dreadful look toward the front of the shack, in the direction of the well. Her voice was forlorn when she asked, "Where to, Lee?"

"You said you wanted to see the ocean. The Gulf close enough?"

The girl nodded, feigned a reassuring smile. She reached up and placed her hand over Mortimer's left ear. "The Gulf would be just fine as frog hair, Lee."

There was another shot. She drew a sharp, anxious breath and then coughed into her handkerchief. Blood drops flecked her nostrils. The sheriff muttered a curse.

"Oh, Wanda," Mortimer said, pulling the dying girl to his chest.

7

MEAN AND UGLY nickered eagerly as Prophet drew rein before the stone well coping and dismounted in the broad semicircle of shade that angled west of it, stretching toward the large hotel that looked like some kind of ungainly bird that had been trapped and painted by a madman.

Prophet could smell the cool, coppery odor of the water issuing up from below. Deep in the purple shade cast by the peaked roof over the stone coping, it beckoned to the parched and weary bounty hunter. His throat contracted and expanded at the thought of a long, cool drink of the stuff.

He placed his hands on the top of the stone coping that Chisos La Grange had laid himself one stone at a time in the hot West Texas sun. La Grange had been a loner, with not even a woman around, as far as Prophet knew. The old desert rat had dug the well and laid the stones himself. Prophet had ridden through here about the time La Grange had finished the coping, and he and a Mexican bull team had enjoyed the first gourd dippers full . . . as well as a good bit of tequila later.

There hadn't been much out here then. Certainly not the

big hotel. La Grange had built a much more modest flop-house. A homey place—albeit a flea-bit one and one without percentage gals—in which a dragged-out traveler could kick off his boots and enjoy a few drinks and La Grange's pinto beans and roasted javelina.

A strangely silent man, Chisos La Grange. But one who'd been easy to be around. Prophet had liked him, the few times he'd seen him. With his grubby duck pants, deerskin serape, expressionless eyes, and tangled bib beard, La Grange had seemed as much a part of the desert as the coy-otes and the hawks.

Prophet started to reach for the winch handle but stopped when he saw the signpost standing before him, along the side of the stonework around the well. He'd seen the signs before, when he'd first ridden past the well, though the brunt of his attention had been on the two faces peering at him from the hotel window.

Now he read the sign facing him. He scowled. He'd ex-pected it to say merely something on the order of, PLEASE RETURN THE BUCKET TO ITS NAIL WHEN FINISHED or DON'T WASTE NONE, AS THIS IS THE DESERT, STUPID! Because, re-membering back, that was the sort of sign Chisos had put up.

This one was nothing like those had been. This one indicated that some asshole was charging for water out here in this parched and rocky land.

Prophet looked around, his pale blue eyes spoked at the corners with exasperation, his broad forehead brick red beneath his hat brim, his thick nose with a bulge in the bridge nearly crimson with incredulity. The street was de-serted. The fresh breeze was shepherding a small dust devil toward him from the north, and a couple of tumbleweeds were skipping along both sides of the street.

But no one was out. They likely would be soon after sup-per and the hot sun had finally gone down behind the moun-tains, and, like Mortimer had mentioned, when the bull and mule trains with their burdens of freight heading either to or from Mexico had rolled in.

Prophet wanted to scold someone for charging for

water—hell, why don't they tag a price on every breath of air a man breathes?—but his and Mean's thirst drove him to ignore the sign and to winch a bucket up from below. His anger faded, and he smiled as he turned the crank and heard the tinny sounds of the water slopping down over the sides of the wooden bucket and splashing back down into the well below. It sounded like distant coins being dropped on a counter.

The air wafting up against his face was cool and moist, and it smelled like damp earth and lemons. The water flashed like the skin of a silvery dark snake as it rippled below the bucket rising toward him.

Mean shook his head so hard he nearly threw his bridle and bit and loosed an eager whinny. Prophet chuckled as he lifted the bucket out of the well and set it on the coping. He removed Mean's bridle and bit, hung it on a nail protruding from the signpost, and filled the rusty ladle for himself. He set the bucket down in front of Mean, and then he poked his hat brim back off his forehead, lifted the ladle to his mouth, and closed his upper lip over the side of it.

The tin was cool. The water was cooler. Prophet didn't think he'd ever tasted water so cool and pure and refreshing. It cut through the leathery dryness of his tongue and plunged on down his throat, spreading its bracing coolness throughout his belly. The vigor instantly began returning to his extremities. Suddenly, he could breathe better, and he could see better, too, as, taking a break to relieve the start of a slight headache at the water's deep-rock chill, he looked around at the growing purple shadows and the splash of red velvet in the west, where the sun was dropping.

He was only vaguely aware of movement on the broad gallery of the saloon behind him.

He lifted the ladle to his mouth once more, but he saw that he'd nearly drank all the water in it. He'd just started to stoop to refill the ladle from the bucket that Mean was still drawing water from when he heard a froglike, angry croaking. "Griselda said you didn't pay first, mister, and by God that's my water, and I say everyone pays!"

He turned to see a man with a child-sized body but a devil's face—likely the same man he'd seen in the window earlier—standing atop the gallery steps. He was decked out in a clawhammer coat and checked, patch-kneed trousers, a scruffy brown bowler hat with a ragged red feather sticking out of its band.

The little devil man wore a child's black boots. However, the brown fist he extended toward Prophet now, his index finger jutting angrily out from around a fat cigar, was nearly man-sized. A gold band ringed the middle finger. His eyes were pinched up, and the colorless whiskers tufting the spade-shaped chin completed the little man's satyr-like appearance. Prophet wouldn't have been surprised if small horns were concealed beneath the bowler hat.

The girl stood behind him and slightly to one side, arms crossed on her chest. Long, dark brown hair hung in two straight queues forward down her shoulders. Her pale face was rescued from plainness by a patrician nose, prominent chin, and lustrous brown eyes, which were rife with sultry mischief beneath her man's felt Stetson. Her lips seemed well suited to the jeering smile that now quirked them.

She was a small girl—Prophet guessed no taller than five feet, *maybe* a hundred pounds—but beside the dwarf she nearly appeared ungainly.

There were three other men on the gallery, but Prophet didn't pay them much attention except to note they wore shabbily gaudy suits and pistols, and that they seemed to be there to back the little man's play. They stood like grim giants behind the dwarf and the girl.

Nevertheless, Prophet couldn't keep the anger from his voice as he said, "You're the one chargin' for water?"

"That's right. I'm the one chargin' for water," the dwarf said in his frog-like croak from between gritted teeth. "It's my well, see? It's on my land. So I'm chargin'. Now, kindly pay the box."

Prophet dropped the ladle in the dust at his feet. The thud caused Mean to jerk his head up out of the water bucket, drops tumbling from his snout and beading the dust at his hooves. The horse swished his tail angrily as he stared back at the little man standing atop the porch with the three hard-faced gunmen flanking him. The girl stepped out to one side of the dwarf to have a better view of the stranger at the well.

Prophet's voice sounded hard and flat and strange even to him. "If it ain't against the law, chargin' for water in the desert, especially when you obviously don't need the money, and especially when there ain't no other water around, besides the muddy Rio Grande, outside of a two-day ride, it oughta be."

It wasn't that Prophet couldn't pay it. He had a fair-sized pouch of gold coins in his saddlebags. What galled him was the moral injustice of charging for drinking water in the desert. The little man might have had a hard life, being so small and ugly, but he obviously didn't need the money. Not if the gaudy saloon was his, and something told Prophet it was.

Chisos La Grange had dug the well and never charged a dime for anything but grub, tequila, and his half-dozen beds. Everyone from the Mexicans who lived in the shacks around his place to the bull and mule trains passing through on regular runs to and from Mexico drank for free.

Just like they breathed the air. For free.

The man standing before Prophet now was just a greedy little bastard who thought he could throw his proverbial weight around.

The dwarf glanced over his shoulder at the men behind him, and jerked his head forward. He limped down off the steps, slung the flap of his clawhammer coat back behind the Colt Lightning holstered on his left hip, and stomped toward Prophet, his little boots pluming the dust around his hemmed trouser cuffs. The girl held back, her faintly delighted grin remaining on her red lips, arms crossed on her chest.

The three obvious gunmen tramped leisurely down off the steps and followed the little man with the airs of overgrown attack dogs awaiting the command to kill.

Prophet stood facing the group, his back to the well, head canted to one side, squinting against the red sunset bleeding in over the western mountains and the big hotel flanking the dwarf, the girl, and the dwarf's lackeys.

The dwarf shook his head sadly. "Mister, I sure am sorry it's come to this, but . . ."

Faster than Prophet thought the little man capable, the dwarf filled his fist with the short-barreled Colt. A hair faster, Prophet snapped his own Peacemaker from its holster and squeezed the trigger.

The shot exploded the somnolent, late-afternoon silence, and the dwarf stopped in his tracks and gave an indignant scream as his hat went sailing off his head as Prophet's slug caromed between two of the men flanking the little man to plow into a porch post behind them.

All three gunmen stopped suddenly, dropping their hands to their holsters but apparently knowing instinctively that if they started to raise the weapons, it would be them stopping the next bullets and not the dwarf's porch.

"Drop it, mister," Prophet snarled, glaring through his own wafting powder smoke as he aimed his Colt straight out from his right side at the satyr-like creature still holding the Lightning.

The dwarf returned the glare, his pasty face mottled red with exasperation. His head was almost bald; only a few strands of dead-looking hair straggled across the top between slightly thicker, fuzzier patches on the sides, above his large ears whose lobes hung down like thumbs.

Prophet said with quiet warning, "The next one's gonna give you a second belly button about six inches above the first."

The dwarf gasped, glanced at the pistol, as though he hadn't realized he was still holding it, then flung it down into the dust like a hot potato.

The gunman flanking the dwarf on his right jerked his hand toward the pistol he carried in a shoulder holster, under his long, faded blue denim duster. Prophet slid his Peacemaker slightly right and fired.

The bullet slammed through the gunman's right hand as

he began to slide the gun from its holster. He screamed and
jerked sideways as the bullet ricocheted off his gun, tore
through the side of his coat, and puffed dust in the street
beside him, about two feet in front of the girl.

She wasn't smiling now.

The man clutched his bloody right hand with his left and
turned back toward Prophet, bending forward and grimacing, his eyes spitting javelins of raw fury.

Prophet stared back at him, his Colt cocked and ready
once more. The bounty man looked at the others, including
the dwarf.

They all appeared flabbergasted, indignant. The dwarf's
lower jaw hung in shock. The two unwounded men seemed
to be awaiting orders from the dwarf. The little man appeared tongue-tied.

Behind the men, the brown-haired girl lowered her
arms, canted her head to one side, and drew a ragged breath.
"Mister," she said just loudly enough for Prophet to hear,
wagging her head slowly. "You oughtn't to have done that."

Prophet looked at her and then at the men. "Toss those
guns in the dirt." He looked at the girl again—at the pistol
riding high on her left hip with the butt angled back toward
her hip. "You, too, honey."

"Don't *honey* me, mister."

Prophet raked his eyes over all of them. They stared back
at him, silent and angry, fuming over the prospect of the humiliation of giving up their guns. Prophet knew he couldn't
ride out of here until they did, however. Not without risking
getting drilled between his shoulder blades.

He triggered the Colt again blowing up dust to the right
of the gunmen, causing them all to jerk with starts. He
waited a few seconds and then plumed more dust to their
left.

The dwarf glanced at his men, rasped out a couple of
harsh words that Prophet couldn't pick up against the gust-
ing breeze. Reluctantly, regarding Prophet owlishly, they all
tossed their guns into the street.

The girl stood atop the steps as she had before, saucily defiant. The dwarf followed Prophet's gaze to her. "Throw the iron down, Griselda!"

She waited another couple of seconds, then slid her pistol out of its holster, held it up high by two fingers, mocking Prophet with her eyes, and then dropped the pearl-gripped Smith & Wesson into the dust at the side of the gallery steps. It hit with a thump, causing dust to rise.

Prophet glanced at the water bucket a couple of feet from his right boot. Mean had drunk nearly all of it. There might be a half a dipper left. He couldn't risk drinking it, though, and taking his eyes off the men and the girl.

He'd have to get more water later, though he'd first have to secure a canteen. He wasn't leaving town without a full canteen, however, or he'd be in the same fix he'd been in when he'd left the Rio Grande.

Keeping his pistol on the group before him, including the girl on the gallery steps, he gathered up Mean's reins, turned the horse sideways to the hotel, and stepped into the leather. Staring grimly at the crew before him, he backed the horse down the street in the direction from which he'd come. He wasn't sure where he was going; he only knew he'd worn out his welcome at the well.

As he backed the horse, he spied two men standing on the opposite side of the street from the hotel, up near the jailhouse. The salmon and green light angling over the town from the west revealed the tall, rangy frame and pinto vest of the Rio Bravo Kid. He stood spraddle-legged, thumbs hooked behind his cartridge belt. The barber stood near him, head canted skeptically to one side, watching the grim doings by the well. The barber drew on the cigar he was holding and blew out the smoke as he turned to the Kid and said something that Prophet couldn't hear.

Prophet looked around. Where was Mortimer?

The real threat here had switched to the unseen sheriff. Was the former gunman, Lee Mortimer, trying to plant a pair of rifle sights on Prophet? Prophet knew the man's reputation as a cold-blooded Killer, so it wasn't out of the realm of possibilities that he might try to bushwhack a man.

The bounty hunter looked at the dwarf, whose lips had acquired a faint smile, telling Prophet that he might have the drop now, but this wasn't finished.

Prophet knew that, too. It could have been finished if he'd had a canteen, but the Rurale sniper had drilled a bullet through the bounty hunter's flask at the river. The loss of that canteen was even more significant now than it had been before.

Prophet backed the horse up as far as the Rose Hotel and Saloon, and then he turned Mean around and booted him on down a break between the saloon and a stone, brush-roofed hovel with chickens pecking around the barren yard. A young Mexican woman stood in the shack's open back door, holding a small baby to her breast and regarding Prophet apprehensively.

"Everything's all right, senorita," he said, automatically pinching his hat brim to the nervous mother.

But he heard the lie in his own words.

Nothing much was all right here in Moon's Well, least of all himself.

8

WHEN PROPHET'S PISTOL had spoken the first time out in front of the hotel, Ruth Rose had been putting a fresh pajama top on her husband, Frank, and she'd jumped with a start, releasing one arm of the top so that it hung off Frank's bare, pasty shoulder.

"Oh, god!" she said, backing into the dresser beside the bed, nearly knocking over the unlit Tiffany lamp. *"Now what?"*

Ruth looked at Frank as though for help. He stared up at her as if seeing right through her, as though he hadn't heard the gun report, as though he'd neither heard nor been aware of anything at all. He'd been this way since his stroke eighteen months ago, after Moon had come for his monthly tax payment along with a ghastly amount of rent for the land the hotel stood upon. Frank's eyes were sunken, his cheeks sallow. If he'd heard the reports of the dwarf's pistol, as when the vile little man had shot the Rangers only a few hours earlier, he'd shown no sign of it.

Ruth's heart thudded as her thoughts turned to what was happening outside, and what it might mean for her and Frank. The town of Moon's Well was a powder keg that would surely soon explode and take her and Frank and the hotel—all that they'd worked for—right along with it. The hotel wasn't really theirs, for the dwarf owned the land it stood upon and had even imposed a tax on every penny the hotel brought in. Ruth would have abandoned the place and fled the town if Frank had been able to travel.

She glanced at him once more, quickly buttoning his pajama top as she listened with a keen, raking dread to the men's voices pitched with anger up the street toward Mordecai Moon's place. Frank wasn't capable of dressing himself or feeding himself. Sometimes he didn't even use the chamber pot she kept beneath the bed for him. He couldn't speak. At times, she wasn't even sure he knew her.

How could she ever get him across the desert and across the panhandle back to Missouri? In a year and a half, he hadn't stepped foot outside even once.

"Oh, Frank," she said, as though gently calling him back to her. Their home was as far away as Missouri, but Frank was as far away from her as a distant planet. Leaving her alone to run the hotel and to deal with Mordecai Moon and his curly wolves, as Frank had called them before the stroke had taken his mind.

Quickly but gently, Ruth shoved Frank back down on the bed and against the pillows she'd fluffed for him. When his skinny legs were stretched out against the lumpy corn-shuck mattress, she drew the single sheet up to his chest and felt the searing burn of anguish once more as she stared into those liquid brown eyes that were only vaguely familiar and as opaque as those of a dead man.

Outside, a gun blasted.

Ruth gasped, slapping a hand to her chest. She hurried over to the window, stepping to the far left of it so she could see up the street on her right. She frowned as she stared, taking in the scene—a tall, burly-looking stranger in buckskins holding a gun on the dwarf and his men in the street between the dwarf's House of a Thousand Delights and the well.

Ruth lifted a hand to absently finger the silver flower-

and-leaf locket pendant hanging around her neck. Whoever the man was, he'd had Mordecai Moon toss his pistol down in the street, and the others, even the inscrutable and somehow terrifying Miss May, followed suit with their own weapons. One of the three curly wolves was bent forward and clutching his right hand in his left, as though he'd been wounded.

"Who . . . in God's name . . . ?" Ruth breathed, her fear now making way for a buoyant sort of surprise, a hushed and subtle jubilation at the sight of Moon's men and the dastardly girl being cowed so by a stranger who'd apparently been taking water at the well.

Was this a third Ranger, an associate of the two who'd ridden into Moon's Well earlier and had foolishly refused to pay for the water?

Ruth gasped at a near sound, and she turned sharply to Frank. Her nerves were taut as piano wire, and her heart drummed.

Frank sat back against the bed's scrolled wooden headboard, his jaw sagging as he snored. Heart still fluttering, she looked back into the street. The stranger was backing his horse toward her, moving slowly, keeping his pistol aimed at the dwarf and his three gunmen and Miss May, who glared at him with menace.

Fear nibbled again at Ruth Rose. She'd just started to wonder what this meant, but now it occurred to her that it only meant more killing. Ranger or not, the big man in the skintight, sweat-stained buckskin shirt might have the upper hand at the moment, but it wouldn't last long. He'd go the way of the other two.

Mordecai Moon and his curly wolves—there were more than just the three on the street with him now—had a stranglehold on the town. The town's two lawmen were not really lawmen but merely two more of the dwarf's hired killers— a gruff-looking albeit aging hombre named Lee Mortimer, and Mortimer's deputy who called himself the Rio Bravo Kid. Separately, they made a mockery of the law. Together, in the employ of the dwarf, they were like two curs guarding the gates of hell.

The dwarf had the well, and the well was everything in a land of so little water. He also had a saloon full of relatively good whiskey and the kind of doxies whom men traveling through this vast, hot desert paid good money for, just as they did the water.

Women and water. With those two things, Mordecai Moon ruled the world out here.

Which meant the big man wasn't long for this or any other world. Still, as she watched him back the horse from her right to her left in front of the saloon, she couldn't help feeling grateful to him, as well as sympathetic. For a moment there, he'd given her hope that there would soon be an end to the dwarf's stranglehold on the town and on her and Frank.

Ruth turned away from the window. Frank was sleeping now, lower jaw hanging, his face sagging like a pale sheet hung on a line to dry. Slow, loud snores rose from his open mouth. Ruth smiled sadly.

He'd been such an alive, handsome man not all that long ago. They'd come out here to forget their miseries in postwar Missouri, to start another life after Ruth's parents died, and Frank and Ruth, who were not farmers, lost her parents' farm to creditors. While Frank had not been a farmer, and had looked as out of place behind a plow as would a Missouri riverboat gambler, he *had* been a man with a strong will, humor, strength, and hope for the future . . . even after their only child, Grace, had died from a milk fever.

His hope had been for him and Ruth to move west and to start a new life by opening their own business in this unfettered land of opportunity—the western frontier.

They'd bought a lot from Chisos La Grange and built the saloon and hotel here along the oft-busy old Chihuahua Trail, near La Grange's old place. Chisos had been growing old and he'd welcomed the competition. But then he sold his land grant to the dwarf, and Ruth and Frank had found themselves slave tenants to a ruthless land baron who not only made them pay rent for the land their business stood upon but for water, as well.

And then he'd built himself a hotel that their own humble place couldn't begin to compete with.

Now, because of Mordecai Moon's vile business practices, Frank was a mere shell of the man Ruth had married. Fingering the locket in which she'd tucked away a fringe of their dead daughter's hair, Ruth glanced once more out the window, and then she walked past Frank's bed to the door.

She glanced once more at her sleeping husk of a husband. She listened to his quiet snores and felt the raw ache of guilt once again. How many times had she found herself wishing Frank's snores were death rattles, so she would soon be finally free of this place? Turning to the hall, her face pinched from all her sundry miseries, Ruth closed the door quietly behind her.

A moment later, she found herself hurrying down the rickety wooden stairs, her long, spruce green skirt swishing about her long legs. She walked past her desk and through the small lobby where Chisos La Grange used to sit with the old prospectors who frequented the saloon back when it was the only thing here and the town's name had been Chisos Springs, and glanced out the window behind the single potted palm between two chairs.

She frowned, feeling a vague disappointment, and then opened the door and stepped out onto the saloon's narrow stoop, and looked to her left, in the direction of Moon's imposing place and the well. Moon and his men were no longer there.

A bull train was just now thundering into the town from the north, heading straight for the big hotel, of course, as they always did. Dust was billowing as though a cyclone were near, men were bellowing, and the oxen lunging forward against their yokes were braying and trying to get over to the water they smelled.

Soon the animals would be watered from the well—after the train captains had paid Moon, of course, unless they'd already contracted for the water—and then the beasts would be led around behind the place to the enormous corrals constructed of woven ocotillo stalks, where Chisos La Grange's old hotel had once stood before the dwarf had torn it down to make way for his own.

Ruth looked to the south. There was no rider there. Feeling the lines of befuddlement cutting deeper across her forehead, she walked out to the south edge of the stoop and peered down the side of the Rose Hotel and Saloon toward the back. There he was, back by the woodshed. He'd dismounted from his horse and was crouched forward, inspecting the horse's left front hoof, just now sliding his pistol from its holster and flipping it in his hand to use as a hammer.

She turned away and, with another cautious glance back toward the dwarf's place, glad that none of his men were heading toward the Rose, she slipped back inside and walked through the small lobby, between the dusky, vacant saloon on the left and her desk on the right, and into a narrow hall that cleaved two separate storage rooms. She unlocked the back door and went out into the backyard.

The big man gave the horse's left front shoe another tap with his pistol butt, muttering to the beast and glancing cautiously back the way he'd come. He jerked around, flipping the pistol in his hand and gripping it by its butt as he faced Ruth.

"Whoa now," he said, aiming the pistol at her and holding his left gloved hand up, palm out, in grave reprimand. "Best not sneak up on a man in that fashion, missus . . ."

"You can put the gun away," Ruth said. "I mean you no harm."

She hesitated, a little frightened now. He was awfully big and sort of crude-looking, with a broad face that was neither handsome nor ugly. There was no Ranger badge pinned to his buckskin shirt. He appeared to be wearing half the desert on that sweaty shirt and on his faded denim trousers, the cuffs of which were pulled down over badly worn boots.

His nose bulged at the bridge, as though it had been broken several times. The pale blue eyes, however, were pleasant. She sensed a humor lurking far back in them, a funny side that could easily move forward and lighten the grim set of his mouth with a handsome smile.

He looked around, cautious as a wild animal, his eyes flicking to the open door behind her and then up the break between the saloon and the small shack beside it in which a Mexican family lived.

"All right," she said, taking a step back in retreat, reaching for the door handle.

"Sorry, ma'am." The big man raised his pistol's barrel and there was the *click-clack* of the hammer being depressed. He smiled, and she realized she'd been right about it drawing out his humor, showing a gruff but tender brand of kindness. "There's just a few more of them than there is of me."

He gave the gun, which looked no larger than a derringer in his big hand, an absent twirl before dropping it into its holster and snapping the keeper thong closed over the hammer.

Ruth released the door handle. "Where are you heading?"

"Back into the desert."

"I don't see a canteen on your horse."

"I lost it to a Rurale bullet and the Rio Grande."

When she frowned curiously, he offered his mildly disarming smile again. The expression comforted her. The largeness of him, the muscularity of him, did now, as well, because she sensed no threat in it.

Only . . . what? Her own female attraction to it?

A man like that could be a real companion to a woman, she thought. That smile and those big arms would make a woman feel safe, not like she were teetering over a deep precipice every minute of her life out here.

She'd so vaguely entertained the thought that she felt no shame or guilt for having had it with her bedridden husband only a few yards away, upstairs amongst the for-rent rooms. Even more vaguely, only half consciously, she felt the physical desire awakening within her, like a warm hand on her belly. It had been a long time since any man had made her feel that way. She'd been too busy, too frightened . . .

"Well, you can't go off without a canteen, Mr. . . ."

"Prophet."

She nodded at this, liking the name for some reason she wasn't sure of. Because it sounded biblical? Her parents' piousness had for some reason never infected their daughter, who'd never really known what she believed in. But Ruth supposed some of the Good Book had rubbed off on her.

"Don't worry," the man called Prophet said, turning to his horse and glancing over his shoulder at her again, as he stepped into the saddle, "I'll be back to get one. I seen a mercantile down the street. And I'll be back at that well. I don't mind payin' a penny or so for a canteenful to good folks needin' it, but that little half-ounce son of a . . . well, pardon me, ma'am."

His grin spread wider this time, his pale blue eyes slitting with a boy's delight edged with a man's righteous anger, and he added, "Don't worry. I'll be leavin' Chisos Springs tomorrow, and I'll be leaving with a water flask filled from that well, and I won't be payin' out any more than I did today."

He pinched the funneled brim of his ragged, sweat-darkened hat to Ruth, and then he started to rein the dun away before stopping and turning back to her. "Pardon me," he said affably, "but I didn't catch your name."

"Ruth. Ruth Rose. I run this saloon, which"—she lifted her chin toward the upper story—"is also a hotel. You're welcome to stay here, Mr. Prophet."

His eyes flicked to the sashed, second-story windows. "Oh, I don't know. Kind of a tight fit for me. Especially when I haven't exactly made any friends here in Chisos Springs."

Ruth's lips quirked a smile. She liked the way he stubbornly refused to call the name Moon's Well.

"I saw what you did at the well, Mr. Prophet. And you've certainly made yourself a friend of mine . . . and of my husband," she added, feeling another keen edge of guilt, because the invisible hand on her belly was growing warmer and softer.

"Like I said—pretty tight fit. Wouldn't want to be responsible for either you or your husband to get whipsawed in my affairs."

"Moon won't look for you here," Ruth said. "He's busy over at his own place with the bull and mule trains just now rolling in from Alpine. He keeps a sharp eye on all the faro and roulette games, and he makes sure none of his bartenders are skimming off the top . . . and that every man pays for his girl." She shook her head. "No, he won't look for you here or anywhere. Not tonight. Maybe tomorrow."

The man called Prophet looked around with a troubled, hunted look. She had a feeling it was one he was accustomed to, because it seemed as at home on his face as his smile.

"Well, shucks . . . maybe . . ." Prophet looked east across the formidable-looking desert turning dark green and purple now as the sun fell. It would be cold out there tonight, she knew he was thinking. Cold and dry. He probably couldn't have a fire—not with men possibly looking for him.

"I have water," Ruth said, suddenly very much wanting this man under her roof tonight, though she tried hard to keep the desperation from her voice. She suddenly felt so terribly alone . . . even more alone than before she'd met him. "And I'll walk over first thing tomorrow, and get you a canteen from Soddermeyer's Dry Goods."

Prophet looked interested. "You have water?"

"Yes. Everyone in town has water. But of course we have to buy it from Moon. On contract. He gives me a break, though, because my husband's sick, and . . ." Ruth was aware that she was prattling on indecently but couldn't stop herself; it had been a long time since she'd talked like this. ". . . And because he pretty much owns this place despite our having bought it from Mr. La Grange. Wouldn't do him much good if Frank and I died of thirst, now, would it?"

"Well, hell, if you're offerin' . . ." Prophet swung down from Mean's back. "I reckon I'll light and lay in here. If you really don't mind. I could take a drink of water. But, like I said, tomorrow I'll be fillin' a canteen at Chisos's old well."

"If that's your pleasure, Mr. Prophet." Ruth heard herself sigh.

"How much?"

"A dollar for both you and your horse. Is that too expensive?"

Prophet frowned a little suspiciously and canted his head to one side. "That sounds right cheap. You sure that's all you charge, Mrs. Rose?"

"I keep my prices low to encourage business, because Mr. Moon, of course, gets most of it. I get only the traveling families, few as they are, and the overflow from Moon's Place. I make a little more on supper and breakfast, because Moon doesn't have a very good cook. His Chinaman is a little heavy on the spices for most folks around here."

"I'd give you two dollars and fifty cents if you throw enough water for a sponge bath into the bargain."

Ruth smiled, her heart light, a faint excitement tingling like a man's intimate whisper in her ears. Not to seem overly eager and give this innately suspicious man reason to become suspicious of her intentions, she arranged a serious, businesslike expression as she smoothed her cream apron across her thighs. "Supper's an extra dollar, however. Breakfast an extra fifty cents."

He nodded, studying her obliquely. She could see his soft eyes flicking across her body, which she thought even at twenty-eight years was still relatively firm and shapely, not unkind to a man's gaze. She might have been fooling herself, but she thought she noted a subtle but authentic appreciation in his eyes, a quiet male interest.

"You may stable your horse in the barn, then, Mr. Prophet," she said, glancing at the mud brick stable standing back in the brush a ways, behind the plank-board, one-hole privy with the obligatory half-moon in its door. "I hope there's enough hay. Unfortunately, I employ no hostlers, so you'll have to tend the gelding yourself."

"Fine as frog hair, Mrs. Rose."

"Ruth."

"Well, then, I reckon it's Lou, Ruth."

His smile returned that warm, soft, masculine hand to her belly once more. Feeling the warmth of a blush rise in her cheeks, she turned quickly through the saloon's doorway. "I'll get that bath . . ."

9

GRISELDA MAY WALKED slowly through the brush behind Soddermeyer's Dry Goods store, glancing cautiously behind her toward the big purple saloon and hotel looming darkly against the spruce green sky, her hands lightly touching the polished pearl grips of the double-barreled derringers holstered on her waist.

She didn't think she had anything to worry about. Mordecai Moon had been plenty busy since the bull train of Cap McCormick had rolled into Moon's Well, and she knew from the deep, crimson flush in the dwarf's pasty cheeks that he was thoroughly distracted at having been, for all intents and purposes, whipped to a frazzle by the stranger in denim and buckskin and wielding a Peacemaker.

A boy caught peeping through the door of the girls' schoolhouse privy couldn't have been feeling any more chagrined than was Mordecai Moon, walking around with that bullet hole in the hat he was so proud of. He might have changed the hat if he'd had a spare, but Griselda had never seen any other hat around the room they shared on the hotel's third floor. "The King's Chambers," Mordecai Moon called the room, appointed with furnishings shipped in from all over Texas.

She had to chuckle a little at that, but there was no mirth in it. The whole thing between her and the ugly, old dwarf was about as disgusting as finding a rattlesnake in the coffee beans.

But somehow she'd managed to rise to the occasion. Somehow, she'd even found herself enjoying playing the little man, giving him pleasure until she thought his blood-shot eyes would shoot out of his skull, setting him up to watch him fall like a stone dropped from a high cliff over the Rio Grande.

It was a game with her, this thing she had with Moon. A deadly game. She liked how it took her breath away and made her chuckle at times with giddiness.

This little outlaw girl, an orphan child raised by half-breeds in the Indian Nations, was going to take down the most formidable little devil riding roughshod over a large chunk of southwestern Texas.

"Rio," she said now, stopping and shoving a mesquite branch aside, so she could see the little, ancient stone cabin hunched on the dry wash littered with skull-sized, sun-bleached stones before her. "Rio, you in there, hon?"

Only silence issued from the stone hut that had been sitting there along the wash for as long as anyone native to these parts could remember. Some believed an old Apache who'd been exiled from his tribe had lived in it around the time that Chisos La Grange had dug the well, but no one was sure anymore. Others said an old Mexican padre had built the place over a hundred years ago, when he—according to the legend—had been exiled from his church for breaking his vow of celibacy when he'd fallen in love with a young Kiowa girl.

Griselda liked that story the best. It gave her a bittersweet feeling. To think that someone, even a preacher, could feel such love for another person that he'd been willing to sacrifice his soul . . .

Griselda moved past the mesquite tree and crossed the rocky wash. "Come on, Rio, I know you're in there."

Just after the big man in buckskins had backed his horse down the street to the east, and when Cap McCormick's train had been clattering into the town, she'd seen the young man limp away from the jailhouse, cross the street in the dust from the train, and slink off like a wounded dog between the dentist's office and Green's Saddlemaker's though Green had left when he could no longer afford Mordecai's water contract and hefty monthly tax on profits.

Griselda had waited on the hotel gallery until she was sure that Moon and his men had gone into the hotel with Cap while Cap's men tended their oxen, and in all that confusion, she'd slipped out away from the hotel, heading for the little cabin hunched here along the wash.

She could hear the bawling of the oxen now as they were fed hay from Mordecai's barn which was kept stocked with hay and oats by his Mexican tenants, and watered from his well.

She walked up to the door and stood upon the three flat rocks embedded in the ground for a stoop of sorts, and then lightly rapped on the door. "Rio, I know you're in there," she said, holding her lips up to within an inch of the door, speaking in a breathy, sensual tone.

"Go away," came the Kid's muffled voice from within.

Griselda smiled. If he'd really wanted her to go away, he wouldn't have said anything. She knew everything there was to know about the Kid, having grown up with him back in Nebraska, on farms only a few miles apart. That was before he was known as the Kid but merely as gangly young Vernon Cartwright.

Griselda pulled the leather string. The bolt fell from its plate with a clank, and the leather hinges creaked as the door sagged open. Griselda pushed it open halfway and peered into the earthen-floored hovel's dank shadows.

The Kid lay on his cot on the far side of the low, arched adobe fireplace. He was fully clothed, wearing even his boots and his gun, and he lay facing the stone wall, weak light pressing in where the chinking had crumbled away. His hat was on the floor near his small eating table.

Stepping inside, she said, "You okay, Rio?"

She walked in slowly, hesitatingly, for she'd seen how the big man in buckskins had hauled Rio into town, thrown him over his own horse like a sack of potatoes. Sharing the horse's back with a dead man, no less!

Rio was a prideful young man, and she knew his temper. He could very likely be in a very bad temper right now, maybe fixing to take out his rage and humiliation on someone, anyone—even her. He'd grown from a gangly boy into a rangy, powerful man. Maybe not as powerful as the big man in buckskins, but powerful in his own right.

Dangerous . . .

The danger gave Griselda one of those thrills she was so addicted to, and she felt her breasts swell slightly behind her cream cotton blouse and thin chemise.

"Rio . . . ?"

"Go 'way."

"Ah, come on, Rio. How bad you hurt? Want I should fetch the doc?"

"I'll shoot any goddamn pill roller you bring around here, Griselda!"

Gently, she sat down on the edge of the cot, and placed a hand on Rio's shoulder. He had his right hand on his gun, and he was squeezing it so hard that his knuckles were white.

"We'll settle our accounts, Rio," she said quietly, rubbing his arm. "But you're the deputy sheriff, now, you know, so you'll have to do it within the law. You'd best leave that big gunny to the dwarf."

Rio turned to her now, and she stifled a gasp at the massive, blue bump on his forehead, right at his hairline. "You don't think I can do it? I can take him. He just got the jump on me—that's all!"

"Oh, poor Rio."

Griselda reached up to caress the lump with her fingers,

but Rio shoved her arm down. It was a powerful shove, and she fell back against the wall.

"Don't! Leave me alone, damnit, Griselda! It hurts like hell. Feel like some jake's pressin' a hot iron against my head, and inside I feel like someone's smashin' rocks against my brain."

The Rio Bravo Kid rolled onto his back and pressed his fists to his temples. He chuckled, then drew a deep, painful breath. "Seen what he did to that little pecker, the dwarf." He laughed again, sucked another painful breath, but continued to laugh and groan at the same time as he said, "Seen it all. Blew Moon's hat right off his head. Shot Bannon's gun."

"Where was Mortimer?" Griselda wanted to know.

"Hell, I don't know. You know him. Can't figure him sometimes. Probably off worryin' over that girl of his." Rio drew a breath. "Christ, that big feller's good. I only hope I can get to him before Moon does. Injuns say when they shoot a big ole griz, they acquire his power. Must mean, then, if I were to shoot a man like that, I'd take *his* power." He furrowed a brow at her. "You believe that?"

"I guess." Griselda hiked a shoulder. "Why not?" She was smiling at the Rio Bravo Kid, whom she knew better as Vernon Cartwright, but she was thinking about the big man now, too. About his power. About how maybe it was worth trying to acquire, like the Indians acquired a bear's power . . .

Rio rolled his pain-racked eyes to Griselda. "You see where he went?"

Griselda's thoughts were a mile away, and it took Rio to fashion an impatient look before she said, "Who? Oh, the big fella? No, I didn't see where he went."

That was a lie. She'd suddenly become very interested in the big jake in the buckskin shirt who could get the drop on the Rio Bravo Kid and suddenly make him look less like the cold-steel artist he fancied himself and more like the scrawny farm boy Griselda had grown up with.

And who'd cut Mordecai Moon down to his real size. Who'd made Moon look foolish. And scared.

A simpering idiot there for a few seconds—that's how he'd made Moon look.

The big man had even scared the hard-eyed border toughs who'd once run with the dwarf when Moon was nothing more than a border bandit himself and who now worked for him around the saloon and hotel and helped him tax the entire town and make it pay dearly for his water.

"What are you thinkin' about?"

Griselda jerked a little with a start, finding Rio's critical, faintly suspicious eyes on her. "I was . . . I was thinkin' about how we were gonna get that fella back for what he done to you, Rio."

Rio continued to study her as he rose up on his elbows. His head looked oddly misshapen by the bruise—so much so, in fact, that if Griselda hadn't been all too aware of his violent temper, she would have snickered.

Rio said, "You sure that's all you were thinkin' about?"

"Of course. What else would I be thinkin' about?"

"I don't know, but I seen that look in your eyes before, and it always made me feel a little funny about you, Griselda. Like maybe you were in this whole thing for just yourself."

Snapping into action, she gave him a slow blink and let her right eye wander slightly, with a foxy prettiness, toward her nose. Men just melted when they saw that, for some reason.

Just as slightly, she slid her shoulders back, feeling her blouse tighten against her small, pert breasts. She smiled to herself when Rio fell for it, as every man she'd ever known always did, dreaming of opening her blouse and nuzzling the tender, youthful orbs.

His eyes flicked downward, and she saw a very faint color rise in his cheeks. The bruise on his forehead even darkened a little.

He swallowed.

Griselda caressed his right cheek with her thumb. "You know I'm in this whole thing for us, Rio. You know that. How long have we known each other? Since we were five years old? I'm in this world for you, Rio, and you're in it for me. We ride together. Always have, always will."

There was that thrill again. Like a draw of strong Mexican tobacco. The danger . . .

Rio's eyes dropped to Griselda's shirt again, and his lower jaw loosened. She let him get a good look at that lightly tanned valley between the mounds of her supple flesh, and then she said in a soft, intimate voice, "Now, it's understandable, you bein' jealous, with the situation bein' what it is. But you know, don't you, that nothin' happens between that little urchin and me? I've never let him lay a hand on me, just let him go on thinkin' I will"—she gave a devilish smile—"when the time is right.

"In the meantime, the time's gonna get right for you and me, Rio. That's gonna happen soon, maybe in a few days or next week, when that wagon of fresh meat rolls in, and then he takes it on down to the border and comes back with all that Mexican gold!"

She really let her breasts swell now. It wasn't just a show, either. Thinking about all that gold made the girl randy, made her feel as though her bosoms would fairly explode . . .

She studied Rio. He was drunk on her again, just like he usually was, just like she wanted him to be. He believed the lie that she'd never actually slept with Mordecai Moon. He had no idea that she, in fact, actually enjoyed sleeping with the dwarf. Oh, not because he brought her pleasure, but because she enjoyed playing the little monster like a violin.

Whenever she did it, and climbed down off the stubby mound of pasty flesh, she couldn't help giggling to herself as she imagined how he'd look when he realized what she'd been doing all along. Propping him up to watch him fall. Setting him up, learning the ins and outs of his business here in Moon's Well, to rob him blind and head for the border, never to be seen or heard from again.

She and Rio had come here with that in mind. No, they'd come here on their way to the border, for they'd robbed a bank up in Kansas and believed a posse were after them.

They hadn't made off with much from the little farm town bank, however, so when Griselda May and the Rio Bravo Kid, as he made himself known two days after they'd ridden into Moon's Well, saw the dwarf's fancy setup, they just knew they had to learn more about it.

And see what they could get of it for themselves.

It just so happened that Moon's personally appointed sheriff, the broken-down old gunman, Lee Mortimer, was in need of a cheap deputy to keep the peace around the town when the freight trains rolled through. Also, border toughs like the dwarf's men themselves often stopped here for whiskey and women, and they needed to be controlled by men who at least called themselves the law.

That way, word wouldn't get around that there wasn't any *real law* anywhere in or around Moon's Well. The dwarf didn't want word to get out that the town was wide open, because that would attract the attention of the Texas Rangers, like the two whom the dwarf had killed in a foolish yet typical fit of fury earlier in the day.

So, here Griselda and the Rio Bravo Kid were, sitting on a veritable gold mine of riches—as long as she could keep the lid on the powder keg she knew the Kid to be. Young Vernon Cartwright had, after all, locked his parents in their cabin back in Nebraska, shot them both through a window, doused the roof with kerosene as they lay writhing and screaming, and set the place on fire.

Of course, Griselda had pushed him toward it, because his folks were mean as rabid dogs and would soon as whip Vernon as feed him, but he hadn't been all that hard to push. Griselda had known even at that young age that the apple didn't fall far from the tree.

She smiled now as she looked down to see Rio sticking his nose between her breasts. He wrapped his arms around her, drew her close. She felt his warm breath on her skin, one of his hands on her skirt, the warmth pressing into her thigh beneath it.

Careful to avoid the ugly bruise on his forehead, she ran her hands through his hair. "Oh, Kid," she cooed. "It's gonna be all right. That big bastard who slapped you down will be dead soon, by tomorrow, most likely, and the dwarf—why, he'll be dancing in hell soon, too!"

She pressed her lips to the top of the Kid's head, feeling one of his hands kneading her bosoms through her blouse, the other squeezing her thigh. "And you and me, we're gonna be richer than our wildest dreams!"

"Nasty, *ugly* rich?" Rio said, his voice muffled by her blouse.

She smiled, remembering how they'd described how rich they were going to be, back in Nebraska.

"Nasty, ugly rich, Rio!" Griselda said.

She thrilled to the danger as she let the Kid slide her skirt farther and farther up her legs. . . .

10

LOU PROPHET SAT back in the warm, sudsy water, hands on the sides of the copper bathtub, a quirley dangling from his mouth as he listened to the whooping and hollering from up the street, in the direction of the dwarf's giant saloon and whorehouse.

Occasionally, now that he'd scrubbed the filth from his bones, he'd hum a few bars of "When Johnny Comes Marching Home," but not for long. He was too distracted by the obvious party rising from Mordecai Moon's place, and by contrast, the noticeable lack of clientele here in the Rose Hotel and Saloon.

He was in a street-front room in the Rose's second story, soaking in a tub that Mrs. Rose had insisted on half-filling with warm water, so Prophet could have a proper bath. She assured him she had plenty of water, for everyone in town bought a barrelful each week for a dollar—the price the dwarf allowed the town's citizens, since he apparently didn't want to drive everyone away. He saved the outlandishly high prices for the freight trains and other non-citizens passing through, like Prophet himself.

Prophet bit down on the quirley in anger, then sucked the

acrid but satisfying smoke deep into his lungs, blew it out through his nostrils, casting his angry gaze toward the curtained window over the bed on his left.

No man should be charging that much for water in the desert. The idea of it graveled Prophet no end. It was none of his business, and he'd likely ride out of here tomorrow, for he'd had enough trouble south of the border to last him a good long year north of it.

But he'd leave here hoping that Mordecai Moon eventually got his just deserts.

He drew another lungful of air, and his thoughts drifted to the dead Texas Ranger he'd found in the desert, not far ahead of the blond younker who called himself the Rio Bravo Kid. The bounty hunter had been so preoccupied with his trouble with Moon that he hadn't had much time to consider the Ranger. But when he'd been winching up the water bucket from the well, just before he'd been so rudely interrupted by the dwarf, he'd absently noticed several deep scuffmarks in the dirt as well as a thick, dark-brown substance that was undoubtedly blood.

The Ranger's blood?

Footsteps sounded in the hall beyond Prophet's closed door, interrupting his dark speculations. He looked at his walnut-gripped Peacemaker .45 hanging off the hide bottom chair he'd positioned within an easy reach of the tub. He took the quirley in his left hand and started to stretch his right one toward the revolver, but stopped when Mrs. Rose said, "Mr. Prophet?"

He rested his right hand on the side of the tub and looked at the door. "Yes, ma'am. I'm still appreciatin' the bath. Can't tell you how good it feels after that long ride up from Mexico."

"I have some more hot water for you, Mr. Prophet. Can I come in?"

"Oh, you shouldn't have done that, ma'am. I don't . . ."

He let the sentence drift off when the door opened and Mrs. Rose stumbled in, wrestling with a steaming wooden bucket, water sloshing over the sides. Self-consciously,

Prophet sat up straight and squeezed his legs together to conceal his equipment that the soapy water only partly covered.

"Now, ma'am," he said, "you shouldn't be wastin' water on this old bounty hunter. I'm clean enough as it is."

"Pshaw," the woman said, sidestepping to the tub and raising the bucket. "I've plenty of water left in my barrel. Don't get that much business, and if I took a bath every day, there'd be nothing left of me. Living out here, you become half dust, you know."

She chuckled as she dumped the water into the tub between his legs, and he drew a sharp breath as the plenty-hot water threatened to boil his oysters. He rose up a little, making a face.

Mrs. Rose gasped, horrified. "I didn't get it too hot, did I?"

"Nah, no . . . it's fine," he said, quickly revising a wince into a smile and easing back down in the tub. He felt as though a rat were nibbling at his scrotum, but it would die down soon.

"Oh, good. It's hard to judge." She held up a finger as she turned to the door. "I'll be right back. I hope you're hungry!"

With that, she was gone.

He sat back in the tub, frowning curiously at the door and puffing the quirley, hearing her descending the stairs to the first story. When she came back, she gave the half-open door a cursory knock and then came in holding a steaming plate, a bottle, and two water glasses. He could smell the food instantly, and his stomach rumbled audibly. His mouth watered as he flicked his gaze from the plate of steaming food to the whiskey bottle labeled Old Kentucky, and then back to the food.

"Good Lord," he said, letting the quirley drop from his mouth to sizzle out in the water between his knees. "What have you done there, Mrs. Rose?"

"Ruth, please," she admonished him gently. "I thought you'd like to eat in your room where you wouldn't be as conspicuous as you would downstairs. Not that Mr. Moon or any of his men are likely to show up here this evening. They usually have their hands full at night, serving the men from the freight trains. A stage just pulled in, as well, so Mr. Mordecai Moon is doing a right smart business."

She leaned forward to hand him the plate, and he was aware that she'd changed from the more conservative, plain gray dress she'd been wearing before to a red dress that was cut considerably lower. The edges of the bodice were trimmed in white lace. A gold locket dropped down into her cleavage, as though consciously directing his eye.

He felt abashed when, after handing him the plate, she straightened, her eyes on his, which meant she'd seen where his own gaze had strayed. "Mrs. Rose, you really shouldn't have. A hot bath, food—"

"And whiskey," she said, setting the bottle and the two glasses on the dresser. She popped the cork on the bottle and filled each glass nearly half full. "Please, Mr. Prophet, the pleasure is all mine. Like I said, I don't get much business . . . or company."

She shoved the cork back into the bottle and then leaned down again, lower than before, to set the glass on the floor beside the tub. In the corner of his eye, he saw her cleavage yawn, her breasts jostle.

They were indeed lovely, as was the rest of her, he'd noticed. She was a dark-skinned, brown-eyed brunette, her skin lightly freckled. She was full-figured, and the dress she now wore accented it to damn near perfection. Her thick, attractively sun-bleached hair was piled high atop her head, with several sausage curls dangling about her cheeks.

As he dug into the two thick slabs of roast beef and mashed potatoes drenched in dark brown gravy and complimented by a small portion of boiled greens, he reminded himself she was married. Lonely, apparently, or she wouldn't be in a man's room while said man sat in a bathtub naked— but married.

She'd said something about her husband having taken ill . . .

"These here vittles is sure a sight for sore eyes, ma'am," he said, forking a thick chunk of meat into his mouth. "And they taste even better."

"I'm glad you like it, Mr. Prophet. The beef was supplied by a rancher from the other side of the Chisos Mountains. The greens came from my neighbor's irrigated garden."

"Mhmmm—Mhmmmm!"

She took the second glass of whiskey, dragged the chair over by the door, and sagged into it.

He glanced up from his plate—he couldn't stop himself from shoveling the food in, as he hadn't realized how closely his belly had been snuggling up to his backbone—and couldn't help noticing the faint longing in her brown eyes as she watched him.

He wasn't sure what to say, if he could say anything with all the food that was constantly in his mouth, so he said nothing but simply let her watch him eat as she sat there in her low-cut red dress, slowly sipping her whiskey and watching him.

When he finished, he licked his fork, dropped it onto the plate, set the plate on the floor, stifled a belch, and scooped up his whiskey glass. He tossed back half the whiskey in two swallows, and then looked at her again, watching him with a hard-to-read expression.

Longing? Sadness? Desire?

Then her brown eyes slid slowly across his exposed chest and his shoulders, and her lips parted slightly. The color in her cheeks darkened.

This woman, he silently, idly opined, had been alone for a long time. Her husband might be here, but she was as alone as if he'd been planted months, maybe years ago.

She must have read his thoughts. Her eyes jerked to his with a self-conscious start, and she lifted a hand to the locket dangling against her breasts. "Good Lord, look at me—sitting here with a strange man! A naked man!"

She stood, her cheeks flushing, fingering the locket with one hand, holding her whiskey glass in the other. "My husband is just down the hall, Mr. Prophet."

She stared at the curtained window beyond him, above the bed.

Prophet sipped his whiskey. "You said he took to his sickbed."

She stared at the window as though it were the only place she now dared place her gaze, and then walked around Prophet to the window and stood staring through the sheer curtain at the street. He watched her narrow shoulders and slender back. The dress had no sleeves, only straps, and the backs of her light brown arms were as speckled with tiny freckles as was her face and neck and what he had seen of her bosom.

"Yes," she said quietly, with a soundless sigh that lifted her shoulders. They lowered again slowly as she exhaled. "He's very sick."

"A brain stroke?"

She nodded, keeping her back to him. She took another sip of the whiskey. He could hear her swallow.

"Mr. Moon came calling on us here about a year and a half ago. The little man and his big tough nuts, as Frank called them. Our tax payment was a couple of months past due. We'd had a bout of business, then . . . nothing. But the dwarf still wanted his money. The water contract money, as well. Frank tried to put him off, as he'd been doing successfully for a few months, but this night Mr. Moon threatened to tar and feather Frank if we didn't pay up, and to burn our place to the ground."

She paused.

When she spoke again, it was even softer than before. "That night, I woke up to Frank moaning and stumbling around the room. He'd had his stroke."

Prophet felt his shoulders slump. He stared at his hands resting on the sides of the tub. After a time, he said, "If you bought the land from Chisos La Grange, how does the dwarf think he can tax you, let alone charge you for water?"

"Simply because he has the curly wolves to back his play here in Moon's Well." Ruth accentuated each word in the town's new name with a hard irony. "We'd saved our money to buy a business, preferably in West Texas. Frank had found the place a couple of years ago and thought it would be a good place to come for his health. Frank had lung problems, and the doctors in Missouri thought the dry air out here would help. Also, the water of West Texas is supposed to be particularly healthful."

She chuckled with more irony at this.

"So, after my parents died and the farm went under," she continued, "we came out here, bought the lot for the hundred dollars, and, with the help of the Mexican tenants, built the hotel. A month after it was operational, Mr. La Grange got sick and sold his claim to Mr. Mordecai Moon for one thousand dollars. He became our landlord. We were sure, however, that our business arrangement with Mr. La Grange would be honored, so we were willing to remain here despite the town's sudden name change. We were making money, with all the freight traffic on the trail."

"But then the dwarf built his own place."

"It went up almost overnight," Ruth said sourly. "He employed the local Mexicans for next to nothing, and in a month the place was up and running."

"And he didn't honor your and Mr. Rose's deal with Chisos."

"No, he certainly did not. Not only did Mr. Moon take most of the business, he taxed us an outrageous fee for our own business and charged us for water. Of course we couldn't afford it. I still can't. Oh, I make every other payment, but . . . in the meantime what we owe grows. Frank and I are sinking into a deeper and deeper pit of ruin. Before Frank got sick, we could have at least cut our losses and gone home, but there's no doing even that now."

Ruth turned toward Prophet and took another sip of her whiskey. The whiskey had emboldened her, and she looked right at the big bounty hunter sitting naked in the tub before her. "I guess I shouldn't be so hard on Mr. Moon, Mr. Prophet. He has given us one way out of this mess we find ourselves in."

Prophet waited, but she seemed to want prompting. He

wasn't sure he wanted to hear what she had left to say, but he dipped his chin, and said, "And that way is . . . ?"

"Me going over and working for him," she said with what almost appeared a genuine smile. But her brown eyes owned a very thin sheen of tears. She tossed the rest of her whiskey back, held the empty glass straight down at her side, lifted her chin, and swallowed.

Suddenly, her face bunched with anger. With an enraged wail, she threw her glass against the closed door, where it shattered and fell to the floor. She stepped toward the tub. Prophet stared up at her, tongue-tied. He watched her hands unbutton the corset of her dress and then slide the dress's straps down her arms.

Both heavy, freckled breasts sprang free of their confines.

Reaching up, she removed the pins from her hair. When she shook her head, the rich waves tumbled down across her shoulders.

"What do you say, Mr. Prophet?"

Prophet only vaguely realized that his lower jaw was hanging. He had to clear his throat to rediscover his voice, and then he said thickly, "What do I say to what?"

"To killing him for me, of course. I'll pay you with everything I have!"

11

PROPHET STARED UP at the bare-breasted woman standing before him, her face in her hands, sobbing. Her breasts jostled as she cried, the small, gold locket jerking at the top of her cleavage.

Slowly, he rose from the soapy water, grabbed a towel off the bed, and wrapped it around his waist. He climbed out of the tub, and walked over to her, his chest and arms and even his hair dry now in the dry desert air.

He stood before her, looking down at her, and then very slowly lifted the straps of her dress up over her shoulders. She lowered her hands and looked at him, puzzled, tears streaking her cheeks. She looked down at her breasts that were mostly covered now, the dollar-sized nipple of one exposed by the unbuttoned corset. Gazing up at him again, the skin above the bridge of her nose deeply creased, she said, "You think I'm a harlot."

Prophet shook his head. "No, but you would, if I took what you offered. And I ain't an assassin for hire."

"What about all that I told you?"

"Oh, he deserves to be kicked out with a shovel, I'll give him that. But if I kill him, I'll kill him for me." Prophet

shook his head. "I won't saddle you with that. You're in a
bad place, but I got a feelin' I could handle killin' a man a
whole lot better than you would. I'm a bounty hunter, Mrs.
Rose. I do it for a livin'."

Her half-covered breasts rose and fell as she breathed,
staring at him, her lips parted, the flush still in her cheeks.
Her eyes held his, and as she continued to breathe heavily,
he said, "What about your husband . . . ?"

She reached down for one of his hands, lifted it to her
right breast, used it to slide the corset open, and pressed it
over her nipple. "You can't betray a dead man, Mr. Prophet."

She pressed his hand to her breast. The nipple came alive
against his palm. With his other hand, he removed the towel
from around his waist. He wrapped his arm around her
shoulders and pressed his lips to hers. They were warm and
open, welcoming and pliant.

A couple of hours later, she lay tight against him, her head
on his chest. Outside, he could hear wild laughter beneath
the strains of what sounded like a four-piece band. Women
screeched and men guffawed. Infrequently, a pistol barked
flatly. A dog barked intermittently.

Hooves clomped past the Rose Hotel and Saloon. There
were occasional shouts of anger but mostly everything
seemed friendly, albeit raucously so, over at Moon's House
of a Thousand Delights.

During the infrequent lulls in the party, Prophet could
hear coyotes yammering in the hills around the town.

"They're havin' a good time over there," he said, waking
from a brief doze and lightly running his fingers across Ruth
Rose's bare back.

He felt the warm moistness of her lips on his chest. She
groaned luxuriously. "Soon they'll be having even more fun,
when the fresh batch of girls rolls in."

Prophet frowned.

Ruth said, "I don't know where he gets them, but every
so often a wagon rolls in. A jail wagon with anywhere from
five to ten young women in it. It's escorted by soldiers, if

you can believe that." Ruth chuckled darkly and raked his chest very lightly with her thumbnail. "I've been here for three years now, Lou, and there's nothing I won't believe anymore. Especially where the dwarf is concerned."

"You mean he buys slave girls for his place?"

"That's how I figure it. Of course, I haven't heard. No one around town talks much about the dwarf's activities. We're all pretty well cowed by the little fellow and his tough nuts. Besides, he brings business to Moon's Well. Men come from all over to visit his place. Sometimes the freight trains stop over for three or four days."

"Slave tradin's illegal."

She only laughed at that.

"Soldiers bring the girls in?"

"Uh-huh."

Prophet chuckled without mirth. "What a perdition you got here, Ruth."

"Oh, yes."

Prophet slid her hair back from her cheek. "Ruth, what happened to that Ranger I brought into town with the Rio Bravo Kid?"

She rose up a little, the locket hanging down between her sloping, freckled breasts to dangle against his chest. "You don't really want to know, Lou. What I said before, about you killing Moon? Forget it. It was just that . . . watching you out there, how badly you cowed him . . ."

"What happened?"

"Like you, they refused to pay for water."

"They?"

"There were two. The one you found ran after the dwarf shot him. They probably tossed the other into a nearby ravine. That's probably what the coyotes are singing about."

Prophet lay back against the pillow and considered that. The little man was only evil but crazy, to mess with the Texas Rangers.

"What if others come, looking for the first two?" he said, thinking out loud.

"Men disappear out here all the time, Lou," Ruth said,

rolling off of him and dropping her legs to the floor. Walking over to the dresser, she said, "He has a chokehold on this town, and enough men to keep it good and tight."

She splashed whiskey into the glasses on the dresser, and came back and offered one to Prophet. He took it and looked at her, her hair mussed and wild in the soft light of the lantern flickering on the dresser.

He touched her hair, brushed his fingers across her shoulders.

"How often does he pester you to go to work for him?"

"Every time he sees me he just laughs in his seedy way to remind me," she said, giving a little shudder of revulsion. "He could force me, of course, but he likes terrorizing me, making it my decision. Having to think about what it would be like with him and the others."

Prophet lowered his hand from her shoulder. She grabbed it with both of hers and kissed it.

Holding it taut against her cheek, she continued in a sad, bleak tone, "I've been able to make enough money serving food to the occasional few who make their way over here, and to Moon's overflow. But I'm just barely making it. I would, however, put a gun to Frank's head and then to mine before I'd walk over to that demon's place and throw myself on his mercy."

Prophet's mind was reeling from all he'd learned of the dwarf's depredations here in the town he'd named after himself. A dark voice told him, however, that there was much more to learn.

Ruth looked at him, and her eyes brightened in alarm.

"Oh, no," she said. "Please forget about what I said earlier. About you killing him. You can't. He has a dozen gunmen working for him—his old gang from his outlaw days. And the girl. You mustn't try. I was drunk and feeling lonely and helpless. I don't want you to die. I want you to ride out of here tomorrow and not look back."

Prophet was incredulous. "A *dozen* men?"

"Yes!"

"How does a little rooster like that manage to rule such a

large roost? Why any one of 'em could stick a boot so far up his . . ."

Ruth shook her head, genuinely befuddled. "I reckon some men have an air about them. Despite their size. With just a look, they can command others, hold others, hard men like those who ride for Moon, sort of how a snake holds a rabbit with its gaze."

"Mesmerized 'em," Prophet said, thoughtful, then adding with a hard edge, "Well, he didn't mesmerize this old jack-rabbit buck."

"Apparently he's got quite a grip on Miss May."

"May?"

"The girl with him. Griselda May. The one who goes around sneering and twirling those little pistols on her fingers. Apparently, she's plumb gone for that wretched demon. Her soul is as black as his is."

"That's even harder to swallow." Prophet remembered the girl from the hotel steps. She'd been no raving beauty, but she'd been young and sexy in a crude sort of way, and he couldn't imagine her genuinely finding Mordecai Moon attractive.

Ruth was studying him. She sandwiched his hand in both of hers, drew it to the deep valley between her breasts. "Please?"

Prophet continued to stare up at this pretty, lonely woman so terrorized by a merciless hard case in a town she was trapped in. But he was a bounty hunter, not a lawman. And even if he were a lawman, his going up solo against the dwarf and his men would be certain suicide. He'd likely end up in the same ravine as those two Rangers.

His death would accomplish nothing.

Prophet sipped his drink. "I reckon," he said without conviction and took another sip of the whiskey.

She leaned forward and kissed him. "Thank you for tonight."

"Ah, hell," he said, his ears warming in embarrassment.

"No, you gave me a gift. It's been . . . lonely."

"No regrets?"

She smiled and shook her head. Rising from the bed, she walked over and picked her dress up off the floor. "I'd best check on Frank and stoke the range. Some of the business from Moon's place might be heading over here soon, and they might be hungry."

"I can get you out of here." Prophet had said it before he'd even thought it through. "You and Frank—I can get you out of this town. That much I can do."

She held her dress against her breasts, and she looked beautiful standing there in the lantern light, in front of the door. Her brown eyes sparkled as she furrowed her brows.

She appeared to be on the verge of both sobbing and smiling at the same time. "No." She shook her head. "Don't be silly, Lou." She paused, staring at him, considering it. "How could you?"

"I'd have to leave here first. Just me. I can go up to Alpine, enlist a passel of Rangers. We'll bring a wagon, park north of town a ways, and then slip in here and fetch you and Frank under cover of darkness. Give me a week, maybe two. Likely, it'll take that long for Moon to forget about the man who drilled that hole in his hat."

Ruth stared at him, fear creeping into her gaze now as she considered the possibility.

"Of course, you'd be losing everything," he said. "You'd have to start over."

"I've already lost everything."

"Let's give it a try, then. Like I said, give me a week, two at the most, and I'll—"

Rising voices cut him off. Beyond the open window, he could hear foot thuds and the ring of spurs.

"They're coming," she said, looking at the window. "The dwarf must have run out of rooms. I'd better go." She came over and kissed him and then pulled away.

He clutched her shoulders as the voices and the spur chings grew louder. "All right?"

She looked nervous, but she smiled. "All right, yes."

Still clutching her dress to her breasts, she hurried to the door.

"You need help down there, splittin' wood or anything?" he asked.

"No, you stay here, out of sight." She opened the door. Downstairs, someone was pounding on the saloon's front doors. She looked back at Prophet. "Thank you, Lou."

She gave him another nervous but hopeful half smile, and then went out and drew the door closed behind her.

Prophet rose just after dawn the next morning. He dressed quietly in his room, in no hurry. The mercantile where he'd buy a canteen likely didn't open until after sunrise.

With his saddlebags draped over his left shoulder, his Winchester on his right shoulder, shotgun hanging down his back, he stole quietly downstairs and outside to the small barn of vertical pine planks behind the saloon.

Mean and Ugly was happy to see him. The horse tossed his head a few times in greeting before dipping his snout in an oat bucket. When Prophet had tended the horse and saddled him, he led him outside and around to the front of the saloon, where he paused to let the sun climb a little higher over the Del Carmens in the southeast.

He sat on the edge of the Rose's porch, building a smoke.

He fired the quirley and was smoking it leisurely when one of the bull trains that had pulled into Moon's Well last night came up from the barn and corral behind the dwarf's place. The four big wagons with tarp-covered boxes churned the dust in the street in front of Prophet as the bleary-eyed, scowling teamsters wearing broad sombreros and colorful bandannas up over their noses, continued their journey south toward Mexico.

A white, black-speckled dog was loping into town from the south, tongue drooping as though it were thoroughly exhausted from its nightlong hunt in the ravines and washes. It stepped off the trail to watch the teams pass, a malicious glint in its eyes. It lunged at one of the turning wheels and then leaped back off the trail, just beyond the lash of a driver's blacksnake, and gave the last cabin-sized, double-axle Burnside freight wagon a couple of parting barks.

The dog continued on to the Rose Hotel and Saloon where it let Prophet scratch its ears, groaning and swatting at its shoulder with a hind leg. It gave Mean and Ugly a perfunctory growl before continuing on up the street for a nap under a boardwalk.

Prophet had smoked the quirley halfway down when he started hearing voices around the town, some rising from the direction of the dwarf's place. The mercantile was two buildings down from Moon's House of a Thousand Delights, a man in a long, green apron sweeping the loading dock. Prophet took one more drag from the quirley and had dropped it in the dust when the hotel's front door opened.

Ruth stepped out, her hair down, squinting against the intensifying light. She wore a powder-blue robe and deer-skin slippers. She'd just gotten up.

"Lou? What are you doing out here?"

"Waitin' for the mercantile to open, which it looks like it just did." Prophet grabbed Mean's reins from the hitch rail.

"Hold on," Ruth said. "I'll get dressed and fetch the canteen for you."

"You don't need to fetch no canteen for me," Prophet said with a dry chuckle.

She gave him a look of reprimand, shaking her head. "Lou, no."

"I've always bought my own canteens in the past, always fetched my own water." Prophet swung into the leather. "Don't see no reason under the sun to let you do it for me now."

He pinched his hat brim to her and touched spurs to Mean's flanks. He did not look at Ruth as he rode on up the street, though he could feel her apprehensive gaze on his back. He probably should have let her buy the canteen for him and fill it from her own supply. That would have made more sense. It would have been practical.

But something in him—something stupid and mulish, which too often won out when pitted against his better judgment—wouldn't allow it.

12

PROPHET RODE UP past the well in the middle of the broad street and looked at the three-story, gaudy, purple hotel with its lime-green gallery on his left. A small Mexican man in a red serape slept in the street, slumped back against one of the gallery's stone pilings, an empty bottle lying at one of his steel-toed boots. He was a remnant from the previous night's festivities.

Prophet merely glanced at the hungover Mexican. The brunt of his attention was on the small, brown-haired girl sitting at the top of the steps in a cream blouse and long, wool skirt, smoking a quirley. Her Stetson hat with conch-studded band was hooked over her left knee. She held the quirley between the long, slender fingers of her right hand.

Her sharp, devious face brightened when her eyes found the big man riding past the hotel. "Good mornin'!"

"Good mornin' your own self," Prophet said, keeping Mean moving in the direction of the mercantile.

The girl turned her head and narrowed one speculative eye at the Rose Hotel and Saloon at the south end of town, and then turned back to Prophet once more, her smile turning foxy. "Have a good night, did you?"

"Slept like a rock. You?"

"I reckon I did okay for it bein' so hot."

"Well," Prophet said, grinning and pinching his hat brim to the girl he'd seen with Moon the day before, "be seein' you."

"Most likely." The girl grinned again, foxily, and lifted the quirley to her thin lips and took a deep drag, exhaling the smoke through her nostrils as she continued to watch the bounty hunter.

Her grin faded. Her eyes turned cunning.

Prophet continued on over to Soddermeyer's Dry Goods and reined up in front of the loading dock. The man he'd seen earlier was no longer on the porch but was standing just inside the door he'd propped open with a barrel bristling with picks, shovels, and scythes.

He was lean, bony, his skin tanned a dark, rosy hue. He had thick, black hair streaked with gray, and a mustache of the same color. "I don't need your business," he said throatily, canting his head to his left. "Keep ridin'!"

Prophet swung down from the leather, glanced over at the dwarf's place, seeing only the girl still sitting on the steps, smoking and watching him, and then tossed Mean's reins over the hitch rail. He smiled affably at the shopkeeper scowling before him and climbed the loading dock's wooden steps, his spurs ringing loudly in the quiet morning air that was heating up quickly, foretelling another scorcher.

"Mornin', there, amigo. Looks like it's gonna be another hot one. Just a few things I'll be needin' before I shake a rein."

Prophet crossed the dock and stood before the lean, dark-haired gent with the bushy mustache. A full head taller, the big bounty hunter loomed over the man, grinning.

Soddermeyer looked up at him apprehensively, his eyes flicking nervously from the Peacemaker thonged on this stranger's thigh to the fierce double maw of the coach gun peeking up from behind his right shoulder and then to the width of his shoulders that stretched the buckskin tunic taut across his chest.

The shopkeeper glanced toward the dwarf's place and

then stepped back into his shop, beckoning with a quick, impatient sweep of his arm.

"Make it quick. I don't got all morning to spend on drifters who aggravate Mr. Moon!"

Ten minutes later, Prophet walked out of the mercantile with two canteens for the long ride to Alpine, a bag of Arbuckles, and a pouch of jerky. He slowed his stride as he walked across the loading dock, seeing first the two local lawmen, Lee Mortimer and his deputy, the Rio Bravo Kid, standing in the street to Prophet's left. Mortimer scowled beneath the brim of his black Stetson, his eyes like steel above his knife slash of a nose and his steel gray mustache. Despite the menace in his gaze, he had a bored, worn-out air.

The Rio Bravo Kid scowled beneath his hat that was tilted up an angle to accommodate the blue goose egg on his right temple. The two men cast long shadows, for the sun had just risen above the roofs on the east side of the street. The Kid didn't look good, and he didn't seem happy, either. Eagerly, again and again, he raked his thumb over the hammer of one of his holstered Colts; his teeth shone white between his thin lips.

Mortimer drew up one side of his mouth. "Why couldn't you just ride the hell out of town?"

Prophet continued on down the loading dock steps and glanced to his right, where the dwarf stood with the three hard cases he'd had out there the day before as well as four others, including the man whose hand Prophet had punched a slug through. The bandaged hand hung down by the man's side. His other hand rode atop the big Remington holstered on his other hip.

The additional four looked just as mean and hard as the other three. They all wore at least two pistols on their suited frames.

The dwarf stood at the head of the group, only a few yards from the well. He had his thumbs hooked in his vest pockets—a severely ugly child in a very bad mood. As he stared at Prophet, who dropped the coffee and jerky into his saddlebag pouch, Moon rose up and down on the balls of his child-sized black boots that looked as though they'd gotten a recent polish. He wore the shabby bowler with the small, ragged hole in its crown.

Casually sliding his shotgun forward, so that the sawed-off popper hung down to around the middle of his belly, Prophet hung his two new canteens from his saddle horn, swung into the leather, and neck-reined Mean and Ugly toward the well. From his higher vantage now, he could see Ruth Rose standing on the steps of her saloon, one arm hooked around a porch rail as she stared worriedly toward Prophet.

As Mean clomped slowly toward the belligerent group of men standing in a pie-shaped wedge between the well and the hotel, Prophet saw Miss May sitting where he'd last seen her, on the porch steps of Moon's hotel. She was no longer smoking her quirley, though Prophet could see its stub smoldering in the dust near the empty bottle of the Mexican still passed out beside the steps.

The girl wrapped her arms around her knees, staring at him gravely now, pensively, with none of the mocking humor of before. She almost appeared to be waiting to see what would happen, maybe wondering if it would turn out the same as the day before.

Or different. Almost as though she had a stake in it.

"You got a lot of nerve," the dwarf said, rising up and down on the balls of his boots, jutting his knobby chin toward Prophet. "A lot of damn nerve . . . hangin' around my town after what you pulled yester—!"

He cut himself off abruptly and snapped his eyes wide, startled, as Prophet's two silver nickels winked in the air as they caromed toward him. He threw up his hands a split second too late, and both coins bounced off his chest and dropped to the street near his boots.

Prophet held his shotgun by its neck though he kept the barrel down, not wanting to bait anyone into slapping leather but wanting to be ready in case it happened. He turned his head slightly to one side, and saw the two lawmen standing where they'd been standing before, apparently out here to merely back the dwarf's play.

Or maybe cut off their quarry if Prophet chose to light a shuck to the north?

"There's your ten cents," Prophet said, pulling back on Mean's reins with his left hand, squeezing the gut shredder's neck with his right. "Now, kindly vamoose."

He squeezed his shotgun's stock even tighter, having a hard time holding his fury in check. Being made to pay for a canteen of water graveled him no end, and the only reason he did it now was so he could ride out of here and return later for Ruth and her husband.

The dwarf glared at Prophet. He looked down at the coins at his feet. He looked up at Prophet again, and both his eyes shone as red as a devil's eyes.

At that moment, Prophet fully realized the dunderhead-edness of his own move. As though to confirm it, the hard case with the wounded right hand jerked his left hand toward the big horse pistol on that hip. With a snarled curse directed mostly at himself this time, Prophet raised the gut shredder's barrel, thumbing both hammers back, and tripped the left trigger.

The coach gun fairly exploded, the concussion of the blast sounding like near thunder and rocketing around a narrow canyon. The man who'd been going for his revolver was lifted two feet in the air and tossed straight back, as though he'd been lassoed from behind by a cyclone dead-heading for the Rio Grande.

He landed in the street, lifting a grunt and a great swarm of tan dust.

All six of the dwarf's other men, and the dwarf himself, sprang into action. Prophet decided to take the bull by the horns, and slid the coach gun's barrel at Moon, but then revolvers began belching behind him. A slug raked the left side of his head and across his left temple, fouling his aim.

When the shotgun thundered a second time, it blew a pumpkin-sized hole in the street two feet in front of Moon's black boots. The little man screamed, *"Ach!"* and leaped back so quickly that he got his boots tangled, and he fell on his ass.

At the same time, several more revolvers barked, curling the air around Prophet's head. Mean and Ugly whinnied shrilly and pitched, rising high off his front hooves. Prophet, who was suffering the effects of the bullet that had carved a furrow along the side of his head as well as dropping the coach gun and reaching for his Colt, was thrown back so quickly that he had no time to reach for the horn to steady himself.

"She-eee-ittt!" he heard himself cry as he turned a backward somersault off Mean's back, feeling the tail rake his face. He hit the ground hard on his back, one of Mean's scissoring rear hooves clipping Prophet's right boot and causing pain to bark in that ankle.

Groaning, seeing Mean twist and turn and edge off to the far side of the well, lifting a thick dust cloud painted butter yellow by the morning sun, Prophet sat up, reaching for his holster.

The Colt wasn't there. It lay in the dust several feet away, half covered with dirt and bits of straw.

A cold stone dropped in his gut as he switched his gaze to the group spread out before him, all grimacing and squinting against the dust, all with one or two pistols leveled on him. All but the man with the injured hand, that was. That gent now had another injury—a bad one that had left him flat on his back in the street yards away in the direction of the Rio Grande, an astonished expression on his face, a gaping hole in his chest and belly. His limbs quivered as though he'd been touched by lightning.

"Hold your fire! Hold your *goddamn fire!*" the dwarf shouted, sitting on his butt in the dirt, about ten feet from Prophet. His hat was off, his thin hair mussed about the pale, bulb-shaped top of his head. Dust hung in the ragged tuft of his spade beard.

His men held their positions, crouching, resembling a pack of wolves about to pounce. Behind Prophet, running footsteps sounded as well as the raucous chinging of spurs.

He turned a quick glance to see Mortimer walking toward him and extending a pistol straight out from a shoulder while the Rio Bravo Kid ran toward Prophet, grimacing, a hogleg in each red fist.

"Ease up, Kid," the dwarf ordered. "I don't want him dead. Not yet, anyways." He laughed raucously, kicking his little, crooked legs, dust rising around his boots. "First, we're gonna show him just how unwelcome he made himself here in Moon's Well!"

Prophet, who had also lost his hat, stared grimly through the wafting dust at the gang surrounding him. They all had guns. He had only his empty barn blaster. He saw Ruth Rose standing in the street fronting her hotel, staring toward Prophet in shock and dread, holding both hands to her face.

He glanced over at the girl, Griselda May, who sat as before on the gallery steps of Moon's hotel. She had turned the corners of her small mouth down and was slowly, darkly shaking her head.

She seemed genuinely sad about Prophet's imminent demise.

He felt sad about it, too.

13

PROPHET BRUSHED A hand across the side of his head and saw the blood on his glove. Not a lot. It was just a crease. Likely nothing compared to what he was in store for. . . .

The dwarf walked up to within a few feet of Prophet, trying to look cocky, but his movements betraying the hesitation of a man walking up to the edge of a snake pit. Moon, dusty, bedraggled, and now sporting his bullet-torn hat, dipped his fingers into his glove pockets and again rose up on the toes of his little boots.

"If we had some tar and some feathers, you know what you'd get. Since we don't . . ." Moon turned aside and swiped his short, stubby arm toward the big man on the ground. "Boys, I want you to beat the shit out of this son of a bitch, but stop just this side of killin' him. Strip him naked, tie him over his horse, and send him out into the desert to die slow."

He squinted one eye up at the rising sun shedding heat like a locomotive with a freshly stoked boiler, and then cackled his wicked laugh and sauntered over to join the girl on the gallery steps.

Prophet looked at the six men before him. They were all

hard-eyed, bearded, and decked out in gaudy wool or broad-cloth suits with checked or striped trousers and bowlers or slouch hats. The guns and knives they wore conspicuously were very well cared for.

There were two Mexicans, one who appeared a half-breed Apache, and three white men, one with the white skin and yellows eyes of an albino. He was the biggest of the lot—Prophet's size or bigger, with long, cottony-white hair hanging down from his black derby hat trimmed with a stamped-copper Indian talisman of some kind. Maybe a witch's totem. Purple-tinted spectacles hid his eyes.

He spat to one side and, grinning, his pale, gaunt cheeks making him look dead, he came in hard and fast on Prophet, his freckled hands held out in front of him as though he were preparing to swing them in chopping motions. Prophet shrugged off the searing pain in the side of his head and scrambled to his feet, spinning to get a look at the two lawmen.

They appeared to be content to watch from a distance, Mortimer filling his pipe while the Rio Bravo Kid stood grinning eagerly, maliciously, hands on both his holstered pistols. The purple bruise dipped down from beneath his hat.

"Shoulda left while you could, Lou. Reckon the trail ends here," Mortimer said. "Too bad we're so far off the beaten track. Many a man with paper on his head would love to see this." He shook his head and swiped a match across his black leather holster, firing it.

Mordecai Moon clapped and yelled, "Give it to him good, boys! Make him feel it, now, hear?"

Prophet swiped his shotgun's leather lanyard up over his head and right shoulder. Shuffling just beyond the albino's reach, setting his feet and grabbing the gut shredder by its barrels, wielding it like a club, he made a mental note to save his last ounce of strength for breaking the dwarf's neck.

"Hey, that ain't fair!" the Rio Bravo Kid shouted, pointing at the shotgun in Prophet's hand.

"Since he's outnumbered," the dwarf said, sitting down

beside the girl, "I'm gonna let him use it. Otherwise, I'd shoot him in the knee."

Moon cackled and looked at the girl, who laughed then, too.

The albino lurched toward Prophet, who saw it for the feint it was, and smacked the stock of his shotgun hard against the side of the big man's head. The albino opened his eyes wide in surprise and stiffened, a muscle in his cheek twitching as blood ran down the side of his head from his badly ruined ear.

"Ah, damnit all, Hans!" bellowed the dwarf in disgust as the albino's knees buckled.

Prophet swung the shotgun at the next man coming toward him—an Anglo with a gold earring and two Green River knives sheathed on his hips—but the bounty hunter was distracted by the half-breed circling around behind him, and the coach gun whistled through the air over the man's head as he ducked.

Prophet lurched forward and rammed his knee against the ducking man's forehead, sending the hombre stumbling straight back, cursing and clutching his temple. The half-breed jumped on Prophet from behind, wrapping his arm around the bounty hunter's neck and doing a good job of pinching off Prophet's wind. His head felt as though it doubled in size as the half-breed hung on his back, closing off the carotid arteries in Prophet's neck, whooping and hollering and grunting and jerking back with his hooked left arm.

In the upper periphery of his vision, Prophet saw a Mexican storming toward him and swinging his right fist far back behind his shoulder, intending to slam it against Prophet's head. The bounty hunter wheeled, turning full around, and the Mexican's fist slammed with an audible, crunching smack into the half-breed's back.

That caused the half-breed to loosen his grip enough that Prophet got both his arms up beneath the half-breed's arm and, throwing himself forward into a deep crouch, sent the half-breed tumbling into the air over Prophet's head.

The half-breed bounced off the well coping and piled up

in the dirt at its base, instantly rising to his hands and knees and shaking his head.

At the same time, Prophet swung around to see the Mexican throwing a haymaker at Prophet's face. The Mexican was a short, wiry man, and Prophet reached up and stopped the fist with his own hand, hammering the Mexican's face twice—two resounding left jabs that turned the Mexican's nose sideways against his face and exploded it like a tomato splattered against a stone wall.

Prophet hit him again, but then, to his right, the half-breed came at Prophet with the bounty hunter's own gun, which Prophet had dropped when the half-breed had jumped onto his back. Prophet saw the stock growing bigger and bigger so quickly, that he only got his hands up after it had smacked with savage force against the dead center of his forehead.

The bounty hunter stumbled backward, leaning forward and grabbing his forehead in both hands. He stopped, the street pitching and wheeling around him and under him, bells tolling in his head.

From somewhere, a woman was screaming.

As he dropped to his knees, he opened his eyes beneath his hands pressed to his forehead. Ruth Rose was running toward him, her own hands pressed to the sides of her head, her face crumpled in terror, tears glistening down her cheeks. She'd thrown her gray dress on but her hair wasn't brushed, and it hung in messy waves across her shoulders and down over her bosom.

"No!" the woman screamed.

"Stay there!" Prophet shouted raspily, and then heaved himself off his heels and bulled forward into the half-breed's knees, lifting the man off his feet and slamming his back to the ground.

Prophet was only about three-quarters conscious after that, only vaguely aware of the fight continuing, his fist slamming against flesh and bone and hairy scalps, only vaguely aware of many more fists hammering his jaws, cheeks, ears, the back of his head, until, after what he suspected was his own shotgun butt slamming into his head once more, just above his left ear, all turned black and hot and quiet.

It remained that way for he didn't know long, until he heard what sounded like someone smashing an ax handle against a barrel a hundred yards away.

Boom! Boom! Boom!

The sound kept getting louder until he was sure that whoever was wielding the handle was now smashing it against the top of his head. Then against the back of it. Then the top of it again, as though he were trying smash Prophet's head to a bloody pulp.

The misery was almost unendurable, and he tried to run away from it but he had no legs or feet with which to run. He could do nothing but lay there, against what felt like a rough-cut board raked back and forth across his belly and groin, while his tormentor continued to beat him, as hard as he could, about the head and shoulders with the ax handle.

The torture continued for a long time, and with it were other tortures, like that of a second tormentor setting hot irons against his back, between his shoulders, on the tops of his shoulders themselves, and against his ears and his ass. He could hear himself groaning and struggling, trying to flee these savage, merciless captors, but his hands and his feet were bound together.

The hammering continued, as did the raking of the crudely sawn board against his belly.

Gradually, the heat in the irons dwindled, and for a time he felt relief from that torment only to gradually feel a hard chill coming, as though a winter storm were descending.

It was just one more thing to endure, and he wished only that the horrible injuries he was surely suffering from all the abuse if not from the hombre wielding the stick would go ahead and kill him. Time to see the Devil, Ole Scratch, and start paying back the loan that Prophet had received for extra party time up here on the green side of the sod in return for Prophet's shoveling coal down below for all the rest of eternity.

He'd hoped he'd be able to stay up here longer, enjoy the green side of the sod for a few more years, but, oh, well, all good things must come to an end. Thinking back on it, they really hadn't been as good or as much fun as he'd hoped, anyway.

Ole Scratch had really taken him for a ride on that one. That would teach Prophet to sell his soul to the Devil . . .

Truth be told, though, he was ready. Oh, Christ on a merry-go-round—he was truly ready. Just toss him a shovel and show him the coal pile. And for the love of God and all that's holy, tell the bastard with the ax handle to light and sit a spell!

He heard himself mewling like a whipped coyote, but then, mercifully, he lost all sensation for a while, as though his brain had been shut off.

Vaguely, he became aware of being able to separate his hands and his feet, and to move freely, and then he groaned luxuriously at a cool—not cold, but *cool*—soft, soothing feeling as though mud were being rubbed into his back and butt, relieving some of the tenderness from the irons that had been pressed there.

The hombre with the stick was still in business, but he seemed to be taking a smoke break now and then. When he was back at it, smashing that stick against Prophet's head and shoulders, he seemed to ease up slightly. Maybe he was getting tired or a little bored. Whatever the case, the pain in Prophet's throbbing brain was easing.

Later, or what must have been later in this timeless, dark world he found himself in, he was aware of soft hands on him, making him feel wonderfully, soothingly cool, gently massaging that mud into his back and butt again. Then soft breasts pillowed his head while a feminine hand fed him soup with a spoon. He couldn't see the woman when he opened his eyes a little, only a snapping fire radiating warmth and light in a stone room, a wall of blackness beyond.

Then he was aware of being alone for a time.

He'd awaken now and then and look around the stone room, which he gradually realized was a cave with his gear spread around. He was resting against his saddle, and he was naked beneath his blankets. Sometimes he was alone, and sometimes he wasn't. When he wasn't, he could hear a woman's soft, soothing voice in his ears, though he couldn't seem to pry his eyelids open far enough to get a good look at her.

He smelled something foreign, which set his nerves on edge. It was the rancid odor of long-unwashed men and leather. Horses snorted. Men were speaking around him in Spanish, and when he opened his eyes, he saw two Mexicans kicking through his gear.

One turned to him. He had a big, dark face with a long mustache and one white eye with a scar above and below it. He lifted a big pistol with a deer horn handle. There was the loud *click-clack!* of the hammer being cocked.

"Amigo!" the Mexican said, smiling to reveal a gap where his front teeth should have been, the fang-like eye-teeth giving him a serpent-like, predatory look.

He aimed the cocked revolver at Prophet's head. "You wake up only to die, huh, amigo?"

14

OUTSIDE THE CAVE, a horse whinnied. The Mex with the cocked pistol jerked his head toward the dark night gaping on Prophet's left. The other man, who'd been crouched over the fire to add another log, straightened and turned his head in the same direction.

Prophet had been wrong about him. He wasn't a Mexican but an Anglo dressed in the bright colors and leather of the Mexican border bandito. He slid his Schofield from its holster angled across his belly and clicked the hammer back.

The horse whinnied again. Another one nickered. Hooves clomped as the horses shifted around nervously.

"Someone's out there," said the Anglo in a deep, raspy voice, working his nose like an animal aware it's being stalked.

"Si!" said the Mex, who turned his molasses-dark eyes on Prophet. "Who's out there?"

Prophet wondered if he was dreaming. As in a dream, he tried to speak but he had no voice.

A gun barked loudly. Prophet saw the flash to his left. The Mexican gasped and staggered backward, triggering his pistol into the floor of the cave about a foot left of

Prophet. The impact on Prophet's ears was like two open-handed slaps. There were two more quick flashes.

The shots outside sounded like heavy branches broken across rock.

The Anglo flew back into the cave's shadows and lay still. The Mexican lay groaning and shifting his feet, raking his spurs against the cave's stone floor. Prophet's ears rang. The ringing started that rapping in his head again, though mercifully less violently than before.

In front of him, between him and the fire, powder smoke wafted, smelling like eggs left too long in the sun. The Mexican continued to groan and rake his spurs. Outside, the horses shifted nervously though Prophet could not see them, as his night vision was compromised by the fire and his brain-addled state.

Foot thuds sounded, spurs ringing. Gravel crunched beneath leather soles. As if out of a dream, a figure materialized—slender and curvy, long, blond hair tumbling over shoulders clad in a striped brown serape. As the stranger stepped closer to the cave entrance, Prophet blinked, trying to clear his vision.

He looked down at brown boots trimmed with silver spurs and followed the slender, denim-clad legs up to a cartridge belt and two cross-draw holsters strapped to slim hips, over the serape. A kid-gloved hand still held a smoking, silver-chased, pearl-gripped .45, gray smoke curling from the barrel.

Prophet looked up past the gun to the serape swollen with a pair of full, round breasts, to a long, slender neck that was tanned to the color of fresh-whipped, buttery cream. He took in the sharp chin, the long, fine nose, and a pair of oblique hazel eyes set atop tapering cheeks and peering out from beneath the brim of the man's tan Stetson.

Prophet cleared his throat and raked out, "Fancy meetin' you here, Louisa."

The blond twirled the pistol on her finger and held it low by her denim-clad right thigh. "Friends of yours, Lou?"

Prophet looked at the two dead men lying on the far side

of the fire in pools of their own blood. Gun smoke still wafted in the air around him, mingling with that of the snapping fire. "Mere acquaintances. We were just startin' to get friendly when you came along."

As the young woman stepped into the cave, raking her flinty hazel eyes from one bandit to the other, she said, "Sorry to intrude."

"Ah, well."

The Mexican was still alive, blinking up at the ceiling in shock, his chest rising and falling sharply.

Prophet had risen onto his elbows, pain raking him from head to toe. He was too confused and in too much pain to try to wrap his mind around any of what had just happened. He cleared his throat several times before he managed to say, "They . . . didn't . . . introduce themselves . . . but I reckon they was banditos."

"Banditos." She'd said it slowly, letting each syllable roll of her tongue.

Louisa Bonaventure, the blond bounty hunter and Prophet's sometime partner, had become notorious in her own right for hunting down and killing the men who'd murdered her family on their small Nebraska farm and then gone on to hunter other child- and women-killing men of their ilk across the western frontier.

Over the past several years, her harrowing exploits had become known nationwide, and somewhere along her bloody trail some pulp writer had tagged Louisa with the handle of "Vengeance Queen." Prophet had once seen a subtitle in a *Police Gazette* story about her that read, "The Hazel-Eyed Queen of Vengeance Rides Again!" Beneath it, in slightly smaller print: "As Beautiful as She Is Deadly!"

The prose might have been a tad on the purple side, but for once the writer hadn't been gilding the lily. Louisa was about as comely a pistol-wielding vixen as a man could find, and when she rode, it was usually in an all-out effort to serve a nice plate of cold revenge or just deserts.

Louisa walked over and gave the Mexican's boot a kick.

The Mexican groaned more loudly. "You a bandito, amigo?" she asked him, staring down at him, aiming her pistol at his head.

He didn't say anything, just stared up at her, breathing hard.

"Best say a prayer, if you've a mind," she warned him.

Louisa walked around the fire to inspect the unmoving Anglo and then walked over to the Mexican again, who beseeched her in Spanish to spare him. She spread her feet and aimed the silver-plated Colt at an angle. Prophet winced and covered his ears as she drilled a bullet through the Mexican's head.

The head bounced, turned to one side, and lay still.

"There you go," the girl said. "That's what you get for trying to kill my old pal Lou."

Lowering the smoking pistol, she turned to Prophet, her eyes oddly uncertain, maybe even a little haunted. "We are still pals, aren't we, Lou?"

He rested his head back against his saddle. "Why wouldn't we be?"

Louisa stepped over Prophet's legs as she walked back to the cave door and pressed her back to the side of it, hard to Prophet's left. She stood staring out, her pistol in her right fist. She stood silently for a long time, staring into the darkness and listening for possible friends of the men she'd killed.

Finally, apparently deciding there'd been only two intruders, she holstered her pistol and stole out away from the cave, disappearing into the darkness. When she returned, she was a little breathless, as though from a medium-hard hike.

"Nothin' but two good horses out there, each stocked with a carbine." She went over and picked up a mesquite log from the small stack beside the fire and added it to the flames. "They laid a nice fire, anyway. We're all good for somethin', I reckon. Eh, Lou?"

Prophet nodded. He knew what haunted her but he didn't

want to talk about it just now. Later, when the man with the hammer in his head took another smoke break.

She swung around to Prophet, her slender, curvy figure in the poncho and denims silhouetted against the fire that was shooting a column of sparks toward the cave ceiling, which was about seven feet above the floor. The firelight reflected off a crenellated rear wall about ten feet away from Louisa and the two dead men.

"How you feelin'?" the girl asked, both pistols in their holsters, her gloved fists on her hips.

"Like I had a Dutch ride over sharp rocks."

"You look like you did."

Prophet scowled at her, wincing against the hammering in his head that wasn't so much like an ax handle anymore, but just your average pine branch. He still wished the demon wielding it would go away, though. Even worse was the agony of his bladder that appeared ready to explode if he didn't drain it straightaway.

She must have read the look on his face. "Coffee can to your right."

He glanced at the empty coffee tin, suppressed the warmth of embarrassment creeping into his cheeks. Again, she must have read his thoughts.

"It wasn't the first time I saw it, you know, Lou." Louisa gave a provocative grin. "Need help?"

"I can manage."

As he worked his way to his knees, he realized he didn't have a stitch on. He looked at her again. She stood in the cave entrance with a lopsided, faintly jeering grin on her pretty, lightly tanned face that still owned the smooth flaw-lessness of a girl. And a deceptive innocence.

Those pretty, peaches-and-cream features had been the downfall of many a bad man who'd died hard, staring at them.

Prophet sniffed, raked a thumb across his thigh, lifted it to his eyes. Greasy.

"Arnica," she said. "Got a fresh tin from the dry goods

store in Moon's Well. Put it on all your cuts and bruises, which means it about covers every inch of you."

Prophet groaned as he knelt there on his blanket roll, trying to keep his balance against the cave floor's pitch and roll. "What a sorry state for this old Georgia reb." He held the coffee tin in front of his crotch and looked up at Louisa, who continued to smirk down at him.

"A lady would avert her eyes."

She turned toward the night, and he lifted the door on the dam inside him. The coffee tin rattled as his bladder emptied. As he continued the evacuation, he glanced at the night beyond Louisa.

An escarpment or something rose about six feet beyond the cave, but to the left of it he could see a few stars twinkling between dark, jagged-edged peaks. All he knew was that he wasn't in Chisos Springs, and he wasn't out on the plain, either.

He grunted blissfully as he continued filling the can. "Where the hell are we?"

"My camp in the Chisos range."

As the piss stream dwindled, he gave another grunt, but before he could ask his next question, she answered it for him. "I've been keeping an eye on the town. Was looking it over this morning when I saw some big, dumb-looking hombre getting his proverbial hat handed to him out by Mr. Moon's well."

She clucked and shook her head. "What'd you do to make those men so angry, Lou? Cheat at cards or diddle the wrong whore?"

"Here." Prophet held the filled container up in both hands. "Don't spill."

Louisa turned the corners of her lovely mouth down as she took the nearly full can between her gloved hands, and tossed its contents into the night. She tossed the empty vessel down beside Prophet, who drew his blanket back up over his battered, naked body.

"Or maybe you're trying to cut in on my dance," the girl

said, leaning against the side of the cave, arms crossed on her breasts. "You might have asked . . . like a *civilized* bounty hunter."

"Dance?" Prophet leaned back against his saddle. "I don't know what you're talkin' about. You got any whiskey?"

"With all the lumps on your head, how can you think of tangleleg?"

"I always think of tangleleg. Besides, painkiller . . ."

She walked out to where Prophet could now see her brown-and-white pinto and Mean and Ugly hobbled about twenty feet down the slope from the cave. He saw her shadow move around her horse, heard straps whipping free, the squawk of leather, and saw her walk back up the incline toward the cave with her saddle on one shoulder, saddlebags over the other.

She dropped the saddle on the other side of the fire from Prophet, then reached into a saddlebag pouch and pulled out a flat, corked, smoky blue bottle.

"Go easy," she said, tossing the busthead to him. "It's all I have."

Prophet scowled at the bottle, shook it. Only half full. "Why, hell, there ain't much more than a thimbleful in there! What's the point in carryin' any whiskey at all if you ain't gonna carry any more than *this*?"

"Don't look a gift horse under the tail, Lou."

She said it wryly, for it was Prophet's own line. "I carry it for medicinal purposes only," she added.

Prophet popped the cork on the bottle, and took a conservative sip. "How long I been here?"

"This is your third night."

"Christ!" He took another sip. "Where'd you find me?"

"I caught up to you after they stripped you naked and tied you over your horse. They tossed your clothes out in the brush behind the dwarf's pleasure parlor. They're not exactly clean, but they're behind you, if you ever feel like donning them again."

"Oh, I'll don them again," Prophet said and tipped the bottle back once more. It was good forty-rod, not the usual snake venom he carried. There wasn't much of it, but it oozed sweetly over his tonsils and made him yearn for more.

That was like Louisa—nothing but the best no matter what it was, be it guns, ammo, horses, hair pins, or forty-rod, though he remembered a time when she'd indulged in nothing more potent than sarsaparilla, albeit *good* sarsaparilla. That was before their last adventure together, in Mexico, when they'd taken on a gang of killers led by Tony Lazarro and his beautiful, blond sidekick, Sugar Delphi, and ended up in one hell of a dustup in a desert mountain town called San Gezo.

Prophet and Louisa had separated after that. In the hardest of ways. Without saying anything about it. Just forking trails.

Prophet hadn't thought he'd ever see her again. He hadn't been sure he'd wanted to see her again, after what she'd pulled on him in Mexico.

Hard to deny a girl who'd saved your life, he thought now, studying her, wondering what it had been—just blind luck?—that had brought them together again. Lucky for him, anyway.

Sometimes he wondered if it wasn't just meant to be. Him and her. Together. On the other hand, being who they were, staying together as anything more than trail partners would have been impossible. They were just too much alike in all the wrong ways, and too different in all the right ones.

"You're thinking about Mexico, aren't you?" she said, hauling her cooking gear from her war bag, not looking at him.

He didn't want to talk about Mexico. Not yet. His head ached too badly for him to think straight, and thinking about Mexico only made it pound harder.

"Where were you just now?" he said.

"Moon's Well."

"Don't call it that," he said, irritation in his voice, resting his forearm over his eyes. "It's Chisos Springs."

"Whatever it's called, I've been keeping an eye on it."

Louisa was slicing salt pork into a skillet into which

she'd poured a good portion of soaked beans. She set the pan on a rock amongst the dancing flames, added another mesquite branch to the fire, and sat back against her own saddle, regarding Prophet darkly.

"Trouble there, Lou. The dwarf has been hauling in kidnapped women from New Mexico and Arizona, most of them Apache orphans kidnapped off reservations or monasteries, as sex slaves for his whorehouse. Several Indian agents are in league with him, point out the best girls to take, those who won't be as missed as those with kin. That's what brought me here. I heard about such deviltry in Las Cruces and rode over to see what I could do."

"Moon's ridin' point on this deviltry?"

She nodded.

"Wouldn't doubt it a bit," Prophet said with a sigh. He wouldn't put anything past the vile dwarf, after what he'd heard about him from Ruth Rose. "How many does he think he needs, anyway? How many can he house?"

"Quite a few, apparently," Louisa said, leaning forward to stir the bacon and beans around in the popping, snapping pan. "He keeps each girl for only a couple of months. When he figures his customers have tired of the same ones, he ships them down to Mexico and sells them to a corrupt Rurale colonel, who in turn—"

"Campa?" Prophet interrupted her.

Louisa looked over the crackling pan and the flickering flames at him. "How did you know?"

"Lucky guess."

"Who, in turn, as I was saying, sells them to brothels down in Chihuahua and northern Sonora. It's a big money-making proposition for them. The Mexicans might not like the wild Apache men much, but they like their young girls just fine."

Prophet shook his head and lowered his arm over his eyes again, trying to push down the pain behind them. "Forget it, Louisa. It's too big. You're one girl. Not bad with a pair of matched hoglegs—I'll give you that. But I won't be any use for at least a week, and even if I was, we're talking the dwarf's men—he's got a big role—and the old outlaw sheriff, Lee Mortimer."

Again he shook his head. "That's a job for the Texas Rangers, U.S marshals, the cavalry. . . ."

"There's one more thing, Lou, which might hasten your healing."

"What's that?"

"Moon has made a slave of Mrs. Rose, now, too."

Prophet snapped his head up.

Louisa nodded slowly, darkly. "I saw her tonight through a window. Her and the dwarf and that brown-haired girl of his."

"The *three* of them?"

Louisa nodded again slowly, pursing her lips, her hazel eyes reflecting the umber firelight. "But only two seemed to be having any fun."

15

THE DWARF CLIMBED off of her, wheezing, thin strands of hair in his eyes. He grinned down at her, his little pig eyes rheumy and red-rimmed from exertion, as he crawled to the edge of the bed and dropped to the floor with a slapping thump.

Ruth Rose drew her legs together, scrubbed the back of her hand across her mouth with a grimace. Revulsion rippled through her.

"Don't lick my spittle off your lips!" the dwarf said, standing naked by the bed and poking an admonishing finger at her. He was so short that Ruth could only see his large head, bug eyes, and his spindly shoulders. "That's nectar of the gods!"

Laughing, he turned to where Griselda May was dressing near the door of the large, sparsely furnished room—the dwarf's and the crazy girl's own room. "Ain't it, Griselda?"

The girl had stepped into her skirt and dropped her lacy chemise over her head. Her small, cone-shaped breasts poked against the thin garment. She looked at Moon, stuck her tongue out, curled the tip, and ran it slowly, lasciviously across her upper lip.

That got him laughing harder.

His croaky, raspy voice was as revolting as the rest of him, including the heavy, fishy odor of his breath. Ruth could still smell it. It made her stomach clench, and for several seconds, she thought she'd be sick. She drew a deep breath and scrubbed her hand across her mouth once more, when the dwarf's back was turned as he gathered his clothes from the floor.

"Can I go now?" she asked, unable to keep her fury from her tone. "I have to see to my husband."

The dwarf was hopping around, pulling his pants up over his balbriggans. "Hell, no—you can't go. I done told you, you was a permanent fixture in these parts. When me an' Griselda's done with ya, we're turnin' you over to our payin' customers. When they tire of ya, you're goin' to Mexico with the Apache girls!"

He winked as he straightened, then bent both knees, crouching a little to bring his pants up over his paunch, sucking in his gut and buttoning the child-sized denims.

"Me," Griselda said, "I'm tired of her, Mordecai. She just lays there. Don't even pretend to be havin' any fun at all."

The dwarf reached down for his shirt and said with a grunt as he straightened once more, "Maybe she just needs a little more practice. She ain't never whored before, Griselda. Not like some others. . . ." He snickered meaningfully.

Griselda stopped buttoning her cream blouse to swat Moon's shoulder with the back of her hand. "I done told you, Mordecai, I ain't never whored a day in my life! I done told you that! And I don't like bein' called a *whore*!"

The dwarf chuckled in devilish delight as he dodged another swat, sort of sidestepping and dancing around the sharp-faced, brown-haired girl, whose cheeks were red with rage, as they often were, Ruth had noticed. Rage and jealousy.

Ruth had seen it just a few minutes ago, when the dwarf was toiling over Ruth herself, and, bored, Griselda had climbed down off the bed and started washing herself at the porcelain basin.

An odd, funny girl. A dangerous one, too. Even more dangerous than Ruth had once thought.

And whatever fondness she had for Moon was faked.

"Please," Ruth said, covering herself with a pillow and dropping her legs over the side of the bed. "My husband has been alone for two days. He needs food and water. He needs his *medication*!"

"Ah, keep quiet," the dwarf said. "Your caterwaulin's growin' right tiresome. And when I get tired of you, you know what that means." He pointed an admonishing finger at her again.

Before she could respond, the clatter of wagons and the thunder of many hooves rose in the street outside the hotel. The cacophony grew louder amidst the whistling and yells of bullwhackers or muleskinners. Another freight team rolling into Moon's Well, Ruth knew. She'd grown so accustomed to the din that she often no longer even heard it.

"Ah, that'd be Chaz Burdick's train from Amarillo," the dwarf said. "His crew always comes in thirsty and girl hungry. We're gonna make us a killin' tonight, my dear Griselda."

Moon ambled toward the window and stopped in front of Ruth. He placed one of his big, horny hands on her cheek, lifting her face to meet his wretched, leering gaze.

"You shouldn't have piss-burned Griselda, Mrs. Rose. For that, I'm gonna turn you over to ole Burdick. He's just rollin' in money, and he's asked about you before." He winked. "Before you was in my stable."

"You son of a—!"

"Oh, hush!"

The dwarf removed his hand from her face, hopped up on a chair fronting the window, and looked out. He yelled down a greeting and waved, then said with a big grin over his shoulder, "It's him, all right. Burdick and his half-dozen skinners from the panhandle. They look even thirstier an' hornier than usual!"

Leaping off the chair, he looked at Griselda as he stuffed

his shirttails into his pants. "What do you say, honey?
Would you like that—me turnin' her over to ole Burdick and
his boys! They'd pay a purty penny for her, too. Virgins and
married women. Nothin' turns a man's wheel faster!"

Griselda was strapping her derringers around her narrow
waist. She looked at Ruth still sitting on the edge of the bed
and curled her lip evilly. "I'd like that just fine, Mordecai."

The dwarf ran over to her. wrapped his little arms around
her legs, rose up on the balls of his stocking feet, and
pooched out his lips. Griselda glanced once more, propri-
etarily, at Ruth, and then leaned down and pressed her lips
to those of the dwarf. She tried hard to appear as though she
were enjoying herself.

Moon groaned and cooed. When Griselda pulled her
head away from his, he chuckled as she turned and walked
toward the door. He stared at her butt until she'd left, leaving the door open behind her. Moon shook his head and
sighed, thoroughly smitten by the girl who was every bit as
demonic as he himself was, and then turned to Ruth.

"Ain't she somethin', Mrs. Rose? Ain't she just *somethin'*?"

Ruth's heart felt as though it had been torn to ribbons in
her chest. She'd been violated with the promise of more vio-
lations to come. On top of everything, her husband was
likely dying in the most ghastly way back at the Rose Hotel
and Saloon.

"Why are you doing this, Moon?" she asked. "What did
Frank and I ever do to you?"

The dwarf sat on a footstool to pull one of his little,
black boots on. "You didn't pay your taxes, Mrs. Rose. You
know that. And you barely even been payin' on your water
contract."

"You don't need our money," she said, her voice dull with
shock and bewilderment as well as the torment and degrada-
tion she'd just endured—the wet lips and pawing, clawing
hands of both him and that evil girl of his. "You make
enough here to satisfy every need you could possibly have."

"Yeah, I do, don't I?" he said, buckling his shell belt and twisting his rounded hips this way and that, adjusting the holstered Colt.

He smiled so that his pasty, craggy cheeks dimpled and his little eyes narrowed to slits. "I do it 'cause I *can* do it."

Moon scooped his hat off a chair, frowned at the hole in its crown, and then set it on his head. He walked toward Ruth, stopped about a foot away from her.

He said, "When you *can* do something—a man like me—you *do* it, no matter what it is. No matter how bad. Fuck *good*! To a man livin' in a body like mine, eye level with crotches all my life, raised by folks who'd as soon spit on me as treat me even halfways decent, who kept me locked in a cellar when neighbors came cause they was embarrassed—laughed and called me the *devil in the hole* or *hell's little angel!*—there ain't much good in the world to begin with.

"See how it is? Well, I found out early that my body might be small. But my spirit was big, bad as it was. Big and *bad*! And for one reason or another, small as I was body-wise, I could command men. Get 'em to do just whatever I wanted. Don't ask me how. But I could do it then and I can do it now. And by God, for a man like me, that's *everything*!"

Moon rocked back on his heels and poked the first two fingers of each hand into the wool vest he wore under his black clawhammer coat. He considered her for a time. Ruth stared back at him, through the screen of hair hanging in her eyes. Pity only slightly tempered her loathing for the man. In her mind, she could still hear him grunting on top of her, staring down at her and grinning maliciously, his bug eyes crossing as he toiled.

"I could never win the heart of a woman like you," he continued, raking his eyes across her, his little chest rising and falling slowly. "No, I could never make a woman like you—purty and upright and well-mannered and sophisticated in a country kind o' way—feel anything but disgust for me. I seen it all my life. But I can put the fear of God into you, can't I?" He grinned broadly, showing his yellow, crooked teeth. "And I have, haven't I?"

Ruth said nothing, only stared at him, knowing that sooner or later, after he'd had his fill of torturing her simply because he could, he'd kill her. Or cause her to want to be dead in the worst way possible.

He winked, turned on a heel, and sauntered to the door. He stopped with one hand on the knob and looked back at her. He frowned as though troubled.

"Tell me somethin' from your woman's point of view, will you, Mrs. Rose? You think Griselda really loves me, or is she just playacting?"

"I think she had far more fun with me than she's ever had with you, Mr. Moon." The automatic response, spoken with quiet satisfaction, caused a devilish thrill to ripple through Ruth. She felt the ripple again when, for a fleeting half second, she witnessed genuine injury darken the dwarf's eyes like a cloud sweeping the ground on a sunny day.

He covered it with a sigh, smoothed the colorless whiskers dangling off his chin, and turned to the door. "Get yourself ready for Burdick. He'll be up shortly."

He gave her another menacing wink and went out. She heard the key turn in the lock on the opposite side of the door, locking her in.

16

THERE WAS A knock on Ruth's door.

The key in the lock clicked. She turned from where she'd been brushing her hair in a standing mirror, to see the door open and a man's hatted head appear between the door and the jamb. The man had a thick mustache with upswept ends and three or four days' worth of beard stubble on his sunburned cheeks.

Ruth flushed. So did Chaz Burdick behind the bright pink on his broad, fleshy cheeks, above the mustache that had a fine coating of trail dust. His eyes were blue beneath dark brown brows. The fetor of mules, the man's own sweat, and wheel grease was an almost visible cloud about him.

From downstairs came the tinny clatter of Moon's four-piece Mexican band, one of the men singing along with a girl. There was clapping and the stomping of feet, yells, and ribald laughter.

Burdick doffed his broad-brimmed Stetson as he came into the room, looking sheepish but also randy, his eyes raking Ruth up and down. She'd cleaned herself at the washbasin and donned the dress the dwarf had given her, likely shipped in from Fort Worth, as was most everything else here, including professional whores who worked for percentages. The dress was red and extremely low cut with very slender shoulder straps. It was the only dress Ruth had, and she wasn't about to receive Burdick naked.

She looked down at the gun belt hanging down his right, denim-clad hip. A walnut-gripped pistol jutted from the worn, brown leather holster. Her heart thudded, and she quickly lifted her gaze to Burdick's flushed, pink face.

"Well, Chaz," she said, softly. "Fancy meeting you here."

He came in and closed the door, holding his hat down low by his side. His thick hair was sweat-matted to his head, with an indention line caused by the hat's sweatband. The din from downstairs was loud now. Burdick had the key in his other hand, and now he stuck the key in the lock and turned it until the bolt clicked and left it there.

Burdick turned to her, still wearing that sheepish, eager look of a nasty schoolboy about to do what he'd been dreaming of doing for a long time and finally got his chance.

"Ruth," he said, dipping his chin politely. "Quite a place here, huh?"

"You don't really expect me to indulge in polite conversation . . . like the *real* percentage girls, do you?"

Burdick chuckled and glanced at the hat in his hands. "Well, the Apache girls mostly just grunt and groan."

Ruth let the smile turn dark. "Is that who you prefer? The little Apache girls here against their will? Moon's *sex* slaves?"

Burdick let his arms drop to his sides. "Now, Ruth, goddamnit . . . !"

"You know I'm here against my will—don't you, Chaz?"

Burdick swallowed, glanced at her breasts half-revealed by the low-cut dress, and then lowered his gaze to the floor. "Figured."

"But you still want to do this?"

Now he looked up, angry, and she could see that his dark blue eyes were glassy from drink. "I paid the little man, fer chrissakes, Ruth! And, hell, I got needs! You know how far I come today?"

"You were friends with Frank, Chaz." Ruth's voice was quiet, vaguely incriminating. All she really wanted was to be able to get out of this room, and she thought she had a chance, but she still couldn't help badgering the man, torturing him a little, seeking a little revenge for the humiliation he would visit on her.

Burdick had stayed at her and Frank's place several times, eaten the food she'd cooked, had always acted pleasant enough. He and Frank had often played cards together. Ruth had always felt his eyes on her backside, but now he'd gone much further than that.

Now he was about to, for all intents and purposes, rape her.

And she couldn't help needling him about it.

She glanced once more at the gun on his thigh and then she set the brush on the dresser by the mirror and stepped back from him, letting him have a good look at her body. Shaming him with his own lust.

"You're married, aren't you, Chaz?"

Burdick's face turned pinker. He curled his thick upper lip and angrily tossed his hat on the brocade-upholstered chair to his right. "Enough talkin', Ruth. I'm sorry about Frank, but you're workin' over here now, and by God I paid two silver cartwheels to that little fucker for only an hour with you. Now, you get outta that dress before I get mad!"

"All right, all right," she said, feeling an odd pleasure at the power she wielded.

She'd always thought that whores were the only ones victimized by the transaction, but maybe that wasn't entirely true. Maybe the men who used them were also victimized in a way. Victimized by their own ugly vulnerabilities and unrestrained cravings.

Slaves of their own desire.

She unbuttoned the dress. He watched in eagerness and awe as she slid each strap down off a shoulder, slowly lowered the top of the dress to her waist, her breasts springing free.

She wore nothing beneath it. She let the dress drop to the floor and stood before him, naked but not ashamed. Her nakedness shamed him. He felt the embarrassment. She could see it flicker amongst the male lust in his eyes—the lust that overpowered everything.

"Is this what you've been wanting to see?" she asked Burdick. "Am I what you'd imagined I'd be?"

"Holy shit," he whispered, and then, with a near-manic grin, keeping his eyes on her naked body, kicked out of each boot so quickly that he nearly lost his balance and fell.

She crawled into bed and stared at him coolly while he removed his gun and shell belt, looped the belt over a rear bedpost, and then shucked out of his shirt and trousers and then his socks and his balbriggans. He fairly ran over to the bed, manhood at half-mast, and crawled under the covers, instantly pressing his sweaty, filthy, hairy body to hers, smashing his lips down on her mouth.

He tasted like tobacco and tequila.

"Wait," she said, feeling his rod press against her belly. "Hold on."

"You hold on to this!" he said through gritted teeth.

"I'd like to be on top," she said and smiled up at him.

"Oh. You would, huh?" Burdick said, looking at her slightly askance, vaguely suspicious. Then he grinned. "Well, all right." He chuckled and rolled off of her.

She rose to her knees and straddled him. He grinned up at her. One of his teeth was grayer than the others, slightly chipped. His doughy, pale chest was matted with thick, dark brown hair.

"All right, then," he said, bucking beneath her. "Here we go!"

"Close your eyes."

He frowned up at her again while she sort of hovered above him, reaching down beneath her for his organ. "Why?"

She squeezed it, smiled at him beguilingly. "I'm shy."

He snorted. "I reckon this is a little strange." He laughed

again and squeezed his eyes closed, keeping his lips parted so that she could see the white line of his teeth between his furred lips.

Downstairs, the singer was singing more loudly. Someone was banging on a kettle with a spoon while many feet pounded the floor of the main drinking hall.

"Come on—hurry up, damnit," he said, creasing the skin at the bridge of his nose.

She grabbed the free pillow from beside the one his head was resting on. When she had it, she reached back and jerked his revolver from the holster hanging from the rear bedpost to her left. She clicked the hammer back at the same time that she pressed the pillow over Burdick's head, leaned forward, bringing all her weight to bear on the pillow, and pressed the revolver's barrel hard against it.

He'd just started to lift his head and to struggle, grunting, when she pulled the trigger. Against the pillow and beneath the raucousness rising from below, the report sounded little louder than the popping of a dry knot in a wood stove.

Burdick's head jerked.

Ruth's heart fluttered. She wrinkled her nose against the stench of gunpowder and charred goose down. A small round spot of blood shone in the pillow. It grew quickly, soaking the pillow and the cotton case. Ruth recoiled from the blood, drawing the pistol back away from the pillow.

Beneath her thighs, she could feel the convulsions in the dying body. She gasped in horror and revulsion.

She climbed off Burdick so quickly that she got a foot tangled in the bedcovers, fell onto the side of the bed, bounced, and struck the floor with a heavy thud.

"Damn!" she hissed, freezing as she sat naked on her rump, pricking her ears to listen.

The music and the singing and foot stomping continued downstairs as usual. She heard no doors opening and closing around the room she was in, no footsteps in the hall.

Quickly, she rose, wincing at a slight bruise on her left hip, and picked up Burdick's revolver from off the rug it had

fallen upon. She set it on the dresser, picked up the red
dress, and drew it on over her head.

She looked around for a pair of shoes, but there were
none in this part of the two-room suite that the dwarf and
Griselda called their own—one that was too large for its
sparse, expensive but practical furnishings shipped in from
Fort Worth. The walls were of unadorned vertical pine
boards still rife with the smell of resin.

It was almost as though the dwarf and Griselda merely
camped here and did not really call the place a home despite
the money the little man had obviously put into the sprawling building. From what she'd seen, the parts away from the
main drinking hall were as bare as caves, though of course
the whores' cribs were furnished with beds.

Moon and Griselda had few clothes besides those they
wore, it appeared. Certainly no shoes that would fit Ruth.
She had no idea what had happened to the ones she'd been
wearing when the dwarf's men had removed her from her
home.

Going barefoot might be better anyway. Quieter. And she
had to flee the dwarf's place quietly, lest she should get
caught. She had to get back over to her own place and see
about Frank. The poor man must be starving, his bedclothes
soaked with urine.

If he was still alive . . .

The thought of him dying so tragically, from neglect,
swelled her heart until she felt it rise in her throat, drumming horrifically. Her pulse hammered in her temples.

Ruth glanced once more at Burdick. She could see his
pasty belly, both arms, and one bare leg. The bloody pillow
covered his face. His hands rested to either side of it, palms
up, fingers curled like claws.

He was the first man she'd ever killed. Strange how she
felt absolutely no remorse whatever. Only revulsion. It was
what she'd had to do to so save herself and Frank.

What she would do once she'd returned to the Rose Hotel
and Saloon, aside from tending Frank, she had no idea. The

dwarf would find her in such an obvious place, of course, but what else could she do?

She hefted the pistol in her hand. She ran her thumb across the dimpled cylinder, heard a single click as the wheel turned.

She'd kill him. He wouldn't expect her to. That's how she'd get the drop on him. Drill a slug through his ugly heart. Of course, she'd probably die, then, too. And so would Frank. But at least she'd make sure the dwarf never saw the light of another day, either.

Holding the pistol low in her left hand, she walked over to the door, twisted the key, and winced when she heard the bolt click. She drew the door open and looked into the hall.

It was dark as dusk, no candles lit. And vacant. The only light was that issuing up from the saloon. Ruth could hear, beneath the constant din from below, the moaning of a girl behind one of the doors to her right and on the hall's far side. A man was saying something to the whore in a soft, snarling voice.

One of Moon's Apache girls was with a customer.

Behind another door, one of the professional gals was laughing as though at the funniest joke she'd ever heard.

Ruth did not know her way around the sprawling building, but she knew that stairs ran along the outside of the rear wall. Doubtful that there was a way to it on this side of the building. She had to risk crossing the place to the other side.

Quickly but quietly, walking on the balls of her bare feet, she made her way toward the broad wooden stairs that led down to the main drinking hall. She could hear the sounds of lovemaking behind the doors she passed, and the clatter of a man stumbling around drunk while a girl berated him in what Ruth assumed was Apache.

A glass dropped to the floor behind Ruth, and she slapped her free hand to her chest with a startled gasp. A man laughed and said, slurring his words, "Now, did *I* do that?"

Tiptoeing past the top of the stairs, brushing a shoulder along the wall, she glanced down the steps quickly to see tobacco smoke, aglow with lantern light, boiling up toward her. Men and brightly dressed whores were vague, jostling figures inside the billowing smoke plume. If anyone saw Ruth from down there, she doubted they'd recognize her through the fog.

Someone was playing a piano. Ruth recognized the dwarf's croaky, raspy voice singing along while a man in the gambling section of the hall spoke loudly in Spanish above the clattering of a roulette wheel.

Ruth finally found a downward slanting corridor bisecting what appeared several unfinished rooms, to the far back wall. Here, after some frantic searching, she found an outside door, and dropped quickly down the two tiers of steps to the ground.

At the bottom, she stopped and crouched to the left of the stairs. Straight out away from the building were two barns and a maze of corrals in which the hulking shapes of horses and mules milled, one mule braying raucously and causing a horse to whinny. To Ruth's right, she could see the silhouettes of three men as well as the small, red-glowing coals of their cigarettes or cigars.

The men, likely the dwarf's hostlers, were speaking Spanish and laughing. They were also passing a bottle. Ruth could hear the sloshing liquid each time they drank.

Keeping to the building's dense shadow, Ruth sidestepped off to her left and then looked around the corner of the building toward the main street and the well. Lights from the lower-story windows revealed several men standing around on the street fronting the dwarf's saloon. A couple were crouched and playing a traditional Mexican bone-throwing game not far from the well—and not far from Ruth's destination, her own forbiddingly dark hotel.

She could see the dark window behind which poor Frank very likely lay slowly dying.

Ruth groaned in frustration. Then she took off running straight west of the hotel, paralleling the main street but crouching behind brush, rocks, and cacti. She winced as her bare feet came down on cactus thorns and sharp rocks, but she kept running. She had to get to Frank.

Finally, she'd traced a semicircle around the main part of the town and approached the Rose Hotel and Saloon from the rear. She entered via the back door.

"Frank," she heard herself mutter, her voice strained with apprehension. What condition would she find him in?

She moved through a storage room and entered the lobby. In the darkness, she saw the front desk. The stairs angled down from the second story on her left. As she made for the bottom of the staircase, something brushed the top of her head.

Instinctively, she cowered from the cold touch, stepped to one side, and turned. She looked up to see something long and pale hanging suspended in the air beneath the second-story balcony. Nearly level with her eyes, two bare feet turned slowly in midair about five and a half feet above the floor.

She heard a creak. Like the complaint of a straining rope.

Frowning, vaguely feeling her lower jaw dropping, she stared up past the bare feet to two, floury white, skinny legs ridged with fine, light blue veins. Then she saw the rest of the hanging body and stumbled back against the wall. As her own eyes met the heavy-lidded, death-glazed eyes of her husband, and saw the rope coiled around his neck, the tongue protruding from between Frank's thin lips, a scream began to burst from Ruth's throat.

An arm wrapped around her from behind. A hand clamped back hard across her mouth, rendering the scream stillborn on her tongue.

17

RUTH GRUNTED AGAINST the hand across her mouth and, panicking, struggled against it. The hand wouldn't budge. She was surprised when she heard a female voice say very calmly into her left ear, "I am friend, not foe. I'll remove my hand if you promise not to scream."

Ruth slid her eyes to the left. A pretty female face stared at her from beneath the brim of a tan Stetson. Blond hair hung down both sides of the girl's heart-shaped face to spill across her shoulders.

Ruth frowned, incredulous, and nodded.

The girl took her hand away.

Ruth drew a sharp breath, her heart still hammering. "Who are you?"

"Not the person who did that." The girl lifted her chin toward the naked body of Frank Rose hanging from the balcony rail above the lobby. He'd turned to one side and now hung slack and still in pale death. "I can promise you that."

"Oh, Frank!" Ruth knees buckled, and she fell to the floor.

She sobbed as she stared up in horror and heartbreak, pulling at the skirt lying snug across her thighs. She cried softly for a time and then crossed her arms on her breasts, lowered her chin, squeezed her eyes closed, and shook her head. "How could he?"

"Rather easily, I would think . . . from what I've learned of Mr. Moon so far." The girl's voice was soft and oddly emotionless. Looking down at Ruth, she said, "I'm a friend of Lou Prophet's."

Ruth looked up at her through tear-soaked eyes, curiosity only slightly tempering her grief. "Lou? He's . . . ?"

"The old boy's still kicking. No thanks to his own damn foolishness. He keeps pulling stunts like that, I expect he'll be giving up his devilish old ghost soon."

"Who are you?"

"I'm Louisa."

"You're a friend of Lou's . . . ?"

"That's right. Trail pards, he'd say."

Even through her grief and terror, Ruth knew an instant's pang of jealousy. The girl before her, though crudely garbed in rough trail clothes, was young and evenly, attractively featured. A man would say sexy, even erotic in her man's clothes and her pistols. Ruth had come to know Lou Prophet well enough to know that if any young woman as lovely as this one called herself Lou's friend, she'd been much more than that.

The girl called Louisa hooked her thumbs behind her cartridge belt and said, "I've got him tucked away in a cave up in the Chisos Mountains. It'll take him a couple days to get back on his feet. I came down here to see what Mr. Moon was up to, figured I could do that from your place. Just found this man, who I assume is your husband, a few minutes before you came."

She paused. Ruth heard her exhale with what seemed genuine regret and sympathy. "I am sorry, Mrs. Rose."

Ruth looked up at Frank once more. His feet looked so vulnerable and exposed. So pale, with light blue veins showing through the papery skin. She imagined what had happened, the dwarf's men coming in here, dragging him out of his bed, tying that noose around his neck. . . .

"He was utterly defenseless," Ruth said, her voice shrill. She tightened her jaws with a raw fury that burned up from deep inside her, remembering hearing only a few minutes ago the dwarf singing at the tops of his wretched lungs over at his House of a Thousand Delights. Singing and cavorting with his whores and that vile Miss May, with poor Frank hanging here alone in this dark hotel.

Ruth rose slowly and stared up at Frank but what she saw in her mind's eye was the grinning face of the dwarf.

"I'll get him down." Louisa swung around and began climbing the stairs, sliding a knife out of a sheath on her left side, behind a holstered revolver.

At the same time, with fury searing a hole through her heart, Ruth picked Burdick's gun up off the floor where she'd dropped it when Louisa had grabbed her.

"Hey, there," Louisa said from the balcony's dense shadows, over Frank's hanging body, "where you going with that, Mrs. Rose?"

Ruth strode tensely out from behind the desk, hefting Burdick's gun in her hand. "I'm going to see about killing a dwarf," she heard herself say in a weird, strained, faraway voice as she made for the hotel/saloon's front door.

Behind her, Louisa said, "Uh . . . I don't think I'd do that, if I were you!"

Ruth didn't hear that last because she'd just then walked on out the front door and was crossing the front veranda. She dropped down the steps and angled across the dark main street toward the dwarf's hotel that was lit up like a Missouri River gambling boat against the velvet desert night.

Ruth held the pistol down low against her right side.

Ahead of her, several men conversing in groups turned to look at the woman in the red dress striding toward them from across the street. She was barefoot and they probably saw that she was carrying something but they probably couldn't see what. Gradually, all of the men around her stopped talking to cast her incredulous, amused looks, their drink-sharp eyes raking her up and down.

She pushed between two men who did nothing to stop

her, and mounted the big hotel's broad front gallery steps.
There were several more men on the gallery, as well as several Apache and Mexican whores doing their best to look as
though they were enjoying themselves, decked out as they
were in their corsets and bustiers or spangled dresses.

One Apache girl stood in front of two bearded Mexicans.
The men had slid the straps of the girl's dress down her
slender, brown arms. One of the men was cupping a pointy
breast in his hands and laughing with the other man though
now both men as well as the Apache girl turned to watch
the woman in the red dress stride purposefully across the
gallery.

Ruth walked through the two front doors that had been
propped open to the fresh night air, and into the saloon-
brothel's main drinking hall. She stopped just inside the
bustling tangle of men, looking around the vast hall that was
the size of three of her own saloons together. It was crudely
furnished though it boasted a giant, horseshoe-shaped bar
curving out from the room's left side, manned by two burly
bartenders. Girls in black or wine red corsets and with
matching feathers in their hair ran drink trays to the men
sitting or standing about the room.

There were all types here. Outlaws from both sides of the
border. Freighters, mule skinners, bullwhackers, drovers in
shotgun chaps, and several bearded men who appeared to be
prospectors. There were Anglos, Mexicans, Indians, half-
breeds, and blacks. The dwarf did not discriminate. He'd
take a man's money whatever his skin color, size, or what
language he spoke.

Roulette wheels clicked. Craps dice rattled. Cards were
shuffled, and coins and poker chips clattered.

The band was still playing. Men and whores danced.

The dwarf was resting, however.

Ruth picked him out of the crowd, sitting about halfway
down the long, deep room on a large brocaded couch with
his little boots propped on a long, low table before him, a
skimpily dressed whore to each side of him. The girls appeared giants in contrast to his wizened, diminutive frame.

One of the whores, a big-bosomed Mexican girl, was wearing his hat and laughing while he spoke loudly, gesturing with the fat cigar he held in his gnarled hand. The other girl, who appeared a half-breed Apache, balanced what was probably his half-filled water glass on her thigh. She, too, was feigning to enjoy the dwarf's monologue, for the more adaptable of the man's whores learned to loosen up and at least pretend to enjoy themselves lest Moon should tire of them more quickly and ship them off to Mexico faster, where their lives would be even worse.

Both girls' lips were set in too-bright smiles.

Ruth pushed through the crowd, heading for the dwarf.

He'd just turned to the girl holding his drink and patted her thigh, and she was lifting the glass in both hands to his lips, when Ruth stopped about four feet away from the wretched little man. He looked at her over the glass that the whore had lifted to his lips.

His brows pinched. His eyes widened.

Ruth raised the Colt conversion .44 in both hands, raking the hammer back with both her thumbs, one atop the other. The click was drowned by the cacophony echoing off the room's walls and high ceiling.

Moon's eyes widened more, grew bright with horror.

He raised a pudgy hand as though to shield his face. He loosed a reedy scream a half second before the Colt roared, smoke and flames lapping toward the little man sandwiched between the two whores on the couch. The bullet punched through the dwarf's palm and into his forehead, slamming his head back against the couch.

As the whore to each side of him screamed and scrambled away from him, Moon's lower jaw slackened. His eyes rolled back in his head, and he sort of slumped down on the couch, his paunch swelling behind his shabby vest, his little black boots dropping toward the floor.

He slumped still lower, convulsing, his tongue poking out the corner of his mouth, and his head sort of wobbled on his shoulders. He gurgled as he died.

• • •

Louisa had sheathed her knife and run down the stairs of the Rose Hotel and Saloon as soon as Mrs. Rose had strode with such eerie purpose out the front door. Louisa ran down the steps to the front door, saw that the woman was already halfway to the dwarf's rollicking, brightly lit gambling parlor and whorehouse.

She was about to call out to the woman again but nixed the idea. Her yell would only attract attention.

Louisa uttered a rare epithet as she dropped down off the Rose's veranda steps and hurried after the woman who disappeared amongst several silhouetted clumps of men on that side of the street, directly across from the well. Ruth Rose reappeared a moment later atop the dwarf's broad front gallery, making a beeline for the open front doors.

"Ah, hell," Louisa said, pausing about halfway across the street.

What should she do?

There wasn't much she could do, she thought as she slid her matched Colts from their holsters, clicking the hammers back. Except die tonight.

18

LOUISA RESUMED WALKING forward.

She stepped up her pace, wended between two clumps of smelly men who eyed her with glassy lasciviousness typical of their breed, and mounted the gallery steps. She'd just stepped through the two front doors when she heard a hoarse cry above the din of the Mexican band and the conversation and gambling, and what sounded like a branch being broken over a knee.

More, shriller screams followed.

Oh, crap, Louisa silently exclaimed to herself. *She did it!*

A thrill rippled through her, pinching her wind, as did a vague admiration for the woman's pluck. She'd die now, of course, but Louisa wasn't about to just stand by and watch it happen.

She couldn't see much because of all the men milling between her and the source of the gun's report and the screams. She hurried forward, both her Colts in her fists, and elbowed men aside until she could see, about two-thirds of the way down the room, the dwarf slumped on a long couch from which two dark-haired girls were scrambling.

The band had just stopped playing and men had just

started yelling. Two or three men appeared to be wrestling with someone in red. Louisa knew that the men were taking Ruth to the floor, and just then she saw the gun come up in Ruth's hand around which one of the men's hands was wrapped.

The gun roared, spat smoke and flames toward the ceiling. Ruth screamed. One of the men ripped the gun out of her hand while two more drove her to the floor while several others—the dwarf's own men, probably—raced toward the commotion.

Louisa gave a wild rebel yell, which she'd adopted after learning how well it worked for Lou in momentarily paralyzing and befuddling his opponents. She ran forward, leaped onto a table heaped with bottles, glasses, coins, and playing cards, and triggered one of her pistols into the ceiling.

"Get away from her, you apes!" she screamed.

Louisa leaped onto the next table toward the rear of the room and kept on leaping tables until smashing the barrel of one of her Colts against the side of one of the men who'd wrestled Ruth to the floor. Still atop a table near the couch on which the dwarf slumped and before which the three men were crouched over Ruth on the floor, Louisa saw one of the dwarf's men aim a pistol at her.

Louisa shot the man through the dead center of his chest. He yelped as he triggered his own revolver at the ceiling and flew back into a table behind him, causing the men seated there to scurry. One of the men there had fallen to the floor on his ass, and now he scrambled away on all fours, losing his sombrero in the process.

Now the room erupted in earnest, though with such a large crowd it was hard to tell from which quarter Louisa and Ruth's next threat would come. They were two women against an entire roomful of men, all armed, many in the dwarf's employ.

She heard a woman shrieking, *"Get her! Get her!"* and saw Griselda May running toward her from the dance floor, where she'd been dancing with a big, buckskin-clad freighter with a beard hanging to nearly the buckle on his cartridge belt.

Louisa triggered a shot at the girl. Griselda was moving too quickly and erratically for an accurate shot, and Louisa's slug shattered a bottle well beyond Miss May. Louisa reached down between the men, grabbed Ruth's arm, and jerked her to her feet.

"Let's go!" she shouted.

At the same time, several pistols popped around Louisa, shattering bottles and glasses on her left and right and causing Ruth to grab her arm and yowl and fall hard against her rescuer. Louisa pushed off a table and triggered a shot at one of the dwarf's men closing on her, crouching and shooting. She hit one but missed another one, though a pistol popping somewhere behind her drilled a bullet through the shoulder of the man she'd missed, and he fell forward over a chair, cursing.

She vaguely wondered if that bullet had been an errant shot fired by one of the dwarf's other men, as she reached down to grab Ruth's unwounded arm, dragging the woman to her feet.

"Let's go!" Louisa yelled.

But as Ruth gained her feet, clutching her bloody upper left arm, Louisa froze. She'd holstered one of her pistols when she'd grabbed Ruth. Holding the other one in her right hand, she looked around, breathing hard, her heart drumming in her ears.

Every man and woman in the room had frozen in various positions. At least a dozen had their guns drawn, and they were aiming said guns at Louisa and Ruth. Some were the dwarf's men. Some were obvious border toughs—Anglos as well as half-breeds and Mexicans. Most of them likely had no idea what all this was about, but they knew that the ugly little man who provided them whiskey and women had been shot by a feisty brunette in a red dress, and that a feisty, hazel-eyed blond had come to her rescue, triggering lead in every direction.

These men were like coiled rattlers, ready to strike.

Louisa swept her gaze at the hard-eyed faces set above maliciously grinning mouths. One Anglo was aiming a Remington revolver at her and smoothing his long, yellow mustache with dirty, brown fingers, fairly licking his chops at the prospect of the two women before him.

The only question on these men's minds was how to keep the two women alive long enough to gain some physical satisfaction from them.

An eerie silence had fallen over the room. Powder smoke wafted. One of the wounded men grunted and rolled on the far side of a table to Louisa's right. Griselda May stood ten feet toward the rear of the room, aiming two derringers at Louisa and grinding her jaws together, dimpling her cheeks and hardening her eyes.

She held fire as though she, like the men, wanted to savor the killing.

Someone grunted on the far side of the room from Louisa, in the direction of the horseshoe-shaped bar. She glanced that way to see one of the burly bartenders sag to one side before dropping out of sight. A thin young man with long, red hair and what appeared a nasty scar on his face climbed up onto the bar. He wore brush-scarred chaps over blue denims, a calico shirt, and suspenders. He was holding a pistol in one hand, a Winchester in the other.

"Now this whole thing has done got *way* out of hand!" he said, his voice sounding loud in the heavy silence.

Most of the customers wielding guns had their backs to the redheaded kid atop the bar. The kid stood at a crouch, rifle in one hand, pistol in the other, narrowing one menacing eye as he slowly tracked each gun across the room.

"First one to trigger another shot gets one through the brisket," the kid said. He looked a little ridiculous, gangly as he was, freckle-faced, big ears showing through the copper-red hair hanging straight to his shoulders. He even sounded ridiculous, as his voice had not yet reached the pitch of a full-grown man's.

There was something commanding, though, in the easy,

assured way he held that carbine and revolver, Louisa absently thought. Something even halfway reassuring, though she was also quite certain that the redhead would die right along with her and Ruth Rose tonight.

A man sitting with five others at a table near the redhead said in a raspy monotone, "Why, I recognize you. You're that kid with the mark of Satan on his face. You got two thousand dollars on your head, boy!"

On the opposite side of the table from the speaker, another man jerked back in his chair and thrust up a gun in his right hand. The kid slid his Winchester toward the man with the gun, and the Winchester's roar sounded like a keg of detonated dynamite in the cave-like room.

The man dropped his gun and stumbled backward, kicking his chair backward, as well, until he fell over the chair to the floor. He gasped like a landed fish until his breathing suddenly stopped at the end of a raspy sigh.

"Anyone else wanna buy two thousand dollars' worth of lead?" the kid asked loudly enough that he could be heard throughout the room.

Smoke wafted around the redhead's battered tan Stetson. Louisa could see now that the scar on his face was shaped like an *S* under his right eye, angled slightly. It looked very much like a cattle brand. No one said anything.

He turned to Louisa, who found herself regarding the kid incredulously. "If you ladies would like to make your way to the front door, I'll make sure none o' these fine gentlemen tries to back-shoot you."

Louisa said, "You sure you want a piece of this, kid?"

"No, I reckon I don't. Ma always said I tended to act first and think later, and I guess that's just what I done here, doggone it."

"Gotcha."

Louisa wrapped an arm around Ruth's waist, turned her, and began leading her through the tables and the men standing around with their hands in the air, toward the front door. Ruth shuddered a little from the pain of her wounded arm, and she held the wounded appendage across her belly, walking at a slight crouch. She looked around warily, as did Louisa, expecting more gunfire to break out at any moment.

When the two approached the front doors, Louisa looked at the scar-faced redhead again. He stood as before atop the bar, rifle in one hand, revolver in the other, sliding both guns slowly from right to left and back again.

The men in the place were still as statues. Most of the whores had gone to the floor. A few were looking up warily over the tops of tables.

Griselda May held her own pistol straight down by her side as she flared her nostrils at the redhead atop the bar. Her brown eyes were glassy with rage.

Louisa continued on out the open front doors, extending her Colt straight out in front of her in case any of the men outside tried to make a play for her. She led Ruth across the gallery and down the steps, pivoting on her hips to keep all the men clumped around her at bay. None of these appeared to be part of the dwarf's cutthroat gang. They were mostly Mexicans—probably freighters, judging by their dusty buckskins and billowy neckerchiefs, as well as their seeming reluctance to make any moves toward a sidearm.

They watched Louisa and Ruth stonily.

When the women were out in the middle of the street, right of the well and nearly in front of the Rose Hotel and Saloon, Louisa glanced back to see the redhead walking backward out of the dwarf's sprawling place, the Winchester and revolver extended before him. He turned suddenly and leaped down the steps to the street, hurried over to a coyote dun tied to one of the hitchracks fronting the place, and slid his rifle into the boot strapped to the saddle. He mounted up and, keeping his pistol in his hand, backed the horse away from the hotel.

Louisa headed down a break between the hotel and another, smaller adobe-brick building, toward where she'd tied her pinto. The kid turned his horse and trotted up behind her as she continued leading Ruth through the dark gap toward the rear of the Roses' hotel.

"I gotta warn you, Kid-with-a-Price-on-Your-Head," Louisa said, "I'm a bounty hunter."

"I'll take my chances, Miss Bonaventure."

Louisa looked at him riding up beside her and Ruth. "You know my name?"

"Sure, you're the Vengeance Queen who rides with Lou Prophet—the bounty hunter who done sold his soul to the Devil after the War of Northern Aggression."

"I'll be hanged," Louisa said, using another of Prophet's expressions. "We're just getting too famous for our own good, me an' Lou."

Louisa could hear voices and a general commotion rising from the direction of Moon's saloon. Apprehension raking her, knowing she'd be hunted soon, she led Ruth toward the pinto ground-tied behind the woodshed flanking the hotel and helped the woman onto the horse behind the saddle.

"Which way you headed?" the kid asked Louisa.

She looked at him again, suspicious, as she climbed up onto the pinto's back. "West," she said, her voice pitched with a cagey reluctance.

"If you'll ride south with me a ways, you two can branch off a mile or so out of town, and I'll keep heading toward the Rio Grande. We'll maybe fool 'em for a little while."

"Yeah, a little while." Louisa glanced at Ruth perched behind her. "Hold on tight, Mrs. Rose. We're gonna ride like the Devil's hounds are on our heels."

When Ruth had wrapped her arms around Louisa's waist, Louisa batted her heels against the pinto's flanks. They took off, trotting past the rear of the Rose Hotel and Saloon and up the far side. They turned onto the main street and then continued south along the main trail, heading in the direction of the Rio Grande.

They galloped hard along the trail that was a pale ribbon stretching out across the starlit night. But it wasn't long before they heard the thunder of many hooves chewing up the desert behind them.

19

A SHRILL SCREAM cut the night wide open.

Louisa's scream.

He'd recognize her voice anywhere, even pitched with horror and agony. He'd heard it pitched that way many times . . . when she'd been having her nightmares, in her sleep reliving the bloody murder of her family back in Nebraska.

The scream echoed, sounding like a million panes of shattering glass.

Prophet jerked his head up from his saddle. He looked around, blinking. The fire was out. The cave was nearly as black as the inside of a glove. He looked around, blinking, trying to penetrate the darkness.

"Louisa?" His own voice sounded eerie in the dense silence.

No reply.

He called her name again, louder. Still, nothing.

As his eyes adjusted, he saw the fire ring about three feet to his left. He lay with his feet toward the cave opening, saddle behind him. Louisa's gear was nearby, on the same side of the fire, and he could usually see her blond hair in the darkness, but he did not see it tonight.

Prophet flung his blankets aside, heaved himself to his feet. In the four days he'd been here, he'd healed enough that his head no longer felt like an old, cracked bell tolling incessantly in a bitter wind. He still had plenty of bruises, but they'd heal in time.

It was his ribs that graveled him. He didn't think they were busted, but they felt like they were not only broken but grinding around and chewing into his lungs. The raw ache made it hard to breathe. The old shirt Louisa had cut up and wrapped around him had helped some. Now he drew a breath and looked around the cave.

No sign of the Vengeance Queen.

"Louisa?"

The silence of the deep, desert night.

He walked to the cave entrance and called for her softly, not loudly enough for anyone nearby to hear. Sound carried on such a night as this. It didn't carry to her, however, which meant she must be a ways away.

Where?

He stomped into his boots. Dressed in only his hat, boots, and balbriggans, he walked down the rocky slope to where Mean stood, hobbled in a hollow amongst cabin-sized boulders, head and tail drooping as the horse slept on his feet, knees locked. The horse winded Prophet and gave a wary whicker, swatting his tail.

"Easy, hoss," Prophet said, going over and running a hand down the horse's neck that owned several rough scars from tussles with other horses and, once, a mountain lion before Prophet had managed to shoot the beast.

That had been up in Montana. How long ago? He couldn't remember. Sometime before he'd run into Louisa and they'd ridden after the Handsome Dave Duvall gang and she'd acquired her reputation that was now even bigger than his own, her being a beautiful, blond, and especially savage *pistolera* and all.

Prophet glanced over to where he'd last seen the pinto, hobbled a cautious twenty yards from Mean and Ugly. The horse was gone.

Apprehension raked at Prophet.

He moved back out of the hollow and looked off through a velvety black pass over which stars were sprinkled like Christmas glitter, clear as sequins on a fat whore's black dress, in the direction of Chisos Springs.

The stars were bright. They showered the nightscape with a soft, lilac light that seemed to pulse up from the ground itself, but all he could see were sand-colored rocks and cactus spikes dropping gradually away from him before rising just as gradually toward the pass, beyond which lay Chisos Springs.

Or, Moon's Well as the little demon was calling it now.

Louisa had most likely ridden to the town, as he'd suspected she would though he'd tried to convince her to wait until he was able to accompany her, and they'd see about prying Ruth Rose free of the dwarf's clutches. How long ago had she left? No way to tell. Again, apprehension was a monkey riding his shoulders. He drew another deep breath.

The ribs were better now that he was standing. Louisa's bandage had helped more than he'd thought. Could he ride?

He'd just have to see. He sure wasn't going to stand around out here with his thumb up his ass while she called down only God knew what kind of hell on herself in Chisos Springs.

He opened his fly to evacuate his bladder. Then he walked back into the cave, dressed, wrapped his shell belt and Peacemaker around his waist, thronging the holster on his right thigh, and then tenderly hauled his gear out to the hollow where Mean was fidgeting around now, knowing Prophet was up to something.

He saddled the horse, strapped his rifle scabbard to his saddle, and slung his shotgun over his shoulder to let it hang barrel up down his back. Grimacing, he mounted, drew another breath, suppressed the raw ache like a rat chewing his lungs.

"Not bad," he said, touching spurs to the dun's flanks, heading out. "Not bad at all. I'll be plum spiffy as a half-growed calico colt in no time."

To suppress the pain of his battered ribs and to alleviate his fear of what was transpiring with Louisa, he sang an old song that, with the singing, always made him feel better about whatever situation he was in:

> *Away from Mississippi's vale,*
> *With my ol' hat there for a sail,*
> *I crossed upon a cotton bale*
> *To Rose of Alabamy.*

He paused. Mean's hoofs clomped along the rocky trail, shod hooves ringing off stones. Prophet held him to a moderate pace to lessen the risk of injuring the beast on this dangerous night ride. From somewhere near and sounding sad and all alone in the mountain quiet, a lone coyote wailed, yipped wildly for a time, and then gave another mournful wail.

Prophet increased Mean's pace a little, and sang:

> *Oh brown Rosie,*
> *Rose of Alabamy!*
> *A sweet tobacco posey*
> *Is my Rose of Alabamy . . .*

He was a hundred yards down the pass and heading toward the broad, arid valley in which the town and the well sat, when he reined the horse up sharply.

He'd heard something. The distant clomps of riders moving toward him.

He kept the reins taut, listening, looking around to make sure he wasn't outlined against the sky. Reining Mean off the trail a ways, he stopped in front of a tall stack of boulders and pricked his ears again, listening.

The riders were moving toward him. The hoof thuds were growing gradually louder. Occasionally he heard the metallic ring of a shod hoof kicking a rock, the clatter of a bridle bit in a horse's mouth.

Just one rider. He could pick out each footfall.

He squinted straight ahead along the old Indian trail he'd been following down toward the valley. Movement there. An inky smudge jostled against the powdery tan of the terrain around it. Amidst the ink was a pale splotch that, as the rider drew closer, appeared blond hair bouncing on narrow shoulders.

Prophet's heart began to lighten, but then he heard more, quieter thuds behind the first rider. He shuttled his gaze farther down the grade and saw more inky shapes moving against the dark tan of the surrounding rocks and sand, climbing toward him.

Prophet eased out of the leather, ground-reined Mean and Ugly, and slid his Winchester from its boot. Quietly, he levered a round into the rifle's breech and strode down the slope a ways, about twenty yards wide of the trail, and walked out onto a broad oval boulder cropping out of the slope. This vantage offered a good view of the trail rising toward him from downhill and stretching past his left side and over that shoulder.

The first rider came on along the trail, the horse showing its fatigue in its loose-legged, lunging gait as it galloped up the hill. It was blowing raspily. Its rider was indeed a blond. The horse was a brown-and-white pinto. A second rider, dressed in red, rode behind the first.

Prophet dropped to a knee and doffed his hat, afraid it might show against the sky or the upslope behind him. The splay-kneed pinto was near when Prophet yelled, "You make some new friends, Louisa?"

She whipped her head toward him, hair flying, and closed a hand over her right-side Colt. After a second's scrutiny, and recognizing his voice, she shook her head. "No friends of mine. In fact, I'd admire if you took care of them fellas, Lou."

"Keep ridin'," he said, keeping his voice low as he dropped prone against the boulder.

When Louisa had drifted on up the slope and out of sight behind him, he set the rifle down beside him, and swung his shotgun around to the front. He broke the big blaster open, made sure he had a wad in each barrel, snapped it closed, and drew both rabbit-ear hammers back to full cock.

He hunkered lower, pressing his chest down fast against the rock.

The riders kept coming, pushing hard. Their horses were fresher than Louisa's, but not by much. Their gasps sounded like several blacksmith bellows being pumped hard at once.

The hoof clomps grew louder. Prophet could make out around five jostling shapes on various-colored horses and in various-colored and -styled garb, various-shaped hats. There were a couple of palm-leaf sombreros.

Gun iron winked in the starlight.

When the riders were at the ten o'clock position before Prophet, he said in a softly menacing voice just loudly enough to be heard above the thudding hooves and the squawking of tack, "Go back home, fellas, or get right with your maker. You got about two more strides to make up your pea-pickin' minds!"

"Whoa!" the lead rider shouted, hauling back on his reins.

He turned his head toward Prophet. The other riders brought their own mounts to skidding halts behind him.

"There!" he yelled and raised a carbine.

Prophet tripped the coach gun's left barrel.

Ka-booom!

The lead rider blew straight back off his horse with a scream.

The rider nearest him also raised his rifle.

Ka-booom!

Both riderless horses whinnied shrilly, turned sharply, and galloped off into the desert away from Prophet. Their riders lay behind them, motionless along the side of the trail.

"Hold on!" one of the three survivors shouted, throwing both hands up, including the one holding a Winchester.

At the same time, one of the other two triggered a rifle at Prophet. The slug whistled past Prophet's left ear. The bounty hunter had already raised his cocked rifle, and now he thumbed the hammer back, squeezed the trigger, and emptied a third saddle.

The third rider's hat danced in the air for a few seconds and then landed atop the back of its prone rider while its horse shot straight up the trail, whinnying and buck-kicking wildly.

The other man still had his arms and carbine raised. The second survivor wisely tossed his own rifle out away from him. It clattered onto the trail and bounced atop one of the dead men.

"Yours, too!" Prophet shouted, "or your saddle's gonna get empty mighty quick, amigo!"

The man tossed away his rifle and yelled, "We thought we done kilt you!"

Rage burned through Prophet like a wildfire. He was apparently looking at one of the men who'd given him his sore ribs, not to mention his other sundry complaints, and tied him bare-ass naked over Mean and Ugly's back. Hazed him off in the desert to die painfully slow. He planted a bead on the man's forehead, just beneath the brim of his broad-brimmed black hat.

"Best vamoose, friend! My trigger finger is *real* itchy tonight!"

The one-eyed man glanced at his partner, who looked back at him. At the same time, both riders turned their horses and galloped back the way from which they'd come.

Prophet cursed as he climbed heavily to one knee. He stared after the riders dwindling down the slope in the starry night. Gradually, their hoof thuds died.

"You should have killed 'em both, you stupid bastard!" he grumbled to himself. "'Cause now it's just a chore you're gonna have to face later!"

20

TWO MURKY FIGURES milled ahead of Prophet, up the hill and against the inky darkness of the cave mouth. A horse whinnied—a familiar-sounding greeting. Mean and Ugly answered his old friend in kind, the report echoing off the rocks around him and rattling the bounty hunter's eardrums.

Louisa's disembodied voice knifed out of the silent darkness. "Name yourself!"

"William Tecumseh Sherman."

Prophet reined Mean and Ugly to a halt behind the pinto.

"If wishes were wings." Louisa was helping the woman in the red dress off the pinto's back. Prophet jogged up to help, wrapped his big hands around Ruth Rose's slender waist, and dragged her down off the horse.

Ruth slumped against him, her arm bloody. She slurred her words as though drunk. "Oh, Lou—" she said. "You were alive. I couldn't believe it!"

Prophet picked Ruth up in his arms and groaned against the raking pain in his ribs. "Ah, hell, I been hurt worse fallin' off Mean 'n' Ugly drunk."

He brushed past Louisa and headed toward the cave. "What the hell happened?" he said in a pinched voice.

"Oh, Lou—they killed Frank," Ruth sobbed, her arms around his neck. "Hanged him from the balcony in his own hotel!"

Prophet crept into the cave, looking around so he wouldn't stumble and fall with the woman in his arms. Louisa hurried in behind him, her saddlebags over one shoulder, her canteen looped over the other one. He set Ruth down gently, leaned her back against the cave wall. From what he could see in the cave's near-pitch darkness, her face was pale and drawn.

He felt the oily wetness of blood streaking down her right arm.

"Who shot you?"

"I don't know."

"She shot the dwarf," Louisa said, kicking branches into the fire ring behind Prophet.

Prophet looked at her sharply, certain he must have heard wrong. "Huh?"

"That's right," Ruth said, satisfaction in her voice as she sat back against the cave wall, breathing heavily. He saw the line of her mouth twist in a self-satisfied smile. "I drilled him right through his head. It was terribly easy. I wish someone would have done it a long time ago."

"The dwarf is dead?"

"Got that right." Louisa was laying a fire. "Mrs. Rose gave him as good as he's ever given. Walked right into his own hotel, strode up to him barefoot and wearin' her red dress, and pumped one right through his ugly head!" She leaned forward to blow on the tinder comprised of strips of paper and dry pine needles. "You'd have been proud of her. I know I was . . . though I'm surprised either one of us got out of there alive."

Ruth said, "It didn't bring Frank back, though, did it? Oh, well." She grimaced as she closed her hand over the bullet hole in her upper arm. "Moon killed him a long time ago."

"I'll be damned," Prophet said, shaking his head slowly, slow to comprehend that the little demon was dead. He still harbored so much rage for the dwarf that he felt a slight disappointment, knowing he himself would never now exact his own brand of vengeance on the man.

His selfishness chagrined him.

Behind Prophet, the fire grew. He could see Ruth leaning back before him, wearing only the thin, red dress cut low enough to expose a good third of her freckled bosom that had been full and supple in his hands. Her legs beneath the dress's dusty hem were bare.

He leaned in close to inspect her arm. He didn't think the bullet had struck the bone but ripped clear through.

He sandwiched her hand between his own, a little self-conscious about showing affection for the woman with Louisa so near. "You'll be up and around in no time."

She frowned, her eyes raking his face and acquiring a tender, horrified cast. "Poor Lou—look what they did to you." She touched the still-swollen flesh around his right eye, ran a finger along a deep, scab-crusted cut under that same eye. "Poor man!"

"Ah, hell," Louisa said ironically, kneeling beside Prophet with a red handkerchief, a roll of cotton bandages, and a canteen. "He's looked worse after falling off his horse drunk. Might even be an improvement." She shouldered the big bounty hunter aside. "I'll tend that wound for you, Mrs. Rose, and you can get some sleep."

Louisa glanced at Prophet. "Any of my *medicinal* whiskey left?"

"Oh, there might be a drop or two."

Prophet fetched the bottle, held it up to the fire to see how much was left, shrugged, and handed it over to Louisa, who got busy cleaning Ruth's bloody arm.

Prophet heard something. At almost the same time, one of the horses whickered. Prophet walked outside the cave and slid his rifle from its saddle scabbard. He levered a round into the breech.

After a short time, hoof thuds rose, clear on the quiet air. Prophet stepped away from the horses, held his Winchester up high across his chest, and gave a silent curse.

Had the dwarf's men followed him?

"Name yourself!" His gruff voice echoed.

Silence.

The loudening hoof clomps stopped. A young man's voice: "Don't shoot, Mr. Prophet—it's Colter Farrow."

"You'll like him, Lou," Louisa said behind Prophet, standing with her own Winchester across her chest in the cave entrance, the fire dancing behind her. "He wears the stamp of your old friend Satan on his mug."

"What in the hell do you three think you're doin'?" Griselda May asked three strange riders the next morning after the sun had risen over the Del Carmens in the east. "I don't believe I seen any one of you pay the box, like the sign says to. Or . . . maybe you can't read . . . ?"

The three were winching up the bucket from the bottom of the well out in front of the dwarf's House of a Thousand Delights. They all wore leggings and ragged shirts and frayed neckerchiefs.

They were dusty enough to have been dragged through the desert at a hard gallop. They looked uncouth and ugly, and Griselda could smell them from where she stood a good fifteen feet away, between the well and the gambling parlor and whorehouse, which, after the previous night's activities, including Mordecai Moon's untimely demise, she now considered her own.

They all looked at her incredulously from beneath their sweaty, dusty, weather-beaten hats. The beefiest of the three—a cow-eyed man with a double chin tufted with gray brown beard—said, "We heard the dwarf done gave up the ghost."

"God rest his soul," said the man standing to the far left and holding the reins of a skewbald paint gelding and grinning.

"Yeah, rest his soul," said the beefy man. "So we figured

the water was free again . . . just like it was when Chisos ran things out this way."

Griselda sighed and crossed her arms on her little breasts. "Well, Chisos La Grange doesn't run things out here anymore. And while the dwarf no longer does, either, I do. I'm taking over the House of a Thousand Delights as well as ownership of this here well. And I fully intend to leave the cost of water the same as when Mr. Moon was alive, though I'll probably be inching the prices up after the first of the year. So you may consider the prices indicated on the sign there a bargain."

Griselda smiled icily.

The two drifters let their own smiles droop. The third man, and the tallest of the three, had been scowling from the first. He stood to the right of the other two.

His face was so hairy that Griselda couldn't see his lips move when he said in a low but distinct voice, "I'll be damned if I'll pay a fuckin' little bitch like you fer water."

Griselda's pistols were up in her hands before the last word had left the string bean's mouth. Both derringers cracked like Mexican firecrackers. They cracked again, in unison, and then all three men were piled up in the street at the base of the well, dust wafting around them.

"And I'll be damned if you won't," Griselda said.

Behind her, a high-pitched laugh rose. She glanced behind to see the Rio Bravo Kid standing on Moon's gallery, thumbs hooked behind his cartridge belt, grinning.

Other men lounged along the gallery, some sitting on the rail—freighters and drifters who'd decided to stay over another night and see how the dwarf's killing played out. Several had signed up with the "posse" that Griselda had sent out after the two women—the girl called the Vengeance Queen and Ruth Rose—who'd barged into the place and killed him.

Griselda didn't mind so much that Moon was gone. She just wished it would have happened later, after they'd sold another batch of whores down in Mexico. Mordecai had known how to deal with the Rurales down there, and the transaction would have gone much smoother if he'd been at the reins.

Also, Griselda hadn't yet coaxed him into telling her the combination to his office safe in which she knew a good thirty thousand dollars in gold nestled—profit from the House of a Thousand Delights as well as his slave-running business and his water contracts.

No, she didn't mind so much, really, but she had to avenge his killing just the same, to win the respect of his men. She knew she could only take his place as gang leader and ramrod of the House with their blessing. Even after three of his horses returned riderless to Moon's Well the night before, he still had a good fifteen on his roll, including Sheriff Mortimer, who was striding toward Griselda now from the direction of his office.

"Good Christ," Mortimer said, scowling down at the most recent batch of dead men. "When is all this killin' gonna stop, Griselda? Good Lord—Moon's *dead*!"

"No thanks to you, Sheriff," she said. "Where were you last night when you should have been over at the House, preventing such a thing from happening? In fact, where are you most nights, Sheriff? Does that consumptive have to take up *all* of your professional time?"

Mortimer's cheeks flushed above his salt-and-pepper mustache and goatee. "Listen here, you—"

"No, you listen, Sheriff. I run things now. The House and this town and this water are mine. That makes you mine, too." She looked at the Kid still standing atop the gallery steps, grinning, and jerked her chin.

The Kid strode over to her and Mortimer.

"Sheriff Mortimer, I'm afraid you are now *Deputy Sheriff* Mortimer." Griselda removed the badge from Mortimer's vest, inside his black frock coat, and pinned it to the Rio Bravo Kid's shirt. She gave the Kid a wink and then removed the deputy sheriff's badge from the Kid's vest and started to pin it to Mortimer's vest.

"Forget it," Mortimer said, stepping back away from her and waving his hands, palm out. "I've had enough."

Griselda tightened her jaws and put fire in her glare. "Wear it, Sheriff!" She glanced over at the men on the gallery looking on at the doings by the well with mute, vaguely threatening interest. "You will assist the new sheriff in the carrying out of his duties here in Moon's Well."

Griselda cast an unctuous smile toward the hotel and the gallery filled with Moon's supporters, grateful for the whiskey and women and gambling opportunities so far out here on hell's rear doorstep. "Yes, the name will remain the same, in honor of Mr. Mordecai Moon, the founder of this desert oasis."

Mortimer glanced at the men. Most were or had been outlaws at one time. They ran in packs. Dangerous packs. If he didn't wear the badge, they'd consider him a traitor.

Griselda offered another wicked, icy smile. "Think of your consumptive friend, Deputy. How well would she fare here without you?"

Mortimer's face swelled and his nostrils flared, but he said nothing.

She pinned the deputy sheriff's star to his vest and stepped back.

She glanced between Mortimer and the grinning Rio Bravo Kid and said, "There, that looks better. Now, won't you lawmen join me inside for the funeral? Shortly, we'll be burying Mr. Moon on the hill behind the hotel, under his favorite mesquite."

21

THE CORPSE OF Mordecai Moon lay on a table inside the main drinking hall of Moon's House of a Thousand Delights.

Two Apache girls and one Mexican were just now finishing dressing him after they'd given his little, gnarled, pasty body a sponge bath scented with rose water. They'd cleaned the bruised dimple that Ruth Rose's bullet had made in his forehead. They'd pomaded his three or four fringes of colorless hair, so that they lay pasted against the top of his bullet-shaped, lantern-jawed head. And they'd cleaned and wrapped his bullet-torn hand with a cotton bandage.

Griselda stood over Moon now as the Mexican girl finished wrestling the little body into his age-coppered claw-hammer coat, which, like the rest of Moon's attire, was no different than his customary garb, only they'd laundered his shirt and pants and given the coat and his bowler hat a thorough brushing. The Mexican girl lay Moon back against the Indian blanket spread out across the table beneath him and started to button his coat.

Griselda leaned down and slapped the girl's hands away. "He never wore it buttoned, stupid greaser!"

The Mexican girl jerked her hands away with a gasp and regarded Griselda like she would a coiled and rattling diamondback.

There were a dozen or so of Moon's men in the room, as well as transient freighters, gamblers, down-at-heel drifters, shopkeepers, and Mexican residents of Moon's Well. They'd come to pay their respects and some were having drinks in Mr. Moon's memory, but now they all regarded her incredulously, frowning. A Mexican in customary peasant pajamas and rope-soled sandals, holding his frayed sombrero down low before him respectfully, shook his head and sucked air through his teeth.

Many of the residents of Moon's Well had seen the value in Moon's being here, despite the water tax. For it was Moon and his small army of gunslingers and desperadoes who held the bronco Indians and other desperadoes from both sides of the border at bay. After Moon had come and built his big hotel and gambling parlor, the Mexican residents no longer had to flee to the mountains at the first sign of trouble, which they'd always had to do in previous years.

Looking around the room, Griselda realized her mistake. She wasn't looking properly grief-stricken.

"Oh, Lord," she said, bringing a hand to her temple. "I'm sorry, Esmeralda. It's just that . . . oh, *God, Mordecai!*"

Griselda threw herself atop the little, suited body, smashing flat his hat resting beside him.

She feigned a half-dozen or so convulsions and then straightened, wiped her invisible tears from her cheeks with the backs of her hands, sniffed, and lifted the dwarf's little hat still wearing the bullet hole in its crown. She reshaped the crown, set the hat on Moon's chest, and nodded at the two Mexicans waiting nearby with a five-foot-long box they'd hammered together for a coffin.

The Mexicans—Indian dark, withered, nearly toothless men, one with a corn-husk cigarette smoldering in one corner of his mouth—set the coffin on the table beside the dwarf. They lifted the little suited body with the feathered hat on its chest into the coffin.

"Here's to Mr. Moon," said a beefy, Irish bartender, standing behind the bar and lifting a shot glass in salute. His voice was thick as he added, "He was the only man who offered me a job when I bailed out of Yuma pen. God bless you, squire!"

The others muttered and nodded, raised their own glasses, and sipped their beers or tequilas or whiskies, and then the Mexicans lifted the coffin lid from off a separate table.

"I'm going to miss you, my love," Griselda said, glancing at the Rio Bravo Kid, who stood beside his new deputy, Lee Mortimer, near the open double doors. He and Mortimer both stood with their hats in their hands, chins dipped to their chests. Mortimer's jaw was set tight in silent anger. Meeting Griselda's glance, the Kid quirked a faint, conspiratorial smile, dimpling his cheeks, and winked.

That bit of foolishness annoyed Griselda. What if the others had seen? She'd admonish the big, stupid firebrand later, maybe even withhold her body for a night or two in punishment. After their celebratory tumble of the preceding night, he'd miss it for sure!

The Mexicans held up the coffin lid, waiting for Griselda's order. She stared into the coffin at Moon's slack face, his eyes tightly closed, what appeared a faint grin on his thin lips mantled by his scraggly mustache, with a fringe of goat beard sagging off his dimpled chin.

She sighed, nodded. The Mexicans placed the lid on the coffin and then each grabbed a rope handle on either end. They began carrying the coffin toward the open doors.

Griselda said, "We'll have a brief service at Mr. Moon's grave, gentlemen and ladies. Just a few words, maybe a prayer. Any more than that would only embarrass him. As you know, Mr. Moon was not a God-fearing man."

A couple of the Mexican peasants and Mexican freighters shook their heads regretfully at that. One crossed himself and moved his lips as though in prayer for Moon's lost soul.

Griselda suppressed an urge to roll her eyes.

She donned her hat and walked to the front of the saloon,

avoiding eye contact with either the Kid or Deputy Mortimer, and headed out into the bright sunlight. The other mourners followed her out of the saloon, and they all formed a procession, Griselda following the two peasants carrying the dwarf's coffin, the Kid and Mortimer behind her, the others behind them.

Several more people who'd been holding a vigil of sorts out in the street followed, as well, so that there were a good thirty, forty people striding mournfully behind the sprawling saloon and past the corrals and barns and up a rocky hill sparsely stippled with mesquites and sotol cactus.

Griselda had sent out two other Mexicans—an old man and a boy of about twelve—to dig the dwarf's grave. The grave was dug, and now the pair lounged in the shade of a lone mesquite, the middle-aged Mexican taking a drink from the bladder flask looped around his neck, the boy sitting against the same tree and playing with a black and brown mongrel puppy between his spread legs. The boy and the puppy were playing tug-of-war with a knotted rag.

When the puppy saw the little wooden box and the crowd filing up the hill toward the hole in the ground, it growled and barked and then gave a yip and ran down the side of the hill to the north.

The man and the boy gained their feet as Griselda and the two peasants carrying the coffin approached. The peasants set the coffin down, and Griselda looked into the hole. It was only about three feet deep. A pile of ash-colored soil liberally sprinkled with gravel lay beside it.

Griselda frowned at the old man, who doffed his battered felt hat, and said nervously in halting English, "Bad rock. Very shallow. Too hard dig. Should bury Senor Moon there." He turned to indicate a higher hill about two hundred yards farther west, the starkly forbidding Chisos range rising beyond. "Not so rocky," the Mexican said.

Griselda shook her head. She hadn't wanted to walk that far in the blinding sun and searing heat. It was so hot that she didn't even sweat, but she felt as desiccated as a hunk of beef jerky.

"This was his favorite tree," she lied. "This is where we'd often come to look over his holdings. This is where he wanted to be planted. He told me so."

Mortimer gave a little snort but did not meet Griselda's silent glare. The Kid stood beside Mortimer, keeping his own head down, his hat in his hand, but still looking as though he were about to jump up and down and whoop with joy at being named sheriff of Moon's Well.

Griselda doffed her own hat and held it before her as she waited for the other mourners to circle around the grave. No one said anything. There was only the sound of the hot, parched wind rattling the mesquite leaves and kicking up dust here and there around this godforsaken stretch of ground west of Moon's Well. She kept her head down but looked toward the Chisos range and then south across the painfully bright, white, lunar-like landscape toward the Rio Grande and Mexico.

What a god-awful place this was. All dust and rock and blazing sun and hot wind and Gila monsters, and hardly anything green at all. Even mesquite leaves weren't really green, but more of a silver, as though there wasn't enough water to nourish them properly.

What Griselda wouldn't give to see a sprawling red oak again in the humid, green hills of Missouri. . . .

Soon, very soon, she'd have Moon's money from the safe and from the sale of the slave whores, and she'd be off in search of an ocean somewhere, or at least some green hills.

"All right, let's get on with it," she said, too quickly, indiscreetly returning her mind to the task at hand. "I mean . . . go ahead and set him in the hole, *por favor.*"

The peasants dropped to their knees and, each taking an end of the coffin, slowly lowered it into the shallow hole. The hole wasn't much deeper than the box itself. Coyotes would probably dig Moon up in no time, but what the hell? At least he was gone and out of her hair. If only she'd learned the combination to his safe first, and he'd sold the slave whores . . .

Oh, well. Things might be turning out in her favor despite all of that. A couple of sticks of dynamite would likely blow the safe open. She'd simply have some freighted in.

"Anyone know a prayer?" Griselda asked, when the man and the boy had lowered the box into the grave and gained their feet, dusting themselves off with their hats.

She looked around at the mourners of every shape and size surrounding her—a ragged, dusty lot, some armed, some not. There were more than a few Mexican women from town here to pay their own respects to Moon despite his expensive water contracts, despite his using them for mostly slave labor.

They all looked at her. Most of the Mexicans hadn't understood her. None of the Anglos appeared to know any prayers, except Mortimer, who said with a faintly cunning grin: "Sure, I know a prayer."

"Oh, Deputy Mortimer," Griselda said. "How nice!"

Mortimer held his eyes on her with that faintly wry, decidedly insolent grin as he recited "The Lord's Prayer." When he was finished, he snugged his flat-brimmed, black hat on his head, turned and strode down the hill toward the town, his string tie blowing back over his shoulder in the wind.

"All right, cover him," Griselda said to the Mexican man and his son. To the others she said, "Funeral's over, folks. Mr. Moon is planted. Everyone back to work!"

The gravediggers had just picked up their shovels and started to toss dirt into the hole when there was a hollow thud. Griselda had just started to walk down the hill, but now she turned back to the hole, frowning.

She'd thought that the Mexican man or the boy must have tossed a stone onto the coffin, but the thud had sounded duller than the sound a rock would have made.

The Mexican man and the boy leaped back from the grave as though they'd just spied a rattler slithering out of the hole.

There was another thud.

And another.

A man's hoarse, muffled voice shouted something incoherent. It seemed to come from the hole.

But that couldn't be.

Griselda grew weak in the knees.

The lid flew up off of the coffin. The dwarf crawled up out of the hole, looking haggard, holding his bullet-torn hat in one hand, and standing up on the side of the hole. He canted his head, glowered up at Griselda, and said through gritted teeth, "Surprise, surprise—I ain't dead!"

22

THE PREVIOUS NIGHT, Prophet had watched the strange horse and rider move slowly up toward him, causing Louisa's pinto and Prophet's lineback dun, Mean and Ugly, to snort and blow.

Prophet could see only the young man's silhouette—at least, his voice had told him that the rider was young—so he couldn't tell much about him except that he was slender and he wore a calico shirt and suspenders, and that long hair hung straight down from his hat.

"Who the hell is Colter Farrow?" Prophet said, holding his rifle across his chest, always cautious. "And what's he doing here?"

"Stand down, Lou," Louisa said. "Mr. Farrow gave me a hand in Moon's place earlier. In fact, if he hadn't intervened with rifle and hogleg, I and Mrs. Rose would likely be snuggling with snakes, as you would so colorfully put it." She raised her voice. "Take a load off that horse, Mr. Farrow. We've coffee and food here by the fire. It's not much, but it'll do for these quarters, I reckon."

"Don't mean to muscle in on your camp," the young man said, sitting tall and straight in his saddle. Firelight flickered across a grisly scar in the shape of an *S* on his left cheek. "I just wanted to make sure the ladies was all right, is all. I led Mr. Moon's riders straight south for a time, but they sniffed out the ruse and picked up your trail to the west. I seen what they got for their trouble. I take it that was your doin', Mr. Prophet?"

Prophet walked down the slope until he stood a few feet from the kid's coyote dun. He could see the young man better from this distance. He could see the long, copper-colored hair, the long, pale, slightly freckled face, and the *S* brand that had been seared into his cheek, just under the left eye.

He'd seen the kid a few days ago back in San Simon, airing his paunch out back of the whorehouse.

"Well, well," the bounty hunter said, setting his rifle on his shoulder and giving a soft, wry chuff. "I see you survived your encounter with whiskey, women, and tobacco."

The kid shook his head. "Whew—I'll never do that again!"

"That's what I keep sayin'. Like Miss Fancy Britches over yonder says, light an' sit a spell. I thank you for helping the ladies out. Can't let 'em go anywhere alone without 'em makin' trouble of one stripe or another, callin' rabid coyotes onto their trail."

"Like I said, I don't mean to intrude."

"Kid, you ain't intrudin'," Prophet said. "You helped me out in Mexico, and you helped my lady friends out in Moon's . . . I mean, *Chisos Springs*, and we'd like to offer some coffee and hardtack, maybe a few beans boiled in rattlesnake. That's Louisa's favorite."

"Well, dang," the kid said, quietly droll. "Beans boiled in rattlesnake. Shoulda said so right off!"

He swung down from the saddle. He was a full head shorter than Prophet, and probably fifty pounds lighter. He wore what appeared an old Remington revolver for the cross draw on his right hip, a knife on his left. His long, thin hair blew around his face in the night breeze.

"Kid, I like your style," Prophet said. He held out his hand. "I guess you already know my name. Louisa must've told you."

"Nah, I just knew," the kid said. "Before I took to the trail myself under circumstances less favorable than those I would have preferred, I used to tip an ear to such matters and outlaws and bounty hunters an' such."

As he began stripping the tack off his coyote dun, he said, "I grew up in the Lunatic Mountains above Sapinero, in Colorado, and there wasn't much to do but listen to the old punchers who worked at my foster parents' place, and the men who ran cattle around us. Your name came up more'n a few times, Mr. Prophet."

"Either before or after a cuss word, I'd fathom," Louisa said from where she was preparing a meal over the fire in the cave.

Young Farrow glanced at her over his shoulder. "Heard Miss Bonaventure's name, time or two, as well. More so after I hit the trail myself."

"Men mention Louisa's name in fear and trembling," Prophet said as he hauled the young man's saddle into the cave. He set it down on the far side of the fire and looked at her. "Leastways, I do."

Louisa tossed some bits of jerky into a pot of boiling beans, and slid a steaming coffeepot onto a flat rock out of the flames. "You best sit for a while, Lou. You don't look well. I'll pour you a cup of coffee."

"Ah, don't get all nice, now, or you're gonna rattle me." Prophet took the cup of coffee that Louisa handed him and walked over to where Ruth lay back against the cave wall, a blanket pulled up to her chin. She looked worn and haggard as she stared toward the ceiling, a stricken cast to her gaze.

"Here, Ruth—drink this. Good, hot coffee'll do you good."

She shook her head slowly. "I don't care for coffee, Lou. Food, neither." She looked at Louisa. "I do thank you, Miss Bonaventure, for saving my worthless hide tonight. You shouldn't have endangered your own, however. I'm not worth it." She gave a sad, sardonic smile.

"What you did tonight makes you worth it, Mrs. Rose."

"Please . . . Ruth."

"Only if you call me Louisa."

Ruth lifted her mouth corners at that, crinkled the skin around her eyes. Prophet sat down beside her and took a sip from the smoking coffee cup.

He said, "I reckon you cut the head off the snake floppin' an' coilin' around down there in Chisos Springs. Gotta admit I'm a little disappointed I never got a chance to drill a hole through that little bastard's head my own self . . . uh, pardon my privy talk, Ruth . . . but I reckon now the rest of the beast will die soon, too."

"Don't bank on that," Louisa said, stirring the bubbling pot of beans as young Colter Farrow walked into the cave with his saddlebags on his shoulder, bedroll under his arm, Winchester rifle in his hand. "What about that little polecat girl of his—Miss Griselda May? She's got enough cunning to keep the dwarf's spirit alive in Moon's Well."

"It's Chisos Springs," Prophet corrected her. "And before I leave here, by God, I'm gonna go down and change the name back. Or, hell . . ." He glanced at Ruth. "We'll call it Rose's Well from now on."

Ruth shook her head. "I'm not going back there for any length of time. Oh, I'll bury Frank, and I'll grab a change of clothes. But after that, I'm closing down the hotel, and I'll be heading back north. I've had enough of this dry desert. Even with Moon dead, it's still a perdition."

Louisa poured another two cups of coffee. She offered one to Colter Farrow, who had laid out his gear with his saddle and then hunkered down on his haunches at the end of the fire near Prophet.

He accepted the coffee with a gentlemanly bow—the gracious nod of a polite young cowpuncher, Prophet thought. A young man who'd been raised good and proper.

The kid had that quiet, country air about him—he probably knew horses better than he knew people—though the bounty hunter doubted most cowpunchers would have the sand to stand up to the dwarf's breed of killer, as he'd apparently done in Chisos Springs.

"Mr. Prophet misinformed you, Mr. Farrow," Louisa

said. "No rattlesnake stew tonight. Just beans and jerky and a little side pork."

"Don't mind me. I done ate before I rode into Moon's We—" Farrow glanced at Prophet, flushing slightly with cowboy-bashful chagrin. "I mean, Chisos Springs."

Louisa sat back on her rump, arms around her upraised knees, and sipped her coffee. "What about that bounty on your head, Mr. Farrow? You must be one mean, cold-blooded killer to stack up a whole two thousand dollars. And, heck, I bet you're not yet twenty!"

"I am just twenty, Miss Bonaventure. And about that bounty, well . . ."

"That ain't the mark of Satan on your cheek," Prophet said, resting back on an elbow, ankles crossed before him. "That's the Sapinero brand of Bill Rondo. I'd know it anywhere. He threatened me with it one time. I promised if he wagged that iron at me one more time, he'd get it shoved up his ass."

Colter Farrow stared into the fire. "Well, I didn't shove it up his ass." The kid spoke evenly, quietly, in somber tones, staring into the fire. "But I did burn the *S* into his own face though not before he used it on me first. When I found out it was him who killed the man who took me in when my parents died of a fever before I was out of rubber pants, and sent his body home nailed to the bed of his own supply wagon, I went after him. Broke his legs. Crippled him. Blazed his own brand in his cheek, just like he done me. I hear he's confined to a wheelchair now, wearin' the same scar as me. Rondo was a poison-mean hombre, but I reckon he had enough friends back in Sapinero that this bounty will ride with me for a while."

"It ain't ridin' around here, Red," Prophet said. "Don't sweat it."

Young Farrow appeared to take umbrage at this, beetling his brows and flushing again, causing the *S* on his cheek to turn a shade paler. "I don't sweat nothin', Mr. Prophet. I can take care of myself. Me an' that horse out yonder—I call him Northwest 'cause at home he always grazed facin' that direction—and this here old Remington pistol of my pa's . . . we dusted a lot of trails together. And I expect we got a few more to go."

"Running," Ruth said, though Prophet hadn't even realized she'd been following the conversation. She shook her head as she regarded young Colter Farrow fondly and sadly. "You're too young, and you obviously have too much good in you to live such a life. If you weren't good, you wouldn't have helped us out back at Moon's place. Hearing that about you, young Colter, makes me sad."

"Don't be sad for me, ma'am. There's a lot more people got better reasons for folks to feel sad for 'em." Colter Farrow sipped his coffee, a pensive cast in his gaze. He lowered the cup, cast a quick glance at both women, and brushed a hand self-consciously across the scar on his cheek. He continued to stare into the fire.

He was lost and lonely. A reluctant drifter who had likely become handy with that six-gun and Winchester because he'd had no choice. Prophet didn't feel sorry for him. He sympathized with him because of his hard luck and that nasty brand he was doomed to wear on his cheek for the rest of his days.

That brand had scarred the boy in more ways than one. How could it have done anything else?

But you couldn't feel sorry for a young man as tough as Colter Farrow obviously was. Tough at least when it came to men, but apparently whiskey, women, and tobacco were still bobcats that, taken all together, he hadn't yet learned to wrestle with much success.

Prophet inwardly chuckled at the remembered image of the kid throwing up his guts outside that whorehouse in San Simon, like just another young drifter trying to learn the ways of men and stake his own claim in that rugged territory, and climbed to his feet.

He shucked his Peacemaker, checked the loads, and rolled the cylinder across his forearm, enjoying the solid clicks of the filled chambers. "I'm gonna go out, tend my hoss, take a look around. I'll keep the first watch, in case

Moon's men keep comin' after us, which we best assume they'll do. Louisa, you're next. Colter, then you. Two hours apiece."

Prophet slung his double-barreled coach gun over his shoulder, grabbed his Winchester from where he'd leaned it against the cave wall, and walked out of the cave and down the slope toward where Mean and Ugly stood ground-tied.

"That's Lou for you," Louisa told Colter behind Prophet. "He always just *assumes* he's ramrod."

"I reckon with a man as big as he is, Miss Louisa," Colter said, "and with a popper the size of the one he carries, it's probably a purty safe assumption."

Even Ruth chuckled at that.

Prophet continued walking toward Mean and Ugly and suppressed a grin as he scratched his lumpy nose.

The kid would do.

23

UPON SEEING MORDECAI Moon climb up out of his grave with his bullet-torn hat in his hand, most of the Mexican women and even a few of the men fainted straight away.

A shocked roar sounded as the entire crowd stumbled back away from the grave with a horrified start.

Griselda May staggered two steps back, as well, her lower jaw sagging and her mouth forming a near-perfect *O* with shock, disbelief, and more than a little dismay. Her heart thudded. Her knees threatened to buckle.

Standing beside the grave, covered in dirt, the entire middle of his pasty forehead the deep purple of summer storm clouds, Moon scowled angrily at Griselda. Quickly, realizing that what she was seeing was not some nightmare figment of her imagination, she manufactured a look of un-bridled jubilation and tearful relief.

"Mordecai, you're alive!" Griselda screamed, throwing herself at the dwarf's feet as though in prayer and wrapping her arms around his waist. She even surprised herself with how authentic-sounding her cries were, how violently she managed to make herself convulse against the dwarf's

small, muscular, paunchy little body. "You're alive, you're alive! Oh, God, you're *alive!*"

She looked up at him scowling down at her. "What?" she said, shaking her head in genuine amazement and befuddlement. "How? I . . . I don't *understand . . . !*"

She forced a giddy laugh and was again amazed at how authentic it sounded, at least to her own ears. But then, she really was amazed!

Moon looked around, his own eyes befuddled, as though he'd suddenly found himself walking in his sleep. Griselda turned to look at the others standing around them, shock still showing on the faces of even the most hardened of Moon's hardened criminal gang.

Some of the Mexican men were crouched over the women who'd fainted. Babies were crying. A dog was barking as it backed down the hill with a haunted look.

The two gravediggers had backed several feet away from Moon and Griselda and the grave, and the boy stood with his chin sagging nearly to his chest. His father was crossing himself over and over again, looking at the sky with shiny, silver eyes, as though he were seeing the face of Madre Maria up there against that brassy blue vault.

Suddenly, one of the other Mexican men shouted in Spanish, "Senor Moon is back from the dead—it must mean he is a saint!"

More shocked gasps. A loud, perplexed hum of conversation rose from the onlookers as they turned to each other to confer, their voices pitched with amazement.

"Santo Senor Moon!" cried the Mexican—a wizened old man with thin hair and a tangled, gray beard—who had deemed the dwarf a saint. *"Santo Senor Moon!"*

The other Mexicans, including the well-armed border toughs in their leather leggings and drooping mustaches, picked up the chant, pumping their fists in the air. *"Santo Senor Moon! Santo Senor Moon!"*

The dwarf looked around at them, stitching his brows. He placed his hands on his temples and muttered, "Crazy damn bean eaters are causin' a nasty bell to toll in my head."

He staggered to one side, away from Griselda, and would have tumbled back into the grave if the girl hadn't grabbed him by both lapels.

"Hold on there, lover! You just came from there!" She looked at the Rio Bravo Kid and Mortimer, who both stood staring in shock at the resurrected dwarf. "Don't just stand there!" Griselda cried. "One of you come over here, pick up Mr. Moon, and carry him back upstairs to our room!"

The Rio Bravo Kid looked a little frightened, tentative, as he stared down at Moon. The Kid couldn't seem to work his mind around what he was seeing, or wasn't yet sure that he wasn't seeing a ghost.

Mortimer knelt down beside the dwarf. "You all right, Mr. Moon?"

"Feelin' kinda peaked," Moon said, kneading his temples. He cradled his bullet-torn, bandage-wrapped hand in both arms. "And this here paw o' mine purely hurts like *the blazes*!"

"Didn't you hear me?" Griselda yelled above the chanting around them. "Take him back over to the hotel!"

Mortimer crouched and easily picked the dwarf up in his arms. As he did, Moon tipped his head toward the badge on Mortimer's vest, partly concealed by his frock coat.

"Say, why's you wearin' that deputy's badge, Mortimer?" the dwarf asked as the demoted sheriff began carrying him down the hill, Griselda taking long strides beside them to keep up.

"A few changes been made after your demise, Mr. Moon," Mortimer said, casting a devilish look at Griselda practically running along beside him. The Rio Bravo Kid was walking behind, still wearing that boyishly sulky, incredulous expression.

The Mexicans and all the other mourners were following behind the Rio Bravo Kid, chanting and singing, some of the women dancing.

"Oh, there were changes, were there?" Moon cast a hard look at Griselda. "So soon after . . . my . . . uh . . . *expiration*?"

Griselda kept walking as she wrinkled her nose at Mortimer. She glanced behind her at the Rio Bravo Kid, who merely threw his shoulders up in a show of exasperated bewilderment while the Mexicans sang and chanted along behind him.

Several of the dwarf's main men—Steele, Toma, and Kinch Brautigan—came running up around Mortimer. "Hey, Boss, you all right?" asked Brautigan through his pewter-colored beard still flecked with foam from the beer he'd been drinking in the dwarf's honor a few minutes ago.

"I don't know," the dwarf said, jostling in Mortimer's arms. "I think so. Hell, my hand musta slowed that bullet and the bullet bounced right off my old wooden noggin!" He laughed at that, flopping his arms against Mortimer's, but then he sucked a sharp breath and squeezed his eyes closed as he cradled his bandaged hand against his belly once more.

"Damn glad to see you still kickin', Boss," Tobias Steele chimed in, patting one of Moon's little black boots. "We was afeared your dyin' would be the end of the whole gang. You know how none of us got nothin' but mush between our ears. Can't lead worth shit! At least, not the way you do. O' course, Miss Griselda, she was gonna take over, but seein' as how she's just a girl, and—"

"Ah, shut up, Steele!" Griselda intoned. "Before this girl blows your head off your shoulders, you hairy-necked ape."

Steele scowled, indignant, and fell back in line with the others, as did Toma and Brautigan. Griselda and Mortimer and the dwarf were moving up along the House's left side, tramping through a swatch of purple shade and kicking empty bottles, cans, and tumbleweeds. Griselda ran ahead, turned the front corner, mounted the gallery, and threw both doors wide.

She stepped aside as Mortimer and the dwarf passed through the doors and started down the long, relatively cool main drinking hall. A couple of Apache girls were cleaning up the place, as none of the slave whores were allowed to leave the premises save for hanging wash on the outside line. When they saw the dwarf being carried into the building—alive!—by Mortimer, one screamed while the other sidestepped quickly out of the way and broke out in some kind of Apache hoodoo chant.

The faces of both skimpily dressed, brown-skinned girls turned pale as death.

The mourners remained outside on the street, still raising their joyful ruckus. *"Santo Senor Moon! Santo Senor Moon!"* One of the old, brightly dressed Mexican women stood near the well, thrust both her long-fingered brown hands into the air above her head, and sang a prayer loudly in Spanish.

"Upstairs," Griselda said, trying to sound more concerned than troubled, trying to figure out how she was going to explain her forcing Mortimer to exchange badges with the Rio Bravo Kid.

She ran ahead, mounted the stairs, and soon she was opening the door of her and the dwarf's private room. "In here. Get him on the bed. Hurry up, Mortimer, for chrissakes! The poor man's in *pain!*"

Griselda peeled the covers back from the bed, made a face at the blood that had soaked up through the mattress to lightly spot the sheets. The dwarf's men had hauled Chaz Burdick's body away, but he'd left a barrelful of blood behind him. All the covers had had to be burned.

As for Chaz himself—he'd likely fed a couple of mountain lions known to prowl the village's far northern perimeter, along a sandy dry wash home to Mojave green rattlers and chaparral cactus. To Griselda's way of thinking, it served him right.

The fool had let himself get shot through a pillow with his own gun. . . .

Mortimer lay Moon on the bed. The dwarf clamped his little fists against his head and moaned, bending his legs and grinding his heels into the mattress.

"Whiskey," he said. "Whiskey. Oh, God, *whiskey!*"

"Coming right up!" Griselda ran over to a dresser on which many bottles and glasses, mostly dirty, stood.

"Like the others said, Mr. Moon," Lee Mortimer said with his wry air, standing over the bed. "Good to have you back amongst the living." He cast Griselda another of his sly grins. "If you need anything, you'll know where to find me."

He pinched his hat brim to Moon, though the dwarf had his eyes squeezed closed as he continued to moan and writhe. As Mortimer left, Griselda said, "Indeed, we'll know where to find you, Deputy Mortimer—over at that stable you share with that consumptive whore!"

Mortimer stopped at the door. He stood stock still for about three seconds, staring straight ahead.

When he turned back to Griselda, who was handing Moon a water glass half filled with whiskey, his eyes were cold and hard. "She has a name," Mortimer said, just loudly enough for Griselda to hear him above the dwarf's moaning. "It's Wanda. Next time I'd admire if you used it."

He held Griselda's gaze for another two seconds, pinched his hat brim to her coldly, and went out.

As Moon slurped whiskey from his glass, Griselda said, "Well, what do you know—looks like ole Mortimer might just love that consumptive saloon doxie."

She wasn't sure why, but the realization that the old outlaw appeared to be in love made her feel a fleeting heartsickness, a half-conscious but poignant jealousy, maybe, as she stared down at the wretched Mordecai Moon, who was taking long sips and smacking his lips and lolling his head from side to side on the pillow.

Outside, Griselda could still hear the chanting Mexicans. A din was growing in the drinking hall below as the dwarf's men celebrated Moon's return from the dead just as they'd been drinking to his memory less than an hour ago.

Another dark feeling swept Griselda. She looked down at Mordecai Moon. He was more powerful than ever now, having defeated death and become *Santo Señor Moon*.

How would she be able to follow through with her plans to rob the man blind? Oh, she'd find a way. But how . . . ?

Moon polished off the glass and held it up to her in his clawlike hand. "More!"

"Of course, Mordecai."

She refilled the glass and gave it back to him. He stared up at her, a hard cunning returning to his eyes. "Get undressed and crawl in here." He patted the bed beside him. "I'm gonna play with your little titties. Make me feel better."

He winked.

"And, uh"—an evil grin showed all his black teeth—"you can tell ole Mordecai what you been up to around here while I been dead, startin' with how come you made that *Kid* full sheriff. And then you can tell me what you done with the head of that bitch who killed me!"

24

PROPHET BREECHED THE coach gun. In each barrel a paper wad of double-ought buck nestled.

He snapped the gun back together with a soft click, drew each hammer back to full cock, and pressed his back against the side of the rock wall.

He heard the faint ching of spurs as the man hunting him approached. Gravel crunched faintly beneath boot soles. Breath raked in and out of laboring lungs.

Sound traveled well inside this little devil's maze of ancient lava walls and stony escarpments that Prophet and his ragtag team of trail partners had found themselves in when Moon's small posse had descended on them.

Prophet's heart beat slowly as the spur chings grew gradually louder. He pressed his back harder against the rock wall, felt sweat dribbling slowly down his dusty cheeks carpeted with several days' worth of brown beard stubble.

"Hey, asshole," said a burly voice. "You in there?"

A shadow filled the mouth of the narrow stone corridor that Prophet was in.

"Yep."

Prophet turned the coach gun across his belly and tripped

the left trigger. The bounty hunter could just barely hear the man's shrill scream beneath the gut shredder's roar as the fist-sized cluster of double-ought buck lifted the man up off his feet and sent him flying back with a cracking thud against the stone wall behind him.

He dropped down the wall, leaving a large, thick smear of dark red blood on the rock, and fell to his knees. He squeezed his eyes closed, sighed, and fell forward to grind his forehead into the ground.

He knelt there, head to the ground, shivering as life left him.

Prophet spied movement to his left and ahead of him and jerked his head back a half second before a rifle blasted a slug into the rock wall behind his right shoulder, peppering his shoulder, neck, and cheek with sharp stone shards.

He raised the gut shredder toward a face shaded by a dusty cream Stetson with a snakeskin band, and a rifle barrel poking up from behind a thumb of rock, ahead and to his right. He tripped the coach gun's right trigger and saw the face turn the red of a ripe tomato smashed against the side of a white privy.

The man hadn't even had time to scream before his head was pulverized. The lower jaw sagged a little, but then the crimson-splattered head, suddenly minus its hat, dropped back behind the thumb of rock and out of sight.

Prophet heard the shooter's rifle clatter against the rocks.

Crouching, slinging the shotgun back behind his shoulder, Prophet grabbed his Winchester from where he'd leaned it against the wall he'd hidden behind when he'd heard Moon's man stealing toward him. Now he racked a fresh round into the chamber and looked around, crouching, ready for another attack.

He saw no one to either his right or his left along the dusty corridor in the mass of strewn boulders. Gunfire prattled off to his right, so he headed that way, turned, and tramped quickly down another corridor, the gunfire growing louder before him.

He stopped suddenly. Colter Farrow was shooting from

atop a bluff ahead and to Prophet's right. The kid was shooting down the bluff's opposite side. Prophet recognized him by the long, red hair hanging straight down from his tobacco brown Stetson.

A man was slinking up the slope behind Colter, just now lowering the rifle in his hands and sliding a knife from his belt sheath. The man was tall and thin, with long, blond hair, green silk neckerchief, and a bright yellow shirt and deerskin leggings. Prophet remembered the distinctively dressed gent from the gallery of Moon's House of a Thousand Delights, when Prophet was getting the shit kicked out of both ends.

The man was about seven steps away from Colter now, and he was lowering the knife while angling the point for a quick upthrust into the kid's back.

Prophet snapped his Winchester to his shoulder. "Hold it!"

The man turned suddenly, awkwardly on the gravel-strewn slope, rocks tumbling down and away from his spurred boots. He'd dropped the knife and was starting to raise his rifle when Prophet stained his pretty yellow, bib-front shirt with two round, red holes across his chest. The blond-headed hombre grimaced, fell back against the slope, dropped his rifle, lost his hat, and rolled, limbs akimbo.

Prophet stepped aside as the blond-headed hombre rolled past him to pile up against a boulder on the far side of the corridor he was in. The dead man had lightly splattered the gravel in his wake with red.

Colter Farrow had jerked around quickly at the shooting behind him. He looked from Prophet to the dead man, flushed with chagrin, and shook his head. "Shit."

"Yep," Prophet said, climbing the blood-splashed slope.

"Maybe I can return the favor some time."

"Hope not." Prophet looked over the slight gap in the rock through which the kid had been shooting. "Who you shootin' at over here?"

Then he saw the stocky Mexican lying just beyond the wagon-sized boulder he'd apparently been crouching behind, his rifle and a pistol lying nearby. A horse stood ground-tied about fifty yards beyond him, along a rocky wash tufted with lemon green brush.

"Think that's all of 'em," Colter said as he stood beside Prophet, plucking cartridges from his shell belt and punching them through his Winchester's loading gate.

Just then another shot sounded from the north, ahead of Prophet's and the kid's position.

"That must be Louisa," Prophet said, and he slipped between the rocks at the top of the bluff and began slipping and sliding, holding his arms out for balance, down the other side.

They'd come upon Moon's riders earlier that day, in the early afternoon, when they'd been traversing the Chisos range looking for another place to hole up while they waited for the furor over the dwarf's demise to die down in Chisos Springs. The riders had taken Prophet's group by surprise, and they'd split up in this badland area on the eastern slopes of the Chisos, Ruth remaining with Louisa because they'd both been riding Louisa's pinto. Moon's men had split up to come after them, and during his brief game of cat-and-mouse amongst the rocks, Prophet had lost track of the others.

Until now.

He and Colter ran through this relatively flat stretch of desert in the heart of the rocky badlands, climbing up and over low hills and dashing across two dry watercourses. Rifles continued prattling before him. A man was shouting. Louisa was shouting back at them though Prophet couldn't hear what they were yelling beneath the rifle blasts, but he had a feeling that Louisa and the man weren't complimenting each other's bloodlines.

When Prophet and Colter gained the crest of a low hill near the shooting, they dropped to their bellies and doffed their hats. On the far side of the hill, smoke puffed and guns crashed behind two nests of rocks about thirty yards apart from each other.

A dead man lay in the gap between the two shooting factions, facedown and spread-eagle, his hat lying far beyond him against a clump of Spanish bayonet. Prophet saw Louisa and Ruth hunkered behind scattered boulders to his left, while he glimpsed two men shooting from the rocks clustered on his right—both parties about sixty yards away from him and Colter.

"Come on out here, you little bitch!" one of Moon's men shouted. "And sit on my *face*!"

The two men laughed as they each triggered another round toward Louisa and Ruth.

Louisa's cool retort was, "I've seen privy seats more attractive than your face, amigo. They probably smelled better, too! But I'll make a deal with you. You both walk out here in the open instead of cowering like a couple of yellow dogs back there in those rocks, I'll sit on *both* your faces!"

"You *will*?"

"I *promise*!"

The two Moon shooters conferred briefly and then one of them shouted angrily, "Lyin' little *bitch*!"

Prophet laughed.

On his left, Colter said, "She always talk so nasty?"

"Ever since Mexico. Don't ask."

One of the Moon shooters half stood behind his blocky covering boulder, and raised his Winchester. Louisa triggered a shot at him, blowing his hat off, and he gave a yelp and dropped down the boulder.

Prophet raised his own Winchester and started firing one shot after another, peppering the rocks and dust and cacti around the two shooters until his rifle's hammer pinged on an empty chamber.

During his fusillade, he could hear the men yelling and yelping. They hadn't expected an attack from Prophet's quarter. Now they scrambled around and took off running through the rocks and shrubs farther off to Prophet's right, deciding, the bounty hunter supposed, that they weren't about to die like their pards had died—for a dead man.

Louisa leaped to her feet and emptied her Winchester at the two retreating shooters though her bullets merely plumed dust behind them. When her rifle fell silent, she whipped her head toward Prophet and shouted, "Shoot 'em down, Lou! Shoot 'em down like the dogs they are!"

Prophet lowered the Winchester.

Colter was staring toward Louisa. "She does have some chili pepper in her, don't she?"

"My dear old pa would've said she had fire ants up her skirt."

Prophet began reloading the Winchester as he and Colter began walking down the hill. Louisa walked out from the rocks and rested her own repeater on her shoulder. "You have a soft spot for slave traders?" she asked Prophet snidely.

He walked past her to the man lying belly down in the dirt, planted a boot on the man's back, between his shoulder blades, to see if he was still breathing. He wasn't.

"We've killed enough of the dwarf's men to discourage any others, most like. Most outlaws I know aren't loyal enough to die for a dead man."

Ruth walked out from the rocks, dressed in Louisa's spare trail duds of a wool skirt, checked shirt, half boots, and a yellow neckerchief tied over her head, bandanna-style. Her brown hair dropped down from the bandanna to hang across her shoulders. She had a stricken look on her face as she regarded the dead man and shook her head.

"He was one of those that Moon sent for me. Probably one of those who hanged Frank." She'd spoken in a dull, emotionless voice, her eyes opaque. But now she lifted her gaze to Prophet, wrinkling her brows with a faint desperation. "I have to go back and cut him down and bury him, Lou."

Prophet shook his head as he plucked the spent wads from his barn blaster. "Too dangerous. We'd best hole up out here for a few days. I'll head into town soon and see what's happening at the dwarf's place, maybe fill our canteens. If I can, I'll bury your husband, Ruth."

"What?" she said. "We're just going to hole up out here like desert rats?"

"I'm not leaving," Louisa said, staring south, in the direction of Chisos Springs. "Not until I've seen about the dwarf's slave-trading operation and done what I can to bring it down."

Prophet shook his head wearily. "Leave it for the Rangers."

"You saw what happened to the two Rangers who merely wanted to fill their canteens at Moon's well, Lou!"

"Most likely, with the dwarf dead, his men will pull out soon. Hell, they can't run a business! They'll tire of the girls and probably turn them loose."

"Maybe," Louisa said. "But I'm not going to count on it." She turned and walked away.

Prophet sighed, scratched his temple with the barrels of his coach gun. "That girl's gonna be the death of me yet." He sighed again, turned to Ruth. "I do believe we might have gotten you a horse. You can ride, I take it?"

Ruth was still staring down at the dead man in that cold, bitter, emotionless way of hers. She nodded.

Prophet glanced at Colter. "You wanna fetch our horses? I'll see if I can't run down an outlaw mount for Mrs. Rose, and then we'll find us a cave to hole up in for a few days . . . if you've a mind to hang around, that is?"

Colter considered Prophet with a brow raised in surprise. "You'd want me to? Hell, I almost let that fella stick a knife between my shoulder blades!" He scowled with incredulity and kicked a stone.

"Ah, hell, I've done that! Truth is none of us has eyes in the back of his head. I'd admire if you hung around and helped me watch her back, though"—Prophet jerked his chin in the direction in which Louisa had gone—"because she's liable to get herself killed trying to free them slave girls from Moon's whorehouse, and I could use a hand backing her. She's a handful, that girl!"

The truth was, Prophet genuinely liked Colter Farrow, who reminded him a little of himself at that age, trying to make his way solo in a strange, forbidding land. The boy had obviously been alone a long time, and he could use a friend, just as Prophet could have used a friend out here at Colter's age. His only friend, however, had been Ole Scratch . . . and all the doxies he could afford.

"Well, if you need the help, Lou," the kid said, hiking a shoulder, maintaining a calm expression but with the light of pride flashing silver in his brown eyes, "it wouldn't be right for me to pull foot on you." He narrowed a suspicious eye. "You ain't just askin', though, are you, 'cause you think I got nowhere else to go?"

"Hell, kid," Prophet said, slinging his double-barreled barn blaster behind his back, "if you had a place to go, I'd have you take me there!"

Colter smiled. "All right, then." The redhead held out his hand. "Pards."

Prophet shook it. "Pards."

Colter walked away. Prophet watched him. After a time, he felt Ruth's eyes on him, and he flushed with embarrassment.

She walked over to him, rose up on the toes of her borrowed boots, and pressed her lips to his cheek. "Not hard to see how a woman could fall head over heels in love with you, Lou Prophet."

"Pshaw!"

"Oh, she has." Ruth glanced toward where Louisa had disappeared to fetch her horse. "She's been plum gone for you for quite some time." She gave a wry, almost longing smile. "You must know that, Lou."

"Sure, but that's done and over with," Prophet said, a little surprised to hear the steel in his voice when speaking of his blond partner. He'd never heard that before. What's more, he'd never felt it. But the girl's recent, unforgiveable transgression down in Mexico still raked him.

It would likely rake and nettle him for a long time to come.

Down there, south of the border, for some reason that Prophet himself couldn't quite fathom, the Vengeance Queen had crossed over to the other side. The side of the men and women she and Prophet had always fought against.

She might now have returned to Prophet's side, and she might have returned to Prophet, but he'd never be able to trust her again.

Not fully. That saddened as much as angered him.

A bounty hunter couldn't ride with someone he couldn't trust.

He tramped off to fetch Ruth a horse.

25

THE MAN HAD been crucified a long time ago.

Only a few shreds of clothes clung to his bones nailed to the makeshift cross fashioned from cedar logs and stuck in the ground facing south and the heat of the desert sun. His eyes had likely burned out before he'd died from heat stroke and thirst, possibly hunger or blood loss. His hands had been nailed to the crossbar, feet into the upright, and the nails had held him all this time—at least a year, possibly two.

He was mostly bone thinly covered in jerked skin. His long hair still dangled from his desiccated skull. A green neckerchief, badly weathered and torn, still dangled from around his neck.

"Oh, boy," Prophet said as he reined up in front of the grisly spectacle. "Now that ain't how I wanna go!"

"Play your cards right, Lou," Louisa said.

Ruth, straddling a piebald mustang, scowled up at the dead man. "He obviously didn't play his right." She looked at Prophet. "What on earth . . . ?"

"Bandito justice."

"Must be a lair around here somewhere," Colter said, looking around at the parched hills they'd been riding through. Steep ridges, as bald as anything else out here, rose all around them.

"Best keep our eyes extra peeled." Prophet looked toward a thin fringe of green off to the west. "Come on," he said, touching spurs to Mean's flanks. "I sorta like how it looks over there."

They'd been riding for over an hour since the shoot-out with Moon's men, looking for a protected place in which to camp, and Prophet had been looking around desperately for water. He knew that this neck of Texas had dried up considerably over the years and had led to the demise of the hacendado who'd once run the sprawling hacienda located around here somewhere, on these northeastern slopes of the Chisos range. But certainly a spring or two, fed by the infrequent rains, had to remain.

Ten minutes later, reining up in the thin patch of willows, he discovered that one did. The water trickled up out of a layer of shale just beneath the desert's sandy topsoil, along the bottom of what appeared an ancient riverbed that had probably carved the broad, arid valley they were in and that was hemmed in by forbiddingly steep ridges to the west and east.

All around were the dingy tan remains of tree groves and patches of dead brush, all of which had probably died during the long drought that had plagued this stretch of western Texas. About all that had remained of living plants were the sotol, pipestem, prickly pear cactus, and the occasional patch of Spanish bayonet.

The spring bubbled up so slowly from a crack in the rocks to trickle down over the natural stone shelves that it would take them over an hour to fill the seven canteens they had between them. Colter had wisely ridden out of Mexico with two, Louisa had two, and Prophet had the two he'd bought in Chisos Springs. He'd found only one on Ruth's outlaw horse.

Letting the others fill their flasks first, Prophet slipped his Winchester from its boot and walked away through the rolling, tan hills to the north. He stopped on the shoulder of a barren hill and saw down the other side, in a broad, rocky bowl, a massive adobe ruin to which dead vines clung like the sun-bleached tendrils of a giant, long-defunct octopus.

The massive, barrack-like affair with tall, arched windows and red clay tiles on its pitched roof had to be the Spanish land grant's original hacienda, built around two hundred years ago by the man to whom this stretch of the Chisos had originally been granted by a Spanish royal.

The ruins of a few outbuildings huddled around the place, as well as that of a bright, white adobe bunkhouse whose roof appeared to have fallen in. There was a covered well on the casa's far side, in the center of what appeared an old patio paved in flagstones and bearing the remnants of what had once been flowers, shrubs, possibly nut or orange trees.

As far as Prophet could tell from his vantage and with his naked eye, there was no one around. He saw no sign of men or horses.

He tramped back to where the others were sitting around the spring, told them about the hacienda, and then filled his canteens. They'd watered their horses when they'd first come upon the spring, so they now mounted and rode off through the thin green brush and over the low, brown hills. They reined up about a hundred yards from the hacienda, and Prophet took another good, long look at the villa.

"Imagine a place this size," Ruth said. "Out here on this barren desert."

"Wasn't so barren when the place was built," Prophet said. "Let's ride in. We'll hole up here if it don't look like banditos are usin' the place frequent-like for a hideout. We got enough folks to tangle with back at Chisos Springs."

He glanced at the sky, the blazing sun just beginning to slump toward the dark, western ridges. It would be damn nice to get shed of the sun for a while. He couldn't remember when he'd ever been so tired of it, save when he'd been strapped naked to Mean's back, that was.

Those adobe walls and the cool shadows they likely harbored beckoned to the sweaty, dusty bounty hunter astraddle his sweaty dun from which a hot, horsey musk emanated.

"Mean," Prophet said as he booted the horse on down the last slope, heading for the sprawling case, "I do believe you smell as bad as I do."

The horse snorted, shook his head, and twitched his ears. Sometimes Prophet thought that Mean and Ugly actually understood what he was saying in his bored way, mostly just to have the comfort of hearing his own voice. A frightening damn thought . . .

Prophet circled the casa, the others following, looking around warily and glancing frequently up at the two-story building looming over them. Their horses' hooves clomped on the old paving stones. The horses snorted and blew warily, as though they were unnerved by the place whose arched, casement windows stared out at them like giant, empty eye sockets.

The building was ringed with a five-foot adobe wall and a patio, but now all the flags were cracked or had heaved up out of the ground. Some had disintegrated altogether.

Around them were the charred remains of at least three campfires, and many piles of horse apples. The building inside the wall had sheltered men and horses over the years. Probably bandits of one stripe or another, on the run either to or from the border. None of the horse dung was new; the moisture had been seared out of it so that it had returned to more or less spare piles of ground, sun-bleached hay, and white oat specks.

No recent tracks around, either.

A hot wind rose. Dust lifted, pelting the riders and the big, seemingly empty building with sand. One of the horses whinnied indignantly.

Prophet dismounted and dropped his reins. "Ya'll wait here. I'll check it out."

He slid his shotgun around in front of his belly, held it by the neck of its rear stock, and headed through one of the several openings in the adobe wall. Ten minutes later he came back out of the place, having given it a cursory inspection, finding nothing but a ruined husk of what had once been a grand, Spanish-style casa that had probably known the tears and laughter of several generations of the original patron's family.

The place, riddled with the trash of transient men and feces of pocket mice and other animals including rabbits and coyotes, gave him the willies. He had enough of the old superstitious hillbilly in his soul, raised around southern-style hoodoo, conjure, and rootwork, to have sensed ghosts peering at him from every corner of the run-down hacienda.

He found himself almost wishing he could remember one of the old hoodoo ladies' spells to placate the spirits of the place.

"All clear," he said. "If you don't mind bats, that is. Heard 'em roostin' upstairs."

The hacienda's stable, flanking the casa near the bunkhouse, was still sound enough, so Prophet's party housed their horses in the low-slung adobe structure, rubbing them down, watering them, and giving them each a small portion of oats.

The horses were all stalwart and broad-bottomed, accustomed to extreme climates and severe situations, so they'd be able to make do with smaller rations for a short time with few ill effects. Mean might be a little meaner, Prophet thought, but maybe he'd show a little more appreciation for his next bale of green timothy.

Despite the animal scat and spiders inside the casa, they threw their gear down in front of the fireplace in the old great room, which combined the parlor area and kitchen. There was a pile of mesquite and juniper beside the hearth, obviously left by recent visitors.

While Prophet wasn't sure he could trust that the chimney was clear, it was big enough that he decided to risk laying a fire in the wagon-sized, fieldstone hearth. He was pleased to see that very little smoke issued into the room, the bulk of it curling up the chimney. He could hear some bats scurrying out, squealing, when the first tendrils of smoke hit them.

Prophet plucked a burning brand from the fire and used

it to light a quirley, then walked around outside, wanting to get a good sense of the layout here before darkness descended.

He and the others might have to defend it, after all, and a place could look a whole lot different once the sun went down. Not only did they have to worry about the dwarf's men but other banditos. And last he'd heard, there was still a band or two of Kiowa giving this stretch of western Texas occasional fits. Given the vastness of the area, there were damn few cavalrymen and Texas Rangers to go around.

As the sun sank behind western ridges, long shadows puddled in the hacienda's yard, and the intense heat lost some of its edge, Prophet and Colter headed off to find meat for supper. There wasn't much game around, though they flushed a couple of armadillos out of a thorny wash. Prophet had eaten armadillo down in Mexico, but he hadn't much cared for it, so he was glad when he and Colter each managed to bring down a jackrabbit apiece.

They'd quickly field dressed the animals and started to carry them back toward the lodge when Prophet said out of the side of his mouth, "Stop and bend down to brush something off your pants cuff, will you, Red?"

Colter glanced at him, frowning, but he'd been out in the high-and-rocky long enough to realize the bounty hunter's intention.

Colter bent forward and swatted at his left pants leg, down around his boot, as though to remove ocotillo thorns. Prophet took a step beyond Colter and then turned toward the kid, looking down to watch what the redhead was doing. But instead of watching Colter, Prophet quickly scanned the desert flanking them, picking out a shadow sliding back behind an escarpment about fifty, maybe sixty yards away.

"All right, them thorns are gone," Prophet said in an almost whimsical tone.

Colter straightened, and they continued walking toward the casa whose cracked adobe walls and red stone tiles fairly glowed in the fast-fading light, under a sky of periwinkle blue.

"What was that about, Lou?" Colter asked, keeping his voice low.

"Seen somethin'. Not sure what. Maybe one of Moon's men skulkin' around."

Colter started to turn his head.

"Keep lookin' forward, Red. I may not have a third eye in the back of my big, ugly noggin, but I got a sixth sense, and it's tellin' me our shadower hasn't moved again since I first seen him. Once we get back to the hacienda, you go in and tell the ladies to keep their eyes open. I'm gonna circle around and come at the escarpment from the other side, see who or what's out there."

"Want me to come?"

"Nah, I make enough noise, cast a large enough shadow for two men the way it is."

Strolling casually, they entered the casa by one of the rear doorways, the door itself having long since disappeared. Prophet handed his rabbit to Colter and then stole out through the same door by which they'd all entered the place.

He removed his spurs, set them atop the adobe wall, then made sure his Winchester was loaded. The shotgun swinging barrel up behind his back, he tramped off to the north of the villa, weaving through spindly shrubs, cacti, and boulders. He walked about a quarter mile east and then slowly made his way south until he was in the same general area in which he and Colter had shot their supper.

There was more shadow than light on the ground now, so he felt he was able to move with less chance of being seen. As he moved toward the escarpment behind which he'd seen the shadow slide, he scoured the terrain around him and the ground before him. As he stepped between two catclaw shrubs, he stopped and dropped to a knee.

With the index finger of his gloved right hand, he traced the indentation in the ground before him.

It was a very faint boot print.

26

THE BOOT THAT had made the print was maybe size ten with a round toe. The sand here wasn't very soft, as there was no moisture to speak of, so Prophet couldn't gather much beyond that the track was fresh. Probably not more than an hour old, if that.

With all the wind around here, a print that faint would disappear quickly.

Even more slowly and purposefully, Prophet made his way to the escarpment, coming at it from its northeastern flank. The man was gone. But two relatively clear boot prints remained. He'd been standing right where Prophet had thought, sort of shouldered up against the scarp where, looking around the north side, he could have kept an eye on Prophet and Colter.

Prophet looked all around the scarp, the hair under his collar prickling. He saw no one. The only sound was the breeze brushing the escarpment, scratching shrub branches together, and the cooing of a faraway dove.

Nothing moved.

There was no longer enough light to be able to track the hombre from the scarp. Prophet would give it another try come morning. Until then he and the others would have to keep a night watch.

Since there appeared to have been only one man out here, he was likely just some lone pilgrim scouting the hacienda to see if it was vacant. Maybe some harmless old desert rat and saddle tramp looking to throw down in the same old ruin he'd camped in before.

But Prophet hadn't come to his thirty-odd years taking foolish chances. He knew Ole Scratch was waiting for him to start shoveling coal, but he'd just as soon keep his boots planted on this side of the sod for as long as possible. He didn't much care for the smell of butane, anyway, and he'd heard that Ole Fork-tail wasn't much of a talker. . . .

He went back to the hacienda and told the others about the lone set of boot prints. Louisa's only response was to drag her gun oil out and start taking apart and cleaning her pistols and Winchester. After they'd roasted and eaten the rabbits with hot coffee, though Prophet could have done with a couple shots of tequila . . . in a cool adobe cantina, say . . . and Louisa had rewrapped Ruth's bullet-torn arm, Prophet took the first night watch.

It was good dark, and an owl was hooting. Prophet could see the flickering, black shadows of bats darting about— probably the long-nosed and ghost-faced bats native to the area. Coyotes yodeled in the distant ridges.

He walked out to a thicket of spindly mesquites and sat against a rock amongst them. He was out there about an hour, his keen senses finely tuned, watching the stars slowly pinwheel in the velvet sky, when he heard footsteps behind him.

"Name yourself," he said.

"Lola Montez."

"Ain't that a snort," Prophet said, watching Louisa approach on his right, her rifle on her shoulder.

Senorita Montez was his favorite opera house entertainer, though he knew he wasn't alone in fantasizing about the exquisite beauty from afar despite her "evil eye." It was said that the raving Spanish beauty's many lovers had dropped like flies from suicide, duels, and consumptive exhaustion. She'd even caused some mucky-muck royal across the ocean to renounce his throne.

Imagine renouncing your throne for a woman!

Louisa stood about six feet to Prophet's right, staring toward the east where stars flickered over the black wall of a steep mountain. Usually when she was silent for that long, something was on her mind.

She'd get to it when she was good and ready, though it always made him a little uneasy, wondering what in hell it was *this* time.

It was a humdinger.

"Lou, you don't love me anymore, do you?"

"Ah hell."

"I guess that's answer enough." She turned her head to stare down at him, her rifle on her shoulder, the light, fresh breeze nudging her blond hair back. "I don't blame you, Lou."

"Louisa, goddamnit, what happened to you down in Mexico?"

She sighed. They hadn't talked about this before except in a roundabout way, but now they had the calf down and the iron hot. It was probably as much of a relief for her as it was for him.

"What part of it—Sugar or . . . my turning . . . ?"

He knew she'd had a dalliance of sorts with the blind pistolero, Sugar Delphi, and that had rankled him, to be sure. He was only a human male. But what had really twisted his tail was her changing sides—riding with Sugar's bunch of killers and bank robbers whom Prophet and Louisa had chased across the Mojave desert in western Sonora and had ended up holing up with in San Gezo, to join forces against a rampaging band of Mojave Apaches.

"Your becoming one of them," Prophet said. "Don't you know I'll never be able to trust you again after you pulled a stunt like that? Hell, I should have *shot* you!"

Now she was rankled, too. She turned full around to him, balled her free hand into a tight fist at her side. "You should have *tried*!"

Before Prophet realized what he was doing, he scissored his left leg sharply, rammed it into the side of her right foot, kicking both her feet out from under her. She gave a squeal as she smacked the ground on her rump.

Her hair flew. She dropped her rifle, and her hat rolled off her shoulder.

The sudden violence shocked her. She glared at him, gritted her teeth, and then threw herself at him. He grabbed her by the front of her striped serape, pulled her across his chest, and rolled on top of her. He held both her arms down on the ground and used his body to pin the rest of her, though he could feel her muscles expanding and contracting beneath him as she struggled.

Prophet had lost his hat, and a wing of hair hung down over one eye.

He glared down at her. She glared back at him.

But then she blinked.

Prophet had no idea what he was going to do next until he'd pressed his mouth hard against hers, ground his lips against hers. She instantly stopped struggling. He released her arms, and she wrapped them around his neck, returning his kiss hungrily, groaning and wrapping her legs around him, clinging to him desperately as they kissed.

He could feel her breasts swell under the serape and her calico blouse.

He felt himself come alive.

With both hands, she pushed her face away from his. Her eyes were bright as lights in the darkness. Her chest heaved beneath him. Breathily, pleadingly, she said, "Lou!"

She was like the strongest top-shelf liquor he'd ever drunk. His blood was flooded with her, with the need to couple with her. It frightened him a little, but tempering the fear was his raging desire. He rolled off of her, lifted her poncho up over her head, and tossed it away. She immediately started unbuttoning her blouse.

Prophet rose. She sort of groaned, lifting her chin, watching him, her desire bright in her eyes.

"I'll be right back."

He picked up his Winchester, moved away from the rocks and mesquites. He stood listening, was damn glad when he heard nothing but the yodeling coyotes beneath the thudding of his heart in his ears. Returning to her, he leaned his rifle against a boulder, lifted his shotgun's lanyard up over his head, and rested the barn blaster against the boulder.

Louisa was out of her blouse. Her firm, pale breasts jostling, she kicked off her boots and then pulled off her socks, and wriggled out of her pants. Prophet was a fool for doing what he was about to do out here when he should be keeping watch, but there was no stopping either of them now.

Not when the wildfire had been smoldering for this long.

He peeled off his longhandles. Louisa leaned back on her elbows and spread her knees.

Prophet dropped to his knees before her. He could hear her breathing beneath his own fervent rasps. He leaned forward. She lifted her head to meet him, and they mashed their mouths together once again as he entered her.

Her mouth was ripe, wet, and soft.

Her breasts mashed against his chest, distended nipples raking him thrillingly. He bucked against her, and she lay back, lifting her own hips to meet his in their old, practiced love dance. They didn't make much noise, not like they wanted to, and to keep from groaning aloud Louisa pressed her mouth against his shoulder. His feeling the sharpness of her teeth added to the excitement of their love tangle.

Prophet grunted quietly, thrusting . . . thrusting. . . .

"Lou?" she said, her voice quaking with the passionate violence of their coupling.

He made an unintelligible sound, half growl, half wail.

"I'm bad medicine."

"Uh-uh." He grunted, toiling over her, Louisa thrusting her groin up hard against his.

"Yes . . ." She swallowed, tugged at his ears with her hands, glanced down between them as she rose and fell beneath him. Her hair slid back and forth across her shoulder. "I'm evil. Deep . . . inside me, there's a bad rot, and . . . it . . . came out . . . in *Mexico* . . . !"

"Shut the hell up, girl."

"You've known . . . all along . . . haven't you?"

Louisa squeezed her eyes closed, dropped her jaw in a soundless scream. She lay back in the sand, quivering, grinding her heels into his back. As Prophet spent himself, she turned her head to one side and bit down on her knuckles to keep from screaming.

He rolled off of her, sucking the cool, dry air into his lungs, catching his breath. "Louisa," he gasped, "you ain't bad medicine. Confused, yeah. After what you been through, hell. . . ."

"Lou?"

"What is it?"

She was sitting up on his left, knees bent, propped on her hands and staring straight out before them. She lifted her right hand and pointed. "Look."

Prophet looked off to the south and slightly right. A faint umber glow limned the ridgeline of a distant hill, silhouetting the hill against it. Prophet sat up straighter, staring.

"Fire."

Louisa glanced at him. "Campfire, you think? Or wildfire?"

Prophet continued to stare at the faintly pulsating umber glow and shook his head. A wildfire out here, and that close, could very well be deadly, as most wildfires were in the west where there was plenty of dry fuel to keep them burning.

"If that's a campfire, it's a damn big one," Prophet said. "And it might just belong to the hombre whose tracks I picked up earlier." He rose stiffly and brushed sand and grit off his butt and his knees. "Best check it out."

He stumbled around, wincing at the sand chewing at his tender feet, dressing. When he'd donned his hat and was tucking his shirttails into his denims, he heard footsteps coming up behind him. He turned and was about to reach for one of his weapons when he saw Colter walk around the far side of the rocks and mesquites—a slender, long-haired silhouette in the darkness.

"Lou?"

Prophet glanced at Louisa, who had sat down to pull her boots on, and felt a flush of embarrassment rise in his ears. "Yeah."

"You see that?"

Colter was looking toward the dark orange glow in the sky.

"Yeah. We're gonna check it out." Prophet buttoned his fly, ears growing even warmer with chagrin, and then looped his shotgun over his head and shoulder, sliding it behind him. "You'd best stay here, keep an eye on Ruth."

"You got it."

When Louisa had wrapped her pistols around her hips, Prophet grabbed his Winchester, and, adjusting his Colt tied low on his right thigh, he began walking south, toward the glow. Louisa came up from behind him.

"You think he saw?" she asked, keeping her voice low.

"I don't know. You think he did?"

"How would I know?"

Prophet cursed their foolishness and shook his head, lengthening his stride, picking out obstacles in his way, as he and Louisa made their way to the distant hill.

Damn stupid, them carrying on that way. Sometimes he wondered how in hell he'd kept his boots planted on the green side of the sod as long as he had, cork-headed fool that he was.

They rose up and over one low hill and then crossed a shallow wash, bats winging through the air about ten feet above their heads, making whirling sounds, like slow bullets. Only one coyote was yammering now, somewhere off to Prophet's left.

They walked another half a mile across the rocky desert, meandering around cacti, and then started climbing the steep rocky hill behind which the light appeared to be emanating. When they'd come within about sixty yards of the ridge crest, Prophet started to hear voices rising from the hill's other side.

That slowed both his and Louisa's pace some, knowing that other folks were around.

Not a wildfire, anyway. That was a good thing.

But having other folks around wasn't necessarily a good thing, either . . . depending on who they were, of course.

27

PROPHET CRAWLED TO within three feet of the ridge crest, and doffed his hat. Louisa did the same. At the same time, they crawled up just far enough that they could see down the bluff's opposite side.

In the open area near the base of the bluff, a large fire danced. It was more of a bonfire than a simple cook fire though a wrought-iron spit had been erected over it, likely to roast some large animal.

A dozen men milled around the fire, some sitting on rocks or logs, eating with plates on their knees, tin cups on the ground near their feet. The tin cups reflected the umber light from the dancing fire. The flames sent cinders high in the air where they winked out against the stars.

The light also reflected off the stripes and silver or gold bars on their dark-blue cavalry tunics, and off the stripes crawling down the legs of their light blue slacks, the cuffs of which were stuffed down into stovepipe cavalry boots.

Flat-heeled, round-toed boots, like the boot whose print Prophet had spied near the escarpment near the hacienda.

Louisa whispered very softly, "Soldiers?"

Prophet kept raking his gaze around the encampment. At

the far perimeter of the bivouac were two covered wagons. Animals milled in what appeared a rope corral to the right of the canvas-covered Skinner freight wagons.

"That's how it looks," Prophet said.

"Fortune has smiled on us, then." Louisa's face brightened as she stared down the slope toward the men milling around the fire. "They'll help us run Moon's men and the slave traders to ground!"

She started to rise, but Prophet grabbed her wrist and pulled her back down. "Hold on!" he hissed.

"What is it?"

Prophet stared into the encampment. The men were extremely animated, some appearing drunk. They were mostly older hombres—late twenties, early thirties, with beards or mustaches on their sun-seared, shrewd-eyed faces. What's more—a man with a captain's bars decorating his shoulders was laughing and joking around with several privates and a sergeant.

Prophet glanced at Louisa, jerked his chin, and then crawled backward about five feet down the hill. Louisa followed suit and said, "You don't think they're soldiers."

"The frontier cavalry is a young man's army. Some barely twenty, most younger. The man or men leadin' 'em are usually only a few years older. All those men down there are older, and there's somethin' else about 'em I don't like."

"What?"

"Hell, I don't know." Prophet's eyes widened. "Oh, yeah—soldiers on routine patrol or any other kind of patrol ain't normally allowed to drink. At least, not drink till they're drunk. That's why I just couldn't wait to get out and didn't think once about enlistin' and gettin' all reconstructed and becomin' a *galvanized Yankee*."

Louisa scowled at him. "How you do go on! Who do you think they are if not cavalry?"

"I don't know—bandits, maybe dressed up like soldiers to haul loot more free-like across the Rio Grande." Prophet picked up his rifle. "There's only one way to find out." He rose and started long-striding down the bluff. "Come on!"

Halfway down the slope, he swung to his right and walked parallel to the ridge crest, following a faint game trail. Earlier, he'd seen that the bluff was somewhat horse-shoe-shaped, with the bivouac and wagons nestled inside the horseshoe. The east end of the horseshoe was lower than where he and Louisa had surveyed the camp, and that end was farther away from the fire.

When he and Louisa came to it, they climbed to the crest of the ridge once more. He'd been right. This end of the bluff was much lower than the other end, and the fire was about a hundred yards away, on his and Louisa's right. The "soldiers'" silhouettes jostled between Prophet and the fire.

The wagons were nearer Prophet now than the soldiers. He could see the vague, canvas-topped shapes about fifty yards nearly straight out from the base of the bluff. He couldn't see the rope corral but knew it was beyond the wagons.

Prophet glanced at Louisa. "Stay here. If the soldiers or whoever them boys are see me and start actin' all impolite, as federal soldiers tend to do, cover me. I'll be hightailin' it back this way."

"All right," she said, quietly pumping a cartridge into her Winchester's breech. "But don't do anything stupid."

"Me?"

Prophet clambered up over the ridge and dropped, crouching, holding his Winchester low in both hands, down the other side. He weaved between modest-sized boulders. When he was about a hundred feet from the first of the two wagons, he dropped flat and quickly clawed his hat off his head.

Gritting his teeth, he pressed his chin to the dirt. He'd heard something. Animal-like sounds emanating from somewhere up near the wagons.

Prophet lifted his head slowly until he could see the nearest wagon. He could hear the sounds more clearly now—grunting and groaning. Guttural sighing. Savage sounds.

A wounded animal? Maybe a horse?

Possibly a wounded man?

A man chuckled. There was a sharp smack, like a sudden, violent slap. A girl sobbed. The man chuckled again. A buckle clanked.

Prophet stared straight ahead toward the wagon. The sounds were either issuing from inside or close around the wagon, possibly from the other side.

No, from *underneath* the wagon. A shadow slithered up out of the darkness between the front and rear wheels facing Prophet. A hatted man with stripes on his sleeves straightened. On the outsides of his slacks ran the same yellow stripes as those Prophet had seen before, nearer the fire. The soldier, or whoever he was, was breathing hard, as though he'd run a long ways. He turned back to the wagon and crouched down. "Come out of there now," he ordered.

A girl sobbed.

The man said more gruffly, "Come on, now, by God, or I'll whip ya!"

He reached down and pulled the girl out from beneath the wagon. From what Prophet could see from this distance and in the darkness tempered by starlight and thin javelins of firelight, she was small and dark-skinned. Long, black hair hung down past her shoulders. She wore a long skirt. Her shoulders were bare. She held something, probably a blouse, against her breasts.

Tugging brusquely on the girl's arm, the man led her back to the rear of the wagon. He grabbed her around the waist and tossed her easily through the rear pucker. Then he reached up and drew the flaps of the pucker closed and tied them shut.

He turned toward Prophet, who sucked a sharp, nervous breath. The man stared toward Prophet. Prophet ground his jaws together and squeezed the neck of his Winchester, caressing the hammer with his gloved right thumb.

The man bent his knees, adjusted his crotch, chuckled, and then swung around and started sauntering back in the direction of the fire.

Prophet rose slowly, looking around cautiously.

His heart thudded heavily.

He swallowed, took his rifle in both hands, and approached the wagon slowly, pricking his ears, listening. The wagon creaked and groaned a little as someone moved around inside. There was a faint sobbing—probably the cries of the girl who'd just been raped beneath the wagon. Another girl was cooing to her.

Prophet moved up alongside the wagon, crouching low, staying within the wagon's shadow. He looked around again carefully, and then he straightened and unhooked a strap fixing the canvas to the box. He lifted the side of the tarpaulin about three inches above the top of the box, and peered into the wagon.

It was too dark to see much, but he thought he could see six or seven cowering shadows in there in all that pent-up air smelling like sweat, urine, musty burlap, and roasted meat. The girls had probably been fed what the so-called soldiers had roasted over the fire—wild pig, judging by the smell— and the smell of the charred meat lingered in a cloying potpourri.

Prophet wanted to call out to the girls, to ease their misery, their fear, but he knew that doing so might only startle them instead. One or all might scream or call out, alerting their captors to his presence.

Chewing his lower lip, he reluctantly pulled the tarp down over the side of the box and hooked the strap once more. He wanted to try to get them all out of there now, but where would he take them? They were all on foot, and he and Louisa as well as the Indian girls would very easily be run down by the slave traders.

"Wait," he told himself softly. "Just chew the apple one bite at a time, hoss."

Cursing under his breath, Prophet made his way back in the direction of the slope atop which Louisa waited for him. He was nearly to the bluff's base when something flashed in the corner of his left eye. A bullet screamed through the air behind his head. It barked off a rock at the same time the rifle's flat crack reached Prophet's ears.

A man shouted.

The bounty hunter stopped and swung toward the man who'd fired at him but before he could raise his Winchester, Louisa's rifle flashed and thundered atop the ridge straight ahead of him. The man-shaped shadow standing about forty yards from Prophet, between him and the fire, yelped and flew back to hit the ground with a thump and a clatter of his rifle.

As more men from around the fire started shouting and running, Prophet hightailed it up the ridge, weaving around boulders, pumping his arms and knees, raking air in and out of his lungs, and cursing his smoking habit. Rifles popped to his left. Louisa's rifle barked above him. He ran hard, wincing as bullets screamed around him and thumped into the slope around his boots or spanged loudly off rocks.

Louisa was pumping and firing her Winchester handily as Prophet gained the ridge, threw himself down atop it, and rolled several feet down the other side.

"I thought I told you not to do anything stupid!"

"I didn't do nothin' stupider than I always done!"

Louisa snapped as she fired twice more. The second time her hammer pinged on an empty chamber, and she scrambled down beside Prophet, her Winchester smoking. "What happened?"

Rifles continued barking on the far side of the slope, men yelling. The horses in the rope corral were whinnying.

"I'll tell you later," Prophet said, climbing to his feet. "For now, we'd best pull our picket pins. There's far too many o' them fellas to try swapping lead with 'em!"

He ran down the slope, Louisa on his heels. He ran all the way to the bottom of the bluff and straight out away from it. When he and his blond partner had dropped into a shallow wash sheathed in stunted willows, he stopped and dropped to a knee behind the cut bank.

He stared back the way he'd come. The bluff stood dark against the starry sky. Prophet pricked his ears, listening hard to pick out sounds above the hammering of his heart, the drumming of blood in his ears. His breathing slowed.

He thought he could see several jostling shadows atop

the bluff, vaguely outlined against the shimmering stars. Faintly, he heard men conversing. There was no more shooting. None of the so-called soldiers appeared to be coming after him and Louisa.

"Well, maybe that's that," Prophet said, sucking a deep breath.

Louisa knelt beside him. "What was in those wagons, Lou?" Her eyes were as bright as the nearest stars in the darkness of the arroyo.

"Rifles." The lie had been impulsive, only half-consciously considered. But he knew he'd made the right decision. If he told Louisa that there were slave girls in those wagons, she'd no doubt walk right back up that ridge and stir up a showdown with those dozen phony soldiers. She wouldn't do one thing toward getting those girls freed but only get herself killed in the bargain.

That's how impulsive and headstrong—even, yes, *crazy*—she was. Prophet would tell her the truth later, when he'd ironed out his own plan for rescuing those Indian slave girls.

Louisa looked at him suspiciously, as though she'd been reading his mind. "Rifles?"

"That's what I said."

"Where would they be heading with rifles out here?"

"Hell, how do I know?" Prophet was nervous. He'd never been the greatest liar. His eyes always sold him out. That's why he wasn't looking at Louisa but continued to stare up the side of the black bluff. "Maybe Campa's buying 'em down in Mexico. You know Campa, don't you?"

"Heard of him. Outlaw Rurale colonel. You think he's buying those rifles?"

Prophet started to feel some relief in the taut muscles between his shoulder blades. "Most likely. He's probably got the most use for 'em, looting villages and the like down in Mexico."

"And running slave whores." Louisa stared at Prophet as though she were trying to read him. He felt her eyes boring into his right cheek.

"Yeah, he's probably using 'em to help out with his slave running. Lots of competition between bandito bands down in Mexico." Prophet rose, let his gaze slide quickly across Louisa's eyes, which were riveted on him, like the eyes of a young brush wolf about to pounce on a kangaroo rat. "Come on—let's head on back to the hacienda. I've had enough fun for . . . hey, where in the hell you *goin'*?"

She'd climbed the wash's shallow bank and was marching toward the bluff.

"Ah, bless me," Prophet complained.

He caught up to her, grabbed her arm. Louisa jerked her arm out of his grip and started running toward the bluff. Prophet chased her, threw his big body into her legs, and knocked her off her feet.

She cursed like a drunken Irish poet, twisting around and hammering his hatted head with her fists. "Damn, you let me go," she hissed through gritted teeth. "I'm going to—"

"You ain't gonna do no such thing," Prophet said, grabbing her wrists in his fists and pinning her to the ground in much the same way he'd done before they'd seen the fire glow. "You're as dazed as a goose with a nail in its head, and I ain't gonna let you kill yourself. Now, forget it, hear? We'll see to them girls later."

"Just like a man to say that. *Wait till later.* You don't know what they're going through!" Louisa's eyes were fairly glowing now with reflected starlight and the blazing fires of her passion. "If we go up there, grab the high ground, we can shoot all those men, Lou. Or near enough to make the others pull their picket pins and hightail it, leaving the wagons!"

Prophet easily kept her hands pinned to the ground on each side of her head. "Ain't gonna happen."

"You can't stop me, Lou!"

"Louisa, I do apologize."

Shock flashed across her gaze. "You wouldn't dare!"

Prophet released her left hand and smacked her across the jaw. He'd held back so as not to seriously injure the girl but only to cause bees to buzz between her ears as she drifted off into semiconsciousness.

Her eyes rolled back in her head. Her head fell back against the ground. She sighed, and her eyelids fluttered closed.

"Easy does it," Prophet said, rising, pulling the girl up over his right shoulder, so that her head and arms dangled down his back with his scattergun. He wrapped his own big arm across her taut, round rump and began walking back in the direction of the hacienda.

Colter Farrow walked out of the mesquites to meet him, and after inquiring about what had happened to Louisa, shook his head. "You and Miss Bonaventure sure have a strange relationship, Lou."

"Some might say that."

28

GROWLING AND CURSING around the cigar in his teeth, Mordecai Moon peeled the linen bandage from his hand, which he cradled like a sick pup against his spindly chest. He grimaced down at the wounded appendage.

The hand was swollen and blue. Yellow puss issued from the hole in his palm. The misery in his hand made the appendage feel like a twenty-pound exposed nerve hanging off the end of his arm. The throbbing, burning pain had blossomed all the way up his arm and into his shoulder and neck.

He hadn't felt this miserable since his last bout with syphilis. *Syphilis.* Ah . . .

The dwarf dropped down the edge of his bed and waddled over to a dresser. He reached into the second drawer down from the top and pulled out a small brown, rectangular bottle with a cream label, which read in blocky blue lettering: CALOMEL TRITURATES. 1–2 GRAIN. At the bottom the manufacturer was identified in white letters against blue: SHARP & DOHME, BALTIMORE.

The mercury-derived cure-all had been prescribed by a

physician in San Marcos, Texas, who'd assured the dwarf
that it would not only cure his infrequent bouts with syphilis
but apoplexy and sundry other grievances, including the
more common "male" complaints. Moon remembered that
the man had warned him to take only one or two pills at a
time for no longer than three days; any more than that would
cause his hair and teeth to fall out and "drive him mad as a
hatter."

The dwarf must have taken more than his fair share, for
he had lost much of his hair and several teeth, but he'd main-
tained his sanity, by God. And the pony drip had cleared up
right fast!

He shook the bottle in his knobby fist. He still had at least
ten pills rattling around in there. He pulled the cork out with
his teeth and shook two tablets onto his tongue. He washed
the pills down with whiskey from an open bottle on the
dresser, and then ambled back to the bed. He leaped up onto
the edge of it, near the washstand beside it.

He closed his eyes and growled and cursed loudly
through gritted teeth at the misery the jostling movement
kicked up in his throbbing hand.

When the pain had abated as much as he thought it
would, though it was still firing hot javelins up and down his
arm, he poured whiskey from another bottle atop the washstand over his hand that was thick as a modest-sized potato
and the color a ripe plum. He kicked the side of the bed and,
his face swollen and sunset red, eyes appearing ready to pop
out of his head, he waited for that bout of pain to subside
also.

A little pain now was better than having the hand and
maybe his entire arm turn gangrenous later.

He wiped his brow with a swatch of his old bandage
and then rewrapped the hand very tenderly, continuing to
cradle the injured limb against his chest like a kitten, and bit
off the end. He tossed the linen roll onto the washstand, and
climbed gingerly down to the floor.

He walked over to a mirror hanging low on the wall. His

forehead was purple but only slightly swollen. There was a slight hole where the bullet, after piercing his hand, had ricocheted off his stout skull.

Moon chuckled at that. He'd always said his noggin was as hard as a cinder block. Well, there was the proof, by God . . . though he had to admit that the bullet had likely been hurled by a tired-out old pistol and the gunpowder had probably been fouled. That, coupled with his hand softening the blow, had probably really been what had saved him aside from putting him into a twenty-four-hour coma.

Someone knocked on the door.

Moon said, "What?"

"It's Sheriff Rio, Mr. Moon. The wagons is just now heading into town. Looks like Luke Thursday's bunch and a whole passel of new Injun gals!"

"You don't say!"

Moon ambled over to the window and walked up the wooden ramp to the chair he kept perched just beneath the window frame. There were no panes in any of the House's upper-story windows. Both shutters were thrown back from this one.

Sucking on the cigar clamped in the right corner of his mouth and holding his bandaged left hand in the right one, he peered down into the street. Sure enough, men in dusty cavalry uniforms were just now entering town from the north, a half-dozen men riding in front of a covered wagon obscured by the dust wafting up from behind the horseback riders.

The dwarf grinned. His joy at the prospect of a whole new batch of dusky-skinned, black-haired sex slaves eased the throbbing in his bullet-torn hand. New, fresh girls— most probably virgin girls—meant new, fresh money. His customers loved the Injun gals, especially the *virginal* Injun gals.

Moon walked back down the wooden ramp to the floor, strapped his shell belt and Colt Lightning on his hip, took a couple of leisurely puffs off his cigar, blowing the smoke out through his nose, and reached up to open the door.

The Rio Bravo Kid stood just outside the door, grinning down at Moon in that unctuous way of his, showing his too-large front teeth.

"Mr. Moon," the Kid said, pinching his hat brim. His sheriff's badge was pinned to his pinto vest, and it shone brightly, as though he'd spent all night polishing it.

"Yeah, yeah—what is it?" the dwarf snapped.

"Just wanted to let you know that Luke Thursday's—"

"I heard you the first time!"

Moon did not like the Rio Bravo Kid. He also did not like that Griselda had made him head sheriff as soon as she thought that Moon had expired. He'd have reversed the switch had he not wanted to find out what the town's new sheriff and Griselda were up to.

He'd play along as best he could . . . till then.

Glaring up at the tall, blond-haired kid in the tight jeans and pinto vest, Moon barked, "Back up, Stretch. Give me some room here, huh?" He clutched his wounded append-age. "Don't want you brushin' up against my hand. You nudge my hand, even blow hot air on it, and I'll shoot you in both feet!"

The Kid shuffled backward, glowering down at the pug-nacious little man before him.

"Any word on Mrs. Rose and that big bounty hunter she's with?" Moon asked.

"N-no, sir. Just that they're still runnin' free as Apaches up in them mountains, and there's two men and two women, includin' Mrs. Rose, sir."

"You keep men after 'em, hear?" Moon burned with fury. His head and his hand throbbed. "I want them all dead and brung to me strapped over their horses. All except Mrs. Rose. I want her alive, hear?"

"You bet I hear you, sir."

"Tell the men to keep after 'em . . . and to shoot straight, fer chrissakes!"

"You got it, Mr. Moon!"

Adjusting the Colt Lightning on his hip, Moon swung around and started down the hall. A door opened on his left.

One of his Mexican slave whores stared out at him and gasped, jerking her head back, crossing herself.

Moon grinned and pinched his hat brim to the girl.

She quickly closed the door.

Moon continued down the hall, a bemused expression crinkling his eye corners. All the Mexicans in the town and Apache girls in the brothel were in awe of him. The Mexicans thought him a saint. He thought that the Apaches might regard him as demon-like, because they turned pale as Irishmen whenever they saw him. As much as an Apache girl ever swooned, they swooned when they saw Mordecai Moon—the devil risen from the dirt.

Ha!

He went downstairs to find the saloon doing a good business for only ten o'clock in the morning.

Several freighters were drinking while two more were bucking the tiger in the dark gambling layout behind the stairs. Griselda was behind the bar, checking off items on a freight order while the barman, Mort Findlay, set the bottles on the back bar shelves. Through the front windows and open front doors, Moon saw the two covered slave wagons pull up in front of his House, and his little heart quickened at the prospect of fresh meat.

The thunder of many hooves rose. Dust wafted, blazing copper in the midmorning light.

"Mr. Moon."

It was Lee Mortimer. The man was standing at the bar amongst several beefy young prospectors, one of whom was making time with a bored-looking Apache girl—why in the hell do they always have to look so bored?! Still, their smoldering savagery and customary aloofness was what attracted most men, including Moon himself.

"What is it, *Deputy*?" Moon stopped near the front door and grinned at Mortimer. While he took umbrage with Griselda's demotion of the man, Moon couldn't help rubbing Mortimer's nose in it.

"Can I have a minute?"

Moon scowled and glanced at the wagons. He supposed

he could give Mortimer a minute and let the dust settle outside. He ambled over to the bar where Mortimer stood, back to the bar, elbows resting on the bar top. "All right, but make it fast. What the hell is it?"

The deputy poked his flat-brimmed hat up off his high, broad forehead. His eyes glittered drunkenly. That was odd for Mortimer. Moon knew the old outlaw to keep a short leash on his vices, especially this early in the day. Mortimer held a half-finished beer in his fist, however, and an empty shot glass sat on the bar near his left elbow.

"It's about Wanda." Mortimer tipped the heavy beer mug back, taking a drink. His ears were red. He didn't look good at all.

"That sickly woman of yours?" the dwarf said, grimacing. "She still alive?"

Nothing that the dwarf said shocked or offended Mortimer. He'd heard it all before.

Evenly, keeping his face implacable, he said, "Still kickin'. But feelin' poorly. I think it might be that spider-infested hovel I have her in. I was wonderin' if you'd see fit to give her a room here in the House . . . seein' as how you got so many an' all. Many you don't even use."

"*Give* her a room?"

"I'd pay for it, of course."

"Now, you asked me that before, Mortimer. Don't you remember what I said?"

Mortimer's ears turned redder. "You said no, but—"

"But nothin'. Ain't nothin' worse than to have a whinin' sick woman around a bordello. And consumptives are worst of all! They look bad. They smell bad. They cough and spit blood all over the place. No, sir—you keep her the hell away from Moon's House of a Thousand Delights!"

"She's not that bad, Moon. She's getting better."

The dwarf blazed his eyes at the ex-sheriff.

"I meant . . . Mr. Moon," Mortimer corrected, glancing down into his beer glass. Moon thought the man might have hardened his jaws in anger. "She could run a faro table for you. She's good at that. She did that once up in—"

"No."

Mortimer flared his nostrils. "Look, she's on the mend. All she needs is—"

"I said *no!*" Moon was about to cloud up and rain all over Mortimer when he glimpsed Griselda in the periphery of his vision. The girl was looking over the bar at someone behind Moon. He glanced over his shoulder to see the Rio Bravo Kid standing about six feet behind him.

The Kid had been gazing at Griselda, a smirk on his clean-shaven mug. Now he looked at Moon, and his face turned as red as Mortimer's ears. Griselda's own cheeks were mottled red and white. She parted her lips slightly as though she were about to say something but thought better of it.

A wave of raw fury swept through Moon. He felt the flames licking at the backsides of his eyeballs. He balled his fists at his sides and drew a deep breath. He released it slowly, reining in his rage. He wouldn't find out anything about what Griselda had going with the Rio Bravo Kid if he blew his top.

He could not resist doing one thing, however.

Moon walked up to the Kid and plucked the badge from the Kid's pinto vest. "There's just somethin' about you, boy, that wouldn't make a full-fledged lawman if you lived to a hundred and twenty. I owe it to the good citizens of my town to have a capable man in that office."

He swung around and tossed the badge to Mortimer, who snapped it out of the air.

"That's one thing I will do for you, Sheriff. There— you're reinstated. Maybe you can do somethin' about bringin' that Mrs. Rose to me. I'd feel much better about you if you done that, Sheriff. Now, don't go draggin' your tail around here like a whipped dog. You got your old job back. That's as good as it gets around here. You keep that sick saloon girl of yours out of my sight!"

Moon didn't look at Griselda. If he did, she'd likely see by his expression, if she hadn't already guessed, that he was suspicious of her and the Rio Bravo Kid. Moon wanted to keep her and the Kid guessing but not knowing for sure what he himself was up to.

He had a feeling he knew what their ploy was, of course. And the mere thought of what she might have going on the side made his heart ache nearly as bad as his hand, and his belly burn with fury.

Damnit, he loved the girl! And he'd thought she loved him!

Had she really grieved him for the short duration of his death?

He was near the open doors when three men climbed the gallery steps, the sun causing the wafting dust behind them to dance like the fires of hell. All three men were caked in so much dirt that their navy blue cavalry tunics resembled the dove gray of the old Confederacy. Their beards, brows, and eyelashes were coated in it, too.

"Mr. Moon!" said the leader of the slave traders, Luke Thursday, stopping on the gallery and swiping his hat against his trousers, causing even more dust to billow. "Got some fresh . . . say, what the hell happened to you, there, sir? Why, you look like you wrestled with about five Apache warriors in a two-hole privy with the door locked!"

"Just prone to accidents, I reckon," Moon grumbled, stepping out onto the gallery. "Come on and show me what you brung me. Any fat ones? A few o' my freighters been askin' fer some Apache girls with a little tallow on their bones. You know—somethin' they can hold on to!"

"Come on out, and I'll show you!" Thursday said.

He was big and dark with a full, dark brown beard and cobalt blue eyes. He wore a captain's bars on his shoulders and considered himself the captain of the slave train, as did the other curly wolves in his outfit, the dwarf reckoned.

They were a mean and ornery lot from all over, and their specialty was hunting women for the Mexican slave trade, which now, with Moon coming to the Great Bend country, started at Moon's Well and drifted down into Mexico when Moon was ready to send his culls across the Rio Grande.

Thursday had been in the business for a long time, and

he knew his trade very well indeed. He took only the most comely of the Apache and Mexican girls he hunted throughout the southwest, rumbling along with his caravan of phony soldiers and a Gatling gun that Moon knew one of the wagons was armed with . . . in case anyone decided to interfere in his business.

He had several Indian agents in his employ, however, so his operation usually proceeded with few hitches.

"Right this way, sir!" Thursday said as he dropped down the steps ahead of Moon and sauntered to the rear of the first wagon parked in front of the House.

The other slave traders had dismounted and were leading their horses over to the well to draw the water that was part of Moon's and Thursday's business agreement. Free water for the best whores in the country, for which Moon would pay fifty dollars a head.

While Thursday's two lieutenants, whose names Moon had had no interest in remembering, walked up behind the dwarf, so did several of Moon's own gang members who'd been loafing on the gallery. Those who'd survived the hunt for the bitch who'd shot Moon, that was.

Thursday untied the rear pucker and opened the flaps. He then dropped to one knee and indicated the other one with his gloved hand.

"May I, Mr. Moon?"

Moon took the man's hand and allowed himself to be helped up to a standing position on Thursday's knee. Wrapping his good hand over the top of the wagon's tailgate, he stared into the back of the wagon, at the eight cherry-skinned, dark-headed girls crouched there with their hands and feet tied, heads bowed as if in prayer. Long, black hair hung down over their faces.

The wagon box was hot. It reeked of sweat and the burning hay odor of hot burlap.

"Well, I can't see much, but they all look young, as we agreed. And that one back there looks plump enough. Any idea what she weighs?"

"I didn't weigh her, Mr. Moon," said Thursday. "But I'd bet Henry rifles to slingshots she come in at a good one-seventy."

"Ha!" Moon laughed. "You like your beans and tortillas, eh, senorita?"

He looked at Thursday. "Any Mescins? Some of my customers won't lay with an Apache. They think they're all witches. Don't mind Mescins, though."

"Ah, hell, who can tell," Thursday said. "Where I go they're all so inbred you can't tell an Apache from a Mex or vicey-versy."

The dwarf chuckled as he stared in at the girls. "Ain't that the truth. Pretty much the same as you got here in the other wagon?" He glanced at the wagon flanking the first one, behind the sweat-lathered, four-mule hitch.

"Same back there, Mr. Moon. Prime young whore flesh. Eight of 'em. Sixteen total."

"Well, they don't look like much now, but Griselda'll get 'em cleaned up, decked out, and presentable right quick." Moon glanced at his skinny, brown-haired lover standing on the gallery steps, looking vaguely sheepish. The Rio Bravo Kid was nowhere in sight.

Moon grinned, showing all his crooked teeth and flashing his eyes. "Won't you, my sweet pickle?"

"You bet, Mordecai!" Griselda smiled as though relieved by the dwarf's apparent warm feelings toward her and leaped down off the side of the steps. As she strode toward the wagon, Thursday's men lowered the tailgate and began jerking the slave girls out.

Thursday tapped Moon's shoulder, and they walked off together. "You got your herd culled, Mr. Moon?"

"Not yet, but I'll get you as many as you got here first thing tomorrow, and you'll be on your way to Mexico."

"All right. I best be pullin' out soon." Thursday stared back in the direction from which he'd come, an owly look in his cobalt blues above his thick, tangled, dust-caked beard.

"You can't stay awhile?" Moon was miffed. He usually

counted on Thursday's slave traders staying for a mid-trip blowout. That always brought moon an extra two, three hundred dollars in whiskey and beer sales alone.

"Best push on," Thursday said. "Colonel Campa'll be waitin' on me in San Simon. Besides, the boys got careless. We had an intruder in camp last night. Doubt it was anything to be concerned about—prob'ly just some old desert rat skulkin' around—but I haven't stayed in business this long lettin' grass grow under my feet."

"Intruder, eh?" Moon frowned, looking off cautiously.

The bounty hunter and Mrs. Rose, perhaps? Likely, not. What would their little gang want with slave traders?

Thursday chuckled as he scrubbed dust and sweat from his beard with one hand. "Mr. Moon, I sure could use a drink!"

"Well, you come to the right place, Luke. You come to the right place. Intruder, huh? Yeah, well, I had a little problem like that my own self. It'll all get cleared up soon, though. I'm right confident of that. Hell, I got a small army in my employ!"

The dwarf ambled toward the gallery steps behind Thursday, cradling his tender hand and glancing around shrewdly, hopefully.

29

"SENOR MORTIMER—COME quickly, *por favor*! It is Wanda!"

Mortimer swung around from his table in Moon's raucous saloon, where the customers were getting to know the new cavvy of Indian whores. There was still a general excitement in the air, mainly from Moon's own men and the local Mexicans, about Moon's having risen like Lazarus of Bethany from the dead.

Mortimer dropped an instinctive hand to the walnut grips of his right-side Colt but left the gun in its holster when he saw his neighbor, Bienvenida, stumbling toward him through the crowd, breathless, her big bosoms bouncing beneath her gaudily stitched sackcloth dress. She wore a thin cape, also made of hemp, around her head and shoulders.

"It is Wanda, Senor Mortimer," the woman said, grabbing Mortimer's arm and tugging. "*Por favor*—you must come quickly. She is not feeling well and she has a *gun*!"

"A gun?" Mortimer rose a little unsteadily, for he'd been drinking all day, after the dwarf had bestowed his reinstatement on him, though ostensibly he was here to keep a cork on the slave traders and other transient customers, so they didn't get drunk and raze the place in their frenzy over the new girls. "What the hell is she doing with a gun?"

"Vamos!"

Mortimer doffed his hat and followed Bienvenida back through the crowd and billowing tobacco smoke to the front door and out onto the gallery. The big woman fairly dragged him down the gallery steps through the crowd of burly men milling with a couple of loud, professional whores from Fort Worth.

"Got you an old Mex tonight—eh, Sheriff?" said one of the dwarf's men, laughing. "What—you get tired o' the gringa you rode into Moon's Well with?"

Mortimer would have taken the time to belt the man if Bienvenida hadn't been jerking him by his wrist up the street in the direction of his office, and if the words *Wanda* and *gun* hadn't been careening through his head in large red letters.

"What's this about a gun?" Mortimer asked the woman, striding ahead of her now.

"A *gun!*" Bienvenida trilled. "A *gun*, Senor Mortimer!"

The sheriff swung into the break between the adobe hovel that housed his office and the brick-and-wood barbershop. Despite the darkness, he broke into a jog down the break and then across the wash flanking the jailhouse. He saw his and Wanda's shack just ahead and on his right, on the other side of a narrow wash and sheathed in cacti and spindly mesquites.

It looked like a stone ruin, which it had been before they had moved in.

Dim yellow lamplight emanated from both front windows, one on either side of the open front door.

"Wanda!" Mortimer called, his heart thumping.

This anxiety was new and strange to him. Downright off-putting. He wasn't normally a man who allowed himself to get his blood up, but the thought of what Wanda might do with that gun caused his old venom to jet like acid through his veins, and his mouth to dry up like the very desert he and the ex–saloon girl wanted so much to escape.

He burst through the back door and into the casa. "Wanda!"

Her bed was empty, the covers thrown back. A lamp flickered on a shelf above the cold monkey stove in the wall opposite the door. The back door stood open.

As Mortimer heard Bienvenida's quick, heavy footsteps behind him and the old Mexican woman's rasping breaths, he ran across the casa and out the back door. He ran into the desert south of the house, looking around wildly, trying in vain to prepare himself for the crack of a pistol.

He passed several ruined shacks—hunching, pale shapes in the near darkness sprinkled with starlight—and the cemetery-like ruins of ancient gardens. He ran across another wash and between two dead sotol cacti and stopped suddenly.

A figured crouched before him, facing the darkness of a deep arroyo carved long ago by some long-defunct stream. A pale, slender figure in the darkness.

Red hair fell nearly to the small of Wanda's back. She wore the pale night wrap Mortimer had given her before they'd left Kansas. She sat on her knees, rump resting against her heels. She also wore the delicate silk slippers that Mortimer had given her during that time when they'd first fallen in love and which seemed so long ago in a way, but also only yesterday.

The slippers looked especially pale and thin in the darkness, sheathing her small feet, snugged down beneath her rump, toes curled against the dark ground.

Mortimer stopped. She knelt there so motionlessly that he wondered with a tightness in his lungs if she'd already done it and he just hadn't heard the shot.

"Wanda."

A gasp. Wanda whipped her head to one side and glanced at him over her shoulder. "Oh, Lee! No!" She set a hand down on the ground and rose heavily, weakly. "I didn't want you to come!"

In her other hand was an old .30-caliber Warner rimfire pocket pistol with a long, curved handle that a saloon owner had given her, because she'd been beautiful and had needed to protect herself against men who wanted to take her upstairs. But she'd never done that. At least, she'd said she hadn't. It didn't much matter to Mortimer either way.

"I didn't want Bienvenida to fetch you. She promised she wouldn't!"

"She did." Mortimer walked slowly forward. "What're you doing out here with that peashooter, anyway? Give it to me."

Wanda took one step back toward the ravine behind her, holding the little pistol against her side, the barrel angled over her heart. "Stop, Lee!"

Mortimer stopped.

"Please go back to the house, Lee," Wanda said, sobbing now, her shoulders jerking, her wavy hair in her eyes. "It's better this way. You'll be free now. And so will I. It's the only way we can both ever be free of this wretched hell-hole!"

She was drunk. Even in his own half-inebriated state, he could smell it on her, mixed with the sick, coppery smell of her.

"Oh, Wanda, you didn't," he said, making a face. "You know the forty-rod's no good for you."

"I haven't felt this good in a long time." She laughed drunkenly at that. The tears rolling down her cheeks were touched with silvery starlight. "Go away, Lee. Ride on out of here. Head to Mexico. Right now. Tonight!"

"That's not gonna happen, sweetheart."

"You have to, Lee. On your own. I can't travel. I'm too weak. This is the only way."

She lowered her chin and sobbed. The gun dropped from her chest to hang down by her side in her pale hand. Mortimer started walking toward her again.

"No, Lee!" she warned, raising the gun to her chest once more. Her voice was brittle. "It has to be this way, don't you see? We were such fools, you and I. Who did we think we were kidding?"

"What're you talking about?"

"Us . . . hitchin' our stars together. Why, you're nothing but an old killer, Lee. I'm sorry, but you know it's true. You're an outlaw. Why, you're little better than Mordecai Moon. In some ways, you know, Lee, he's even better than you because he's not pretending he's anything other than what he is. A mangy old killer. Thinks about one thing. Money. Well, two things—money and power."

Wanda laughed caustically, and Mortimer knew he wasn't really hearing the girl he'd tumbled for anymore, but some weird, corrupted version of her welling up from beneath the whiskey and illness. "Actually, three things— money, power, and a good tumble in the old mattress sack!"

She laughed at that, but it more resembled a screech. It wasn't genuine. It was sad and desperate. She was merely trying to repulse him, to get him to leave.

And it was breaking his heart. Because that's how much she loved him.

"And I'm just as phony as you are, Lee. You know how I said I merely dealt cards and slung drinks? Never went up- stairs? Hogwash. I just said that because I was too old to do it anymore when I met you, and when I saw you, I saw a man who might be able to get me out of that saloon I was work- ing in. And I was right. But you were a fool to believe me, Lee. A fool!

"I'm as much of a whore as any of those girls working against their will over at Moon's place—only I fucked my jakes *willingly*. And I was damn good at it, too. I was some of the best pussy around. And when I could get away with it, I kept the largest percentage. The men who owned my ass got the short end of the stick!"

She laughed that choking laugh once more and brushed tears from her cheek with the back of her free hand.

Mortimer just stared at her. He felt as though a black- smith's tongs had a pinching grip on his heart.

"That's who we are, Lee. And if we were really any more than that, we wouldn't have stopped here in Moon's Well. And you wouldn't have taken a job with that disgusting little demon."

"We had to stop here, Wanda. You couldn't ride any farther."

"No, but you can, Lee. Prove to me you're more than who you say you are . . . or *think* you are . . . and ride the hell out of here. Start that new life we've dreamed about for so long in Mexico!"

Mortimer shook his head. "Not without you, Wanda."

"You're a stupid man, Lee. A sucker for a lying, cheating old whore! Why, I don't even love you. In fact, when we got to Mexico I intended to steal whatever money you had and drift to some jake who could turn a coin!" She laughed again, her torso wobbling drunkenly on her hips. "What do you think of that, Lee Mortimer?"

"Not without you, Wanda."

"Sucker!" she shouted as loudly as her brittle voice would allow.

Mortimer continued forward, shaking his head, holding his right hand out, palm up. "Not without you . . ."

Suddenly, all the weirdly screwed-up muscles in her face slackened, and her mouth corners fell. She regarded him through the slack wings of her hair falling down both sides of her gaunt, ghostly pale face. "You're going to have to, Lee."

She rammed the pistol against her chest over her heart. Mortimer leaped forward, closing his right hand over the top of the gun. He winced as the hammer chewed into the web-like skin between his thumb and index finger.

"No!" she screamed as he pulled the revolver out of her hand.

He wrapped his arms around her. As she leaned against him and sobbed into his shoulder, he looked down her hair-draped back at the pistol in his hand, the hammer still biting into his skin, which was all that had kept it from igniting the cartridge.

"Why, Lee?" she bawled as he held her more tightly than he'd ever held anyone before. "Why in the world did this have to happen to us?"

"Just doomed, I reckon, Wanda," Mortimer said, rocking her gently. "Just doomed."

30

THE NUDE BODY of Frank Rose hung where Ruth and Louisa had told Prophet it would, at the rear of the lobby—a long, pale shape in the darkness over the main floor. Prophet looked up at it, the poor man's feet dangling in front of the bounty hunter's face.

He could hear the raucous revelry issuing from the dwarf's House of a Thousand Delights. Vaguely he wondered what the celebration was about. Likely, the dwarf's demise. The folks here in Chisos Springs finally had their freedom, not to mention their water, back.

He reckoned that Moon's rudderless gang would move on once they drank up all the liquor in the saloon and finished abusing the whores. Would they release the girls then, too?

"Well, let's get this over with," Prophet said, glancing at Colter Farrow, who'd entered the rear of the hotel behind Prophet. Colter swerved around the dangling feet, glanced up at the dead man.

"Why'd Moon kill this man, Lou?"

"'Cause I reckon he's the demon I'll be shovelin' coal for."

Colter swung around the newel post and headed up the

stairs, unsheathing the bowie knife from the scabbard on his left hip.

"Let that be a lesson to you, Red."

"What's that?" Colter reached the top of the stairs and turned to where the rope trailing up from Frank Rose's neck was tied around the balcony rail.

"Always get to know your demons *before* you make pacts with 'em."

"Would that help, do you think?"

"All I can tell you, Colter, is I woulda thought twice about makin' that deal to shovel coal in hell if I knew that little son of a bitch would be the one crackin' the blacksnake at my naked ass. Never knew so much bad could be wrapped up in such a small package."

Prophet winced against the stench emanating from the putrefying dead man. Poor Frank had been hanging here two or three days in the pent-up heat, and he was beginning to bloat and grow more than a little whiffy on the lee side.

Colter said, "Ready?"

Prophet raised his arms up along the sides of Frank's bare legs. "Go ahead."

Colter sawed through the rope drawn taut against the railing. Frank's body dropped. Prophet wrapped his arms around the cadaver's thighs and, holding his breath, worms of revulsion crawling up and down his back at the cool, rubbery texture of the dead flesh, eased the man to the floor.

Colter came down the steps with a blanket from one of the beds, and they wrapped the body up in it. Prophet picked it up by the head and shoulders while Colter picked up the feet, and they carried it out the hotel's back door to where Louisa and Ruth waited out by a shed.

"All right, we got him, Ruth," Prophet said.

Ruth walked up to the blanket-wrapped body. She stared down at it in the darkness from beneath the bandanna wrapped over her head and tied behind her neck. She placed a hand on the inert shape.

"Let's bury my poor husband," she said. "As best we can—all right, Lou?"

"You bet, Ruth."

She went over and grabbed one of the shovels that was leaning against the outside of the shed and which she and Louisa had retrieved when Prophet had gone into the hotel to cut the body down. Louisa grabbed the second one.

Prophet and Colter, carrying Frank, followed Ruth off behind the hotel. Louisa followed the group with the second shovel. Prophet continued to hear the whoops, yells, sporadic gunfire, and the calamitous music of the Mexican band emanating from Moon's House a block away. It was like hearing the celebration aboard a riverboat from shore.

The din offered a bizarrely disparate backdrop to the grim task of digging the grave and setting the blanket-wrapped body inside it. Prophet asked Ruth if she wanted to say a few words, and she said only, "I killed the bastard, Frank. Rest in peace."

Prophet and Colter covered the body and set rocks on the mound. Ruth said she'd fashion a cross over him later, and they returned the shovels to the shed and filled their canteens, at her water barrel, which sat against the rear of the Rose Hotel and Saloon.

That task finished, the four of them stood around the barrel in the darkness, lights from Moon's place glowing in the sky to the north and west. Someone was shooting regularly, as though taking target practice. It took the shooter several shots before a bottle shattered.

Whoops rose.

Louisa was still piss-burned at Prophet for the punch he'd laid on her the night before, though something told him she realized that the blow had likely saved her life. Maybe all of their lives.

"What now, Lou?" she said, corking the second of her two canteens. "Since you know so damn much, how are we going to get those slave girls out of there without going in shooting?"

"Don't get your drawers in a bunch," Prophet said. "I'll figure it out." He paused. "With your help, of course."

Prophet considered himself a fool in many ways, but he

knew how to strum Louisa's fiddle. She looked at him, arching a skeptical brow.

Handing his canteens to her, Prophet said, "I'm gonna need you and Colter to get Ruth out of here. Wait up by the dead tree and that big rock just north of the dwarf's place that we passed when we rode in earlier."

"That's the help you need," Louisa said, sarcasm rising in her voice. "That's it. Give me time to reconnoiter the dwarf's outfit, see how many men and how many girls he's got on the premises and when and if they're plannin' on pullin' out. I also wanna try to figure out if we have a shot in hell—aside from going in shooting, that is—to bring 'em all down and get the slave girls out."

"Doesn't sound like much help to me, Lou." This from Colter, who stood beside Ruth, his eyes serious beneath his hat brim. "Sounds like you're throwin' yourself into the bobcat den all by your lonesome."

"You three have been in there recently. Several of Moon's men saw me for a short time several days ago, includin' the little forktailed son of a bitch himself. Most of those men, including Moon, are now snugglin' with rattlesnakes." Prophet rubbed his unshaven jaws. "Besides, my beard has grown considerably since then. If I can get my hands on a Mex serape and a sombrero—I might just be able to get in there long enough for a drink or two and a stroll around the place before I'm recognized."

"That's crazy, Lou," Louisa said, wistfully fatalistic. "And it's just like somethin' you'd come up with."

"Why, thank you, Miss Bonnyventure."

Colter stepped forward. "Look, Lou . . ."

"Forget it, Colter." Louisa stuck her hand out in front of the lad, pressed the back of her hand to Colter's chest. "I can already see he's got his mind made up. The big lummox is even more stubborn than I am. If that's what he says he's gonna do, then he's gonna do it and an entire herd of stampeding Texas cattle won't sway him."

Ruth stared at Prophet, a look of disbelief on her face. "No, Lou. They'll kill you."

Prophet grinned. "I'm not as crazy as I look. First sign of trouble, I'm an Oklahoma cyclone headin' for the Front Range of the Rocky Mountains." He winked at Ruth, felt Louisa shuttle her dubious eyes between them. "I just wanna take a quick gander, see how many guns we're dealin' with."

"This is a job for the Rangers, for U.S. marshals," Ruth said, moving up to stand within a foot of the tall bounty hunter, staring up at him, placing her hands on his chest. "Please, Lou, let's ride to the nearest Ranger outpost, and—"

"By the time the Rangers got here, Moon's men might be gone," Louisa said, her tone crisp. "The girls might be sold in Mexico, never to be seen or heard from again."

Prophet placed his hands on Ruth's arms, gave her a gentle, reassuring squeeze. "You three go on now. Take my ugly horse. Ride up to where I told you, and wait there for me. Give me an hour."

Ruth sighed. "He is a stubborn one, isn't he?"

She and Colter walked off in the direction in which they'd left the horses, in an arroyo just beyond the town's southern perimeter. Louisa remained with Prophet, but she was watching Colter and Ruth walk away.

"If you get yourself killed, Lou," she said wryly, "you're gonna make Mrs. Rose very unhappy." She glanced at him, her expression hard to figure. "Good luck."

"Give me an hour," Prophet said as she walked away, the four canteens hanging from her shoulders. "After that, ride out and keep on ridin'. Don't come back here."

Louisa did not look back at him but only threw her arms up in frustration and kept walking.

When she and the others had disappeared in the darkness, Prophet retrieved his rifle and shotgun, which he'd put in the shed before he'd gone in to cut Ruth's husband down. Now he checked to make sure each was fully loaded and then walked up through an alley beside the now-defunct Rose Hotel and Saloon to the main street.

He doffed his hat and edged a look around the front of the next building to the north, toward the dwarf's place.

Business was hopping. Every window in the place was lit up like a Mexican Christmas shrine, and silhouettes of revelers danced in the street. Several bull or mule trains must have rolled in, and the men from the train, as well as the slavers, were overnighting at the dwarf's place despite the fact that the dwarf was no longer hosting them himself.

His death hadn't seemed to hurt his business much.

Beyond the well fronting the dwarf's House there were a good dozen or so figures. They appeared to be holding candles as they knelt in the street kitty-corner to the giant building.

Prophet scowled. What the hell—were some of the folks who lived around here so devoted to the dwarf that they knelt in prayer for the man's wretched soul? How could that be? Why, the little man had whipsawed them all between his water contracts and taxes! A sane man would be celebrating the little bastard's demise!

Let him burn in hell!

Prophet scanned the dwarf's bordello and gambling den once more. There were only a few men on the broad, roofed gallery fronting the place. No one on the street besides those kneeling with candles beyond the well. The wagons sat with their tongues drooping, their teams of oxen or mules in the corral out back.

Prophet walked up onto the boardwalk running along the street opposite from the House and began strolling slowly, keeping to the buildings on his right so he wouldn't be so easily seen. He tried not to appear overly suspicious if he *was* seen, but he wanted to peruse the environs here as furtively as possible.

He needed to find a man alone out here somewhere. Someone whose clothes he could "borrow" for a closer reconnaissance of the House.

He dropped down off one boardwalk and crossed to the one fronting the next building beyond, and kept walking until he was opposite the well, leaning back in the shadows against a dilapidated adobe and looking past the well at the dwarf's gambling parlor.

A couple of men in blue uniforms were milling on the gallery now in addition to the three from before. They were facing each other and moving their lips, conversing, though Prophet couldn't hear much of anything against the music and ribald laughter and the roar of conversation issuing from the saloon. The slave traders were wearing light blue shirts and suspenders, sleeves rolled up to their elbows. They were all well armed with pistols and knives.

Obviously, they'd sold their cargo to the dwarf's men. Most likely they'd be pulling out again soon, and, if Ruth had been right about the dwarf's depraved operations, they'd be shipping out with the same number of slave girls they'd shipped in.

The dwarf's herd would then be culled, his stock refreshed. . . .

Prophet gave a dry chuckle. He'd been around the frontier a long time, but he'd never heard of anything so baldly depraved.

He waited in the shadows. Several of the men on the gallery headed on inside the House, likely to partake of the fresh slave whores. There was no one around from whom Prophet could "borrow" a hat and a serape.

Frustrated but determined to get inside the House to get the lay of the land, he leaned his rifle and shotgun against the side of the dilapidated adobe. He had to leave the big poppers here. Entering the dwarf's House so heavily armed would attract attention, and most likely suspicion.

The .45 and his bowie knife would have to do him.

He just had to hope the beard was enough of a disguise. The person he thought most likely to recognize him amongst Moon's gang was his nasty little woman—Griselda. If Prophet could avoid her, he he'd have a good chance of appraising the place without getting shot so full of lead he'd rattle when he walked

He stepped out away from the adobe and stopped. A man

was dropping down the gallery's broad steps. Prophet could see only the man's silhouette, hear the trill of his spurs. The man stepped into the street and then Prophet watched his murky shadow moving toward him, the crown of his dark hat jostling against the brightly lit bordello behind him.

31

PROPHET'S SHOULDER MUSCLES tightened as the dark-clad figure kept moving toward him. He had to make a quick decision here, because he was about to be spotted if he hadn't been already.

Letting his instincts lead him, he continued toward the well, staggering a little as though mildly drunk, as though he'd been sleeping off a bottle or two outside the adobe across from the well.

He dragged his boot toes over to the well, and leaned his elbows on the stone coping, bowing his head and drawing his hat brim down over his eyes.

"Rough night, killer?" The man approaching chuckled.

Prophet sighed raspily.

"If you can't hold your skullpop, my friend, you really oughta stay home with Mother. Hold her yarn for her while she knits you a sweater."

The man began turning the winch handle, lowering the bucket into the well. Prophet looked across the well, beneath the roof, at him.

He was about Prophet's size—big, rawboned, and bearded, and he wore a cavalry shirt and suspenders. His teardrop-shaped hat was trimmed with gold acorn bands and a crossed-sabers army hatpin. Its wearer looked very much the size and shape of the man Prophet had watched crawl out from beneath the slave wagon the night before.

The bounty hunter's heart quickened slightly. Keeping his hands pressed to both sides of his face as he watched the man crank the bucket up out of the well, he said, "Any chance you'd help a fellow out with some water, there, friend?"

"Gotta pay."

"Huh?"

The slaver chuckled, said jeeringly, "Gotta pay the dwarf's box. You know how he is about folks not payin'."

"Oh," Prophet said, the old rage flickering like still-hot debris from a recent wildfire. "Sure, sure. Yeah, gotta pay the box." He chuckled.

He started walking around the well toward the slaver who was just now pulling the filled water bucket over the coping. He hesitated. Had the slaver said *is* when he'd referred to the dwarf, as though the demon were still alive?

Ah, hell, Prophet thought, continuing around the well. People talk like that all the time. Doesn't mean a thing. Ruth said she shot the black-toothed serpent through his little, mean head. That would have snuffed his candle, all right.

The slaver had set the bucket on the side of the well and he was drinking from the rusty tin dipper. "Mmmm, sure is good," he said, lowering the dipper into the bucket once more. "Damn!" He chuckled, glanced at Prophet, and closed his shaggy mouth over the edge of the dipper, taking another long drink.

"Nothin' like a good, cold drink o' water in the desert, is there? Nope. Nothin' like it." The bearded slaver drank another half a dipperful and glanced at Prophet.

"You pay the box?"

"Did *you* pay the box?"

The man grinned, showing white teeth inside the shaggy, dark brown beard. "Me and Moon got an agreement. Business partners, don't ya know." He tossed his chin at the box on the post behind him. "Pay the box."

While the man had another long drink, snorting it up loudly, really making it sound good, Prophet went over and dropped a coin in the box.

"Okay, there's the coin," he said. "Mind if I have a go?"

"Sure." The man dropped the dipper in the bucket. "Have at it."

He slid his hand behind the bucket and knocked it over the outside of the well coping. It hit the ground with a thud and a splash. Water oozed out around Prophet's boots.

"Now, look what you did, you damn fool!" the man snarled. "A cork head like you don't deserve a drink of water."

He grinned jeeringly.

Suddenly the grin was gone, and he lunged forward, and buried his right fist in Prophet's gut.

The bounty hunter hadn't expected that. He doubled over as the air left his lungs in one long grunt. Memories of the ass kicking he'd taken here were fresh in his mind, not to mention his ribs, which barked and squirmed like small, angry dogs in his chest.

"Why, you son of a bitch!" Prophet said, straightening, sucking air into his lungs, groaning at the miserable ache in his belly and chest.

The man laughed as he stood before Prophet, balling his fists at his sides.

"What'd you do that for?" Prophet wheezed.

The man only laughed louder, more jeeringly. The bully was having a real good time. He'd probably been looking all night for someone he could kick around.

His smile faded sharply, however, a half second before Prophet head-butted him with a solid, resounding smack.

The man grunted and staggered backward, rage flashing in his eyes as he raised a hand to his forehead. Prophet stepped into him quickly, brought a haymaker up from his knees, and laid it resolutely against the left side of the man's face—a hammering, crushing blow.

As the man's head jerked to his right, Prophet welcomed it with his knuckle-out left fist. Another skull-splintering blow. Prophet felt the sharp pinch of a back tooth through the man's bearded cheek.

The man stumbled backward and fell like a windmill in a Kansas cyclone. Blood from his cut cheek oozed out his mouth and down his furry chin.

Prophet glanced at the dwarf's House. Thank God none of the slaver's friends—no one at all, really—was out on the gallery. Prophet glanced behind him. The Mexicans holding their prayer vigil were still muttering and holding their candles, all faces turned warily toward Prophet. He grinned, placed two fingers to his lips, and pinched his hat brim to the small crowd.

Then he crouched over the shaggy-bearded man, who lay sprawled on his back, dead out, bleeding into the dirt, and grabbed the man's arms. He dragged him around the well and into the darkness just left of the dilapidated adobe.

About halfway down the adobe, near where his rifle and barn blaster leaned, and well concealed in the muddy darkness, Prophet quickly removed his buckskin shirt and replaced it with the bearded man's shirt and yellow neckerchief. He replaced his hat with the bearded man's blue kepi, tipping it straight forward over his eyes, cavalry style.

He wouldn't bother with the pants. Hell, everyone inside would be too drunk to notice his denims.

He turned to appraise the lit-up House once more just as a man staggered outside. He was a short man in a palm-leaf sombrero, cartridge bandoliers crisscrossed on his chest. He stopped just in front of the open front doors, staring out at the night for a time, toward Prophet.

Then he staggered sideways, leaned back against the front wall. His hat fell forward down his chest as he slowly sagged to the gallery floor. His head slanted to one side, chin to shoulder, and he sat there, statue still.

"A good time was had by all," Prophet muttered as, adjusting the unfamiliar hat on his head once more, he walked out from beside the adobe and tramped around the well.

As he approached the large, gaudy building before him, he raked his right hand across his holstered Colt, taking a

modicum of comfort from the solid feel of the walnut-butted
revolver that had seen him out of many pinches.

He hoped he wouldn't need it for any such pinch tonight.
Sharp-nailed witches' fingers of apprehension raking the
back of his neck, he strode slowly up the gallery steps, toward the doors yawning before him like the gaping jaws of
a lion's den.

As he stepped up onto the gallery floor, a familiar, raspy,
laugh—like the long, shrill squawk of a chicken-thieving
eagle—rose high above the din. It careened around the
place until it was nearly drowned by an explosion of accom-
panying laughter.

Another weird sound rose on Prophet's left. His nerves
bouncing around just beneath his skin, he glanced sharply
at the man sitting beside the doors. The man's chest rose and
lips pooched out and then rippled like shuffled cards as he
exhaled.

Snoring.

Prophet felt an extra-angry dog nibbling at his sore ribs
as he moved slowly across the gallery, through the gaping
doors, and into the smoky air and flickering lamplight inside
the great drinking hall.

There must have been a hundred men in the place, crowd-
ing the tables as well as the horseshoe-shaped bar to Prophet's left. They were smoking and drinking and talking and
gambling, smoke wafting as thick as summer storm clouds.
Some customers lay in pools of vomit on the floor. Others
sat with bored-looking Apache girls on their laps.

Some of the girls wore so little as to be mostly naked.
There were Mexicans as well as Indians. Even some blonds
and a redhead. Not all of the dwarf's whores were slaves, it
appeared. Some had that look of a veteran professional who
knew exactly how to ply their wares.

Some were topless. Some were overly expressive, as
though they were trying too hard to please their prospective
jakes as well as their employer.

Employer . . .

As the bounty hunter moved into the room and walked

slowly through the crowd, trying not to make eye contact with anyone, he continued to hear the rise and fall of that grating, eagle-like voice. His hands sweated inside his gloves. He missed the security of having his double-barrel gut shredder hanging down his back.

Halfway down the long room, he stopped. He stared, a ringing growing in his ears.

He blinked as though to clear his vision. But, no, his eyes weren't playing tricks on him.

Thirty yards away, the dwarf was standing on a wooden table fronting a brocade-upholstered sofa on which the dwarf's woman, Griselda May, lounged like a queen. The dwarf was standing on a shipping crate atop the table. Unless Prophet was hallucinating, there was no doubt that the little man was Mordecai Moon. No, that big, dome-like head, pig face, long arms, and feet clad in the child's black boots definitely belonged to Moon.

A tuft of colorless goat beard straggled from his chin. He wore his age-coppered clawhammer frock coat and the feathered bowler hat that Prophet had shot a bullet through.

Moon was surrounded by an especially rough-hewn group of men whom Prophet took to be freighters. He was holding court, yelling, flapping his arms like the eagle he sounded like, and then suddenly lifting a bandaged hand to his forehead.

"Bang!" he shrieked and then immediately started laughing. "I thought I was dead, but, hell, no!" He held up his bandaged hand that was purple and swollen to twice its normal size and pointed at the blood-spotted bandage over the palm. "The big ole paw here saved my rank old hide! Took the zip out of the bullet, and she bounced right off my *wooden head*!"

The dwarf laughed and did a little dance atop the crate, pinwheeling his arms.

"And the Mescins all think I'm a saint! Ha!"

Griselda May rose to a half crouch behind him and extended her arms to catch the obviously pie-eyed little demon if he should fall. As he swung his little body back forward, he smacked his bandaged hand against the head of a tall, long-haired man who'd been walking past him and his semi-circular crowd of admirers.

The dwarf snapped his hand to his chest, lifted his furry chin, and sent a brittle shriek hurling toward the rafters.

He lost his precarious footing atop the crate. Griselda screamed as the crate tumbled away beneath the dwarf's scissoring boots. She managed to grab only one of Moon's arms before the dwarf slammed down hard on the table.

He gave a yelp and then rolled off the table to pile up on the floor, Griselda crouched over him, yelling, *"Mordecai!"*

The dwarf half rose, pushing the girl away. As she fell back on the couch, the demon gained his feet, his face swollen and red, eyes wide with rage. The man who had run into his hand stood staring down at him skeptically, swaying slightly on his hips from drink.

"That hurt like *hell*, you lummox!" Moon shouted, his good hand clawing his Colt Lightning from the holster on his right hip. "Teach you to watch where you're *goin'*!"

His voice cracked on that last. The long-haired man took one step back, wagging his head and raising his hands, one with a beer in it.

But the Lightning spoke once, twice, three, then four times.

The long-haired man went stumbling off into the crowd of men beyond him, sending two others to the floor as he fell, the four holes in his shirt pumping blood out of his chest.

The dwarf lowered his smoking pistol as he walked over to the long-haired man, who was fast dying on the floor as several innocent bystanders scrambled away lest the dwarf should cut loose with the Lightning again. The long-haired gent stared up at the dwarf, shock on his face. He blinked his eyes several times. His chest rose and fell sharply. He lifted one big, brown hand as though in beseeching.

Moon spit on him. "Teach you to walk into my hand, you son of a bitch!"

The long-haired man sighed. Blood frothed on his lips

and dribbled out his nose. His arm dropped, his chest stopped rising and falling, and his horrified eyes rolled back into his head until Prophet could see little but their whites.

"Get him out of here!" the dwarf ordered, and three of his men came running from various points about the room.

The dwarf holstered his pistol, clutched his bandaged hand—the bandage was slightly redder than before—to his belly, and winced. Griselda walked over to him and wrapped an arm around his shoulders.

"Can I see?"

"I'm goin' upstairs," he said, turning to rake his gaze across the men who'd been listening to his bullshit only a few moments before. "If you all will excuse me . . ."

His gaze stretched to Prophet, whose heart hiccupped twice. The bounty hunter started to turn toward the bar on his left when the dwarf pointed at him, Prophet.

"You—*Thursday*. Come on up to my room. We best discuss you pullin' out tomorrow."

Prophet's heart hiccupped twice more, thudded, quickened, slowed slightly. He glanced around him, wary as a cat in an attic full of rocking chairs, and dipped his chin in acknowledgment of the dwarf's request.

Law, law, law, the Georgian thought. *What have I gone and done to my old Rebel ass now?*

Griselda glanced at Prophet, but if she recognized him, he couldn't tell. She turned with the dwarf and, keeping one arm around his shoulders, began walking with him through the crowd toward the stairs rising at the back of the room. An odder pair, Prophet had never seen. The girl herself was petite, likely no taller than five-one or so, but still the dwarf's bowler hat came up little higher than her elbow.

The dwarf was soon lost amongst the tables. Griselda faded into the wafting tobacco smoke.

Prophet stared after them.

Should he follow them or hightail it? He had no way of knowing when the real Thursday would come around, but Prophet doubted he'd hit him hard enough to lay him out for over an hour. He needed to get back out there, grab his weapons, and head for the hills.

But as he looked around, he saw several pairs of eyes on him.

If he turned and walked out now, he'd only attract even more attention to himself. Besides, if he could get Moon in a room alone . . . ?

Prophet brushed his hand across his Colt's walnut grips again for comfort as he began pushing and sidestepping through the crowd toward the stairs.

32

PROPHET REACHED THE top of the stairs, the din of the saloon hall receding behind him. He looked to his right and left, just then realizing that he had no idea which room he was looking for though the real Thursday likely would.

A door closed on his far left, at the end of the hall dimly lit by smoky lanterns. There were more jostling shadows than light.

Prophet started that way, boots thumping on the bare pine planks. Nothing about the dwarf's *baglio* was in any way ornate. It was a large, cheaply made barrack built simply and unashamedly to serve the basest needs of men. Behind the doors around Prophet, bedsprings squawked, girls moaned, and men grunted. There was the occasional clink of a bottle against a glass and a man's rough voice.

Behind one door, Prophet heard a girl sobbing.

He pulled up in front of the door he'd thought he'd heard close and tipped his head to listen. On the other side of it, the dwarf was talking in a pain-pinched voice. The girl said something. Prophet's heartbeat quickened.

He glanced down the hall on his left just as a door opened

and a fat man in a badly weathered, Texas-creased Stetson, trail-worn buckskin shirt, and patched duck trousers came out, his cartridge belt looped over a thick shoulder. A freshly rolled quirley dangled from between his lips, dripping ashes into his beard.

The man closed the door behind him, staring straight ahead, puffing the quirley and buttoning his fly.

He turned toward Prophet and scowled. "What the hell are you lookin' at?" His fleshy, weathered face acquired a surprised expression. "Oh, sorry, Captain. Didn't recognize you there for a minute."

He grinned and jerked a thumb over his shoulder, indicating the closed door behind him. "Nice batch of female flesh you brung in. I don't mind payin' double for the new girls, not when they're as tight as that one was!"

He chuckled and began walking down the hall toward the stairs.

Prophet released the keeper thong from over his Colt's hammer and drew the weapon. He clicked the hammer back and knocked twice on the door.

The dwarf said, "Thursday?"

"Who else?"

"Come on."

Prophet opened the door and stepped into the room. Moon sat on the bed on the other side of the room, which was large by frontier standards, though sparsely, crudely furnished. The girl stood before the dwarf, unwrapping the bloody bandage from his hand.

Prophet closed the door. The dwarf stared at him. "You ain't Thursday."

"You ain't as stupid as you look, Moon."

The girl whipped her head toward Prophet. They both dropped their eyes to the cocked revolver in Prophet's hand. Her lower jaw drooped as her eyes rose to Prophet's.

"Oh, shit." She stepped back away from the dwarf, turning toward the big man who'd just entered their room.

The dwarf pointed with his good hand. "I know you!" His colorless little eyes rolled around in their wrinkled sockets as he tried to remember where he knew Prophet from.

"I'm the one who didn't pay for his water, couple days ago. Remember? The one you fed to the desert."

Prophet's voice was unusually low and hard. He gripped the gun tightly in his fist, keeping his finger taut against the curved trigger, enjoying the feel of it, wanting to squeeze it a little harder so he could really feel it and watch his bullet blow a hole through the dwarf's already bruised forehead.

"Shit," the dwarf said. "You been leadin' them women against me!"

"Ah, hell, them two don't need me to lead 'em nowhere, least of all against you, you sick little fucker!"

Griselda shuttled her shocked, wary gaze from Prophet to Moon and back again. Cunning sparkled in her eyes and she stepped farther away from Moon. "Don't shoot him until we have the combination to his fancy safe!"

The dwarf jerked his own shocked, exasperated face to the girl. He and Prophet said at the same time, *"What?"*

"He has a safe in the next room." Griselda jerked her chin toward a door to Prophet's left. "In there. Only he knows the combination. You can get it out of him, big man." She smiled, flushing, as her eyes flicked up and down the bounty hunter's brawny frame. "You can get it out of him if any-one can!"

Moon said, "Griselda, you double-crossing bitch!" The dwarf leaped down off the bed and pointed at her, aiming along his upslanted arm as though it were a rifle. "I knew you was up to somethin'!"

"You're even wiser than your years, Mordecai!" She laughed before turning back to Prophet. "When we have his money, we'll be richer than our wildest dreams!"

"I can dream pretty wild," Prophet muttered, shocked at the unexpected turn of events though he wasn't sure what he *had* expected.

He'd had only a vague idea of what he'd do once he got up here. One half-formed idea involved shooting the little bastard and getting him out of the way once and for all.

Another consisted of kidnapping both him and the girl and holding them hostage until the dwarf's men released the slave girls.

He hadn't counted on the girl turning on the dwarf and wanting to throw in with Prophet in torturing the little demon to get the combination to a safe out of him!

The dwarf ran over to the girl, lowered his head, and bulled into her, driving her back against the dresser.

"Hey, now!" Prophet said, taking one step forward but feeling helpless. "This will not do!"

Ignoring him, the girl grunted and cursed and fought against the little man, who punched and kicked her until his injured hand thudded into the dresser with a wooden knock.

The dwarf loosed a girlish squeal, gave his back to Griselda, and bent forward over his wounded hand. His ears turned as white as fresh linen, and saying nothing, making no sound whatever, he walked slowly back toward the bed.

"What's the combination, Mordecai?" the girl demanded, leaping on the dwarf from behind and driving him straight down to the floor with another squeal, fighting for his injured hand. "Tell me the combination, or I'll make you wish you was *dead*!" She looked at Prophet. "Help me. We'll split if fifty-fif—"

She stopped and shifted her gaze to something behind Prophet. Just then, Prophet heard the door latch click. He glanced behind him to see the Rio Bravo Kid enter the room, his two matched pistols in his hands. The Kid had a hard, indignant look on his clean-shaven face beneath the brim of his hat that still sat at a slightly odd angle to compensate for his still-swollen temple.

Prophet started to swing his own Colt toward the Kid but stopped when the Kid said, "Uh-uh."

His voice was dull, distracted. He stood in front of the door, staring at Griselda sprawled atop the quietly mewling dwarf on the floor. Moon lay sort of curled around his injured hand, shielding it from Griselda's evil intentions.

"Kid!" she said, brightening phonily. "I didn't think you was *ever* gonna get here!"

The Kid was staring at Prophet. "Drop that gun, mister bounty hunter."

Prophet looked at both the Kid's cocked revolvers. They were aimed at Prophet's belly. With a fateful sigh, Prophet depressed his own Colt's hammer and tossed the pistol onto the bed in front of him.

"Well, I never," the Kid said with dull menace, looking genuinely shocked and grieved, shaking his head slowly. "I never seen the like of you, Griselda May. We grew up together, you an' me. I thought you loved me, wanted to spend the rest of your life with me."

"I do, Kid!"

The dwarf turned his own red face and rheumy eyes toward the Kid. "You stupid shaver. She was playin' both ends against the middle." He looked at Prophet. "And then this big, stupid, *wild card* came walkin' into the room!" He lowered his chin to his injured hand and gave another wounded-dog-like howl.

"I know, Mr. Moon," the Kid said. "I was right outside. I heard it all through the door."

Griselda gained her feet. Her hair was disheveled, her cheeks flushed. "Kid, I was just wantin' the big fella here to torture the safe combination out of Mordecai. You don't think I was really gonna *run off* with him, do you? Come on, Kid—I love *you* like I could never love *anyone*!"

"You bitch!" the dwarf shouted, sobbing now. "I loved you, Griselda. *Truly* I did! And look how you *done* me!"

"You pathetic little bastard." Griselda laughed.

"Shut up, Griselda," the Kid said, moving forward now, stepping wide around Prophet, keeping one gun aimed at Griselda, the other at the bounty hunter. "I don't wanna hear one more word outta you!"

When the Kid turned his full attention on Griselda, pointing both his cocked revolvers at her, Prophet saw an opening. He flung himself sideways into the Kid. One of the Kid's pistols barked a half second before Prophet hammered his right elbow into the Kid's belly.

Pivoting, he brought up his other arm and smashed the elbow into the Kid's face.

The Kid twisted around, clawing at the dresser, but merely pulled four empty busthead bottles and several shot glasses down with him as he fell to the floor and rolled onto his back, eyelids fluttering as consciousness left him.

Prophet heard the dwarf's strained, half-crying voice behind him. "Oh, Lordy, Lordy, Lordy!"

Hatless and breathless, down on one knee, the bounty hunter swung toward the room. Griselda sat on the floor near the front of the bed, a strange, wide-eyed look on her face. Her legs were stretched before her, knees bent slightly. She held both hands over her bloody belly.

Holding his injured hand up tight against his belly, the dwarf crawled toward her. He wrapped his arm around her shoulders, his face pinched and red with sobbing.

"Griselda . . ."

"Shit," she whispered and fell straight back against the floor.

"Griselda!" the dwarf howled, pressing his forehead against her small, pert bosoms. "We coulda had a good life together, you an' me, if you hadn't been such a double-crossin' bitch!"

Prophet stared at them lying there on the floor together, the dead girl in the dwarf's arms. He almost felt sorry for the tragic pair, and he probably would have if one hadn't been as evil as the other. The Rio Bravo Kid was out like a light, chest rising and falling slowly behind his pinto vest to which his deputy sheriff's badge was pinned.

Prophet cursed and grabbed his hat. He stuffed it on his head, rose, and walked over and scooped his Colt off the bed. He clicked the hammer back, walked over to the dwarf, and pressed the barrel against the back of the sobbing demon's head.

"Ah, go ahead," the dwarf cried into the dead girl's chest. "Go ahead and put me outta my misery, big man! I fell in love with the wrong girl, that's all!"

As much as he wanted to, as much as he knew he should do it, Prophet couldn't squeeze the trigger. He pulled the pistol back, grabbed the little man's shirt by its collar. "You're ridin' with me, Moon."

The din of the revelry from below had been vibrating through the floor. Now a man's enraged shout cut through the clamor. Prophet hadn't been able to hear what the man had said, but the sheer volume with which he'd said it caused him to tense.

The din died down, and then another man shouted, *"Upstairs with Mr. Moon!"*

"Hell!" Prophet glanced in frustration at Mordecai Moon now grinning up at him, though tears were still rolling down his cheeks. The whites of the dwarf's colorless eyes were red from crying.

"That's where you're headed, big man," the dwarf said with quiet delight. "In about three shakes of a whore's bell! *Hell!"*

As though to corroborate the dwarf's estimation, boots hammered the stairs, causing the floor to leap beneath Prophet's feet. He backed away from Moon, cursing in frustration. That he'd come so far only to turn back now, leaving the girl dead but Moon alive, was almost too much to bear. Still backing toward the door, he raised the Colt once more, clicked the hammer back, and aimed at Moon's forehead.

Grinning broadly, Moon raised his arms above his head and shrugged his shoulders, eyes flashing in mocking delight. It was an open challenge. He knew Prophet wouldn't be able to shoot a man in cold blood, one who wasn't even wearing a gun, and he was taking great delight in the frustration he saw on the bounty hunter's face.

Louisa could do it, Prophet thought. And she *would* do it. He should, too, but there was something in him whose seed had been sown during the war that would not let him draw his index finger back tight against the trigger and kill an unarmed man despite all the voices in his head urging him to do so.

"This ain't over, Moon." His words sounded hollow even

to his own ears as he lowered the pistol and turned to the door.

Prophet turned, grabbed the doorknob, jerked the door wide, and hurled himself out of the room and into a hail of gunfire.

33

GUNS BLASTED TO Prophet's left, bullets screaming around his head and tearing into the wall at the end of the hall on his left. He fired his pistol twice from his hip just before ramming his shoulder into the door of the room opposite the dwarf's.

The door burst open and slammed against the wall with a bang that was nearly drowned by the blasts and shouts from the direction of the stairs.

The naked girl on the bed screamed. The man who'd been pumping away on top of her turned toward Prophet and shouted, *"What in the name of . . . ?"*

"Don't mind me!" Prophet leaped onto the bed, took one step, and leaped to the floor on the other side.

He looked out the open window and nearly sobbed at his good luck. A shake-shingled roof slanted just below him. Making a mental note to stop getting himself run out of hotels, he wheeled, saw several men scurrying around the room's open door, and fired three quick rounds to hold them at bay.

The girl screamed. Her jake cursed him roundly.

Prophet leaped onto the window casing and without a

second thought, sent himself hurling straight down toward the roof below. This roof was considerably sturdier than the last one he'd piled up on, the one in San Simon, with Ramonna screaming and Campa cussing and firing from above. Prophet did not bust through this roof, though judging by the sound, he cracked a few shingles as he landed feetfirst.

He rolled over the edge and saw the charcoal-colored ground come up fast before it smashed into his head and shoulders. He grunted loudly, stretching his lips back from his teeth and rolling onto his side and clutching his right shoulder with his left hand.

"Shit!"

Above, men shouted. Pistols popped. He was shielded by the roof, and the bullets plunked into the shingles, flinging slivers. Prophet stared up at the roof edge and caught a whiff of cigar smoke. He saw a dark-clad figure hunkered on his haunches on the small rear gallery.

The cigar coal glowed in the darkness. Smoke wafted around the black-hatted head. A man chuckled.

"Prophet, you sure burn it from both ends." It was Mortimer. "You best get your ass up and light a shuck, Reb!"

Prophet had grabbed his pistol but did not click the hammer back. He heaved himself to his feet. Mortimer said, "Catch!"

He swung his arm back and forward, and Prophet watched his rifle come hurling toward him. He grabbed it out of the air and switched it to his left hand in time to catch his coach gun with its leather lanyard flapping out to one side.

"Figured you could use those."

Prophet was stunned. "Thanks," was the only word he could find.

Then he stepped back away from the hotel until he could see the window above the roof. A gun flashed in the dark square, briefly lighting a hatted head. The slug thudded into the ground over Prophet's left shoulder.

Prophet raised the gut shredder and tripped a trigger,

hearing a man scream as the buckshot pelted his face. Hearing more shouting throughout the hotel now, and the thunder of running feet as the dwarf's men and likely his savage customers rushed to the doors to give chase, the bounty hunter turned and ran straight back toward the barns and corrals.

He'd run maybe thirty yards before guns resumed blasting behind him. He headed past a barn and a covered wagon and stopped suddenly. He looked back at the wagon.

The maw of a Gatling gun protruded from the rear pucker.

Prophet looked behind, a wistful look on his crude-featured face. Several slugs plumed the dust around him and caused the horses and mules to dance around inside the corrals. He ran over to the wagon and leaped over the tailgate and inside. He set his rifle down beside what appeared an old 1862 model Gatling gun modified for contemporary cartridges and glanced out the back of the wagon.

At least a dozen men were sprinting toward him from the rear of the dwarf's House, jostling shadows in the purple night.

Several wooden cartridge crates flanked the big, fire-belching cannon. Prophet quickly dropped a box of cartridges down the Gatling gun's loading rail and cut loose with a quick burst of what was probably ten .45-caliber, one-inch slugs.

The gun turned on its swivel, hiccupping madly, savagely, stabbing orange flames back toward Moon's place and filling the wagon with a heavy, eye-stinging plume of fetid powder smoke.

He grinned again as the jostling figures were plowed down as though by an unseen scythe. Men screamed and triggered their pistols or rifles into the ground.

Prophet dropped another ten-round box down the Gatling gun's rail and, turning the crank, opened up on the dwarf's house and the men continuing to run out from behind it. Several more shadows dropped, screaming and groaning, while others dashed to safety behind the hulking building.

Prophet waited a couple of seconds.

Silence had fallen like the pall after a bad storm. Smoke wafted grayly in the darkness. Windows in the House's rear wall wore the soft umber of flickering lamplight. Several silhouetted figures dashed around behind them.

Seeing no more men running toward him, only one triggering wild shots from behind a front corner of the House, Prophet grabbed his shotgun and looped it over his shoulder. He took his rifle, hurried to the front of the wagon, climbed over the driver's box, and dropped to the ground.

Trying to keep the wagon between him and the House, he ran between the two stables in which horses and mules and several oxen whickered, brayed, and bellowed against the commotion, including the Gatling's raucous fire. He crossed a wash and ran up a slope, raking breath in and out of his lungs. When he'd run up the next, higher slope, he stopped near the crest and glanced back over his shoulder.

He couldn't see much because of the darkness, but he heard men shouting and running around, though none seemed to be running toward Prophet. They were all likely so drunk and taken aback by the sudden outburst of violence that had left more than a few of them dead that they'd decided to ponder the situation before endangering themselves further.

Prophet picked up a rock with his left hand, tossed it underhanded away from him, and gave another frustrated curse.

The dwarf was still alive. The slave girls were still in the House of a Thousand Delights.

Prophet stood and walked up and over the slope. Hooves thudded ahead of him. He saw shadows moving toward him, milky dust rising behind them. He walked out onto the curving trail that led up into the Chisos, and stopped and watched as the rider crested the next hill and came toward him. Starlight revealed a pinto as well as blond hair bouncing on slender shoulders.

Louisa reined up suddenly, curveted the pinto in the trail fifty yards from Prophet. Mean and Ugly stopped in the trail behind her, blowing and stomping and chewing his bit. Starlight flashed on silver chasing, and in the quiet night Prophet heard the click of a gun hammer.

"I had enough bein' shot at, damnit," Prophet said.

"Lou?"

"Yeah," he growled and walked toward her.

She galloped up to him, stopped, and tossed him Mean and Ugly's reins. As usual, her tone was snooty. "Did you get the lay of the land?"

"Said I would, didn't I?"

Prophet swung up onto Mean's back, the horse feeling good and familiar beneath him. It was so quiet now that all he could hear was the ringing in his ears from the Gatling gun.

"What was all the shooting?" Louisa asked.

Prophet reined Mean around and headed back in the direction from which Louisa had come and in which he knew that Colter and Ruth were waiting. "The dwarf—he didn't like me gettin' it."

34

THE NEXT MORNING, by the light of a new day washing through the fly-flecked front windows of the House of a Thousand Delights, the dwarf saw that Griselda May still wore the same shocked expression she'd worn when the bullet had punched through her belly the night before.

She lay sprawled atop two saloon tables, staring up at him with those eerily wide-open eyes, lips parted. Several flies buzzed around her head and lips and drifted down to investigate the thick blood staining her blouse. Her arms lay straight down against her sides.

Standing atop a chair by the table, Moon looked down at Griselda's right hand. It was small and delicate and slightly tanned, and there were about three freckles splashed across the back of it. It was the hand of an innocent child, not of a young woman as devilish as the one he'd come to know last night during the last few minutes of her life. The hand looked so tender and innocent lying there without any life in it that Moon felt a tear roll down his cheek.

A sob like a frog's croak issued from deep in his chest, and he leaned forward, placed his good hand on the edge of the table—his injured one would bear no weight at all without him caterwauling like a gut-shot coyote—and placed his lips to the girl's hand.

He straightened with a sad sigh and looked at the three stout Mexican girls he'd hired to clean and work in the kitchen, as they were too ugly to whore for him. He waved an arm and said in a voice crackling with emotion, "Take her away. Put her in the hole she had dug for me, and cover her up and let that be the end of her!"

The Mexican girls, clad in shapeless canvas dresses, rolled Griselda up in the blanket she lay upon. Grunting, the three of them picked up the bundle and carried it awkwardly to the front of the room and out the propped-open doors.

Meanwhile, standing on a chair near the front of the room, wearing a noose around his neck, his hands tied behind his back, the Rio Bravo Kid sobbed. His chin was dipped to his chest and his eyelids and lips fluttered as he bawled.

The rope that extended from the noose was looped over a rafter about three feet above his head. One of the burlier of the dwarf's men, a Mexican named Ramon, had the rope stretched across his bowed shoulder. Crouching, he gripped the coiled end tightly in his hands, ready for the execution.

Ramon had long, silver-flecked black hair and a mustache of the same color, its ends dangling nearly to his chest. An uncorked bottle from which he took sporadic sips stood on a table nearby.

Ramon's eyes were sort of hazel, and one wandered. Both eyes were smiling now delightedly as he shuttled his gaze between the Rio Bravo Kid and Moon, awaiting the order for him to lean into the rope to lift the Kid's feet up off the chair.

The dwarf stared up at the Kid and curled his nostril distastefully. "Thinkin' through all your sundry sins, Kid?" he asked. "Thinkin' through all of 'em real good?"

The Kid continued to sob, squeezing his eyes closed, tears rolling down his clean-shaven, sun-pinkened cheeks.

"The main one you gotta think on, Kid, is the one where

you was in cahoots with Griselda to double-cross me—to steal from *me*, the jake who gave you your job and your very *reason for existence here in my town*!—and run out on me with all my loot!" The dwarf pointed furiously up at the Kid. "That there's the main one. I don't care none about the ones that came before that. That there is the reason that when I give the nod, Ramon is gonna play cat's cradle with your *head*!"

Ramon looked at the Kid and chuckled through his teeth.

There were several other men in the room, including the dwarf's own unwashed lot, sitting around several tables. Luke Thursday, head of the slavers, sat with two of his men at a table near the dwarf.

Two of the slavers stared in amusement at the sobbing Kid. Thursday wasn't in a humorous mood, however. His lower lip was cut and swollen, and his left eye was slightly swollen and badly discolored, with a cut just below it. Thursday leaned forward in his chair, smoking and sipping whiskey from a water glass and staring up at the Kid as though he were eyeing the man who'd so insulted him the night before at the well.

Lou Prophet. Thursday had remembered the man's name after he'd come around from the beating he'd been given by the big Rebel bounty hunter from Georgia. The dwarf had heard of Prophet, too, of course, as Prophet was a colorful character who cut a broad swath, but he'd never seen him before.

Not before several days ago, however, when he should have killed him outright instead of merely trying to torture him. That was the start of everything bad here in Moon's Well. That and Moon's killing the Rangers, that was, and Prophet hauling one of them back to town.

How quickly a man's luck could turn.

Now Griselda was dead, Prophet was on the loose and up to no good, and the dwarf's hand was rotting slowly and with excruciating pain at the end of his arm.

Thursday had an ivory-gripped Smith & Wesson Model 3 top-break .44 revolver on the table beside his whiskey bottle, as though keeping the weapon handy in the unlikely event that Prophet made another unexpected appearance.

"What do you think, Thursday?" the dwarf said, sitting down on the chair and then dropping very gingerly to the floor, keeping his big, purple, white-bandaged hand up close against his chest and out of harm's way. "Do you like my tactics?"

Thursday brought a cigarette to his lips. "I'm gettin' tired o' his caterwaulin'." He drew the smoke into his lungs and blew it out at the Kid.

"Yeah—me, too."

The dwarf glanced at Ramon and dipped his chin. Ramon grinned bigger and pulled down on the rope, throwing his shoulder into it. The Kid's chin came up, his face turned red, and he made a strangling sound as his heels rose from the chair. He tried to ground his toes down into the chair as though for purchase, but two seconds after his heels had left it, his toes did, too.

He immediately began choking and wheezing and dancing a bizarre two-step about eight inches above the chair.

"Kid, I never knew you could dance!" the dwarf said.

Ramon grunted as he pulled on the rope, crouching, putting his shoulder into it. The rope creaked and grated against the beam over which it was looped. Dust sifted down from atop the beam.

The Kid grunted and gurgled, sounding like a coffeepot just starting to boil. His wide eyes stared in horror across the room as he jumped and jerked and lunged and turned from one side to the other and then in a complete circle.

His face was as red as a hot iron, and it swelled like a snakebite. The Rio Bravo Kid grimaced as he grunted and jerked and turned one circle after another, his boots only about a foot above the chair, until he kicked the back of the chair and it fell over with a bang.

The dwarf stood and watched the death dance grimly. So did Thursday. The other men in the room watched, as well, some grinning, one snickering, but most just looking bored.

As the Kid's dance began to lose some of its vigor, like a

drunken dancer at the end of a long night, the dwarf turned
to his men gathered at two tables. "Party's over, boys," he
said. "Sun's up high enough for trackin'."

He tossed his head toward the door.

The ten or so men rose from their chairs, grabbing pistols
and rifles, checking the loads and adjusting the holsters on
their hips. Some tossed back the last of their drinks and
scrubbed their mouths with their hands or shirtsleeves,
sniffing and snorting, ready to ride.

They clomped off toward the open doors, spurs chinging.

Thursday turned to the dwarf standing near his table,
watching his men. "Do your boys got anything against me
and my boys joinin' em?"

The dwarf smiled. "More the merrier."

Thursday glanced at the other two slavers sharing his
table as he blew cigarette smoke out his mouth and nostrils,
causing a big, blue cloud to puff around his bearded head. He
mashed the stub out in an ashtray, doffed his gold-braided
hat, and rose, as did the other two, grabbing their rifles off a
near table.

Thursday dropped the Smithy into its holster, snapped
the keeper thong over the hammer, and turned to Moon once
more. "You comin', Mr. Moon?"

Moon looked glum as he stared out the doors at the
bright street and the well beyond. "I ain't feelin' too good.
Believe I'll stay here, have a drink and take a nap cuddled
up to one of your new Injun gals, Thursday. With your men
and mine combined, you got you a posse of at least twenty.
Prophet and whoever's ridin' with him ain't gonna have a
chance with that many tough nuts on his trail."

Thursday snorted angrily and headed for the front doors
with his other two men.

"Try to capture him alive, and we'll hang him up next to
the Kid here!" Moon called. "I'd love to hold a necktie party
in that big bastard's honor!"

"I make no promises, Mr. Moon," Thursday growled and
was gone.

Moon drew a deep breath, winced at the pain from his

badly swollen hand shooting up his arm and into his neck, and looked at the Rio Bravo Kid. Ramon had tied the end of the rope to a leg of the nearby wood stove, suspending the Kid about four feet above the floor.

The Kid was staring glassily down at Moon, turning slowly. He gave one more kick, as though it was an afterthought, his face expressionless, and then he turned very slowly to face the other side of the room.

"There you go, Kid," Moon said, rising up onto the balls of his boots to grab a bottle off a table. "That's what happens when you fuck with Mordecai Moon. Hope you burn in hell, you rotten son of a bitch!"

He ambled off toward the stairs with his bottle. He said without turning around, "And when you see my girl, tell her ol' Mordecai says hi!"

He chuckled at that as he started up the stairs.

Behind him, Sheriff Mortimer crossed the street through a windblown cloud of sand and grit and entered the saloon. He stopped in the doorway and looked around the empty hall and saw the Kid hanging over the fallen chair. The Kid had stopped turning now, and he faced the front of the room, eyelids drooping lazily over his eyes.

"Vernon, Vernon," Mortimer said.

He walked into the room and over to the bar. He leaned over it, grabbed a bottle from a shelf beneath it, and stuffed it into a pocket of his frock coat. Wanda needed a drink. So did he, for that matter.

He looked up at the Kid once more, his own face expressionless. The sheriff was sweating out the bender that he and Wanda were on—probably their last one together—and the sweat beads were dribbling down his cheeks and into his mustache, eroding the dust on his long, leathery neck that hadn't seen a razor in several days.

Mortimer turned his mouth corners down and headed for the door. Halfway there, he stopped, gave a frustrated chuff, and then walked over to where the Kid hung from the rafter. Mortimer set the chair up on its feet, climbed onto it. He produced a barlow knife from a coat pocket, and sawed through the rope over the Kid's head.

When the last strand was cut, the Kid fell to the floor.

Mortimer stepped down from the chair, grabbed the Kid's arms, and dragged him across the room and out the front door. He dragged him down the gallery steps and into the street.

He knew a quiet, shady place befitting the last resting place of the Rio Bravo Kid.

35

ONE OF THE dwarf's men, Leon "Blue Snake" Sumner, halted his Appaloosa and scowled up the slope ahead of him and his partner, Ralph Dodge, until the blue snakes tattooed on both of Blue Snake's cheeks slithered up high under his eyes. He cuffed his low-crowned black sombrero back off his forehead.

"What the hell is it?" Dodge had ridden on past Blue Snake but now, seeing Blue Snake stopped behind him, reined up his chestnut.

"You tell me." Blue Snake stared up the rocky slope from which the orange sunlight and heat emanated like nearly palpable waves.

Dodge followed his partner's gaze to a woman in men's rough trail clothes and a blue bandanna sitting atop a flat boulder that was shaded by another, larger boulder farther up the slope. The boulders were the size of small cabins, and the woman looked tiny against them. That she was a woman, however, was obvious. Two large mounds pushed out her red-and-black calico shirt as she sat with her legs hanging down over the side of the boulder. A pale garment of some kind—an undergarment?—sat rumpled beside her shapely left thigh. Dodge blinked as he stared at the blouse.

It was unbuttoned, revealing the deep valley between the woman's tits!

"Hey!" Dodge said, startled and raising the Colt revolving rifle that had been resting across his saddlebow. "Who the hell are you?"

"I'm from town," came the woman's soft-spoken reply. "And I'm hot and thirsty." She rose slowly until she was standing at the edge of the boulder. "You fellas wouldn't have a drink of water to spare, would you?"

Dodge looked at Blue Snake, who stared up the slope as though mesmerized. "I don't know," he said, grinning. "What's in it for us?"

Dodge laughed at that. The tug in his groin tempered his apprehension.

The woman smiled, slitting her eyes. Then she reached up and slid the blouse off her shoulders, held it out in one hand, and let it sail down onto the boulder a few feet away, near the pale under-frilly she'd already removed. "These do?"

"Oh, my Lord!" Blue Snake hit the ground running.

He bolted up the slope, slipping and sliding and falling and pushing off the ground as he dug his spurred heels into the sand, gravel, and rocks. Ralph Dodge ran up the slope behind him, both men holding rifles, their horses switching their tails warily in the trail behind them.

They were laughing and breathing hard, eyes riveted on the bare-breasted woman standing atop the boulder before them. Blue Snake frowned when the woman suddenly turned and stepped into a dark niche between the two boulders. At the same time, a big man in a buckskin shirt and faded Levi's stepped out of the niche, holding a savagely cut-down, double-barrel coach gun in both hands.

Prophet smiled as the two men ran up the slope toward him, the one with the blue snakes tattooed on his cheeks about six feet in front of the other man who was shorter and wore a fringed elk-skin vest and fringed elk-skin breeches.

"Oh, shit!" Blue Snake yelled a half second before Prophet squeezed the gut shredder's left trigger and watched the man's head turn red and bounce down the slope behind him.

The second man screamed as he watched his headless partner fall forward and drop to his knees while his shaggy head bounced down the slope on his left. Prophet's barn blaster roared a second time, punching buckshot through the second man's chest, lifting him three feet up off the slope and hurling him straight back in the direction from which he and his partner had come.

He landed on his back, turned a backward somersault, and then rolled down to where both horses had been standing only two seconds ago, before the twin cannon-like reports had sent them galloping off across a shoulder of the mountain.

Prophet breeched the smoking shotgun and glanced toward the gap between the two boulders.

"Don't come back out here," he told Ruth, who stood in the shaded gap, holding her hands across her breasts. "This here little cannon is right efficient but what it does to a man ain't purty."

Ruth stared at him from between the rocks. Her eyes dropped to the broken shotgun as Prophet plucked out the spent wads and replaced them with fresh from his shell belt. She lifted her eyes to his. "We work well together, you and me."

Prophet snapped the gun closed. He reached down and picked up her blouse and chemise and handed them to her.

"But then, you and Miss Bonaventure work well together, too, don't you?" She tilted her head to one side, scrutinizing his reaction, as she dropped the chemise over her head, her breasts jostling freely until the cotton undergarment covered them.

"We used to."

He looked around. The large gang that he'd seen galloping up the slopes from the direction of town had split off into twos and threes to scour the mountains for him and his three partners. That's when they'd split up into twos, as well, to fight the gang Apache style in the rugged foothills and rocky mesas of the Chisos Mountains.

Louisa and Colter Farrow were somewhere off to the north.

"Come on," he said, when Ruth had buttoned her blouse. He brushed past her, took her hand, and began leading her out the backside of the niche toward where he'd tied Mean and Ugly. "Let's see if we can't run one o' them horses down for you. And then I'm gonna send you the hell on out of here."

She stopped, jerked her hand from his grasp. "What're you talking about?"

He turned to her, standing in the shade of the boulders, wisps of hair blowing out from the sides of the bandanna tied over her head. The sun had bronzed her freckled skin, and there was an earthy light in her eyes. Her hair flowed freely across her shoulders, touched with the dust and grit of the mountains. How different she looked now from the woman he'd known their one night together in the hotel. She almost looked like a wild Apache, out here in these mountains.

"This ain't your fight, Ruth."

She gave a brassy laugh. "It was my fight long before it was ever yours!"

"I don't want you dyin' out here."

"That isn't your decision." Ruth held his gaze. "You and the others might be better suited to fighting, but I'm going to stay with you, Lou, and do my part, however small it is."

"You've already done that."

"With the only weapons I had at the time." She smiled broadly. "Maybe it's time for me to start shooting. You must have a gun I can borrow. A knife . . . *anything*!"

He saw that wild, confident flicker in her eyes again. It made him think of Lozen, the fierce Chiricahua warrior woman and sister to Chief Victorio. Like Lozen, Ruth didn't care if she lived or died, but she was bound and determined to go down fighting the men who'd made life miserable for her for too long and who'd murdered her husband.

Prophet couldn't argue with her fierce determination. What's more, he didn't want to.

"All right," he said, wrapping an arm around the stalwart woman's waist and kissing her. "You got it." He took her hand again. "Come on!"

Colter Farrow stepped around a thumb of rock, holding his Winchester straight up and down in his hands. He glanced around the rock wall on his right, then jerked his head back behind the rock and doffed his hat.

Two riders were moving along the canyon below his perch here on the side of a sun-scorched bluff. He'd just caught a glimpse of them, but now he could hear the slow clomps and occasional blows of their tired horses.

Colter reached up with his left gloved hand and slid several locks of his long, blowing red hair back behind his ear and then very slowly shoved his head forward until he could see into the canyon with his left eye.

The riders continued moving down the canyon. One was Mexican. One was a black man with a green neckerchief. They both rode slowly, holding their horses' reins taut in one hand, rifles barrel up in the other. They were coming on cautiously, looking from one side of the canyon to the other.

They'd picked up Colter's and Louisa's trail back where Colter had hoped they would, and followed them into the canyon, also as he'd hoped.

Movement to Colter's left. He turned to see Louisa move slowly amongst the boulders at the edge of the bluff and then stop about ten feet away from Colter, pressing her back against the boulder behind her.

She looked at Colter. He held her gaze, and he was thinking that she was the most beautiful, beguiling creature he'd ever known while at the same time he jerked his thumb toward the canyon and the two approaching riders.

She slid her eyes away from him as she nudged her hat

back off her head, letting it hang down her back by her
horsehair chin thong, and squeezed her carbine in her hands.
Her blond hair fluttered about her ears and cheeks that were
both the color and texture of fresh-whipped butter. They
contrasted the deep haze of her bold, lustrous eyes that always seemed to be harboring a secret and that made his
groin literally ache, though he'd suspected she was Lou
Prophet's girl.

Christ, who was he kidding? She may have been only
a few years older than he, but she was older than her
years, heart-twistingly beautiful, and tougher than a hickory
knot. Besides, no girl would fall for a kid with a big, nasty,
knotted-up brand on his face. That wasn't self-pity talking;
that was just horse sense.

He wanted to look good for her, though. It was in his loins
to do that. Hell, you never knew what might happen . . .

Louisa pulled her beautiful, hazel-eyed, fine-nosed head
back from view of the canyon. Colter held his hand up to
her, palm out, waylaying her, and then he slowly raised his
rifle and even more slowly ratcheted the hammer back to
full cock.

"Easy, Red," she whispered.

He wasn't sure he liked her calling him that. With
Prophet, it was all right—it meant they were partners. With
her it sounded a tad patronizing.

"Don't you worry," Colter said silently as he continued to
raise the rifle while Louisa pressed her back against the
boulder behind her, just out of view of the canyon floor. "I
been to see the elephant my own self, Miss Bonaventure.
You just see how it's done . . ."

That thought caused the corners of his mouth to quirk
slightly upward. This girl obviously didn't need to be taught
anything by anyone, much less by him. But he'd become
right handy with his shooting irons over the past several
years. While he'd prefer to be raising and breaking horses
at home in the Lunatic Mountains where he'd been raised,
instead of running from bounty hunters all up and down
the frontier, in this girl's intoxicating presence he felt the

swell of his young man's pride and the need to show off a bit.

He shoved his rifle barrel out away from the thumb of rock and slanted it down toward the riders who were now nearly directly below him, and quickly laid both beads on the head of the rider nearest him. As he started to draw his finger back against the trigger, a bullet screeched wickedly off the escarpment about one foot above him and to his right.

A quarter second later, a rifle cracked on the far side of the canyon, and a man over there who Colter hadn't seen shouted, "Ambush, boys! *Ammm-bushhhh!*"

36

COLTER'S RIGHT EAR rang from the scream of the ricocheting lead. He could feel blood running down his cheek that had been cut by flying rock slivers.

But he stayed his ground and quickly laid his sights once more on the head of the rider nearest him. It wasn't as easy a shot as it would have been a second ago, before the third man had alerted the two riders, but he took it, anyway, and smiled in satisfaction as the rider who'd just started to gallop for cover flew down the side of his horse to pile up on the canyon floor.

In the corner of his left eye, Colter saw Louisa drop to one knee and face the canyon as she raised her carbine to her shoulder.

As she opened up on the man who'd been nestled in the rocks on the far side of the canyon—*Bam! Bam! Bam! Bam-bam!*—Colter fired three more quick rounds, emptying the saddle of the second rider and sending his horse galloping after the first.

"Damn!" he said, staring down through his and Louisa's powder smoke at the man Louisa had shot and who now lay sprawled on his back half out of the niche he must have been hiding in.

"Teach you to stare at a girl's tits when you should be watchin' out for ambushes, Red!"

"Hey, I wasn't!"

Louisa jerked around just as Colter heard the thud of galloping horses behind them.

"Two more!" the girl shouted.

She ran back through the boulders and several yards down the back of the ridge. Colter followed her, his ears burning with chagrin, as Louisa dropped to a knee and aimed at one of the two riders galloping toward them from the south, up a shallow grade stippled with cactus.

She blew the first rider off his horse with ease. Her second shot plumed dust behind the second man. Colter raised his own Winchester quickly. The rifle leaped and roared, spitting fire.

The second rider jerked back in his saddle, dropping one of his reins and clapping that hand to his leather-clad chest, near the long, red tail of his neckerchief. As he started to fall forward, Louisa's Winchester roared, blowing the man back flat against the horse's hindquarters. He started to slide down the horse's left hip but then the horse gave a shrill whinny, dropped to its knees and turned a forward somersault.

The rider must have gotten his left boot hung up in the stirrup, because he flew like a ragdoll, obscured by flying dust, up over the horse's head before the stirrup jerked him violently down once more and out of sight beneath the horse that immediately started to rise. The man gave a shrill, short-lived scream.

As the horse shook itself, causing the saddle to slide down its side, it sidled away unsteadily, addled. The rising dust revealed its rider sprawled on his side, only the long tail of his neckerchief moving as the breeze caught and waved it.

"Damn, Red, we make a good team!" Louisa turned to Colter and planted a soft, wet kiss on his lips, her tongue gently pressing against his own and instantly warming his volatile young loins. She pulled her head away and winked one of those lustrous hazel eyes. "But the admonition of before stands. Come on—there's no rest for the wicked!"

Colter stared after her as she swung around and began running down the ridge toward the canyon floor, meandering around rocks with her rifle on her shoulder. His mind spun. He could still feel her mouth on his, her tongue pressing against his own.

Then he leaped forward and ran after her, breathing hard.

At the bottom of the canyon, one of the five men they'd shot was trying to crawl away. Louisa strode purposefully up to him, stopped, and delivered a single killing shot from her shoulder, causing the man's head to bounce violently as blood and brain matter splattered the ground beneath him.

"Holy shit," Colter whispered, running a sleeve across his sweaty forehead. "I've never known a woman like you before, Miss Louisa."

"And you probably don't know what to think."

Colter looked at the man she'd just sent to Glory. The man's high-heeled, dark brown, silver-spurred boots were still kicking. "No, I reckon not."

"Just don't fall in love with me, Red. Lou did that . . . and paid the price."

She trotted east along the canyon floor, heading toward where they'd hid their horses. "What price is that?" Colter called after her.

"He's not done tallying it yet!" Louisa beckoned as she ran. "Come on, Red. We got more riders comin'!"

Colter heard the hooves and turned to see a triangle of riders galloping toward him from the west end of the canyon. "Shit!" The keenness of the girl's eyes was second only to her ears.

Colter followed her into a narrow canyon that fed the main one, and they mounted up and rode north out of the gap. Once they were in the open desert, Colter, riding beside Louisa, glanced over his shoulder. The riders were hot after them, maybe a hundred yards away and closing.

He looked at Louisa. She must have been reading his

mind, because when she'd glanced back to see their pursuers, she turned to Colter and said, "We'll get shed of them after the next hill."

Colter grinned and turned his head forward, tugging his hat low over his eyes to keep it from blowing off in the hot, dry wind. But when they were halfway up the next hill, winding around boulders and cactus snags, a man's voice shouted, "Keep ridin'!"

Colter and Louisa both jerked looks to their right to see Prophet wave his shotgun from a nest of rocks and scrub brush. He was kneeling on his hat. Ruth Rose was on the other side of the trail and slightly higher on the hill, aiming a rifle over the top of a low, flat boulder. Colter recognized her by her long, brown hair and yellow bandanna.

"Speak of the devil!" Louisa shouted as she crested the hill before plunging down the other side.

Behind them Prophet shouted, *"Keep a-ridin'—there's a half-dozen more o' these curs over the next ridge!"*

Colter looked at Louisa as he galloped just off her pinto's left hip. She glanced back at him, scowling. "I told you he was bossy!"

She crouched low over her galloping horse's neck and batted her heels again the mount's flanks, urging more speed.

Prophet crouched against the boulder, his shotgun in one hand, his rifle in the other. He stared toward the seven riders galloping toward him in a jostling, dusty wedge—seventy yards away and closing quickly.

He looked slightly up the grade behind him and north, where Ruth hunkered behind another boulder, a rifle he'd taken off one of the men he'd killed in her hands. She'd promised she knew how to wield the weapon, had even been a fair shot back in the Ozarks from where she hailed, though it had been several years since she'd fired such a weapon.

He'd told her to take her time, line up the sights on her target, and squeeze the trigger slow.

He hunkered lower, pressing his left cheek up against the

backside of the boulder to make certain he wasn't seen before he wanted to be. He'd let her take the first shot, because she'd probably only get one. He knew it was important to her to get at least one. Then he'd cut loose with his rifle and barn blaster.

He glanced toward her again but could see only her boots. She'd assumed a prone position and was probably lining up her sights on the far side of her covering boulder. Prophet gritted his teeth.

Come on, Ruth, they're gettin' close. . . .

The ground vibrated beneath him as the riders approached to within fifty yards . . . forty. . . .

Ruth's rifle cracked. At the same time the *ka-pewww!* reached Prophet's ears, he heard a metallic thunk. The rifle of one of the two lead riders flew out of his hands. He screamed and clutched his arm, releasing one of his reins and sagging back in his saddle, his hat tumbling back off his head.

Prophet rose to a knee and commenced hastily lining up his sights and firing. The spent cartridges flew up over his right shoulder as, one after another, three riders were thrown from their saddles. Another dropped down the far side of his horse and was dragged by his stirrup on up the trail behind his wildly buck-kicking mount.

Prophet heaved himself to his feet and took a step forward as three still-seated riders brought their horses to skidding stops and turned their rifles on him. The rider on the far right fired a wild shot from his shaky perch, and Prophet punched a round through his throat. As the man tossed his rifle aside as though it were a hot potato and grabbed his throat, Prophet lined up his sights on one of the other three riders and squeezed the trigger.

The hammer pinged on an empty chamber.

He tossed the Winchester aside. As the other two riders galloped toward him, bellowing curses, Prophet ran forward, reaching for his shotgun and swinging it around before him. The two riders came at him, crouched low, one firing a rifle while the other triggered his pistols one at a time.

Bullets screeched around Prophet, who ran ahead to meet the attack head-on.

He triggered his right barrel at the man on the right, blowing him straight back off his horse while triggering a shot from midair, screaming. Prophet dove forward and hit the ground on his belly as the second rider galloped past him on his left.

Prophet swung the gut shredder around and cut loose with the second barrel just as the second rider curveted his horse. The double-ought buck tore into the killer's left arm and shoulder and tore a couple of red chunks from his face.

Prophet slid the empty shotgun behind him, unholstered his Colt, raised it, and fired.

"You fuckin' son of a *bitch*!" the killer screamed, his cream duster billowing as a bullet tore into his side.

He cocked his carbine and ground his heels into his horse's flanks. The white-socked black lunged off its rear heels and galloped toward Prophet, its eyes white-ringed with fear. Prophet fired the Colt again, again, and again, watched dust puff from the rider's duster, and then he dove to his left. One of the black's hooves clipped Prophet's right heel as he hit the ground and rolled as two slugs hammered the dirt and gravel around him.

Ignoring the gnawing pain in his tender ribs, Prophet pushed to his knees. The man had stopped the black and was looking at Prophet. His duster had more red on it than white, and it sagged off his broad shoulders. Blood from Prophet's buckshot slithered down his right cheek.

Prophet shook his head. "You ain't dead *yet*?"

The man grinned, shook his head. With both hands, he raised the carbine.

The man's head jerked sharply to his right. He dropped his arms. The rifle fell to the ground. When the man lifted his head again, his brown bowler hat was gone, and the entire right side of his head was painted red and white from blood and brains.

He sagged slowly to his right. As his horse turned to start running back in the direction from which it had come, the rider fell out of the saddle, hit the ground, rolled once, and lay still.

Prophet turned to see Ruth walking toward him slowly, aiming her rifle from her hip. She held her yellow bandanna in her teeth, and it flapped around her neck in the wind that also tussled her hair, lifted dust, and tore at the lingering powder smoke.

"Now, that," Prophet said, "was the shootin' of an Ozark Mountain gal! Good to know that about you." He gave a devilish wink.

She smiled as she lowered the rifle and strode toward him, taking her bandanna in her hand. She frowned, stopped suddenly, and stared down at his side.

"Oh, Lou!"

"What is it?"

He looked down. Blood spotted his sweat-soaked and filthy buckskin shirt above his right hip.

"Ah, shit," he complained. "I thought I just landed on a pointy ol' rock!"

His seeing the blood and the ragged hole in his side caused the wound to fire war lances of sharp pain all through him. Odd how that was, he absently thought as his right knee started to buckle. He chuckled, a little giddy.

Ruth lurched toward him, wrapped his right arm around her neck, and led him over to a rock. He sat down heavily, winced against the pain, and blinked to clear his spotty vision.

"Oh, Lou!" Ruth said, sandwiching his big face in her hands, her eyes shiny. "Don't you go and die on me, you big bastard!"

37

"WELL IF I *was* dyin', which I *ain't*, I don't think it'd be right for you to curse me so," Prophet said.

He grinned at Ruth, trying to calm her down. She gave a reluctant smile, kissed him, and then knelt beside him to inspect the wound.

"Is the bullet still in there?" she asked, looking around his side at his lower back for a possible exit wound.

"I do believe so," Prophet said with a grunt.

"Water." Ruth rose and began jogging away. "I'm gonna fetch our horses. The canteens. I need water to clean that out and get the bleeding stopped."

"Shit," Prophet said, pressing a gloved hand to the wound and leaning forward against the hot pain flooding his side, making him queasy. "Sure could do with a shot of bust-head."

For some reason, his desire for a shot of whiskey made him think of Louisa. He glanced toward the crest of the hill on which he and Ruth had effected their ambush and over which Louisa and Colter had ridden.

He wondered where they'd gone and how they'd faired

against the six riders who'd been trying to cut them off. As if by magic, two riders came up over the top of the ridge and started down—Louisa herself, and the redheaded younker, Colter Farrow.

Right away, Louisa must have sensed something wrong. She ground her heels into her pinto's flanks and galloped down the hill toward Prophet. "What happened?" she said, jerking back on her reins and leaping down from her saddle, chaps buffeting about her long, slender legs.

Colter drew rein behind her and glanced toward where Ruth was returning with hers and Prophet's mounts.

"Bee bit me," Prophet said. "You wouldn't happen to have a snort of tanglefoot, would you?"

"You drank the last of it." Louisa crouched over him, placed a hand above the fist-sized patch of blood on his side. "Shit, Lou."

Prophet glanced at Colter, who was just now dismounting the coyote dun he called Northwest. "The women in this region are decidedly privy-mouthed."

"Is the bullet still in you?"

"I'll worry about it later. Where're them six that were tryin' to cut you off?"

"We laid for 'em but they stopped suddenly, as though they were spooked, maybe sensing a trap, and swung east."

"Toward town?"

"Well, Moon's We . . . I mean, *Chisos Springs* . . . is east, so, yes, I guess they headed toward town."

"Well, we've cleaned up right good," Prophet said. "They probably think we're more than we are. Don't call me Geronimo just yet, though . . ."

He started to rise. Louisa placed her hands on his shoulders and pushed him back down.

"You just sit there, Lou—you're bleeding bad!"

Ruth was approaching on the grullo they'd appropriated for her, trailing Mean and Ugly. "There's my ride," Prophet said. "We're headin' to town, girl. Gonna finish this, turn them slave girls loose."

"Not in your condition." Louisa stared up at him worriedly and hardened her jaws. "Lou, don't you die on me, you son of a bitch!"

"Never seen such bossy, foul-mouthed women!"

Ruth was walking toward him, holding a canteen by its braided hemp lanyard. "Water, Lou." She shouldered Louisa aside, handed him the canteen, and knelt before him.

"Obliged." Prophet glanced at Louisa, who sidled away reluctantly, looking vaguely miffed at Ruth. Prophet popped the canteen's cork. He took a drink, splashed some water down his side, and handed the canteen back to Ruth.

He rose from the rock, shouldering both women aside, and strode heavy-booted toward his horse.

"Lou!" both women admonished simultaneously.

"Ah, hush up, both of you. Son, hold my horse, will you?"

As Colter held Mean by his bridle, Prophet reached up and grabbed the saddle horn. He heaved himself heavily into the saddle, groaning at the tearing pain in his side and clamping his right hand over the wound, which oozed more blood as he settled into the leather.

He looked at the women glaring at him, both standing side by side, feet spread, fists on their hips. "Christalmighty," Prophet snorted, looking at Colter, who held his reins up to him. "Been ridin' solo all these years, and now a coupla females think they can boss me like we was married."

"Lou, you think you oughta do this?" Colter said. "Maybe you oughta stay here, rest up. We'll go to town—the three of us—and settle things, and be back by sundown." The kid narrowed his eyes resolutely. "That's bond, Lou."

Prophet scowled as he sort of crouched in the saddle, holding his neckerchief against the wound. "Ah, Junior," he complained. "Not you, too!"

He reined Mean around, touched spurs to the dun's flanks, and galloped up and over the rise.

As Prophet's group approached from the south an hour later, Chisos Springs stood dusty, sunbathed, and silent in the still, searing afternoon air. Shadows were stretching out from the southeast sides of the buildings scattered around the low rocky hills stippled with Spanish bayonet and the upright poles of sotol cactus.

Moon's House of a Thousand Delights, standing at the center of the settlement, near the roofed well, looked especially garish in the unforgiving light, like a whore painted way too early in the day. A thick, purple shadow was bleeding out from the front gallery, edging toward the well.

As Prophet's group clomped slowly into the southern edge of the town, approaching the Rose Hotel and Saloon on the broad trail's right side, a dust devil rose beyond the well. It swirled, picked up a newspaper, and swirled it with a couple of handfuls of dust, before the mini-tornado and the dust and paper all piled up against the far side of the steps of the dwarf's front gallery.

As Prophet approached the south front corner of the Roses' hotel, he said softly, "Whoa," and pulled back on Mean's reins, bringing the horse to an easy stop.

The others stopped around him, Louisa on his left, Ruth and Colter Farrow on his right. He'd been looking around cautiously, sensing gunmen waiting for him, but now the brunt of his attention was on the gallery of Moon's House of a Thousand Delights. Several shadowy figures milled there, some sitting on the rail, others in chairs against the House's front wall. Smoke wafted around a couple of the men.

Suddenly, a quirley stub sailed out of the shadows and turned copper white in the sunlight before it landed in the street near one of several long hitchracks. The shadows on the gallery shuffled lazily and then one came down the gallery steps, nonchalantly cocking a carbine one-handed. Four more men filed down the steps behind him. They walked in a line out into the street, heading toward the well.

Prophet continued to turn his head slightly from left to right and back again, scanning all the shadows around stoops and boardwalks, all the windows and rooflines. His gaze held on a second-floor window of Moon's House. A face peered out at him—the round, gray, old-man's face he'd seen when he'd first ridden into town nearly two weeks ago.

The haunting, haunted visage of Mordecai Moon.

Unlike before, no girl stood beside him. Maybe it was a trick of the light, but the dwarf's face looked grayer, more haggard than it had that day when Prophet had first ridden up to the well, wanting only water.

He couldn't see the expression, if any, on Moon's face now, but he detected a simmering rage in the little eyes.

Prophet looked at the five men who had now stopped in the street, standing about four feet apart, between Prophet's group and the well. There were four Anglos and one Mexican.

Prophet looked at Ruth. "Don't argue with me now. You go inside your hotel and keep your head down."

She slid her eyes from the five gunmen to Prophet. There was no defiance in the expression. She knew this was no place for her now. A shoot-out in the street was for seasoned shooters. She'd only get in the way if she didn't get herself killed first.

Ruth drew a breath, nodded slightly, swung down from her saddle, glanced up at him, wishing him luck with her eyes, and then turned, patted Colter's thigh, and then walked around behind the young redhead's horse and over to the hotel.

She climbed the porch steps and then stopped and turned, one hand on the rail post, staring apprehensively at the five men lined up in front of the well.

Prophet swung down from his saddle. He tied his reins to his saddle horn, turned Mean around, slapped his rump, and watched the horse gladly head back along the trail. Mean had been Prophet's horse long enough to know when lead was about to fly.

Louisa and Colter dismounted, hazed away their own horses, and turned toward the men and the well.

Prophet gave a grunt. He'd stuffed Ruth's bandanna into the bullet hole and that had seemed to quell the flow of blood though he knew he must have lost a pint by now. Still, the wound was a raw agony in his side.

Louisa glanced at the bounty hunter. "How are you doing, Lou?"

"Fine as frog hair. Mind your own business."

Staring at the men glowering back at him, all of them holding rifles across their chests, he said, "There were six sons o' bitches before, only five here." He started walking forward, and Louisa and Colter matched his stride. "Keep your eyes skinned for the other son of a bitch."

A thunderous blast sounded on Prophet's right. At the same time, a man came hurling out a shop door in a hail of breaking glass and wood. The man was thrown over the short boardwalk fronting the door and out into the street, his rifle piling up beside him about ten feet to Colter's right.

"Never mind," Prophet said.

The would-be shooter lay belly down. The back of his doeskin vest was shredded, and blood oozed through the pellet holes in the vest as well as those in the back of his head that was a mess of long, tangled, greasy brown hair.

Boots clomped in the shop behind the dead man. Prophet watched Lee Mortimer walk through the door and stop on the boardwalk, holding a double-barreled shotgun in both hands across his chest. Mortimer glanced at the dwarf's men and then turned to Prophet. He lifted his left hand slowly, pinched his hat brim, and offered a grim smile.

His eyes were as shiny as polished, dark blue marbles.

One of the five men near the well pointed at Mortimer. "You're gonna pay for that, Sheriff!"

Mortimer grinned and leaned against the door frame.

The man who'd pointed turned his attention to the two men and one woman standing before him. The two groups were about fifty feet apart. Prophet raked his gaze across each of the rugged faces partly shaded by their hat brims.

He smiled. That caused a couple of his opponents to frown. A smile in such a situation usually caused a moment's confusion and peevish anger in Prophet's opponents, and that's why he did it. Anger could translate to a slightly shaky aim in some. A man, especially a wounded, out-gunned man, needed any edge he could find.

Silence hung over the street. It was so heavy that Prophet could hear Louisa breathing to his left, Colter on his right. In the corner of his left eye, Prophet could see the dwarf staring into the street.

"Sorry I got you into this, kid," Prophet told Colter.

The redhead drew a deep breath. "Me, too."

Prophet felt his lips stretch a wry grin.

The man second to Prophet's left in the opposing group said, "How you wanna do this?"

One of his own men, the man on the far right, didn't wait for Prophet to respond.

"How about thisaway!" he shouted, snapping his rifle to his shoulder.

38

LOUISA MUST HAVE sensed the killer's sudden move as he hoped to surprise his quarry.

The man didn't know Louisa. She was very rarely surprised.

The blond snapped her own rifle up and shot the man outright, and he triggered his own rifle over Prophet's head as he flew straight back with a scream, dust billowing from the dead center of his short, fancily-stitched charro jacket.

All the killers snapped rifles to their shoulders then, as did Prophet and Colter. Louisa was pumping lead as fast as she could, triggering and levering her Winchester from her right hip. Prophet punched a round through the man who'd pointed at Mortimer, and a half second later, Louisa punched one through him as well.

He stumbled back, screaming.

Prophet felt the burn of three slugs and, weakening, he dropped to a knee and continued shooting, empty cartridge casings flying over his right shoulder, until no more outlaws were standing.

At least, not as far as he could tell.

Three were down. Two lay still. One was crawling on hands and knees toward the right side of the street.

Colter fired at him but merely blew up dust and horse shit in front of him. When the redhead triggered another round, the crawling gent screamed and jerked his right hand up as though he'd laid it atop a fiery hot range. Prophet fired two rounds at the crawler, but both slugs thudded into the stock trough he'd just thrown himself over, clutching his bloody hand to his chest.

Prophet glanced at Colter and saw why the redhead had missed his target. He was down on his butt, one leg bent beneath him, the other straight out in front of him, his right arm hanging slack, as though it had a bullet in it. Colter was spitting curses through gritted teeth as he clumsily jacked another shell into his Winchester's breech with his left hand.

When the crawling man lifted his hatless head above the lip of the stock trough, Prophet was ready. His Winchester roared. The man's eyes widened as the .44 rounds drilled a quarter-sized round hole in his forehead, just above his shaggy left brow.

The street pitched and rolled to either side of Prophet. The sun seemed to flicker. When the street rose up steeply on his left, he threw that arm out to keep himself from tumbling sidelong.

Louisa was still on her feet, tracing a broad semicircle around the well. Her hat was off. Blood streaked her right cheek, and her hair danced messily. Her face was pinched with fury as she thumbed a fresh cartridge through her Winchester's loading gate and moved toward the well behind which two of the surviving five shooters were crouched.

"Don't hide like whipped dogs, you slave-running cowards!" Louisa screamed.

A rifle cracked from behind the well. Louisa screamed and jerked sharply to her left, sending a slug careening into the dirt about six feet in front of Prophet. She dropped the rifle, staggered sideways, holding both hands out to her sides in shock, and dropped to a knee.

Wild laughter erupted from behind the well.

Fury blazed through Prophet. Grinding his teeth and suppressing the pain from the wound in his side and his sundry other more recent complaints, he tossed his rifle aside. He heaved himself to his feet, grabbed his shotgun from behind his back, and ran growling like an enraged bruin toward the well. One of the shooters was just now stepping out from behind it, crouched over his Winchester.

Ka-boooom!

The man didn't even scream as the gourd-sized fist of buckshot took him chest-high and blew him off his feet and threw him six feet straight back and down in a cloud of buffeting dust. Prophet ran around the well, saw the other man turn to run, limping, for a break between the barbershop and a dilapidated stable. He was screaming as he ran, his hat bouncing across his back by his chin thong.

"Won't kill you from this distance," Prophet said, spreading his feet and aiming his barn blaster out from his left hip. "But you're gonna wish it *did*!"

Ka-boooom!

The buckshot shredded the running man's hat. The man screamed and threw his head back and threw his arms wide as he stumbled forward before falling prone.

He lay screaming and writhing.

Prophet walked over to him. Pellet holes oozed bright red blood across his entire back, the back of his head and neck, and his shoulders and buttocks.

"Told ya," Prophet said, unholstering his Colt.

He cocked the hogleg, aimed, and drilled a hole through the back of the screaming man's head, silencing his screaming though he continued to kick and claw at the ground with his hands.

"That there was a gift, you son of a bitch."

Prophet walked back over to where Louisa knelt in the street near her rifle. She was clamping a hand over her right forearm.

"How bad you hit?"

She shook her head as she looked around warily. "Is that all of 'em?"

"All except for Moon."

Prophet glanced at Moon's window. The dwarf was no longer staring out. He'd take care of the devil's half ounce in a minute . . . if he could make it up the gallery steps without passing out. All the recent activity hadn't done the hole in his side any good.

He looked at Colter Farrow, who was just now climbing to his feet, using his rifle as a crutch. The kid had several nasty bullet burns on his arms and legs and one across his forehead, but the only one that looked serious was the one in his upper right arm.

"Kid, how you doin'?" Prophet asked.

"Flesh wound—I'll live," Colter said, glancing around, his long hair hanging to his shoulders. He'd lost his hat in the dustup. "What about Moon?"

As if in reply, a shrill scream rose from inside Moon's House of a Thousand Delights. It was Moon's own hoarse, raspy voice. More screams followed. These didn't sound like Moon's. They were shriller and higher pitched.

They sounded like the screams of a half-dozen young women.

The angry screams of piss-burned, young women . . .

"Help!" the dwarf shouted, his voice echoing around inside the saloon. *"He'p meeee!"*

Running footsteps hammered woodenly, echoing inside the place. Prophet, Louisa, and Colter all stared toward the saloon as the dwarf came running out the open front doors to plunge down the steps, leaping awkwardly on his little, bowed legs down each step while holding his bandaged hand, which appeared twice as large as the other one, tightly against his chest.

He wore only red longhandles and dirty white socks. Tufts of his thin hair danced around the dome-like top of his head.

Before he'd reached the bottom of the gallery steps, dark-skinned, black-haired young women dressed mostly in underwear of various styles, some wearing the hair ribbons and feathers that the dwarf had forced on them, exploded out the saloon's open doors.

"*Hep!*" the dwarf screamed, running toward Prophet, Louisa, and Colter. "For God's sakes, help me! I'm an injured man! I ain't *well*!"

The girls were too fast for him. They came spilling down the steps in a tightly clumped group, howling, yowling, and yipping like demon wolves, dark eyes flashing the red of unbridled, renegade fury as they swarmed over the little man.

At least one was carrying a large butcher knife that she must have gleaned from the kitchen. When the dwarf and the pack of enraged slave girls ran out into the sunshine, copper light glinted malevolently off the blade. The girls' running bare feet drummed in the dirt. Halfway between Prophet and the gallery steps, a couple of the girls jumped on the dwarf's back, one wrapping an arm around his neck from behind and driving him to the ground.

Moon yelped, hit the street, and disappeared from Prophet's view as all the dusky-skinned Indian girls leaped on top of him. Moon screamed and begged for mercy. The girls screamed and snarled and did not comply with his pleas except, finally, after they'd pummeled the little demon for over a minute, to raise and lower the butcher knife again and again.

That was all the mercy they had in them.

As they continued swarming over the little man, clawing, punching, kicking, and stabbing him over and over, Prophet felt the street rise suddenly and smack both his knees hard.

"*Lou!*" he heard Ruth and Louisa yell at the same time.

Then he heard nothing at all. The last thing he saw before darkness overtook him was the copper dirt of the street, each pebble and fleck of horse shit clearly defined and growing larger and larger before him.

He woke sometime later to see Ruth and Louisa sitting cross-legged on either side of him, both women scantily clad in thin chemises, bathing his naked body with cool sponges.

He was sprawled on a bed in the Rose Hotel and Saloon. Night had darkened the open windows beyond which stars shone.

Lamplight flickered.

Louisa had a thin bandage across her upper arm down which a strap of her thin chemise had fallen. Otherwise, she looked fine.

Both women looked fine . . .

"Feeling better, Lou?" Ruth asked him and pressed her lips to his forehead.

Groggily, Prophet grinned, said dreamily, "Oh, yeah."

As he let his lids drop gently over his eyes, he heard Colter Farrow grouch indignantly from another room, "I got injuries, too, you know!"

PETER BRANDVOLD has penned over seventy fast-action westerns under his own name and his pen name, FRANK LESLIE. He is the author of the ever-popular .45-Caliber books featuring Cuno Massey as well as the Lou Prophet and Yakima Henry novels. Berkley recently published his horror-western novel, *Dust of the Damned*, featuring ghoul hunter Uriah Zane. Head honcho at Mean Pete Press, publisher of lightning-fast western ebooks, he lives in Colorado with his dogs. Visit his website at www.peterbrandvold.com. Follow his blog at peterbrandvold.blogspot.com.

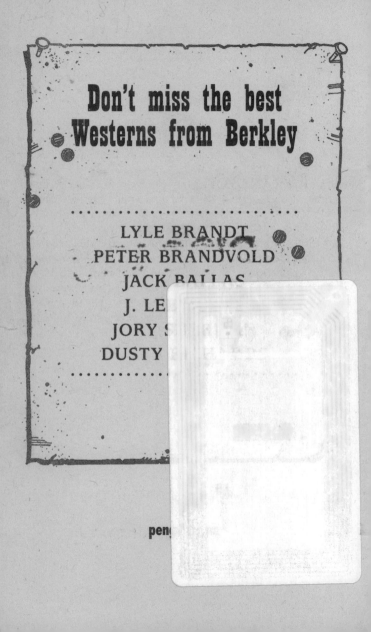

Don't miss the best Westerns from Berkley

....

LYLE BRANDT

PETER BRANDVOLD

JACK BALLAS

J. LE

JORY S

DUSTY

....

peng